Praise for

The Haunting of Rosehill

"One of the most hauntingly beautiful things I've ever read."
- Anni Taumata, Goodreads Review

"In the same league as The Woman in Black and Northanger Abbey."
- Philippa Williams, Goodreads Review

"It made my heart melt into a million pieces."
- Sarah Madeline, Goodreads Review

"A fantastic debut novel from Samantha Blok... *Bridgerton* meets *Supernatural*. If you loved *Crimson Peak*, you will love this read."
- Mollie Smith, Goodreads Review

"So beautifully written. In-depth and thought-compelling... If you like suspense, ghosts and romance, this book is for you. I couldn't put it down."
- Amanda Gold, Goodreads Review

"From the very first page, Blok's prose swept me into a world of eerie beauty, where the atmosphere and setting were almost as alive as the characters themselves... a stellar debut."
- Emily Hidalgo, Goodreads Review

THE HAUNTING
OF ROSEHILL

First Edition: 2024.
Second Edition: 2025.

Book cover design by Samantha Blok

ISBN: 978-1-7637540-0-3 (eBook)
ISBN: 978-1-7637540-1-0 (Paperback)

Published by Samantha Blok
samanthablok.com

THE HAUNTING OF ROSEHILL

A Gothic Regency Romance

SAMANTHA BLOK

Table of Contents

For Michael, who turns every page of life with me.

Prologue

With a grace that seemed almost ethereal, Seraphina glided through the undulating hills. Her chestnut hair flowed behind her like a pair of dark wings, and her eyes shone like glowing embers in the shadows. With every stride, she seemed to transcend the ground beneath her, moving with a fluidity that merged with the earth itself.

Her cottage, nestled in a secluded glade, was surrounded by a garden that flourished under her tender care. The space was alive with a tapestry of colour – a riot of blooms that flourished through the seasons. Towering foxgloves stood alongside delicate daisies, while clusters of fragrant herbs – lavender, rosemary, and thyme – filled the air with their heady scents.

She was known as a healer in nearby villages, and many journeyed from distant hamlets for remedies of both body and spirit – and yet, whispers filled the air. Some believed she held the secrets of nature, while others spoke in hushed tones of curses and witchcraft.

As the autumn wind howled through baron trees, a chill settled in the air, a harbinger of the frigid winter to come. Rosehill Manor stood over her cottage, each tower and turret reaching desperately for the heavens. The very stones groaned under the pressure, already marred by the relentless beating of wind and rain.

Seraphina's heart was heavy. A shadow loomed over her, a bitter reminder of the love she once cherished – a fragile thing, like the flowers she nurtured. His name was Edmund, and he was the very lord whose estate overshadowed her world.

Their love had blossomed in hidden corners, growing quietly away from prying eyes. Beneath the ancient oaks and cherry trees, their laughter mingled with the nightingale's songs as their dreams unfurled like blossoms greeting the moon.

As the sun disappeared below the horizon and dark storm clouds began to roll in, Seraphina stepped into her garden with a sense of melancholy, dreading the impending winter. A flicker of movement caught her eye – a black cat slinking through the shadows, with eyes gleaming like shards of obsidian.

"Stay close, my friend," she murmured, kneeling to greet him.

Even as she sought solace in his sleek fur, her focus was drawn to another figure emerging from the shadows.

Edmund approached with an urgent stride, and Seraphina's heart thundered inside her chest. In that moment, time seemed to slow.

"Seraphina," he breathed, his voice deep and guttural. "I could resist no longer."

"Edmund. You should never have come here. Your wife – "

"Curse my wife," he growled. He was a tempest, his dark hair a wild mane. "Please, Seraphina – forgive me," he pleaded, "for my absence has not been by choice. Every moment away from you was torture. I cannot live this charade, pretending to love another while my body aches for you." His voice cracked, and he lunged forwards to clasp her hands in a desperate grip.

"And of your title? Your vows?"

"My duty may bind me, aye, but my heart knows no chains." He clutched her hands with such force that she felt his fingernails press into her skin. "We shall find a way, I swear upon it – no matter the cost."

"Edmund," she groaned. "Do you believe you can simply cast aside the life laid before you? Your estate, your title, your very legacy? And now, a child – your bloodline."

He paused then, the swirling winds carrying an ominous charge. "Why can't I have it all?" he demanded, and his words rang out like a challenge to fate itself. A low rumble of distant thunder echoed through the hills. His gaze seared into her like a white-hot branding iron. "I long for your touch."

Seraphina breathed deeply, bitterness swelling from the depths of her stomach like bile. "How dare you come here and speak to me of longing," she spat. "Your longing is a beast that consumes all you touch. It is but a pale shadow – a weak imitation – of what love should be." Her heart pounded in her ears. "You seek to dominate and control me, as though I am a mere object to be possessed. You would betray your sacred vows, abandoning the woman carrying your child, to pursue me as though I were a mere dalliance to indulge in? Have you no respect for me? Do you truly hold me in such low regard?"

She wrenched her hands from his grasp, repelled by his touch. She wrapped her hands tightly around her body. "You crave my flesh, but not my heart, my mind, my soul. You have revealed your true nature, Edmund Sinclair. Your heart is as fickle as the winds that howl through these cursed woods." The storm rumbled closer, her chestnut hair whipping in the rising wind. "I am no fool. I will not be the refuge you turn to when your own choices turn sour. You were once everything to me, but you cast me aside for the allure of another, and now you come crawling back, seeking comfort in my bed. How dare you think I would ever embrace you again after the pain you inflicted upon me?"

The wind howled around her, carrying her rage and transforming it into something raw and savage. She stalked forwards, her glare piercing through him like a spear. "You stand there, cloaked in your pretensions of love, yet you remain blind to the poison of betrayal dripping from your lips. What respect could I possibly hold for a man who forsakes his own kin, driven solely by the cravings of his flesh?

"Remember this well," she whispered, her eyes blazing. "Betrayal carries heavy consequences, for it weaves curses that will cling to your very soul. You will rue the day you turned your back on love, for your heart shall know no rest."

She extended her hands, raising her palms to the heavens. "Listen well. Hear me now." As the words left her lips, the wind roared, spiralling around them violently, as though nature itself rose to her defence. "For your treachery and your selfishness, may your heart be cursed to know only the torment of unfulfilled desire, and may your soul be eternally shackled by the weight of your own sins. May you be forever damned to wander through the shadows of your own making, haunted by the echoes of all you have forsaken."

With each word, a deep sorrow entwined itself with Seraphina's anger, a lament for the love that had rotted into betrayal. Hot tears spilled from her eyes, unbidden, as her words flowed forth. "As you chase fleeting pleasures, you will clutch at shadows, only to find the void within yourself. And as you walk this cursed path, your children shall inherit only the sorrow of a father's neglect, and the stain of your name will poison their very blood. And you," her voice dropped to a haunting whisper. "You will watch as every bond slips away, the love you seek always out of reach, forever beyond your grasp."

As she spoke, the wind twisted through the trees, carrying her voice like a dark hymn. Her words settled in the space between the leaves, a solemn vow to the earth itself. Edmund's face blanched as her words clawed at him like unseen hands.

"Let this be the curse you bear," she whispered, her voice soft, almost broken. "The bitter fruit of your betrayal. May love forever slip through your fingers like sand, and peace remain an unreachable shore. You will reach for it, again and again, only to find shadows – echoes of all that is lost, all of which you can never reclaim."

Chapter 1

1815

Evelyn

The carriage rattled along the winding road, the last vestiges of winter clinging to the landscape. Evelyn Ward sat poised across from her father with her sketchbook resting in her lap. Its pages brimmed with delicate lines of wildflowers and frost-laced leaves. Despite the cold and the sway of the carriage, her quill danced across the paper, tracing the curve of a leaf.

Beside her, Charles was a restless bundle of energy, leaning forwards and fogging the window with his breath. "Do you think the gardens will still be blooming, Evelyn? Even with all this cold?"

Evelyn smiled at her younger brother, glancing up from her drawing. "They say Rosehill's gardens are remarkable, even in winter. I'm sure we'll find something to enjoy, even if spring is reluctant to arrive."

Their father peered over his spectacles from his volume of *Flora of the British Isles*. "Rosehill Manor is renowned for its extraordinary flora. We're fortunate Baron Sinclair invited us. But remember, dear children, some plants thrive best in the cold. Nature often surprises us."

Evelyn peered through the foggy carriage window, unable to ignore the stark contrast between the rugged beauty of the landscape and the comforting warmth of her home in London. Their own charming townhouse was nestled in a respectable neighbourhood, boasting a facade draped in ivy and blooming window boxes. Though not nobility, her family commanded quiet respect. Within those walls, the household thrived on intellectual discourse and scientific inquiry. There, she found peace, and a profound connection to the world of knowledge and discovery her father had opened for her.

A second carriage trundled along behind theirs, laden with their luggage and attended by a few servants. As the carriages crested a hill, the grand silhouette of Rosehill Manor came into view.

"Look, Evelyn! Do you see it? We're here!" Charles exclaimed, pressing his face against the glass. Evelyn tucked her sketchbook away as the carriage rolled up the long gravel driveway.

The manor loomed high atop the hill, its towering arched windows framed by old ivy and climbing roses, like darkened eyes watching them approach. Vines snaked around the ornate stonework with tendrils reaching towards the sky as if trying to reclaim the building to nature. Small garden beds encircled the manor's entrance, laying in quiet slumber in the chill of winter. The estate's lawns and gardens stretched far into the distance, disappearing into a line of ancient trees.

As the carriages came to a halt, an unsettling hush enveloped the estate. The driver stepped down, offering a steady hand to Evelyn as she prepared to alight.

"Do be careful, my dear," her father called from behind her. He emerged next, a frown creasing his brow as he surveyed their surroundings. Behind him, Charles jumped down swiftly.

Evelyn's lady's maid, Clara, stepped down from the servant's carriage, smoothing her skirts with anxious fingers. Her eyes darted about, wide and unsettled.

"Shall we proceed?" Evelyn asked. Her father nodded, adjusting his coat as he moved towards the entrance, while her brother lingered for a heartbeat, shooting her a reassuring glance.

Atop the high stone staircase, the great oak doors creaked open, revealing a thin figure clad in dark livery.

"Welcome to Rosehill Manor," the butler intoned, his voice echoing in the expansive foyer. Tall and gaunt, he stood shrouded in shadows. His pale skin contrasted sharply with the tailored suit that clung to his elongated frame, making him appear like a wraith against the rich wood panelling. His eyes, deep-set and unnaturally bright, glinted as though he could see into the very souls of those before him. There was a palpable pause, a breath held in the air, as if the walls themselves were listening, waiting for the next words to break the silence.

"May I take your coats?" he offered as he stepped forwards, descending the stone staircase. "The warmth of our hearth will be a welcome respite from the chill outside." He took their coats and smiled, revealing teeth that were a shade too sharp, before turning away.

The cold settled quickly against Evelyn's skin without her coat. As she ascended the stairs, the heavy silence around them was disturbed by a sudden rustle of leaves. She turned, and her breath caught in her throat as a shadow detached itself from the gloom along the line of trees.

For a fleeting moment, she thought it must be a ghost. The faintest outline of a man lingered – tall and broad-shouldered, unnaturally still against the old trunks. The fading light wrapped around him like a shroud, and a chill ran down her spine.

"Is something the matter, Miss Evelyn?" asked her lady's maid.

"Nothing," she murmured, shaking her head to dispel the image. It was merely a trick of the light – her imagination playing cruel games in the fading light.

"Shall we go inside?" Charles suggested impatiently, unaware of the chill that clung to Evelyn's thoughts. "I'm cold now without my coat. I don't know why the butler took it so soon."

11

As they neared the threshold of the manor, a few servants appeared as if from thin air to assist those already by the carriage. They moved with a hushed urgency, their expressions concealed by the encroaching twilight as they quietly unloaded bags and belongings.

Gathering themselves, Evelyn and her family crossed the threshold into the manor. The oak doors groaned as they swung shut, closing behind them with a resounding thud. Within the grand foyer, the oppressive atmosphere seemed to cling to the very walls, as if the manor itself had drawn them into its dark, unyielding grasp.

"Stay close," Evelyn whispered to her lady's maid who followed behind.

She glanced around the cold foyer that loomed before them, vast and imposing. The high ceilings seemed to stretch endlessly above. A crystal chandelier hung from the centre, casting a ghostly glow across the marble floor, though its brilliance was dulled by dust. The walls were adorned with silk tapestries and dark wooden panels, dulled by age, and a grand staircase spiralled upwards. Gilded frames held oil portraits of ancestors long forgotten, their eyes following any who passed. The manor was grand, magnificent, and yet it felt as though the years had settled into every corner, clinging to the air with a quiet, haunting presence.

"If you would follow me," the butler said, "I shall show you to the parlour room where you may make yourselves comfortable before dinner." His eyes lingered on them for a moment too long before stalking away.

Clara and the other servants lingered outside the parlour, quietly overseeing the placement of the family's belongings. Evelyn glanced back at her lady's maid, who offered a small, reassuring smile before turning away. Evelyn, however, found little comfort in it, and tightened her grip around her sketchbook as if it were a talisman.

To her relief, the parlour room was a haven of warmth. Heavy velvet drapes framed the tall windows, and plush chairs, upholstered in deep burgundy, were arranged around a grand marble fireplace where flames crackled softly.

"Please, make yourselves at home," the butler said, gesturing towards the seating with a slow, deliberate motion. "Refreshments will be served shortly."

Evelyn moved towards the fire, glad for its warmth. Her father, looking pensive, settled into a chair across from her, already lost in thought. Meanwhile, Charles wandered to the far side of the room, drawn to the oil paintings that lined the walls. He peered closely at their sombre faces and scrunched up his nose in disdain.

"Keep your hands to yourself, Charles," Evelyn chided as he reached out to touch. He sniffed and stuck out his tongue. Evelyn sighed and turned back to the fire.

After some time, the butler returned, his movements unnervingly fluid as he set down a tray of delicate pastries and tea. The clink of porcelain echoed through the room, sharp against the quiet. Grateful for the distraction, Evelyn moved closer and poured herself a cup, watching as the fragrant steam curled into the air.

Charles, still inspecting the portraits, glanced over his shoulder. "I wonder what the baron is like," he mused, "I hope he's not terribly stuffy or old. I cannot quite tell which one he is." He pointed to one of the more faded portraits: a man almost obscured by age and shadow.

As if summoned by an unseen force, a hunched figure appeared against the doorway, shuffling slowly into view. The baron's walking stick tapped rhythmically against the polished floor. His frail form was draped in heavy brocade, the fabric rich but worn, much like the man himself.

"Apologies for my tardiness," he croaked, and it seems as though each word was an effort. "I trust you've managed to entertain yourselves in my absence?"

Evelyn's father rose swiftly, the suddenness of his movement making her step closer, positioning herself slightly behind him.

"My lord," her father said, bowing deeply. "It is an honour to finally meet you in person."

13

The baron's thin lips curved into a smile, the wrinkles on his aged face deepening like weathered lines carved by time itself. "The pleasure is mine, Mr Ward," he replied hoarsely. "I have long anticipated this meeting. Your letters have been most enlightening for my poor, ailing mind." His pale eyes lingered on them, sharp despite his frailty, as though measuring their every movement.

Her father practically bounced on his toes, the veneer of formality slipping away as excitement surged through him. "I am eager to share more about my botanical studies," he said, his words now tumbling out. "I believe there are some species in your gardens that would be of particular interest – "

The baron raised his hand, the other leaning heavily on his walking stick. "In due time, Mr Ward. There will be ample opportunity to discuss your findings. For now, let us enjoy the evening's comforts and allow our minds a moment of respite from the rigours of the natural world."

The butler lingered nearby, his presence quietly watchful, as if weighing the exchange between the two men.

"But first," continued the baron, his words slow and drawn, "you must introduce me to your family. It is a rare pleasure to have company in these desolate halls."

"Ah yes, of course." Her father cleared his throat. "It is my pleasure to introduce my children. This is my daughter, Miss Evelyn Ward, and my son, Master Charles Ward."

Evelyn stepped forwards, executing a graceful curtsy beneath the Baron Sinclair's cold glare. As she rose, she noticed his eyes briefly flicker with an expression akin to pure terror, before he swiftly masked it. He studied her, his eyes lingering a heartbeat longer than was comfortable. The hair on her arms stood up as another icy chill ran through her. His slow manner of speech felt directly opposed to the quickness of his gaze, to that sharp intelligence in his eyes.

He turned to Charles, who stood grinning with boyish charm. "And Master Charles. I see you are already intrigued by the history of the manor."

Charles straightened, clearly pleased with the recognition.

"Perhaps you will learn some of those stories during your stay." . The baron smiled as if he appreciated the boy's curiosity, though a glimpse of something darker passed across his features. "Alas, dinner awaits, and I would be honoured if you would join me in the dining room." He paused, his focus drifting, as if contemplating the very shadows that clung to the walls, before it settled once more on his guests. "My grandson, The Honourable Henry Sinclair, ought to be joining us shortly. He tends to roam the grounds, lost in his thoughts – brooding, most likely. I expect you should like to meet him, Miss Ward."

∞∞∞∞

The dining room enveloped them in the rich aroma of dinner, thick with the savoury scents of roasted meats and fragrant herbs. Silver platters gleamed beneath the soft glow of candlelight, casting shadows that danced along the ornate wallpaper. The long table was lavishly set, adorned with seasonal vegetables and delicate pastries that seemed almost too beautiful to eat.

Her father and the old baron were quickly engrossed in a deep discussion of botanicals. Baron Sinclair spoke slowly of his collection of medicinal herbs, particularly the danger of wolfsbane and belladonna, while her rapidly father extolled the virtues of cultivating plants for their healing properties.

"Foxglove, of course, has its risks," the baron droned, his wrinkled hand shaking as he gestured with his fork. "But in the right doses, a powerful healer. And you were right about lavender – nothing better for a restful night when the mind won't quiet."

Her father quickly nodded in agreement, his voice rising as he shared his experiences with rare alpine plants. "I've found that thyme thrives in even the most difficult soils, especially in high altitudes. It's extraordinary how these small herbs survive under such harsh conditions."

As the second course was served, the door swung open with a low creak, echoing through the dining room like a whispered omen. A tall, striking figure filled the doorway, silhouetted against the warm glow of the hallway beyond. Clad in dark, tailored attire that clung to his form like a shadow, the man's sharp features were momentarily obscured in the dim light.

When he stepped into the room, the candlelight danced across his face, illuminating high cheekbones and a chiselled jaw that seemed sculpted by an artist's hand. And yet, it was the depth of his gaze that truly captivated – dark and piercing, as if he carried secrets that could unravel the very fabric of the room. His presence was like a sudden storm, an unspoken force that demanded all attention without uttering a word.

"Henry!" the baron's voice sliced through the room, suddenly sharp with irritation. "You are late. Dinner has commenced, and you have kept our esteemed guests waiting."

Mr Sinclair's jaw tightened at the admonishment, defiance dancing in his eyes. He cast a fleeting glance over the assembled company, his gaze brushing against Evelyn's for but a breath before he advanced further into the dining room.

"Pray forgive me, grandfather," he replied, his tone cool as the chilling draft that swept through the open doorway. "I lost track of time, as is easily done within the estate."

The old baron narrowed his eyes but then waved his hand wearily. He gestured for his grandson to take a seat. "Join us. There is much to discuss."

Mr Sinclair took his seat across from Evelyn, the scrape of his chair on the floor breaking the heavy silence. She was suddenly aware of her every movement, her every breath. She kept her eyes fixed firmly on her plate as she ate, but every so often, her eyes would dart up, and for a fleeting moment, their gazes would meet across the table.

Evelyn could not shake the feeling of unspoken tension, as though he could peer into the depths of her soul. The conversation between the old baron and her father droned on, but for her, the room seemed to constrict, drawn to the quiet storm that was Mr Henry Sinclair.

Just then, Charles leant over, a mischievous grin playing on his lips. "I suppose we should be grateful, Mr Sinclair, that you graced us with your presence. We were beginning to wonder if you'd taken a wrong turn in the gardens."

"Indeed, Master Charles," he replied, a flicker of amusement breaking through his stoic demeanour. He leant forwards slightly, as if whispering a secret to the boy. "One must navigate these grounds with care. They can be as treacherous as they are beautiful. I daresay I might have stumbled upon some hidden secrets had I wandered too far."

Charles' eyes widened, but Mr Sinclair sat back and resumed his meal.

The baron coughed loudly and then cast a contemplative glance among his dinner guests. "And what hobbies occupy your time, Miss Ward? I trust you possess a passion beyond idly wandering in gardens as my grandson does?"

Evelyn felt her cheeks flush under his scrutiny but managed a coy smile. "Indeed, I do take delight in gardens, my Lord. However, rather than idly wandering, I find great pleasure in drawing." She glanced apologetically at Mr Sinclair before continuing. "I seek to capture the likeness of nature in my illustrations. Moreover, I must admit to a keen fascination with scientific pursuits. I often immerse myself in my father's botanical volumes."

"My sister once remarked that she wishes to be a renowned botanist, like Father!" Charles chimed in, earning a warning glance from Evelyn.

At this, the baron let out a derisive chuckle. "A woman in the man's realm of science?" he croaked. "What a quaint notion, my dear. Leave the studying and formal professions to the men!"

He punctuated his dismissal by digging his fork into a serving of roast venison.

Evelyn's heart sank for a moment, but she held her composure. "I find solace in capturing the beauty of nature, particularly flowers and plants, my lord. There is much to learn from them, beyond their mere appearance."

"Yes, of course, my dear," her father interjected quickly. "Your curiosity and pursuit of knowledge is admirable, and I encourage it wholeheartedly."

17

A hush fell over the room, though Evelyn could sense Mr Sinclair's gaze upon her. She looked up to find him regarding her with a thoughtful expression.

The old baron began to rise shakily from the table, the creaking of his chair echoing through the stillness. He gestured to the men. "Shall we retire to the drawing room for a nightcap?"

As they stood, Mr Sinclair leant across the table slightly. "We have not yet had the opportunity to converse properly, Miss Ward. I hope to remedy that soon."

She blinked rapidly before gathering her wits. "I would like that very much."

With that, the baron, her father, and Mr Sinclair moved towards the drawing room, while Evelyn and Charles were led by a servant to their guest chambers.

Once the men had departed, Charles turned to Evelyn with a wide grin, the hole of his missing front tooth gaping. "I would like that very much!" he mimicked in a sickly-sweet voice.

Evelyn could not help but smile as she swatted at him, though he darted from her reach. "Oh, hush! You're insufferable!"

∞∞∞∞

Once in her guest chambers, Evelyn paused to collect her thoughts. The space was cosy, bathed in the soft glow of moonlight filtering through lace curtains. As she approached a gilded mirror, she caught sight of her reflection. Her chestnut hair cascaded in loose waves, framing her gentle features like a halo of warmth against the room's subdued hues. She wore a simple muslin gown, the soft pink hue lending her what her lady's maid, Clara, had once called an ethereal glow.

Clara bustled around the room as she helped to arrange Evelyn's clothes and possessions: finely embroidered handkerchiefs, delicate stays, and small trinkets.

"Did you speak to him?" Clara whispered. "The tall gentleman in dark attire? I believe his name is Henry Sinclair. Quite a sight, is he not?"

Evelyn felt a blush creep into her cheeks. "I suppose he is," she replied, trying to sound nonchalant as she folded a shawl.

"He is certainly an eligible bachelor, miss," her lady's maid continued. "Heir to Rosehill Manor and son of a baron, no less. A fine match, I would say."

Evelyn shook her head, dismissing the notion with a frown. "Marriage is not a consideration I have entertained. It would only serve to hinder my pursuits."

The memory of her first season in the marriage mart still loomed over her. It had been a whirlwind of expectations and disappointment. Under the watchful guidance of her father's older sister, Aunt Beatrice, she reluctantly ventured into the opulent ballrooms of London. Instead of delight she anticipated, she found herself weary of the attentions of frivolous gentlemen, finding their pursuits increasingly concerned with appearance over substance. With each ball, she longed for the solace of Kew Gardens, where she could lose herself in the pages of her botanical volumes or sketch the petals of flowers. These pursuits offered far greater satisfaction than any suitor ever could.

"But you must admit," her maid continued gently, "it would be a fine match."

Evelyn could not help but appreciate Clara's tenacity; her lady's maid had a way of pushing boundaries as only a true friend could.

She sighed. "It is simply that… I wish my only option as a woman were not marriage. It seems a narrow path when there is so much more I long to explore. Did you know there exist women botanists and scientists who have achieved remarkable things… in defiance of society's expectations? Look at Elizabeth Blackwell, for instance." Evelyn pulled a book from amongst her belongings. "She published *The Curious Herbal* in 1737 under her own name! Her descriptions were all aimed at physicians and herbalists." She sighed again. "Imagine, a woman free to explore and study the world around her – without the constraints of marriage."

19

"I admire your determination, Miss Evelyn, I truly do. But you must remember, love can inspire one to achieve wonderful things. Besides, would not marriage bring a sense of security? Surely that would provide a sturdy foundation for your dreams."

"Wise words, Miss Clara," came a voice from the doorway. Evelyn's father rested against the frame with a gentle smile. Clara's eyes widened, and she curtsied stiffly before scurrying from the room.

Evelyn's father chuckled as the maid nearly fled down the corridor. "You should take heed of her advice, my darling. Marriage need not constrain your pursuits. Rather, it might enhance them."

Evelyn slid *The Curious Herbal* beneath her pillow, though her fingers lingered upon the cover. She hesitated for a moment. "What would Mama say to such a notion?"

Her father paused, pursing his lips, before he adjusted his spectacles and rubbed the bridge of his nose. "Your mother... she always believed in following one's passion. She had an incredible talent for music, as you well know... And yet, she set it aside for the sake of our family. I often wonder what she might have accomplished if given the chance." He remained in the doorway, gazing out the window as if searching for answers in the moonlight. "I believe she would urge you to pursue your dreams, as she could not."

He sighed deeply as he entered the room and settled onto the edge of her bed. "Still, I desire security and an advantageous match for you, my dear – and if I may be so bold, a match born of love. Though your mother had her own aspirations, she never lost sight of what truly mattered: our family. You. The new babe she carried." His voice shook with sorrow. He refrained from uttering "me," yet Evelyn sensed that unspoken word hanging between them.

She sat in silence with her father for a time. Some moments require no words at all; they exist in the warmth of shared understanding and the love that binds them together.

"I understand, Father," she replied at last. "I wish for naught but to make you and Mother proud. Yet it feels as though I am being pulled in two directions. I desire a future that honours Mother's legacy and brings you peace, yet I fear that marriage may confine me in ways to which I am not yet prepared."

Her father smiled wistfully, placing his hand over hers. "Perhaps you shall discover a balance between duty and your own aspirations, even if it takes time. There is no need for haste." He pressed a gentle kiss upon her forehead. "Goodnight, my dear. May slumber grant you the rest you require."

22

Chapter 2

Evelyn

Long after her father had left, Evelyn lay cocooned in her blankets, the silence of Rosehill Manor settling around her. Outside her window, the gnarled trees swayed in the night breeze, their branches casting shadows that danced across her chamber wall. A chill permeated the air, one that clung to her skin like a persistent fog. She squeezed her eyes shut, hoping to escape the gloom that seemed to seep through the very walls.

As the clock struck two, the silence fractured, dragging her into a restless sleep.

She found herself ensnared in a garden. A lush bouquet of roses burst forth in an array of colours – crimson, lavender, and gold, each hue more vivid than the last.

At the garden's centre stood a rose, larger and more opulent than any she had ever seen. It possessed a depth that transcended the ordinary – a deep, velvety hue that shifted subtly in the moonlight, oscillating between rich crimson and haunting midnight blue. Its petals glistened with dewdrops, catching the moonlight and refracting it into a dance of shimmering stars.

Suddenly, her dream shifted. All colour drained away, leaving a monochrome world where shadows twisted and curled like smoke. She turned and caught glimpses of figures lurking in the gloom: faces distorted in agony, mouths moving in silent screams.

"What do you want?" she cried out, but her voice only echoed back at her, hollow and empty.

The faces pressed forwards, hands outstretched, their fingers clawing at the air. A cold breeze swept through the garden, rustling the leaves with an eerie whisper, carrying their distant pleas: "Save us! Free us!"

Evelyn stumbled back, catching her foot on the roots of the rosebush, and she tumbled onto the earth with a thud. The ground trembled beneath her, alive with a rhythm that pulsed like a heartbeat.

Her eyes darted to the rose, now blooming with a blinding intensity that hurt to behold, petals unfurling to reveal something grotesque at its centre: a pair of hollow eyes. The eyeballs spun, staring at her in horror, glistening with despair, with an unbearable longing for release.

"Remember us!" The voices rose in a cacophony, growing louder and more insistent, filling her mind with a haunting melody of grief. "You are bound to us. You must remember!"

Amidst the dissonance, a familiar figure emerged, a silhouette materialising from the shadows, weaving through the tendrils of darkness like a ghost. She recognised his face now, drawn and haunted, yet beautiful as a moonlit night – Henry Sinclair. His eyes glimmered like stormy seas, dark and pleading.

He reached out, his hand quivering, as though the very act of moving was a challenge against the unseen forces. "Evelyn! You must save us!"

∞∞∞∞

With a gasp, she jerked awake, the remnants of her dream clinging to her like mist. She lay in her bed, drenched in sweat. The shadows in her room shifted ominously, the moonlight casting strange shapes that loomed and writhed in the corners.

Clenching the covers, she fought against the urge to scream. It was merely a dream, she told herself, a product of her restless mind. And yet the weight of the garden, with its fragrances – too real, too fresh – and the haunting, pleading faces, remained in her senses, refusing to be dismissed as mere figments of imagination.

An unsettling scratching sound echoed from above – in the ceilings, or perhaps the walls – sharp and relentless, as if something was desperately trying to break free from its confines.

It was merely a dream, she repeated to herself. *Go back to sleep.*

And yet, she could not. The scratching sound echoed around her from every direction – the walls, the ceiling, the wooden floors – as if the very manor was alive. Where was it coming from?

Everything can be explained, she told herself.

Gathering her courage, she swung her legs over the side of the bed, the chill of the floor seeping into her bones.

Each step towards the door felt like a plunge back into her nightmare, the whispers of the garden intertwining with the scratching from above, a dissonant chorus of dread urging her onwards. *You are bound to us,* the voices echoed in her mind.

Enough foolishness, she chided herself.

She opened the door slowly, the creaking sound reverberating in the stillness. Portraits of the Sinclair ancestors glared down at her with hollow eyes, their painted faces twisted in expressions that seemed to warn her away.

She halted at the foot of a set of stairs, the worn steps ascending into the heights of the manor. The darkness above loomed, pulsing with a life of its own – a swirling mass of shadows that seemed to breathe, shifting and undulating as if beckoning her to step into its embrace. She took a tentative step forwards, the wood creaking beneath her weight.

A sudden noise shattered the silence. A loud crash erupted from somewhere deep within the manor, and a guttural growl resonated through the hall. Evelyn's heart leapt into her throat as the growl morphed into a chorus of frantic rustlings.

Panic surged within her, primal and urgent, and she fled back down the corridor. Reaching her chamber, she slammed the door shut and pressed her back against it, gasping for breath. With another gasping breath, she ran to her bed and she drew the covers over herself, as if that thin barrier could shield her from the horrors lurking just beyond.

As she lay there, trembling and wide-eyed, the manor outside her door faded into a haunting silence.

It was then that a rustling noise broke through the silence – another terrible sound creeping from the dim shadows of her own room. She froze, clutching the covers in her hands. She could not move if she wanted to, for fear had gripped her too tightly.

The rustling grew closer. She strained to see beyond the darkness of her chamber, to reason the fear away.

There is a logical explanation behind each noise I hear, she told herself. *I need not be afraid.*

And yet, every rustle seemed to inch closer, mingling with the soft creaks of the manor. She clenched the covers tighter, trembling as the darkness danced closer.

At long last, as the rustling drew near and her fear was at its height, a figure slipped from the shadows. A sleek, dark cat emerged, its body flowing like liquid night as it stepped into the faint glow of the moon. It strolled closer, tail held high as its soft purring broke the stillness.

"Oh, you little troublemaker!" Evelyn breathed, shaking her head as the cat settled beside her, mewing softly.

The cat soon settled into a tranquil sleep at her side, and she ran her hand over its sleek fur until, gradually, her heartbeat slowed.

"There is nothing to fear," she murmured into the darkness. "Nothing to fear."

Chapter 3

Evelyn

When Evelyn awoke that morning, the cat was gone, leaving only a faint impression where it had nestled against her. She mused upon its whereabouts, for the door was firmly closed and the window tightly shut.

She sat up and stretched, the remnants of the previous night's fears lifting like morning fog. She glanced around her chamber, noting how the light streamed in with an unexpected brilliance. The sun had ascended high in the sky, a clear indication that she had overslept. A low rumble from her stomach confirmed her suspicions; she had missed the morning meal.

A gentle knock resonated at the door, followed by the soft creak of the hinges as it opened. Two maids entered, the aroma of freshly baked bread and sweet pastries wafting in with them.

"Good morning, Miss Ward," one of the maids said warmly, her cheeks flushed. Her apron was neatly pressed, and her hair arranged in a tidy bun. "We thought we might find you still resting. Your breakfast is served."

Evelyn returned the smile, though she felt a twinge of embarrassment creeping into her cheeks as she sat up. "Thank you. I appreciate your kindness."

The maid placed the tray on her lap. The spread was a comforting sight, but the guilt lingered, a reminder of her tardiness and the etiquette she feared she had breached.

After finishing her meal, she rose and ventured forth to seek her hosts. She glided through shadowy corridors, peering into the dining room where the grand table remained ominously set, untouched. In the drawing room, porcelain teacups gleamed under the dim light. The great hall loomed before her, with its towering ceilings and ornate chandeliers. Her hosts remained elusive, leaving her with an unsettling sense of abandonment as she wandered the halls of Rosehill Manor.

As she continued her search through the dimly lit corridors, something brushed against her leg. She jumped, before looking down to find the black cat. A smile broke across her face as she bent to greet him.

"Ah, there you are! I almost wondered if you were just a dream last night," she murmured. "I shall call you Shadow, for you appear from the darkness like a whisper."

The cat purred in response, weaving around her ankles.

In lieu of her hosts, Evelyn made her way to her father and brother's chambers. She rapped softly on her father's door, but there was no response. She pressed her ear against the wood, straining to catch any hint of life within. She turned the handle and gently pushed the door open, revealing a room awash in golden light that poured through the window. Her father sat at a small table, head buried in the newspaper, the remnants of breakfast laid out before him.

"Father?"

His gaze lifted from the pages of his newspaper, the weariness in his eyes giving way to surprise. "Evelyn, dear! I thought you would still be resting."

"I seem to have overslept. I beg your pardon for missing breakfast."

"Well… yes, quite so. It appears we all did." He gestured to Charles, who sat slouched in a chair, still half-asleep and clutching a piece of toast.

"Good morning, Charles," Evelyn said, stifling a laugh at his dishevelled appearance.

"Morning," he mumbled, blinking slowly. "I thought I heard you scream last night."

"It was merely a troubling dream. And what of you two? Did you also find your rest less than peaceful?"

Her father nodded, peering over the spectacles that rested on the bridge of his nose. "There is an unsettling stillness about this manor. Though the maids kindly brought me breakfast. Will you not join us?"

"Oh, I have already partaken," she replied, though she still made her way to a chair opposite him.

Slowly, as they shared in the morning quiet and stillness, Evelyn felt semblance of normalcy envelope her. She sighed as she watched her father read his newspaper, and Charles nodded back to sleep upright in his chair – and yet, as the sun climbed higher, a longing swelled within her: an aching desire to break free from the confines of the manor. She felt like a caged bird, longing for the open air.

She bid farewell to her father and brother, donning her coat and grabbing her sketchbook and quill. She stepped outside, where the air was crisp against her cheeks.

Clara followed dutifully behind as Evelyn wandered the estate grounds, scanning the landscape in search of specimens to draw. Most of the plants had succumbed to the harshness of the season, yet there were a few stubborn souls clinging to life amidst the cruel remnants of winter. Snowdrops peeked through the frost, while clusters of hellebores pushed through the earth, their deep green leaves framing the dusky petals that hinted at spring's approach.

Evelyn paused at the sight of a few chives daring to sprout. In a sheltered corner, a sprig of rosemary glistened with frost, sparkling like tiny stars, and even jasmine trailed along the stone wall.

"Look, Clara! It's remarkable how some plants endure, is it not?"

Evelyn spotted a kitchen servant with a woven basket, crouched beside a small herb patch. "Hello there!" she called out merrily. "What a splendid selection you have!"

The servant turned, and as her eyes fell upon Evelyn, the colour drained from her face, and she shrieked.

For a moment, Evelyn caught the glimpse of pure terror in the girl's wide eyes, as though she had confronted a ghost instead of a living, breathing soul. The girl's hands, pale and shaking, clutched the sprigs of thyme as though they were a shield.

"Forgive me, miss! I did not mean to startle. I thought – " The kitchen maid sprung to her feet. "It's nothing, only my imagination playing tricks."

Evelyn took a step closer and reached for the woven basket of herbs. The girl recoiled slightly.

"Please, do not be frightened. Whatever did you imagine?"

"Oh, it's foolish, really, miss! I only had a moment of fright, that's all. It's easy to get lost in one's thoughts out here, is it not?" Her eyes darted back to the manor, as if expecting something – or someone – to emerge from its shadows.

Evelyn nodded, sensing unspoken words in the air, but she chose not to pry. Instead, she offered the maid her basket back. "Those herbs look lovely. They would pair wonderfully with a lamb dinner."

The servant girl nodded quickly and scampered off without another word.

Evelyn pursed her lips, continuing her stroll along the garden path with Clara, though as she walked away, the image of the kitchen maid's fearful gaze sat heavily on her heart.

"It is peculiar, don't you think? That kitchen maid appeared genuinely terrified. What could have frightened her so?"

Clara looked up, brushing a loose strand of hair behind her ear. "I dare say, Miss Evelyn, I have known the cold to play tricks on one's mind... yet there was something in her eyes – a true fear."

Evelyn nodded thoughtfully. "It reminds me of when the baron looked as if he might recognise me last night. There was something in his look, too... something unsettling." She paused, her thoughts drifting to the

30

fleeting moment of recognition, like a shadow brushing against the light. "Do you think I resemble someone they knew?"

"Perhaps," Clara sighed. "Perhaps it is the manor's history that weighs on the minds of those who live here. Who can say? I cannot help but feel this place has seen its share of ghosts."

Evelyn nodded, though she said no more.

They walked in silence, lost in their own thoughts, until they stumbled upon a large glass structure nestled among the trees: an orangerie, its panes fogged slightly from the warmth inside.

"Father did not mention a glasshouse!" Her worries all but forgotten, Evelyn turned to Clara with wide eyes. "Shall we?"

Inside, vibrant orchids cascaded from the rafters, while exotic ferns unfurled their fronds, forming a lush canopy overhead. Lining the sides of the orangerie were citrus trees of every variety. It felt like stepping into another world.

"Look at this one, Clara!" Evelyn pulled out her sketchbook and began to draw its likeness.

Clara wandered deeper into the orangerie, the sound of her footsteps fading as she disappeared behind a row of orange trees. She had always been a quiet presence, prone to losing herself in curiosity and melancholy thought. Still, Evelyn expected her to return at any moment, lingering just out of sight.

Evelyn lost herself in her drawing, as she often did.

After some time, she became aware of a presence nearby. She turned slightly and saw a figure amongst the greenery, sitting quietly in the shadows. Mr Sinclair appeared to be brooding, as his grandfather had quipped earlier, yet there was a serenity about him, as if he sought refuge in the orangerie.

She glanced around for Clara, her hand unconsciously tightening around her sketchbook. *Alone without a chaperone.* No, it simply would not do. Evelyn resolved to slip away unnoticed, for the man had not seen her yet.

As she closed her sketchbook, the sound fractured the stillness of the orangerie, like a stone dropped in a pond. Mr Sinclair glanced up, as though surprised to be disturbed from his solitude.

"Forgive me," she said softly, feeling suddenly shy. "I did not intend to intrude."

"It is no intrusion, I assure you." His voice was low and gruff. "This orangerie is not mine; it belongs to the baron – a gift to his late wife. It was his pride and joy; though his constitution no longer permits him to visit as often as he once did. I come here to seek respite from his presence, not to lay claim to this sanctuary."

"You share an affinity for plants as well, I take it?" she inquired absently, while she looked through the foliage for her maid.

"Not especially. They possess a certain morbid fascination for me, if truth be told. What draws you to such things?"

Whilst Evelyn had asked her question to bide time, he asked with genuine interest. She hesitated, tracing the curve of a petal with her finger as she considered how much of herself to reveal. What could he, with his stern countenance and noble bearing, understand of her connection to the natural world? Still, something in his eyes, guarded as they were, invited her to speak.

"It is like the feeling of waking in the morning," she began slowly, "to the warmth of sunlight streaming through the window. When the bite of winter begins to retreat, and the first breath of spring stirs in the air. When you feel the garden begin to awaken. It is... difficult to explain."

He was silent for a time, weighing her words. She felt foolish suddenly, worried he would find her words childish or trite.

"You have conveyed it beautifully," he said softly.

Evelyn felt her cheeks warm at his praise, and for a moment, their eyes met. There was something unexpected in his look: a vulnerability that caught her off guard. She opened her mouth to respond, but before she could, she heard the soft rustle of Clara's skirts. The spell between them shattered.

"Miss Evelyn! You will scarcely believe the strange insect I have discovered near the citrus trees – " Clara's words faltered as she caught the exchange between the pair. Her eyes widened, but she quickly composed herself. "We should be going, miss."

Evelyn did not want to go – did not want the peculiar conversation to end, and yet, she knew it was wise. She nodded and began to follow her maid, but Mr Sinclair's voice stopped her: "Perhaps I might have the honour of showing you the estate gardens soon." His tone was measured, almost too careful. He cleared his throat. "With proper chaperonage, of course."

Her breath caught, though she could not say why. It was odd, the way he looked at her. She could not read his face at all, though something inexplicable drew her to him, to the way his gaze lingered as if she held answers to questions he dared not voice.

He was beautiful, yes, but it was not beauty alone that drew her. It was the way he existed, the gravity in the way he stood, as though he carried secrets heavy enough to bend the earth beneath his feet.

For a moment, she forgot herself – forgot the world, her maid waiting, the proprieties that bound her. Only when his lips quirked – ever so slightly, as though he knew her inner thoughts – did she draw herself back, her cheeks warming a degree.

"That would be... most agreeable," she stuttered.

She cast a final glance his way before turning her back.

He remained as he was, as though the earth itself held him there, his dark eyes fixed upon her with a weight that seemed to see beyond flesh and bone.

As she walked away, his gaze remained with her, like the echo of a melody she could not name and yet, could not forget.

∞∞∞

As Evelyn continued her stroll through the gardens, the cool breeze barely touched the strange feelings stirring within her. Clara had departed to attend to her mending tasks and promised to fetch her when it was time for lunch. After Mr Sinclair's offer of a chaperoned walk, Clara had raised an eyebrow at Evelyn, though her eyes were sparkling. Evelyn only shook her head in dismissal of the silent teasing. She was rather glad Clara had departed and left her in solitude.

Evelyn startled suddenly, for she thought she heard a sound – only a faint whisper carried on the wind. The rustling branches seemed to lean closer, their gnarled forms casting shadows on the ground. She stopped, listening intently, but the garden was silent save for the whistle of the wind through the leaves.

She began walking again, but there it was – soft, almost indistinguishable, like the murmur of voices carried from far away. She quickened her pace, glancing back at the shadowed treeline, where the darkness seemed to writhe.

As she reached the manor door atop the stone staircase, a chill settled in her bones, the warmth of the midday sun offering little comfort against the sensation that something was watching, waiting just beyond the edge of the garden.

Chapter 4

Henry

Rays of golden sunlight filtered through the glass walls of the orangerie, casting gentle patterns on the floor. Henry Sinclair sat on a weathered bench as a tight coil of tension gripped his chest. He had spent the morning in a haze, his thoughts swirling like the wind outside, but now they settled upon a singular figure: Miss Evelyn Ward.

The morning had begun with a storm – namely, a confrontation with the baron. As they sat down for breakfast in the dining room, a tension hung thick in the air. While pouring his tea – a casual act that seemed to ignite a fury in the old baron – Henry found himself at the centre of a familiar tirade that condemned his perceived dereliction of duty. The most recent transgression was his lateness to dinner the previous evening.

"It is high time you comprehended the burden of the Sinclair name, Henry. You are no longer a child to be coddled!"

His pulse had quickened, yet he maintained his composure. When had he ever been coddled?

"I am well aware of it, my lord. But you mistake me if you think I shall be bent to it by your demands alone."

"Demands?" The baron's eyes narrowed. "You speak of duty as if it were an inconvenience. This estate, this title – it will not wait for your whims. You cannot afford indifference – none of us can."

"*You* speak as though I have not borne the weight of these obligations my entire life. Would that I could pursue my own ambitions – be free of this wretched place – and yet, here I am."

The baron had pulled himself to standing. "Ambitions?" he spat, the loose skin of his throat shaking. "It is your duty to uphold this legacy, and yet you squander your it with your childish whims! And pray tell, what have you become? A discontented wretch, sulking in the shadows, unwilling to grasp the reins of your own fate!" He paused, wiping the spittle from his lip. "You will learn, Henry Sinclair, or all that remains will fall to ruin. The price we pay has always been steep." He dropped his voice, as if the walls themselves might hear. "And it shall only grow steeper still."

"I do not wish to be defined by your failures."

The baron's face darkened. "Do you think you can simply walk away from this, boy? It is not for you to decide. You are Sinclair blood. Never forget that."

With that, he turned as sharply as his frail body would allow, his walking stick echoing through the silent hall as the door slammed behind him. Breakfast lay untouched, a mute reflection of their discord.

Seeking refuge, Henry had fled to the glass greenhouse, hoping the gentle sunlight would offer some peace. Instead, he found himself ensnared in a whirlwind of thoughts. His strained relationship with the baron felt like a delicate spider's web, fraying at the edges, and each broken strand was a reminder of all that loomed over him.

Then, as if drawn by an unseen force, Miss Ward had disturbed him. The sight of her, caught as if trying to leave unnoticed, had pulled him from his reverie. He had felt exposed – vulnerable – as her eyes met his.

He had asked her what drew her to flowers, and she just stood there. Her fingers gently brushed the petals of an orchid, the sunlight filtering through the glass and onto her sweet face. Her skin looked so soft, her lips so pink. The auburn of her hair glinted like spun gold, as if she herself was a blossom in the sun.

She had talked about warmth, the slow retreat of winter, and the awakening of the garden. Her words had flowed with a sincerity that drew him in. She had painted an image of renewal and life that stood in such stark contrast to the harshness of his own reality.

"You have conveyed it beautifully," he said, and in that moment, she looked straight into him. He felt a sudden urge to reach out, to pull her closer and share the weight of his existence. Her softness stirred something deep within him, awakening a longing for freedom beyond the constraints that bound him.

When her maid arrived, the spell between them shattered, that invisible thread that had drawn them together snapping like a taut string.

Come back. Do not leave me here.

"Perhaps I might have the honour of showing you the estate gardens one day," he said instead. "With proper chaperonage, of course."

She had agreed, her voice betraying a slight tremor as she cast one last glance in his direction. He noted the flush on her cheeks, the way her breasts moved with the gentle rise and fall of her breath. As she turned to her maid, he caught a glimpse of the pulse in her throat.

Henry had watched her go, drawn in by the sway of dress as she moved. She seemed like a rare bloom, thriving in a world that didn't quite understand her.

He remained in the orangerie, the flowers around him fading into the background, lost in thoughts of her.

Chapter 5

Evelyn

Evelyn wandered through the manor's halls that afternoon, unsure of how to occupy her time, and so she simply kept walking. She felt a pull – an inexplicable longing – guiding her footsteps, until she found herself standing before a heavy oak door.

Pushing it open, she stepped into the library, a grand room lined with dark, towering shelves that seemed to stretch up towards the arched ceiling. Dust swirled lazily in the dim light that filtered through the leaded windows, casting shadows on the ancient wooden furniture. A huge fireplace dominated one wall and its mantelpiece was laden with curious trinkets.

She moved further inside, brushing her fingers over the spines of books, feeling the textured covers and embossed titles. The scent of aged paper and well-worn leather filled the air, wrapping her in a comforting embrace that reminded her of home. As she browsed the titles, her eyes fell upon a peculiar book tucked away on a high shelf. It looked ancient, as if it had not seen the light of day for many years.

Drawn by a strange compulsion, she placed the ladder against the towering shelves, shaking slightly as she ascended. She grasped the old book, pulling it gently from its resting place. Dust cascaded down like tiny stars as she opened its pages, revealing yellowed parchment adorned with flowing script.

The text inside was a mixture of botanical illustrations and cryptic notes, but something else caught her eye. In hurried cursive, it read: *"I have unearthed the truth behind the curse that plagues the Sinclairs. I was but a pawn in a cruel game orchestrated by the spirits of the past."*

Her curiosity piqued, she carefully descended the ladder, settling onto a chaise that creaked softly beneath her. Opening the journal again, she noticed that the ink had smudged in places and entire sections had been hastily rubbed out, as if someone had tried to erase the memories within.

She kept reading: *"I see it in their eyes, the despair and hopelessness that plagues our bloodline. I once believed I could break the curse, but now I fear I have only strengthened its hold."*

The ink bled into the parchment, rendering the rest of the text on the page unreadable. Frustrated, she flipped to the next page. *"I do not believe love to be enough. My son will suffer for the sins of the father, as I have suffered for mine."*

"I see you have found my father's diary," a voice rumbled from the doorway. The baron stepped into the dim light of the library.

Evelyn snapped the book shut. "Your father's diary?"

"Yes." His words were slow, forced through ancient lips. He hobbled closer. "He rambled on about a great many things, most of which were quite nonsensical. This diary is just one example of his madness. He became obsessed with his theories, all stemming from a curse he believed plagued our family."

"It reads like the fevered ramblings of a troubled mind."

"Indeed. You'd do well to think little of it. My father's imagination was far more vivid than his reality." Yet beneath the baron's casual dismissal, a flicker of something darker danced in his eyes. She stood quickly, handing him the book.

"It is just so that I do not believe in curses. They defy rationality."

The baron's lips curved into a slow smile, but his eyes remained cold and sharp. "Ah, but the mind... it can be a trickster, bending reality in ways we scarcely understand. Just because something cannot be explained, it does not mean it cannot exist."

Evelyn felt a shiver run down her spine, not for the first time since arriving at Rosehill Manor. "Surely you do not believe in such superstitions, my lord."

The old baron moved slightly closer, his dank breath washing over her. "I have seen things in this house, Miss Ward – things that cannot be easily dismissed. Secrets buried deep, waiting to resurface. The mind can be a powerful thing, but so too can the past."

"Yet there must be an explanation for all things, my lord. Surely your father's musings were merely that – the disjointed thoughts of a man who had lost his grasp on reality."

A low, humourless chuckle escaped him. "Perhaps. Or perhaps he possessed knowledge he chose to conceal, and in his madness, stumbled upon truths best left undisturbed."

""Best left undisturbed?" Evelyn's eyes narrowed. She cared little for the diary and its words, though the challenge grated at her. "And what if one should choose to seek out those truths?"

The baron straightened as far as his curved back would allow. "One may find that the more they seek to understand, the deeper they find themselves entangled with those very mysteries. One must be prepared for what they might uncover."

The baron began to cough, spittle flying from his lips as he bent over. He turned to leave before pausing at the door, glancing back over his hunched shoulder.

"Remember, Miss Ward," he croaked. "Curiosity is a double-edged sword."

∞∞∞∞

That evening, dinner was served in the great hall, a cavernous cathedral with a ceiling adorned by intricate plasterwork of twisted vines and grotesque faces. Grand chandeliers hung low like jewels, casting restless shadows that danced upon the stained-glass windows. The panes, depicting long-forgotten tales, filtered the waning light into a haunting tapestry of colours.

The atmosphere was formal and the conversation stilted, interrupted only by the muted clinking of cutlery. Mr Sinclair – seated opposite Evelyn – was withdrawn, eating in brooding silence. The baron spoke of mundane matters – weather, politics, local matters – but beneath his words, Evelyn sensed an unspoken tension that hung in the air like a cloud.

At one point, Mr Sinclair's fork clattered against his plate, and for a moment, their eyes met. In that fleeting exchange, she sensed a storm brewing behind his dark eyes. She wondered at the strained relationship between the baron and his grandson.

When dinner had finally adjourned, Evelyn trailed behind the butler as he ascended the grand staircase. The oil lamp he carried cast wreathing shadows against the walls, the ornate carvings and gilded edges seeming to come alive. Mr Blackwood moved with an unsettling grace, his dark suit blending seamlessly into the gloom, as if he were more a part of the shadows than the living world.

They reached the landing, and Evelyn hesitated at the threshold of her room. The glow of the lamp revealed the faintest tremor in the butler's hand, as if he too sensed the terrible tension of the evening.

"Good night, Miss Evelyn."

She offered a smile, feeling both grateful for his presence and unnerved by his watchful demeanour. He retreated down the corridor, the light from his lamp slinking into the shadows.

She lit a solitary candle by her bedside, the flame flickering in the quiet darkness. The scent of wax mingled with the faint aroma of night-blooming jasmine from the gardens below.

Clara entered the room with a soft rustle of fabric. "Shall I help you prepare for bed, Miss Evelyn?"

She nodded, grateful for the familiar routine.

Clara guided her to a cushioned stool before the mirror, taking the brush in hand. As the lady's maid worked, she hummed a quiet tune, weaving a thread of warmth through the room.

44

Once her hair was neatly secured, Clara helped her into her nightclothes. "There you are, Miss," she said with a satisfied nod. "All ready for bed."

Evelyn managed another small smile. "Thank you. Goodnight, Clara."

"Goodnight, Miss Evelyn. Do remember to keep the candle close at hand should you require its light."

Before the door closed, Shadow slipped through the narrow gap of the door, padding silently into the room. The cat leapt onto the bed, curling beside her with a soft purr.

"Ah, there you are, Shadow. Keeping watch, I see."

Evelyn settled onto her bed, the lace curtains fluttering slightly, as though stirred by an unseen breath. She opened her sketchbook in the dim light of her candle, hoping to find solace in her drawings, but the recollections of the evening's tensions remained. Even the air in her room felt stifling, as if the walls themselves were closing in around her.

Her mind flickered back to the orangerie, and Mr Sinclair's piercing gaze. The library had only deepened her unease, the baron's words echoing in her ears like a sinister refrain: *Curiosity is a double-edged sword.* What secrets did the baron have to hide?

Evelyn closed the sketchbook with a sigh. She picked up a novel, but as she began to read, the scratching began.

It was just like the previous night. At first, it was faint, a mere whisper against the walls, but soon it grew louder, more insistent – a relentless scuttling sound that seemed to burrow into the very fabric of the manor.

She set the book down, her hands clammy against the cool wood of the nightstand. The scratching was unyielding. But from where did it originate?

Evelyn rose from her bed, drawn to the window, peering into the inky abyss of the night. A chill swept through her, a breath of air that felt impossibly cold. Though she searched the room, the source of the scratching remained elusive.

With a deep sigh, she returned to her bed and curled beneath the thick blankets. She nestled closer to Shadow, who responded with a soft purr, his warmth wrapping around her like a cloak. As the scratching morphed into a rhythmic thrumming, she tried to convince herself it was merely the house settling, as all old houses were wont to doo – but deep within, she felt an undeniable and illogical fear: the manor was alive, and it harboured secrets that clung to its walls like smoke.

Chapter 6

Alistair

The baron sat hunched over a letter, his fingers stained with ink. His study smelled of aged paper and a hint of tobacco, the remnants of a long-forgotten pipe left to languish in a drawer. He dipped his quill once more, and the scratching of ink against parchment was the only sound to break the silence.

Velvet drapes framed the arched windows, allowing only slivers of light to pierce the darkness. He raised his brandy and took a shaky sip, savouring the warmth that coursed through him. It was a moment of solace – brief yet precious.

"Ah, the eternal ebb and flow of light and dark," he mused aloud in a slow drawl, though no one was there to listen but the walls. "A delicate balance, one might say, like the symphony of life itself." He chuckled softly, the sound echoing oddly in the emptiness. "But what is a symphony without its dissonance?"

His mind wandered to Henry, his heir. A twinge of regret gnawed at him as he leant back in his chair, fingers steepled under his chin.

It was then that the glass slipped from his fingers, shattering on the floor. He rose unsteadily and the remnants of the glass crunched beneath his feet.

"I must see him," he murmured. "Henry needs to understand the burden we carry – the legacy that shadows us. Perhaps I have been too harsh."

The door creaked open, and a chill gust of air swept through, causing the candle on his desk to flicker precariously.

"What is it?" he snapped.

Mr Blackwood glided into the room. His pale skin seemed to absorb the light, rendering him almost ghostly against the dim backdrop of the study. Alistair regarded him warily, thinking of how the butler was as old as he was, and yet, Blackwood seemed untouched by the passage of time in comparison.

"I trust you have news?"

"The household remains as it ought, my lord. Yet, this evening, the atmosphere bears a distinct shift."

"Indeed, it does," he replied wearily.

"There are whispers in the shadows." Blackwood's eyes glinted with a strange light. "The night holds a weight, a heaviness that suggests old things may rise again. It is a time when boundaries thin."

"Old things," Alistair echoed. "All that is needed is the right alignment."

Blackwood's smile spread unnaturally wide. "Indeed, my lord. This night may unveil what is destined to be. All it demands is a gentle nudge, a fleeting moment when the fabric of fate permits that which has long been dormant to awaken."

"Do you not think that we should be more forthcoming with Henry? How can he protect himself if he remains in the dark?"

Blackwood regarded him steadily. "Knowledge can lead to fear, my lord, and fear may cloud one's judgement."

As the shadows deepened around them, Alistair felt an unsettling weight envelop him, as if the very walls were drawing in tighter. He knew well what lay hidden beneath the surface; he had awaited this moment for longer than he cared to admit.

Chapter 7

Evelyn

Evelyn had not forgotten Mr Sinclair's promise of a stroll through the gardens, though he had kept his distance since their fleeting encounter in the orangerie. Each morning, she wandered the frost-kissed paths, where winter blooms released their sweet perfume into the chilled air. Her steps often led her back to that glass greenhouse, though she scarcely admitted to herself why.

In the echo of his absence, Evelyn occupied her days in a dance between duty and distraction. She attended to correspondence by the drawing-room fire. She walked the halls, trailing her gloved hands along the banisters as if they might lead her somewhere new. She devoted herself to the art of nature sketching in the gardens, gliding her quill across parchment as she captured the intricate beauty of the blooms. In the absence of a suitable governess, she took it upon herself to guide her brother through lessons of reading and arithmetic. By night, she performed her role at dinner and in the parlour. Still, no diversion wholly occupied her thoughts, which turned again and again to the figure who had not appeared.

One morning, just as she was lost in the rhythm of another sketch, the quiet of the drawing room was broken. The heir to the manor finally reappeared, framed by the pale light that filtered through the windows.

The sight of him – his dark hair tousled as if stirred by a restless wind – sent an unbidden thrill through her. His waistcoat, trimmed in gold, stood against the crisp white of his shirt and the neatly tied cravat at his throat. His stance was rigid, hands clasped behind his back, as though every movement was an act of sheer will.

He cleared his throat. "Miss Ward. I believe I promised you a walk in the gardens. Would you care to join me now?"

Evelyn stifled for a moment. *He has been absent for days,* she thought, *and now he appears, asking me to walk with him?* She ought to refuse. *He can walk by himself.*

Still, before she could voice the objection, she found herself nodding and rising from her chair. Her hands moved to smooth the folds of her woollen gown, and she wrapped a thick shawl around her shoulders.

He extended his arm towards her.

Through the layers of her gloves, she felt the firm pressure of his grip. His touch, though steady, held no familiarity. She could not help but feel the invitation was born from pity, or duty.

They stepped out into the brisk air, their breath rising in soft clouds as they began their slow walk down the gravel paths. Though the air still carried the sharp chill of late winter, the sun shone brightly, casting a pale, almost mournful light across the estate grounds. The gardens, though mostly bare, held a stark beauty, the skeletal branches and muted earth offering an eerie reflection of the silence between them.

Evelyn stole a glance over her shoulder at Clara, who followed at a respectful distance. Her maid's presence, though a comfort, was a subtle reminder of the propriety she must maintain in a gentleman's company.

Mr Sinclair's voice broke the silence, his tone formal and detached. "The gardens in this section of the estate are my mother's legacy. She oversaw the design herself. The roses will begin to bloom in a few months, though it's difficult to imagine them now."

"Her legacy is most beautiful." Evelyn inclined her head, and her words were as stiff as his. "I am certain it must be beautiful in the spring."

Mr Sinclair nodded, though his eyes remained fixed ahead, as if he sought to distance himself from everything, but particularly from her.

As they continued their walk, Evelyn found herself stealing glances at him. He was undeniably handsome with a strong and noble profile, yet beneath that exterior, there was something more: a depth, an intensity, like the hint of a storm behind calm skies. Her heart beat a little faster, aware of his nearness and the strange tension that seemed to accompany his presence.

They rounded a corner and approached the stables, where the rich scent of horses and hay filled the air.

Charles was inside, grinning widely as he mucked out one of the stalls. The sleeves of his shirt were rolled up and sweat dripped down his brow into his brunette locks.

"Sister! Mr Sinclair!" he called out brightly, leaning on a pitchfork. "I did not expect to see you here. I have been helping the stable hands! It's good, honest work."

Mr Sinclair's expression softened, if only slightly. "Not the sort of task one expects a lad of your station to be involved in, Master Ward."

Charles laughed. "Horses don't care if I am a gentleman or not. They appreciate the attention just the same." He paused, casting a glance at Evelyn before continuing. "Might you consider taking me on a hunting expedition, my lord? I've heard there's game in the woods just beyond the estate."

Evelyn noticed the way Mr Sinclair's posture stiffened beside her. His response was swift and clipped: "No. I will not leave the estate."

"Oh." Charles blinked in surprise and resumed his mucking of the stable. "Perhaps another time, then."

Evelyn could not help but feel the sting of Mr Sinclair's rudeness. She stole a glance at him, wondering why he had refused so firmly. Was it possible he simply couldn't ride? Perhaps he felt embarrassed by such a limitation. She considered whether he might harbour a fear of the woods, or if he merely viewed spending time with a child as beneath him.

"I am sure you will find something else to entertain yourself with, Charles," she offered.

He smiled at her, though it didn't quite reach his eyes.

Mr Sinclair, however, said nothing more. His jaw remained clenched, and when she looked at him again, his eyes were shadowed with something odd – perhaps regret, or guilt.

As they made their way back to the manor, the cold seemed to seep deeper into Evelyn's bones.

The drawing room was a sanctuary of warmth that afternoon, with the flames of the hearth casting a gentle glow across the ornate furnishings. Evelyn lounged on a chaise with her sketchbook, watercolours arranged on a small table beside her. A light luncheon of cold meats, cheese and bread was laid to the side.

"It is good to see you, my dear," her father said, nibbling a piece of cheese. His spectacles lay atop a closed scientific volume, likely filled with scribbled notes. "I often wish we could have more relaxed meals like this. The atmosphere in the dining hall is rather stifling, is it not?"

Evelyn returned the smile, though her gaze drifted towards the door. "Indeed, Father. To sit here with you is a pleasant reprieve from the daily routines." A thought crossed her mind. "But where is Charles? He has not yet joined us."

Her father frowned. "He always has such a hearty appetite, especially after his morning in the stables. I expected him to be here by now. Shall we save him some bread and cheese?"

"Perhaps he became too engrossed in his work. I shall check on him. He has the tendency to lose track of time when he is with the horses."

"Shall I accompany you, Miss Evelyn?" Clara asked, standing. She had been tucked away in the corner, silently mending a shawl.

"No – thank you, Clara. I shall go alone. I will only be a moment."

As she stood, a sudden draft swept through the room. The heavy wooden door creaked open, revealing a servant with a pallid face and a brow glistening with sweat. He hesitated at the threshold, eyes darting nervously around the room.

"Pardon the interruption, sir," he stammered. "There's been an... incident in the stables."

Her father set his plate down on the side table with a deliberate slowness. He waited.

"Master Charles. He was – " the servant faltered, casting a quick glance over his shoulder as if fearing unseen eyes. "He was thrown from a horse, sir. He is injured, and they are calling for you."

Evelyn felt her heart drop.

"I shall attend to him at once." Her father rose abruptly, and she caught a glimpse of his expression; something akin to fear crossed his features before he masked it, stalking from the room.

Clara approached, running her quivering hands against her skirts. "I have been meaning to tell you, Miss Evelyn. I cannot help but fear there is something wrong with this place... something that lurks just out of sight."

Evelyn nodded once, and moved to stand at the threshold of the drawing room, the chill of the afternoon creeping into her bones as she peered into the dimly lit foyer.

Should she follow her father? No, she would be in the way. Perhaps she should call for the physician.

Though she had not replied, she knew Clara was right: there was something not quite right at Rosehill Manor.

Suddenly, the grand doors of the foyer swung open, and Mr Sinclair emerged like a giant silhouetted against the light. He carried Charles in his arms, and Evelyn's breath caught at the sight of her younger brother. His face was pale and drawn, and his leg twisted at an unnatural angle.

"Oh, Charles!"

"He was thrown from a bucking horse," Mr Sinclair explained calmly, as Evelyn ran to them. "I witnessed it from the gardens. He landed poorly and has likely broken his leg. We must send for the physician at once."

"Oh, Charles." Her hands trembled as she brushed back his hair, now damp with sweat.

"Just a bit sore, Evelyn," Charles managed through laboured breathing. His eyes betrayed him, glistening with unshed tears.

Their father emerged in the foyer behind Mr Sinclair, breathless and visibly shaken. "Mr Blackwood," he commanded, "fetch the doctor at once."

The butler, who had been lingering in the shadows like a ghost, nodded swiftly before vanishing down a corridor.

"Do not worry so, Father; I will be back to riding soon," Charles whispered, his breath shallow as he lay cradled in Mr Sinclair's arms.

"Let us get you settled in your chamber," Evelyn urged, squeezing his hand gently. "Clara will bring you some lemon balm tea to ease the pain as we await the physician. He will be here soon, I am certain. Rest now, and I shall soon come sit by your side to read you a story."

Charles blinked up at her through his welled tears. "Will you read my favourite? The one about the brave knight and the dragon?"

"Of course, my dearest. I will read it to you from the very beginning, just as you like."

As Mr Sinclair carried Charles up the stairs, she could not help but notice the strength in the man's arms and shoulders – the way the fabric of his shirt stretched taut against the contours of his muscles, shifting with each stride.

Once they had reached the landing and disappeared, she turned to her father. "Do you believe all shall be well, Father?"

She felt a keen sense of motherly love and responsibility for her younger brother. In his ten short years, hers was the only maternal affection he had known.

"My dear, the human body and spirit possesses remarkable resilience, particularly in the young. Charles is strong. I am sure that with the physician's care, he shall mend in due time. We must remain steadfast and provide him with the comfort he needs. Let us not borrow trouble from the future."

She nodded, swallowing the lump in her throat as she pressed herself against her father's chest. She inhaled deeply, drawing in the scent of sandalwood and leather that enveloped him.

As she stepped back from her father, feeling somewhat steadied by his embrace, the sound of footsteps echoed softly from the staircase. Mr Sinclair descended, his brow furrowed deeply.

"I have laid Charles in his bed," he began, his voice low. "A footman has been sent to retrieve the physician from the village. The boy is resting now, but…" His words faltered, caught in the tightness of his throat.

"Thank you, Mr Sinclair," her father said. "You gave my son comfort and strength when he needed it most."

Her breath caught as Mr Sinclair ran a hand through his tousled hair, the movement revealing his weariness. Now that Charles was safe, she could not help but notice the disarray of his attire. Once so pristine that morning, it was now rumpled, his cravat undone, and his shirt slightly askew.

"I should have allowed him to ride with me – at least around the estate. Had I done so, he might have been spared this injury. The blame lies with me for his suffering." It seemed the words slipped from Mr Sinclair's lips with raw honesty before he could rein them in.

"Accidents do occur, Mr Sinclair," her father interjected. "You need not shoulder this burden."

"You cannot comprehend, sir. A darkness lingers within these walls. A weight that bears down upon us all." He paused, and an icy shiver snaked down Evelyn's spine, a familiar sensation since arriving at Rosehill Manor. "I find myself deeply troubled for the safety of those you cherish. It may be prudent to think of a departure from this manor. One cannot dismiss the misfortune that seems to haunt those who reside here."

Evelyn stiffened, her gaze flickering to his. *Misfortune that haunts?* The phrasing struck her as absurd, the sort of sentiment one might find in a ghost tale whispered by servants around a kitchen hearth. Surely, he could not truly believe such things.

"We must not allow superstition to dictate our lives, Mr Sinclair," she asserted, though the edge in her tone betrayed her unease. "From whom, or what, do you believe harm will come? The house is old, yes, but it is only wood and stone. Misfortune is shaped by the choices of people, not the whims of walls."

He offered a tight smile, one that never reached his troubled eyes. "Perhaps. Yet one cannot overlook the relentless pattern of grief that has haunted my family. The thought of further harm befalling anyone within these walls is unbearable."

As if summoned by the words, Shadow emerged from the gloom, its black fur slinking between the shadows. The cat padded silently into the pale wash of light before them. It paused, luminous eyes narrowing as its body stiffened. With a sudden arch of the spine, Shadow let out a hiss that shattered the stillness, a warning aimed directly at Mr Sinclair.

Chapter 8

Evelyn

The moon glowed silver and cold, casting a watchful eye over the grounds of the manor. Snowflakes danced across the night sky, settling on the verdant leaves as reminder of winter's lingering grasp.

Evelyn wrapped her shawl tighter, the thin fabric offering little protection against the night's chill. She had spent hours tossing restlessly in bed, her mind swirling with unsettling thoughts: the ominous entries in the old diary, Charles' accident, Mr Henry Sinclair and his strange warning to leave Rosehill Manor. But mostly, she could not shake the memory of his broad back and muscled arms as he carried Charles to safety.

Frustrated and confused, she had finally slipped out for a stroll, hoping the cool air would calm the tempest inside her.

As she wandered the estate's winding paths by moonlight, an inexplicable pull drew her away from the manor towards the gardens at its edge. While much of the estate lay dormant, here – amidst the quiet stillness – life thrived in unexpected ways.

Striking hellebores and vibrant winter jasmine swayed in the crisp breeze. Amongst them, she spotted flowers that should not have survived the season: delicate delphiniums and foxgloves with petals lush and defiant against winter's chill. She wondered aloud at their resilience even in the coldest of seasons – how was it that this garden was in full bloom? It was not yet spring, and these flowers were not in season. Wonder blossomed within her, and her curiosity tugged her deeper into the garden.

The world around her faded into a soft haze. She paused, her breath visible in the cold night air, closing her eyes for a moment. She could almost hear the soft murmur of the flowers urging her to explore the hidden corners of the garden. She pressed on, weaving through the blooms. It felt as though the very essence of nature conspired to lead her towards something extraordinary.

A subtle glow emanated from a thicket of vines ahead, and an archway of ancient oak trees emerged. With each step closer, the world faded, as if the air held its breath in ancient reverence.

A narrow path wound through the undergrowth, nearly obscured by a tapestry of ivy. She pushed through a curtain of foliage at the archway, unveiling a hidden enclave.

"A secret garden," she breathed.

She slipped off her shoes, relishing the cold air against her skin. The ground was blanketed in a carpet of moss, woven from shades of emerald and jade.

Enclosed by walls of stone and vines, the garden stood against the night like a refuge of beauty. Each flower shimmered in the moonlight, their colours impossibly vivid, as if the very stars had descended to bloom among the petals. How very like her dream it was – yet this time, real.

Evelyn pinched herself to be sure. Oh yes, she was awake.

At the garden's heart lay a patch of untouched snow, and at its centre stood a solitary rosebush. Its thorny branches reached skyward, ancient and defiant, the glossy leaves glinting like polished jewels, and at the top was nestled a single rosebud.

She knelt beside it, her breath hitching as moonlight bathed the bloom. It was just as she had dreamed – perfect and impossible.

She reached out to brush her fingers against the petals, and a shiver coursed through her, though not from the cold. Her heart quickened, caught between wonder and a quiet dread she could not shake.

"Do not touch it."

Evelyn jumped backwards, almost falling, for the voice sliced through the air, sharp as ice. She spun around to see a figure cloaked in shadow, seated on a weathered bench at the garden's edge.

In the dim light of the moon, she caught a glimpse of familiar features: broad shoulders, tousled dark hair, eyes that glimmered a deep blue under heavy brows.

"It will bloom tonight," said Mr Sinclair, his tone gentler now.

The silver light of the moon caressed his chiselled jawline, illuminating the fine lines of worry etched upon his brow. He was both beautiful and fragile, like a dark rose poised to unfurl. There was a watchfulness in his gaze, as if he were attuned to the very heartbeat of the night.

Something unspoken hovered between them in the garden, a thread woven into the fabric of the evening air. They said nothing for a long time. They did not need to.

In the distance, the clock from the manor began to chime, and Mr Sinclair sat up straighter.

As if awakened by the stroke of midnight or the very call of the moon itself, the rose began to unfurl.

Evelyn held her breath, as if caught in a spell, acutely aware of the gentleman close by her, still as a statue.

The first petal unfolded, a deep crimson as rich as blood, glistening like velvet touched by morning dew. With each layer that opened, the rose shimmered, swaying gently in the breeze.

As the rose unfurled completely, it seemed to breathe, to exhale a sound. It was neither song nor noise but something in between, an aching harmony that stirred the air around her. It resonated deep within, like a lament for love lost and love yet to be found.

Evelyn and Mr Sinclair were still, suspended in a moment both eternal and fleeting. Their hearts beat in unison with the gentle rhythm of the rose. Their eyes met across the garden.

Beauty. Fragility. Understanding.

And then, a sudden chill swept through the garden, causing the leaves to tremble and the spell to lift. Time resumed its flow, and the garden was just that – a garden.

The cold caught in Evelyn's throat, and she stifled a cough.

"It is late." Mr Sinclair stood abruptly. "The chill of the night seems to have taken its toll. I would not wish for you to take ill on my account. It is past midnight, and we should not be alone without a chaperone, yet again."

His words stung, the blooming rose all but forgotten.

"Mr Sinclair," she bristled. "I assure you, I am no fragile flower, ready to wilt at midnight's toll or in the night's chill."

"I never suggested you were, Miss Ward. But society has its rules. I would hate for you to become the subject of gossip. A lady deserves respect, and I cannot abide the thought of compromising that."

Evelyn paused, her fingers brushing the edges of a stone statue as she considered his words. A breeze stirred, making the vines tremble like old bones.

Respect? Or is it more about controlling where that respect is placed?

His concern felt more like restriction than protection. She straightened, lifting her chin slightly.

"With all due respect, Mr Sinclair, I hardly think gossip will flourish here, in this hidden garden in the heart of the countryside. Particularly with no guests in sight." She hoped the implication was clear: her actions were her own, not for the world to judge, not to be confined to the roles others had carved out for her.

He shook his head, a smile playing at the corners of his lips, as if her words amused him. He took his place again on the cold stone bench, crossing his arms. "You would be surprised, Miss Ward. Servants can be the worst gossips of all. Reputations only require one stray word to be ruined." He spoke lightly, but the warning beneath his words was clear: she could think this was just a private moment, but it was never that simple. Society's watchful eye was never far behind.

Evelyn sighed. Though she detested it, she understood it all too well. She moved to sit beside him, wrapping her arms around herself for warmth.

"I appreciate your concern, truly. But sometimes it feels as if society cares more about appearances than truth or reason. It is as though the world wants us to wear masks. I long to be seen as more than simply a young woman in need of protection or a mere object for marriage. At times, I feel like a caged animal."

He laughed mirthlessly. "I understand the feeling of being trapped too well. It is suffocating." He paused for a moment. "There is something captivating about your spirit, Miss Ward. It is fierce. Unyielding."

A lump formed in her throat, for it was rare to feel seen. Most saw only what was expected: a young lady to be admired from afar or courted, her worth defined by the expectations of her sex. But here, in this quiet garden, Mr Sinclair saw something else – the restless, unbowed part of her that refused to fit neatly into the mould others had cast for her.

As they sat side by side, an unspoken tension filled the space between them. She leant in, her breath hitching as an invisible thread drew them together. She could feel the gravity of the roles she played, the rules of decorum pressing in, but here, in this stolen moment, she could almost taste the freedom of abandoning them.

Their faces were close now, their lips nearly touching.

"Miss Ward," he said softly, pulling away.

Her heart sank as he turned his face away.

Oh, heavens. She stood abruptly, her feet still bare in the cold of the garden. She lifted her skirts above her ankles and ran, fleeing the garden's confines.

She ran through the winding gardens and hedges, past the silent statues that watched her with knowing eyes, past the line of ancient oaks with gnarled branches twisting like fingers grasping for her. She ran until she reached the manor, climbing the stairs two at a time, pushing open the heavy doors and darting through the maze of corridors. When at last she reached her chambers, she crawled into bed in search of refuge beneath the warmth of her covers.

So foolish, she chided herself, as silent tears traced the contours of her cheeks, spilling into her pillow.

Shadow padded in quietly and settled beside her.

Chapter 9

Henry

Midnight cloaked the secret garden in velvety darkness, only the silver moon daring to pierce the night. Henry had spent countless hours in this sanctuary, perched on a cold stone bench, surrounded by twisted branches and rustling leaves that whispered his childhood secrets. As a boy, he had stumbled into the hidden refuge, captivated by a single rose that stubbornly refused to bloom, luring him back time and time again.

But tonight was different. He stood among the tangled vines, knowing that the rose would finally unfurl. He had overheard Blackwood and the baron speaking of an omen – a shift in the air. Though he could not fathom its significance, he knew instinctively that they referred to the rose.

He felt a kinship with the flower: both trapped in shadows, bound by the legacy of his family and the earth. He felt the weight of the curse woven into the very fabric of the air, a riddle unbroken by the baron's cryptic tales. Each word the old man spoke felt like a fragment of truth, never fully revealing the secrets of the rose – of its magic or its pain.

As the rose unfurled, Henry's breath hitched, but beneath the thrill, a knot twisted in his stomach. *What did it signify, to finally bloom?* He stood motionless, waiting – though for what, he did not know.

Before him, Miss Evelyn Ward stood in bare feet with sparkling eyes. They shared a heartbeat with the rose, a fragile understanding. For a fleeting moment, time itself seemed to pause, encapsulating their souls in a fragile cocoon.

But when a chill swept through the garden, reality returned, and the enchantment dissolved into the mundane. He watched as the cold caught in Miss Ward's throat, a delicate sound that danced upon the night air.

"It is late," he said abruptly, rising from his seat. The crisp night air bit at him, but he felt a different kind of unease – one that had nothing to do with the cold and everything to do with the woman before him. He spoke more harshly than he intended, slicing through the quiet garden like a blade. "It is past midnight, and we should not be alone without a chaperone, yet again."

In truth, Henry cared nothing for the bounds of proprietary. He envisioned taking her in his arms then and there, drawing her close, feeling her warmth against him, all rules cast aside – but the weight of his conscience held him back, as always, like a chain he could not break. The rules he had imposed upon himself were far more binding than those of society.

"Mr Sinclair," she replied stiffly, her chin raised, a challenge in her eyes. "I assure you, I am no fragile flower, ready to wilt at midnight's toll or in the night's chill."

The way she stood her ground, even in such a small exchange, stirred something within him: amusement, frustration, something deeper he refused to name. He met her stare, his voice steady, but his own eyes narrowed as he tried to rein in the emotions that surfaced as she defied him. "I never suggested you were, Miss Ward."

She crossed her arms, her posture tight with defiance. He admired her spirit even as it tested his patience. He could practically hear the quiet murmur of the household staff already. Her innocence on this matter, though admirable, was dangerously naïve.

When she moved to sit behind him on the bench and he caught a whiff of her fragrance: an intoxicating blend of lavender and something earthy, as if she carried a garden with her wherever she went. "At times, I feel like a caged animal."

Her words, laden with yearning, struck a chord deep within him, resonating against the unspoken frustrations that festered in his own soul. The vulnerability she laid bare stirred an instinctive need to protect her, to shield her from harm. Yet even as he yearned to draw her closer, to wrap her in the safety of his embrace, he grappled with the fear of what such closeness might entail.

His laughter was hollow. "I understand the feeling of being trapped too well. It is suffocating." As he observed her, he felt as though he could see the depths of her spirit, the dreams she clung to, even in a world determined to clip her wings. Her words rang with a truth that mirrored his own struggle, resonating in the silence between them. "There is something captivating about your spirit, Miss Ward. It is fierce. Unyielding."

As he spoke, he noticed the way her eyes glistened. As they sat side by side, she leant in.

Henry inhaled sharply. He stood teetering on the edge of hope and despair, love and loss, yearning to love her and yearning to protect her from the darkness.

What if the rose was not a harbinger of hope, but a vessel of doom?

In that charged silence, he wanted to shout his truths, to lay bare the torment that swirled within him, yet words eluded him, trapped within the confines of his fear.

"Miss Ward," he said softly, pulling away. In the depths of his heart, he ached to reach out, yet the fear of fate's cruel hand held him back.

She stood abruptly, fleeing the garden's embrace and leaving him alone beneath the vast expanse of stars. It was what he had wanted, and yet the loss struck him like a blow to the gut. The vibrant rose, blooming defiantly in the dark, mocked him like a painful reminder of the desire he dared not pursue. The garden seemed to whisper of what could have been, leaving him adrift in despair, where hope felt like a distant dream – forever beyond his grasp.

70

Chapter 10

Evelyn

Evelyn wandered to the orangerie each day to draw new and interesting flowers, enjoying the flow of ink and the bright splash of her watercolours, though beneath her focus on her art lay a persistent distraction: Mr Sinclair. She found herself watching for him, uncertain whether she hoped to see him or wished to avoid him altogether. His rejection of her kiss haunted her, a lingering question that festered in her mind. Why had he turned away? Had she imagined the air between them? Was he repulsed, embarrassed by her attention?

Mr Sinclair remained elusive, even taking his meals in solitude. Evelyn wondered how long her father intended to stay at Rosehill Manor, and whether they had overstayed their welcome already.

Her worries subsided one evening when Mr Sinclair finally graced the dinner table with his presence. He sat silently, watchful, his gaze drifting across the room.

Evelyn ate in silence, listening to the ebb and flow of conversation between her father and the baron, who animatedly discussed various plants. Meanwhile, Charles chimed in frequently, chattering about the stable horses.

71

Despite his pain, Charles was slowly on the mend, the physician having skilfully bound his injured leg, allowing him to be moved about with assistance. Each day, the servants carefully carried him to the stables, where the sound of hooves and gentle whinnies lifted his spirits. Watching the horses gallop and frolic in the paddock brought a smile to his face, and Evelyn felt keen relief at seeing him so joyful. Her father was right: her brother was resilient.

Evelyn stole occasional glances at Mr Sinclair, noticing the way his attention rested on Charle's anecdotes. It warmed her heart to see him engage with the boy, though his presence stirred conflicting emotions within her. She could not deny the yearning that swirled in her chest: a desire for connection, for him – and at the same time, she feared losing herself to something she was not ready to embrace.

Marriage was not a pursuit she desired.

She had seen enough to know its demands, its compromises, the way it so often dimmed the spirit beneath its expectations. No, she would rather walk her own quiet path, unfettered, the world hers to explore in ways that marriage could never permit.

And still... still, the memory of his rejection remained as a sharp and stinging pain.

Even so, the evening's simple joys made the burdens of the past few days seem a little lighter. The sounds of laughter – even Mr Sinclair's, as Charles recounted a tale of the stablemaster falling in manure that morning – and the gentle clinking of silverware formed a soothing backdrop of companionship amongst the odd group.

The old baron cleared his throat gruffly.

"My dear Miss Ward," he began, raising his glass with trembling fingers. "I must commend you on your splendid choice of dress this evening. The rose hue suits you remarkably well. One might almost think you were inspired by the very blooms that adorn the garden."

Evelyn blushed. "You flatter me, my lord," she replied, unsure of how else to respond.

Charles chimed in, a twinkle in his eye. "Father says roses thrive on neglect... which is much like the attention my sister has received from gentlemen this past season."

Evelyn cast him a dark look, echoed by a warning glance from their father. Her blush deepened as she felt Mr Sinclair's watchful eyes on her.

"Indeed?" asked the old baron as he leant forwards, narrowing his wrinkled eyes. "And what sort of attention do you seek, my dear? Surely a young woman of your beauty should not find herself overlooked. Perhaps you require a more attentive escort?"

"I assure you, my lord, that I have no intention of burdening myself with the attentions of any gentleman."

The old baron raised an eyebrow as he sipped his wine. "Ah, but my dear, surely, there exists some brave soul daring enough to navigate the perils of courting you?"

Evelyn attempted to muster her composure, but the heat in her cheeks betrayed her. "As you say, my lord, the perils are considerable. I would not wish to see any gentleman suffer unduly on my account."

Mr Sinclair remained still and watchful. Her father exchanged a knowing look with Charles, who wore an impish grin as if anticipating the unfolding drama.

The old baron, seeming to enjoy Evelyn's discomfort, smiled broadly. "Might I remind you, Miss Ward, that not all gentlemen are so easily daunted by peril. In fact, some rather relish the challenge."

"Do they now?" Her embarrassment was morphing to irritation. "If so, I can only assume they possess an extraordinary talent for self-deception."

The baron sat back, the smile still playing on his lips. "Pray, Henry, what would you consider to be the most admirable quality in a prospective suitor for a young lady?"

Mr Sinclair, who sat up as it thoroughly caught off guard, hesitated for a moment before responding, "Well, I suppose one might hope for a gentleman who possesses a certain... resilience in the face of adversity."

"A remarkable quality, indeed," the baron murmured. "And what might that adversity entail, I wonder?"

"Perhaps the ability to withstand the indignities of a challenging conversation," he replied quickly.

"How terribly noble," Evelyn bristled, turning her attention to Mr Sinclair. "I would argue, however, that resilience is hardly necessary. It is quite easy to endure banter when one is not at risk of making a fool of oneself."

"Indeed," the old baron interjected. "But surely, Miss Ward, one must also consider the gentleman's fortitude in navigating the intricacies of courtship. A true test of character, is it not?"

"Perhaps a gentleman's ability to sustain meaningful dialogue without resorting to flattery or vague terms might be of greater merit."

Mr Sinclair raised an eyebrow, his gaze drilling into her. "So, you would prefer sincerity over the artful dance of compliments and ambiguity?"

"Is that not what all women seek?" she countered, now looking across the table at him alone. "A man who speaks with honesty rather than veiled intentions? It is rather exhausting to decipher what one truly means when faced with a labyrinth of words."

Mr Sinclair sat back further, his solemn gaze giving way to a hint of mischief. "Perhaps a gentleman may simply enjoy the art of subtlety. After all, life is far more intriguing when one leaves a touch of mystery in one's wake."

"Such intrigue can be frustrating, Mr Sinclair." Evelyn found herself inexplicably irritated. "A lady may find herself wishing to understand the man behind the mask rather than indulging in riddles. If one must constantly decipher intentions, how can one truly know if the gentleman in question is worthy of admiration?"

The baron smiled, clearly enjoying their exchange. "Ah, Miss Ward, it seems you have laid bare the conundrum of many a gentleman. But tell us, if a man were to abandon his veil of mystery, would he not lose some of his allure?"

Evelyn considered his words. "Allure is a fickle thing, my lord. I would argue that true substance lies not in mystery but in sincerity. A man may be charming, yet if he cannot be trusted to speak plainly, what value does he possess? It is all too easy to cloak oneself in the guise of mystery while saying little of substance. One must wonder whether it is the gentleman's wit or his cowardice that keeps him shrouded."

"But isn't a little banter enjoyable?" Charles chimed in. "A test of wits? Would that not make the experience far more exciting?"

Evelyn regarded her brother with a gentle smile. "I'm sure it would be exciting for some young ladies, Charles, but it can quickly turn into a mere game... a pursuit devoid of meaning. I would rather seek genuine connections than play at being a prize for those who wish to impress."

"My dear Miss Ward," the old baron chuckled. "You will certainly set the stage for a most compelling courtship for a fortunate gentleman. Perhaps in the end, it is the challenge of the chase that shall draw them nearer."

"I shall let them chase, then," Evelyn said with a dismissive wave of her hand. "I shall be sketching roses while they weave their riddles. Life is far too short for games that bear no fruit."

"And yet, Miss Ward," the baron said slowly, "you may find that among the thorns, there lie the most exquisite blooms. Are you quite certain you wish to forgo the pursuit altogether?"

Evelyn looked across at Mr Sinclair for a moment, whose dark glare lingered on her. "If the blooms require thorns to flourish, I would sooner cultivate my own garden than allow myself to be pricked by the entanglements of courtship."

The baron settled further back in his chair and chuckled. "A formidable lady indeed! But do remember, Miss Ward, that not all pursuits are perilous; some may lead to unexpected delights."

∞∞∞∞

After dinner, as the last of the wine glasses were cleared, Lord Sinclair stood with effort, his frail frame showing the toll of age. He cleared his throat loudly.

"My dear friends," he began. His voice was raspy and worn, as if tired from the lively conversation. "It is not often that we are graced with visitors. The quiet of this manor can be overwhelming, and the days seem to stretch on endlessly. I find myself growing weary of solitude, and your presence has been a welcome change." He paused, his pale eyes drifting momentarily, lost in a memory. "In my old age, loneliness has become a familiar companion, and it is a comfort to share meals and laughter, even if fleeting."

Evelyn watched as Mr Sinclair shifted uneasily.

"It is a lonely existence, I assure you," the baron continued slowly. "So, I thank you for brightening my days, even if only for a short while. It is a comfort to have you here, and I do hope that you will not feel rushed to leave us anytime soon.

"The evening grows cold," he murmured, his voice rough with fatigue, "and it seems a storm is upon us." He gestured towards the windows, where dark clouds had gathered. "I invite you all to the drawing room, where we may enjoy the warmth of the fire. It will do us well to find some comfort as the storm settles in."

With that, the guests rose from their seats. They followed him to the drawing room, the soft shuffle of footsteps blending with the distant rumble of thunder that reverberated through the manor's dark halls. A footman carried Charles behind them.

The storm raged outside, its fury battering the windows of Rosehill Manor like a wild beast. Rain slashed at the glass, and the wind howled through the cracks, rattling the windowpanes with an almost unnatural persistence. Inside, however, the drawing room glowed with the warmth of the fire, lighting their faces in amber hues.

Evelyn sat quietly, nestled in a velvet armchair beside her father, who absently swirled the liquid in his glass, lost in thought. Beside her, young Charles fidgeted restlessly with his leg propped up on a cushioned chair. Though his pain lingered, his eyes were wide with curiosity, casting restless glances towards the rain-streaked windows as the storm continued its eerie assault on the manor.

"Will you tell us a ghost story, Father?" Charles pleaded, his voice small but insistent, cutting through the crackling of the fire and the roar of the storm.

76

"I am not sure I have one to tell, Charles. Plants, you see, do not make for good ghost stories."

Charles pouted and Evelyn smiled gently, the weight of the storm lifting for a moment. The darkness, however, still pressed heavily against the windows, as if waiting for an invitation.

Baron Sinclair, who had been sitting silently in his high-backed chair for some time now, cast a sidelong glance at Charles. The baron was cloaked in shadows, his face almost hidden, save for the occasional flicker of firelight that revealed the deep lines etched into his weathered features. His long, gnarled fingers tapped rhythmically against the armrest. He looked as ancient as the manor itself, as though the centuries had shaped him along with its stone walls.

"You want a story, do you, lad?"

Charles nodded eagerly, his eyes wide.

The baron leant forwards, his face coming into the fire's glow.

"Very well," he sighed, his voice like the creaking of old wood. "But be careful what you wish for. Some stories aren't mere tales to entertain. Some linger in the bones of a place like this, in the very stone and soil." His eyes flickered to Evelyn, a look so fleeting that it could have been imagined, before his focus returned to the fire where the flames crackled and popped with a life of their own.

"Some ghosts," he continued, his voice dropping to a near whisper, "never truly leave."

The room seemed to hold its breath, the storm's fury a distant hum as his words settled over them like a chill. Evelyn could not help but feel that his story was more than just a tale for Charles. There was something unnervingly real in the old baron's voice, as though the story was not some idle legend, but a living force that threaded through the walls of Rosehill Manor.

She looked around the across the firelit room until her attention settled upon Mr Sinclair, who stood quietly in the corner, leaning with a casual grace against a mahogany bookshelf. His brandy glass caught the light as he lifted it to his lips, though his expression was anything but relaxed. The flames reflected in his eyes, casting them in an amber glow. Something distant, almost haunted, lurked behind his gaze.

"There is a story," the baron's voice rasped through the stillness, "passed down through the generations, from father to son." His words came slowly, as though he was pulling them from the depths of some ancient, buried memory. "A story of this very estate – of a curse, bound to our blood."

Charles leant forwards, wide-eyed, enraptured by the baron's every word.

"Long ago, in this very garden, a woman named Seraphina tended to her plants. She was a healer, skilled beyond measure, known far and wide across the countryside – though not all came in trust. Some whispered that she was a *Cailleach*... a witch." He paused, not for dramatic effect, but to sip his brandy, his long fingers wrapped tightly around the glass.

"In her care," he continued, "were flowers unlike any the earth had seen before. Seraphina cultivated plants of extraordinary power, blooms that flourished under her touch but withered in the hands of others... and among them was her most prized possession: a rose, dark as midnight, said to possess the power to bind two souls for all eternity, so long as it bloomed in love's true light."

He looked to Charles, who seemed almost breathless with anticipation. Evelyn shifted uneasily in her chair, the fire's warmth now doing little to dispel the growing chill in her bones.

"But," the baron's voice grew darker, edged with a sharpness that seemed to cut through the air, "as with all great stories, love was not without betrayal."

A gust of wind rattled the windows, as if punctuating his words. The room fell into a stillness so complete that even the crackling fire seemed to hold its breath.

"Seraphina loved once, deeply, with all the fire of her heart, but her love was not returned in kind... And when her heart was shattered, so too was the bond she had hoped to create. The rose, that cursed bloom, became a symbol of her anguish. It no longer bound souls in love; it bound them in eternal torment."

Evelyn shivered, her eyes flicking to Mr Sinclair, who stood motionless, his face still half in shadow. Had he heard this tale from his grandfather one too many times? Or perhaps not enough?

"It is said that Seraphina still roams these grounds in the dead of night, the woman in white, drifting through the shadows, searching... always searching for her lost love... and for one who can break the curse.

"They say her steps are soundless, but you can feel her presence – a chill down your spine, a whisper against your ear. She wanders endlessly, drawn to those who come too close to the rose, to that cursed bloom."

Evelyn's mind flashed to the rosebush in the garden, its dark, thorny branches gleaming in the pale moonlight. She did not believe in ghosts or ghost stories, but tonight, in the oppressive gloom of the manor, it felt too real, too close.

"Some servants say they've seen her. Her gown trailing behind her, her face hidden in the dark. But the roses... the roses are always near. Wherever she goes, they bloom – wild, untamed, and bleeding red as though they've drunk deeply of the land's sorrow."

The room seemed to darken as his words settled over them, thick and heavy as the storm outside.

"And that one cursed rose, crimson like her heart's blood – it is said to carry her pain. It blossoms but once in a blue moon, fed by sorrow, by unfulfilled love. They say," the baron's voice dropped even lower, barely above a breath, "if you see her, the woman in white, it means she's chosen you... chosen you to bear her curse, to suffer in her stead until the rose finally withers and dies."

The storm outside roared again, rattling the windowpanes as though in response to the tale. A dread settled over Evelyn's heart, though she knew the tale could not possibly be true.

She glanced at the doorway, half-expecting to see a figure standing there, veiled in white with the scent of roses trailing behind her. She turned once more to look at Mr Sinclair, but he was gone. He had slipped out of the room, unnoticed.

Chapter 11

Evelyn

The next day, the storm had retreated, yielding to a gentle drizzle that cloaked the manor in a silken veil of mist. Evelyn's thoughts remained on the strange rose in the hidden garden and the baron's ominous ghost story. As is the way with all fearful things that lurk in the night, the story had lost its weight by morning. Evelyn was sure there was a logical explanation – some reason the rose could bloom in winter, some reason it shone so brightly at night. Perhaps there was even a rational explanation for the tale of the Sinclair curse, a cautionary fable of love and betrayal, a reminder for those who dared to tread the path of affection that heartbreak could be a dangerous game. She was determined to understand it all.

While Clara helped her prepare for bed, Evelyn seized the moment to search out her thoughts.

"On the day Charles fell from the horse, you said there was something wrong with this place. Pray, tell me: what did you mean?"

Clara brushed Evelyn's locks, pursing her lips for a moment before she leant in slightly and lowered her voice. "I have heard some whispers, Miss Evelyn. The chambermaids speak of strange happenings... flickering lights in the East wing, shadows that move on their own, and the ghost of a lady in white said to wander the gardens by moonlight." She glanced over her shoulder, as if the woman in white might be lurking nearby. "Some say she was once the mistress of the manor, wronged and left to wander in search of her lost love. Others believe her spirit guards the secrets of the estate, revealing them only to those deemed worthy."

Evelyn's eyes widened for a moment before she composed herself with a slight shrug. "Stories meant to frighten, I imagine. The baron told one very similar last night. Likely born of a single tragic event, which, over time, grew into a cautionary tale – perhaps about beauty and power, or love and ambition. These things tend to evolve, especially when passed down through the servants."

Clara hesitated, her tone measured, as though carefully considering her words. "Oh, I ought not to say, Miss Evelyn. 'Tis not my place."

Evelyn turned to her, her curiosity sharpening. "What else have you heard, Clara?"

Clara hesitated again, glancing at the door before lowering her voice even further. "There are tales among the staff. They say the rose you've seen was planted long ago, and it is connected to the family in ways even they do not fully understand."

"What manner of connection?"

Clara fidgeted, twisting her fingers in her apron. "Some believe it was planted to safeguard something, or perhaps to seal a solemn promise. Yet the rose... it is not merely a flower. They say it brings ill will, particularly when it blooms in winter."

Evelyn frowned, frustrated by the riddles and ambiguity. "What do they mean by that?"

"They will not say, though I have asked. But Miss Evelyn – " Clara glanced around once more. "I have heard peculiar sounds at night within the manor... scratching, as though something... or someone were trying to escape."

Evelyn's heart quickened at the mention of the scratching at night. She had not thought much of it lately, though she heard it each night, low and persistent against the walls. It seemed the lesser of the mysteries. "And what of the supposed Sinclair curse?"

Clara let out a soft sigh, her expression grave. "It is said to linger, Miss Evelyn, like a shadow cast over the estate. It is odd, though... the servants will not speak of Mr Sinclair's mother. The chambermaid, Bess, said that some truths are best left undisturbed... I fear it is a delicate matter, indeed."

Evelyn nodded slowly, biting her lip.

Clara regarded her with a blend of concern and maternal instinct, resting a gentle hand at her shoulder. "You must tread carefully, Miss Evelyn."

∞∞∞∞

When the servants had retired for the night and the manor lay shrouded in silence save for the faint sound of ghostly scratching, Evelyn slipped from her bed, quietly grasping her sketchbook and quill. She ventured through the dimly lit halls, each step echoing softly in the stillness.

In the quiet of the night, the garden felt otherworldly. Her breath caught when she saw the rose, its petals shimmering with a ghostly luminescence, pulsing like the heartbeat of some hidden creature in the darkness. She knelt beside it, her fingers tracing the contours as she sketched, mesmerised by its strange beauty. There was something more, a pull deep within her chest, as if the rose was calling to her in some wordless way.

After what may have been minutes or hours, her quiet concentration was shattered by a voice that sliced through the night. "You are awake once more."

She startled and looked up to see Mr Sinclair standing under the low-hanging branches. His eyes, dark and intense, locked onto hers. She rose, gripping the folds of her gown, and in her other hand, she cradled her sketchbook.

"I could not stay away," she said softly, her eyes drawn back to the solitary bloom before her. "There is something about this rose; I can feel it. It is unlike anything I have ever encountered. It does not resemble the *Rosa gallica* or the *Rosa centifolia* – the apothecary rose or the Provence rose – nor any other I have studied. The shape of the petals, the texture of the leaves… it is entirely foreign, almost unnatural. As though it were conjured rather than grown."

She leant closer, captivated by the rose's design, that velvety texture that beckoned her to touch. "The Baron Sinclair's story was haunting," she continued, her thoughts swirling like the fragrance that enveloped her. "But such tales are often rooted in misunderstanding. There is always a logical, scientific explanation for such phenomena."

She brushed along the edge of her sketchbook. "I wonder if it could be a new species, one unrecorded in any botanical journal! What causes it to glow so faintly beneath the moonlight? Is it the oils on its petals reflecting the light, or some other quality unique to this plant? And to bloom in the depths of winter – could it be drawing warmth from the soil in some extraordinary way? I thought – perhaps if I could study the rose, document its structure and behaviour, I might discover something extraordinary."

Mr Sinclair moved closer, his face unreadable. "Foolish girl. You heard the baron. The rose is not something to be trifled with, Miss Ward."

She shook her head in frustration. *Foolish girl?*

The words stung, a sharp affront to her pride, as though he sought to reduce her to a child in need of correction. How dare he presume to define her? Yet, beneath the sting, another feeling stirred – a thrill she could not entirely deny. It was almost captivating to provoke such a reaction from him. Was it folly to feel exhilarated by his reproach? To relish, even faintly, the power her defiance seemed to wield over him?

"Foolish or not, Mr Sinclair, curiosity is seldom without risk. Would you have me silence my mind simply to avoid it? Your grandfather's story was a ghost tale," she said tightly, "intended to scare Charles – to scare us all – in the storm. You do not believe such nonsense, do you? Well, it is of no consequence… I must know the truth behind this rose. Tell me what you know. And do not dare repeat the riddle of the curse!"

"Evelyn," he growled, stepping forwards in one swift motion, his hand clamping around her wrist with a startling urgency. "Are you truly such a fool? It is not a tale made up to frighten you. It *should* frighten you!" The words tumbled from his bared teeth in a raw, pained rush. "It is not

84

something that can be easily explained." His grip tightened slightly, as if he were trying to anchor her in reality.

Her breath faltered at his touch. She should have been unnerved by the ferocity of his tone, the way his fingers burnt through the layers of her sleeve like a brand. And yet... *Evelyn.*

The way he said her name, with such desperate force, struck her deeper than any reproach.

Evelyn.

How much more thrilling it sounded than 'foolish girl,' though she scarcely dared admit it even to herself.

"Then help me understand, Mr Sinclair... Henry."

His fingers slackened around her wrist, though he did not let go entirely. For a moment, the only sound between them was the uneven cadence of their breaths. His name on her lips had stilled him.

"Please..." she whispered. "You cannot expect me to remain in ignorance. I must know. I want only to understand."

"Evelyn," he said again, his voice breaking over her name like a wave against stone. This time, it was not a growl but a lament, an invocation. It held more than urgency – it held a rawness that made her knees weaken.

As suddenly as he had grabbed her, he released her wrist as if scorched, stepping back to regain his composure. "Some things are better left untold."

The sting of his withdrawal pierced deeper than she had anticipated. She shook of that thought, turning back to the rose.

"But why?" she pressed. "Why does everyone repeat that same strange sentiment? Enough of these riddles and evasive answers. Is it such a crime to seek knowledge? Why will you not answer me?"

"Because it is dangerous," he growled. "For you. For me. For anyone who draws too near."

"Dangerous? Is it not more perilous to live in ignorance? I refuse to accept silence as a shield. I will not let fear dictate my understanding of you, or of this place. I care not for danger! It is the truth I seek. I beg of you," she implored, her eyes searching his. "Will you not tell me something true? Will you not tell me of your mother, the baroness?"

The silence stretched between them, and before she could regret it, Evelyn pressed on. "You once spoke of the gardens as your mother's legacy. Will you not share more of her story? Why does no one dare to speak of her? Why is the truth so shrouded in silence?"

She watched as Mr Sinclair's jaw tightened. He looked briefly to the glowing rose between them, its petals shimmering like embers in the twilight, before returning to her. His eyes darkened.

"The truth," he said quietly, his voice edged with warning, "has a way of binding one to it. And once it does, there is no turning back. No return to the world you knew, the *safety* of ignorance."

Without another word, he pivoted sharply on his heel and melted into the shadows of the garden, leaving her breathless in the cool night air, her heart racing in his wake.

∞∞○○∞○

As the night deepened and the chill in the air grew sharper in Mr Sinclair's absence, Evelyn lingered in the garden with her sketchbook balanced on her lap. Her notes – scrawled hastily in the margins of her drawing – catalogued every detail: the strange hum emanating from the stem, the peculiar scent, and the way it seemed to glow and pulse faintly. Time lost its meaning in the stillness, her mind so consumed by the mystery of the flower. Still, even amidst her study, she could still feel the phantom warmth where Henry Sinclair had grasped her arm.

When the manor's clock tower struck three, the distant chime echoing through the air, she was startled from her trance. A wave of weariness swept over her. She closed her sketchbook grudgingly and rose slowly, intending to return to her bed – but as, as she left the confines of the secret garden, something in the air shifted. It was a subtle, unnerving sensation, like the prickling of skin when one is being watched.

Glancing around, she saw nothing but the shadows that crept through the trees. The garden was silent... too silent. The rustling of leaves had ceased, and even the night felt as though it were holding its breath, waiting.

Her eyes drifted towards the far edge of the estate, where the shadows loomed thickest, merging with the blackness beyond the trees. An eerie stillness had settled there, unnaturally quiet.

Logic told her it was nothing – merely the lateness of the hour, the solitude of the night playing tricks on her senses – but the deeper part of her, the one she wished to ignore, felt a presence lurking in the shadows, watching her.

Nonsense, she told herself firmly. *Ghost stories and superstitions.*

Still, even as she tried to reason with herself, her gaze remained fixed there. She took a cautious step closer, narrowing her eyes to pierce through the gloom.

For a moment, there was nothing – only the darkness and the quiet, but then there was a flicker, something pale, almost too faint to be real. It was fleeting, a mere glimmer in the moonlight, like a wisp of mist caught in the breeze, or the hem of a gown, impossibly white, disappearing into the darkness.

Evelyn's heart skipped a beat. She blinked, willing herself to see clearly.

It is just the moon, she thought, begging her pulse to slow. *A trick of the light, nothing more.*

When she looked again, her breath caught in her throat.

There, in the dim light of the moon, she saw it: a figure, pale as bone, draped in white. Its form was barely visible, almost merging with the mist that curled along the ground. The figure did not move, did not stir, but simply stood, watching her.

Evelyn's mind whirled, refusing to believe what her eyes showed her. It must be the breeze stirring the shadows, the silver glow of the moon weaving illusions among the trees.

It cannot be real. I am overtired, seeing things that are not there.

Still, the figure remained.

The baron's warning surfaced in her mind, carried on the wind that tugged at her shawl like a ghostly whisper: *They say if you see her, the woman in white, it means she's chosen you.* His words crept back with chilling clarity, as though he stood over her shoulder, murmuring in her ear. *Chosen you to bear her curse, to suffer in her stead until the rose finally withers and dies.*

Her breath caught, fear tightening around her like icy fingers. She did not believe in such things – ghosts, curses – those were tales spun to frighten the gullible. And yet there *she* was: the woman in white.

The spectral figure hovered just beyond the hedgerow. Her face, shadowed beneath the veil of her flowing hair, seemed to tilt ever so slightly in Evelyn's direction, as if aware of being watched.

No, this was no trick of the light, no idle fancy born of a restless mind. The figure stood there, hauntingly real and impossibly still.

For a moment, Evelyn was frozen. She wanted to look away, to close her eyes and banish the apparition to nothingness, but her eyes remained locked, drawn by some dreadful fascination.

And then the figure moved – just the faintest tilt of her head, a ripple of fabric too delicate to be caught by the night breeze – and it was enough to shatter her paralysis. Evelyn's breath came in a sharp gasp, the sound loud against the silence.

She fled, as fast as her legs would carry her.

The garden blurred around her, thorny branches clawing at her skirts as she stumbled blindly towards the house. Her feet barely felt the earth beneath them, her only thought the desperate need to escape, to be anywhere but under the gaze of that unearthly presence. The towering walls seemed impossibly far away, as if the manor had receded into the night. The cold air stung her lungs, and her heart pounded wildly. The weight of unseen eyes pressed against her as she ran, and she dared not glance back. Only when she reached her chamber door, breathless and trembling, did she stop.

Her hands shook as she latched the door behind her, leaning heavily against the wood as if it could shield her from the terror outside. Her breath came in ragged gasps as she clutched her chest, feeling the frantic pulse beneath her fingers – her heartbeat a wild, erratic rhythm in her ears.

The image of the woman in white – the spectral figure she so desperately wanted to deny – clung to her thoughts, persistent, refusing to dissolve into the safety of reason.

It was nothing – merely my imagination, she told herself. *It had to be.*

But no matter how fiercely she willed it away, the scene replayed in her mind over and over again: that pale figure standing so still, watching her, waiting.

She pushed away from the door, fumbling to light the candle by her bedside. The flame spluttered to life, casting long, distorted shadows that stretched across the room, twisting like phantoms of the walls. Evelyn was afraid, certainly, but she knew fear was the mind's reaction to uncertainty.

I am not a coward, she thought to herself, taking a deep breath.

Forcing herself to move, Evelyn stepped towards the window. With shaking hands, she parted the lace curtains just enough to peer outside. Perhaps, in seeing the truth with her own eyes, her thoughts might be quieted: reason restored, and fear, like fog before the morning sun, dispelled by clarity.

The garden lay still beneath a veil of silvery moonlight, eerily quiet. Her eyes swept over the familiar paths and garden beds, but they were drawn, irresistibly, to the edge of the trees in the distance. A deep, unnatural stillness hung over that place.

Oh, heavens! Evelyn's hand flew to her mouth.

There, at the far edge of the garden, the woman in white stood, her back now turned. A dim glow flickered beside her – an oil lantern, casting a pale shimmer on her ghostly form. The hem of her white gown floated as if caught in a breeze, the fabric rippling like mist. Without a sound, the woman moved, drifting deeper into the trees, her white form fading into the darkness as if swallowed whole by the night.

A cold dread swept over Evelyn, seeping into her very bones as her hand stayed clamped over her mouth. It was a chill that reason could not shake, a primal fear that rooted her to the spot. Her heart raced, her mind scrambling to make sense of the impossible.

As the wind howled against the panes, rattling the glass, Evelyn let the curtain fall, retreating into the shadows of her room. The air was thick with a presence she could not see, but could feel, pressing in around her.

Without warning, the single candle beside her bed sputtered violently and went out, plunging the room into darkness.

Evelyn stood frozen in the pitch-black, her hands now clenched at her sides, her breath coming in shallow gasps.

The silence that followed was deafening, and in that suffocating stillness, she could no longer tell if she was truly alone.

Chapter 12

Clara

As Clara wandered down the dimly lit hallway, the soft light of dawn filtering through the windows, she could hear the distant sound of laughter from the kitchen. The warmth of the hearth drew her closer, promising comfort after a restless night. Sleep had evaded her, each hour stretched thin. She had lain awake for much of the night, her thoughts a tangled web of concern for her mistress and the troubling tales that surrounded Rosehill Manor.

As she approached the threshold of the kitchen, Clara hesitated, pausing to gather her thoughts. Laughter bubbled up like sunlight breaking through a fog, but it felt distant, almost surreal in contrast to her lingering unease.

With a gentle nudge, she pushed the door open, stepping into the warm glow of the kitchen. The rich scent of freshly baked bread wafted towards her, mingling with the smoky aroma from the hearth. She found the other servants bustling about, their spirits lifted by the promise of a new day. Still, Clara felt a weight in her chest, a knowing that remained, and she could not shake the feeling that something was amiss.

"Did you hear?" Bess chimed, her cheeks flushed from the heat of the stove. "Old Mrs Hargrove swears she saw a ghost last night, drifting through the East Wing. She nearly dropped her mop!"

Clara smiled but rolled her eyes. She'd learnt that the best way to fit in was to play along. "Ghosts again? You'd think she'd know better than to listen to her own tales." But in truth, a shiver ran down her spine at the thought. Superstitions were rampant in the manor, and though she feigned indifference, she could not dismiss the eeriness that clung to the place like an unwelcome shadow.

"Ah, but what if it's true?" Sarah, a fellow maid with a penchant for the dramatic, leant in with wide eyes. "What if it's the spirit of a Sinclair, haunting the halls, looking for someone to claim?"

Sarah reached out suddenly to grab Bess, who squealed and then laughed.

Clara's gulped at the notion of spirits haunting the manor, and she instinctively glanced towards the darkened corners of the kitchen. Her mind drifted back to her conversation with Miss Evelyn the previous night. Though she knew her mistress was searching for more information, Clara wanted nothing to do with it. No, far better to do her job quietly and dutifully.

"Best to keep our heads down and our thoughts clear," Clara said, trying to redirect the conversation. "Nothing good comes from stirring up shadows."

The other maids exchanged glances, half-believing and half-dismissing her words, but Clara felt a need to ground them. "If we let fear rule us, we might just invite trouble," she warned, casting a cautious glance towards the window, where dark clouds gathered.

"Trouble or not, I'd rather know than be left in the dark," Sarah replied.

Clara sighed, acutely aware that nothing would quell the superstitions that danced like phantoms in the hearts of the staff. She felt a familiar chill creeping up her spine, like the old tales her grandmother used to tell.

The memory came unbidden: a hand, cool and papery, tucking a dried sprig of lavender into hers by firelight. Shadows danced on the walls of a small, timeworn cottage, flickering in rhythm with her Granny's voice: "There are forces in this world, Clara," she'd say with her Irish lilt. "Old things. Older than the stones beneath our feet, older than the stars above. They walk unseen through the shadows and weave their will into the wind and the earth. They cannot be reasoned with, only heeded. When the air grows too still, and the birds cease their song, that's when ye must be most cautious. The silence isn't empty, child – it listens, watches, remembers. Speak softly when the night presses close, and never turn your back to the dark, no matter how heavy the air grows, or how cold the shadows feel."

Clara sighed, her gaze drifting back to the latticed window as a chill crept along her spine. The gnawing dread inside her persisted, as if some unseen force was pressing against her.

As she ate her porridge, Clara found her mind drifting back to her own life – her hopes and dreams tucked away like the delicate linens in the armoire. She had always known she was meant for more than sewing gowns, arranging hair, and managing the endless tasks of a lady's maid. She dreamed of a life where she could choose her own path, perhaps even run a small shop in town. She imagined herself free, her hands crafting things of beauty – though she had no artistic skill to speak of – not just tending to the whims of others. She longed for the simple joys of motherhood, to cradle a child of her own, to build her own home filled with laughter and warmth.

Yet here she was, bound to the whims of the Ward family. Though she dearly loved Miss Evelyn, a feeling of helplessness settled over her. She often felt like a spectator in a world that spun just beyond her reach, her dreams guttering like a candle in a draft.

She shook her head. It was what it was, and no amount of wishing would change it.

Perhaps it was not just her dreams that lingered in the shadows, forgotten and fading. Perhaps there were other things here – things that never truly left, no matter how deeply they were buried.

Her Granny's voice echoed in her mind again: "There are things that don't leave, Clara," she would say, her fingers always brushing against the worn edges of a faded book or a string of herbs. "Spirits that stay long after the body is gone, curses that are passed down, like family heirlooms."

Clara had always dismissed the stories as nothing more than the ramblings of an old woman – tales spun to pass the long, dark hours by the hearth – but now, in the eerie stillness of the manor, the floorboards groaning underfoot, and the long shadows stretching across the walls, the weight of those words felt different – more real... more urgent.

"Don't ignore them, Clara," her Granny's voice seemed to warn, as it had when Clara was a child. "The silence holds more than ye think. There's a pull in the air, a tug in your bones when they're nearby. You'll feel it. You'll know it."

What if her grandmother had been right? What if the spirits of Rosehill weren't just stories? What if they were watching? Waiting?

"Miss Clara!" The sharp call of Mrs Hargrove broke her reverie. She turned to see the head housekeeper eyeing her sharply. "You're daydreaming again. We'll need those gowns pressed for Miss Ward before dinner!"

"Yes, ma'am," Clara replied, swallowing the last of her porridge and moving quickly to her task.

As she hastened to arrange her mistress' gowns for pressing, she could not help but overhear Bess and Sarah's whispers drifting through the air, their tales of ghosts and curses weaving around her like a chilling fog.

"Miss Ward, she's too good for this place," Bess muttered. "She deserves a life free from all these tales of ghosts and madness."

The first drops of rain tapped against the window, a soft, foreboding rhythm. She glanced out at the garden, where dark clouds twisted in an ominous dance, shrouding the grounds in shadows.

"She has a strength we cannot see," Clara murmured, as if convincing herself as much as Bess.

A chill ran through her, a whisper of warning as old as her Granny's stories. Yes, yes – she must keep watch over her mistress, to remain vigilant against the ghosts of fear, never turn her back to the dark. Whatever haunted Rosewood, whatever waited within its walls – she would face it for Miss Evelyn's sake.

Chapter 13

Evelyn

The haunting image of the woman in white remained in Evelyn's thoughts, refusing to fade despite her reasoning. With every step she took, the vision of the spectral figure, motionless at the very edge of the overgrown hedges, sent a cold tremor through her veins.

She paced the library, trailing her fingers along the spines of books. Each title whispered stories of a world she longed to explore, yet her focus was narrowed to one singular pursuit: the diary.

But as she searched the shelves, her heart sank. The old leather-bound book was gone.

It means she's chosen you.

The baron's voice reverberated through her thoughts, a chilling murmur that wound its way into her consciousness like smoke curling in the air.

Chosen you to bear her curse, to suffer in her stead. His words twisted and contorted in the recesses of her mind, impossible to shake.

What did it mean?

She paused, her breath catching in her throat as the memory of the woman in white pressed in upon her... her white gown, billowing in the night air, the glow of her oil lantern illuminating her form, casting an otherworldly light upon the darkened landscape.

What did she want? What secrets lay hidden beneath that spectral visage, secrets that seemed tied to the very bones of the manor?

Evelyn felt a fierce, unrelenting pull towards the mystery that clung to the woman, to the land itself. It was a compulsion too strong to ignore, a need to understand the past that seemed to echo through the manor's walls, calling her name like an ancient chant.

The baron's ghost story had given the woman in white a name. *What was it? Heavens, what was her name?*

Evelyn's lips formed the word in silence: *Seraphina.*

While she searched for lost diary, Evelyn recounted the story in her own mind, sifting through it for threads of truth. According to the baron, Seraphina had been cursed, bound to the manor for eternity, her soul trapped by forces no one could remember – or dared to name. The curse was no random act of malice; it was tied to her broken heart, and to the blood of the Sinclair family, to the very stones and earth of the estate itself.

With a huff, Evelyn straightened her back and looked around the library, her frustration mounting. The diary held the stories of the Sinclairs. Why has she passed it back to the baron? Oh – but she could not have known, back then, of its importance.

The diary had spoken of a family curse, woven so tightly into their lineage that none had escaped its grasp… If she could find it again, if she could delve deeper into its pages, perhaps she could make sense of it all.

Could Seraphina have been a Sinclair? The thought came unbidden, stirring a chill that coiled around Evelyn's spine. Or perhaps the woman in white was the ghost of Henry's mother, the baroness whose name was not spoken! Had she been murdered by her husband, doomed to wander the manor, seeking justice or some fragment of closure? It was all so absurd – unbelievable even – but the questions clung to her like shadows, dark and persistent.

Evelyn closed her eyes and took a slow, steadying breath, willing herself to remain grounded. She could not let her mind be overtaken by phantoms and speculation.

Logic, she reminded herself. *Logic and evidence.*

The diary was her only hope of clarity. It was a link between the ghost stories, the rose, Seraphina, the Sinclair curse – and Henry's role in it all. She had to find it.

"Where could it be?" she murmured to herself.

She searched every corner of the library. She moved from shelf to shelf, gliding her gloved fingers over the spines of countless tomes, their titles offering no promise of the answers she sought. She knelt before the lower shelves, rifling through the volumes that had collected dust. The old diary was nowhere to be found.

An unsettling prickling sensation crawled along the back of her neck, sharp and insistent, as though unseen eyes lingered on her every movement. She froze and glanced over her shoulder towards the dim recesses of the library.

The crackle of the hearth seemed to deepen the silence rather than break it. The fire's glow spilled weakly into the corners, shadows stretching and recoiling as if aware of her gaze. The air seemed to hum with an unseen current, as though the ghostly woman in white lingered just beyond the edge of the firelight, her eyes burning through the veil of darkness like an unspoken question, unanswered and unrelenting.

"What nonsense," Evelyn whispered to herself, shaking her head to dispel the irrational thought, but still, the fine hairs on her arms stood upright, and she pressed a hand to her chest, steadying the uneasy rhythm of her heart.

Turning back to the shelves, Evelyn forced her mind away from the eerie sensation that refused to fade. Frustration simmered within her as she considered other avenues for answers.

If the diary was truly lost, perhaps there were letters, ledgers, or other artifacts within the estate that might shed light on the tangled threads of Seraphina and the Sinclair curse.

She paced the library, absentmindedly brushing her hands along the spines of books as a memory stirred.. the kitchen maid!

Evelyn recalled the peculiar look the girl had given her, wide-eyed and terrified, as though grappling with something she dared not speak. *What had she seen? What did she know?*

Clara had mentioned it too: the fragmented whispers carried by the staff – kitchen gossip traded in the shadows, scraps of truth mixed with superstition. It made sense. After all, the staff were witnesses to the manor's daily life, their ears always tuned to the whispers of its walls and the secrets of its inhabitants. It was disconcerting to think that the very people she often overlooked might hold the answers she sought.

She left the library and descended the grand staircase, her footsteps echoing in the cavernous stillness.

She made her way tentatively to the servants' quarters, a place she had rarely ventured. The corridors grew narrower, the air thicker, carrying the scent of lye soap and roasting meat. The sound of clattering dishes and murmured conversation spilled through the cracks of the door, and her hand hovered before pushing it open.

A few maids sat clustered around a worn table, their voices low, broken only by the scrape of spoons and the occasional burst of laughter.

Clara looked up in surprise, her cheeks flushed and her dark hair falling in loose curls around her face. "Miss Evelyn! Is all well?"

The chatter faltered as the other servants glanced up, eyes widening. Evelyn felt out of place, as though she had intruded upon a realm that was not meant for her – a world that had its own rules, its own rhythms. For a moment, the weight of their stares made her want to retreat, to flee back upstairs to the comfort of her own domain, away from their quiet scrutiny.

Straightening her back, she pushed the hesitation aside, steadying herself with a breath. She was here for answers, and something told her that these women – these quiet observers of the manor's secrets – held pieces of a puzzle she could not yet see.

With a calm that belied her inner turmoil, she gave a polite nod, forcing a smile that felt too thin, too fragile. "Thank you for your kindness, Miss

Clara. I am quite well, though I find myself with... peculiar questions. I wish to inquire further with the household staff about the history of the estate... about the Sinclair family. I have heard the usual tales, of course, but do I wonder if there are other things, more subtle perhaps, that might have been passed down through the staff. Things that cannot be found in books or ledgers but are known to those who have long lived in this house and heard its secrets."

Her gaze shifted from Clara to the other maids, who had gone unnervingly quiet. "I am aware that you and the others are the silent observers of this estate. Servants see all, do you not? You must know more than any tale told in the drawing room or the dining hall. I would be most grateful, truly, for any insight you might be willing to share – whether it is a forgotten story, a strange occurrence, or even the smallest detail that has stuck with you over the years."

The servants exchanged furtive glances. Two of them rose quickly, their chairs scraping against the floor as they gathered their things in silence and left. The room seemed to close in around her, the remaining maids more wary than curious now.

Perhaps she had misspoken. Oh, but wasn't that just like her? She was bred for politeness and parlour talk, thinking her curiosity a virtue when it might instead be taken as intrusion. She had never worked a day in her life, never scrubbed cold stone floors or risen before dawn to stoke the hearth. What did she truly know of these women... of their fears and loyalties, the things they whispered when no lady was listening? Perhaps she was naive – no, worse, perhaps she was spoiled in ways she had not even begun to understand.

It was then that a younger maid, her posture uncertain and eyes cast downward, spoke. Her voice was soft, hesitant, as though choosing her words carefully. "The manor holds many secrets, Miss Ward. Some things are best left undisturbed."

Evelyn masked her frown at the repeated frame. Henry had said it to her in the garden. Who else? Clara?

It was then that Evelyn noticed the girl's face more clearly: it was the same young girl she had seen in the garden, her eyes wide with something Evelyn could not quite place. Fear? Guilt? Or perhaps something deeper, something darker.

She fought the urge to press further, knowing she would not extract anything if she pushed too hard. *Perhaps I ought to go,* she thought, glancing towards the door. *I came in search of answers, but maybe all I have done is unsettle them… barge in where I am neither wanted nor trusted.*

"Sit down, Miss," an older cook said, firmly but not unkindly, gliding over to pull out a chair for Evelyn. She poured a steaming cup of tea, the rich aroma filling the air as she introduced herself and the younger kitchen girl. "I'm Mrs Abernathy, and this here is Millie."

Mrs Abernathy was not the round, plump figure one expected in a cook. She moved with a weary grace, her thin frame draped in a worn, faded apron that hung loosely from her bony shoulders. Her skin was pale, stretched thin over high cheekbones, and wisps of white hair, once neatly pinned, had escaped in a tangled halo. The pale blue of her eyes flickered with a strange knowing, as if they had seen more than they cared to remember. Despite her age, she stood unnervingly tall, her frail hands steady as they gripped the back of the chair.

This is absurd, Evelyn told herself. *I've dined with barons and scholars without blinking, but here I am unsettled by a kitchen and a quiet woman with haunted eyes.*

Instead, she smiled politely, lifting the teacup to her lips and savouring its warmth before gently placing it down.

Mrs Abernathy moved soundlessly around the table and came to stand tall behind Millie. The younger maid shrank slightly beneath the cook's shadow, though nothing in the woman's expression was overtly cruel.

This is it, Evelyn realised. *This may be the only chance I shall have to ask my questions without being sent away or smiled at like a child asking after ghosts.*

Evelyn leant in slightly, her voice lowering to a soft, coaxing murmur. "Surely you've heard tales, Mrs Abernathy? Stories passed down among the staff? You must have witnessed much in your time at Rosehill."

102

She watched their faces carefully. Millie fidgeted, glancing back nervously at Mrs Abernathy, whose expression remained unreadable – until Evelyn caught the fleeting look in her pale eyes, a glimmer that betrayed more than her stoic exterior. Mrs Abernathy paused, her long, skeletal fingers hovering over the back of Millie's chair, eyes locking with Evelyn's. A silence settled over the room.

"Aye, Miss Ward," she said, her voice soft but weathered, like the creak of an ancient door. "There are always tales in houses like these. Some true, some... twisted by time. I've been here long enough to know that Rosehill has a way of keeping its secrets. Whether or not it decides to share them is another matter." She hesitated, her eyes seeming to measure Evelyn's resolve, as if weighing whether to reveal more. Then, with a slight shake of her head, she turned away, gliding back towards the simmering pot on the stove.

Evelyn's attention shifted to the kitchen maid, who stared at the ground, avoiding her gaze.

She knows something. Fear like that does not come from nowhere.

"And what of you, Millie?" Evelyn's voice was softer now, but no less intent. "When we met in the garden, you seemed... unsettled. What is it that you know? What stories have you heard about this place, about its past?"

Millie's face paled. "Oh, there are stories, aye, Miss. But not all are fit for gentle ears." She cast a glance towards Mrs Abernathy. "There's talk of... the attic. Strange things happen up there."

Evelyn's pulse quickened, but her tone remained measured. "What manner of strange things?"

Millie shifted uncomfortably, twisting her hands in her apron as she glanced towards another maid for support. "Whispers... and shadows. Things that don't belong."

Bess, standing nearby, hesitated before speaking, her voice hushed as if fearful of being overheard. "I've heard it said," she ventured, "that those who go up there come back... changed. Or sometimes, not at all."

"Have you ever been up there?" Evelyn pressed, looking between the maids.

Millie, looking as though she had been caught in a lie, shook her head vigorously. "It's a place best avoided, Miss. Too many stories. You'd do well to stay away."

Evelyn's heart sank at the sight of the maid's distress, a cold knot forming in her chest. It seemed the staff were unwilling to indulge her curiosity. Still, she could not let the matter drop so easily. "I understand your caution, Millie. But these stories – if they are true – are part of the manor's history. I'm not seeking trouble. Only truth. For my own peace of mind, if nothing else."

"It's not for the likes of you to uncover, Miss Ward," Mrs Abernathy snapped, her voice rasping like brittle parchment. "Curiosity is a dangerous thing. This house has its secrets, and the Sinclairs have paid dearly for theirs. You would be wise not to seek the answers that lie buried here."

Evelyn opened her mouth to protest, but the old cook's expression darkened, her face hardening like marble. In an instant, the quiet warmth she had once shown was gone, replaced by a steely glare.

"You would do well to forget those ghosts of the past," Mrs Abernathy said. "The dead don't rest easy here, and some things are better left alone."

Evelyn hesitated, fear gnawing at her resolve.

I have pushed too far, she realised, the room shifting around her, quieter somehow, as though listening. *I should stop now. Take the tea, offer thanks, leave with grace… but oh, I need to know!*

She drew a breath and steadied her voice. "But what of the baroness? Mr Sinclair's mother? There are whispers of a woman in white…"

At the mention of the baroness, Mrs Abernathy's eyes flashed, her lips drawing into a tight line. "That name," she hissed, "should not be spoken lightly. She was a woman who knew suffering, and her fate is bound to this manor in ways you cannot begin to fathom."

Evelyn could feel the tension crackle in the air between them – Millie, Bess and Clara watching on with wide eyes – but she pressed on, unyielding. "I have seen her, Mrs Abernathy. In the garden, last night! I need to understand what it means."

Mrs Abernathy's hands stilled, and for a fleeting moment, the hardness in her eyes softened, as if the weight of past sorrows threatened to break through her stoic façade. "Some mysteries are not meant for the living."

Evelyn's heart pounded against her ribs, the ghostly figure of the woman in white flitting through her mind. "Please, Mrs Abernathy. I cannot turn away now – I have seen too much, heard too much. There are too many unanswered questions, too many threads that refuse to weave together. I feel as though it is just beyond my reach, and I cannot walk away without understanding."

The cook sighed heavily, glancing towards the doorway as if the walls themselves had ears. "You want to know what haunts this manor, Miss Ward?" she said, her voice low and cold. "Then go ahead... climb the attic stairs, open that door, and see for yourself. But know this: once you do, there'll be no turning back. Some doors, once opened, cannot be closed again. And some truths... they come at a cost."

Chapter 14

Evelyn

Rain cascaded against the windows, drenching the grounds outside. Evelyn roamed the manor, her mind a sea of thoughts about the woman in white, the strange rose, and now, a new thread: the attic. Mrs Abernathy's warning clung to her like a damp cloak, yet her determination to uncover the estate's mysteries burnt brighter than the storm raging beyond the walls.

With each step, the floorboards groaned beneath her, echoing through the vast, silent manor. She felt a pang of regret for not having asked the servants the way to the attic. It was a foolish oversight, indeed – but she would not go back to ask again. Pride and impatience: ruinous combination, as any governess would say.

Evelyn sighed deeply, for the sprawling expanse of the manor, with its endless halls and narrow staircases, had become a labyrinth of shadows and forgotten doors.

If there are ghosts in this place, she thought grimly, *then let them show themselves*

She found herself in a new wing, the air thick with age and dust. The walls, adorned with faded tapestries and darkened portraits, seemed to close in around her, their eyes watching her every step.

As she wandered through the eerie quiet, a faint melody floated through the air, delicate and haunting, weaving its way into her consciousness.

What is that beautiful sound? Evelyn wondered. *Where is it coming from?*

It was a melody she could not place, but one that felt strangely familiar, as though it had always been there, waiting for her to listen. It stirred something deep within her, a quiet ache of beauty and sorrow. The notes seemed to beckon her, teasing the edges of her memory, urging her forwards with a gentle pull. Each lilting phrase resonated with the weight of lost dreams, wrapping around her like a gossamer thread, urging her deeper into the manor's heart.

At last, she paused at a half-open door. Through the narrow gap, a figure sat bathed in pale light: Henry, his silhouette carved from shadow and soft illumination. His hands moved with an eerie fluidity over the strings of a grand harp, the notes floating like whispered secrets into the stillness. The light traced the sharp lines of his face, lingering on the curve of his jaw, and his hair fell in gentle waves, half-obscuring his eyes. He seemed almost otherworldly, lost in the haunting beauty of the melody, as though he, too, were a part of the music, drawn from the depths of some forgotten sorrow.

Oh.

In the wake of Evelyn's encounter with the woman in white, thoughts of Mr Henry Sinclair had faded to the periphery, overshadowed by the mystery of the ghost and the attic. But now, seeing him like this – lost in his music, beautiful against the soft afternoon light – he was drawn sharply back to the forefront of her mind.

The melody he wove was both terrible and beautiful, wrapping around her heart and tugging at the very edges of her soul.

Unable to resist the pull of the music, she pushed the door open quietly and stepped inside, careful not to disturb the fragile spell that bound him to the harp and her to the moment.

He sat utterly absorbed, completely unaware of her presence. His expression was softer than she'd ever seen, as though the notes soothed something within him that nothing else could reach. In that moment, he seemed almost ethereal, so entirely lost in the haunting melody he created.

"That was beautiful," she murmured, as the final note sounded.

He sat up and looked at her suddenly, startled. His expression was fleetingly bare, as if she had caught him in the act of unveiling a secret, but the vulnerability vanished in an instant.

"It is merely a quiet comfort," he muttered, moving away from the grand harp, as if to dismiss the beauty he had just created. He rested his hands on his knees, his posture tense, and she could sense the walls he built around himself beginning to close in once more.

Evelyn's heart raced as she took in the sight of him. The remnants of their last night in the garden echoed in her mind, the phantom heat of his grip on her skin. She yearned to bridge the gap between them, to unravel the layers of his guarded heart.

"No, it is more than that," she insisted gently, stepping closer. "Your music carries a depth that speaks to the soul. It holds a truth that is often left unsaid."

He turned to her with curiosity in his eyes, though he remained stiff with his hands on his knees.

"My mother was a musician as well," she continued, settling onto the seat beside him. "She played the piano... sometimes the violin. She had dreams of performing, though life had other plans for her."

Henry's brow furrowed. He was silent for a moment. "You have never spoken of your mother."

"She was my everything. She died bringing my brother into the world."

She watched as he absorbed her words, his expression darkening. He inhaled deeply, then exhaled with a frustrated puff of air.

"That is most unfortunate," he said carefully.

Evelyn offered a sad smile.

"I understand, you see," he continued softly, as they sat side by side. His eyes were fixed on the window, where gentle rain pattered against the glass. "I never knew my mother. She, too, died in childbirth... The curse of bringing heirs into this world, it seems." His voice was a low murmur, as if speaking the truth aloud made it all the more real.

Evelyn's heart sank at his revelation as she processed his words. The late Baroness Sinclair – Henry's mother – had become a ghostly figure in her mind, much like the woman in white.

How foolish I've been, she thought, shame prickling beneath her skin. *Spinning tales of phantoms and restless spirits, when the truth was something far simpler and far sadder.*

The realisation that she and Henry shared such a profound loss struck her deeply. It was not a mystery, nor a haunting – merely grief, plain and human. A silence settled between them, laden with sorrow.

Evelyn was first to break the stillness, her voice thick with emotion. "It is unfair, is it not? That a woman's role is so often confined to being a wife, and that her life can often end in service of that purpose. No one speaks of the cost... the sacrifice."

Henry turned to her, and for a moment, she saw the walls around his heart begin to crack. "Indeed. I have oft pondered upon that. It is cruel... and yet, it is expected. Tradition ensnares us all in roles we never asked for."

Evelyn squinted her eyes at him, noticing the fatigue etched into his features deepening the lines of his face. "What troubles you so?"

"Oh..." He stood, running his hands through his dark hair. "I am merely weary." He began to circle the room, his steps restless, as if pacing could shed the weight of his thoughts. "Perhaps it is the knowledge that I cannot change what is destined."

Evelyn tilted her head, watching him closely as he paced, as if she could see into his very soul – as though she were seeking to unravel the knots binding his heart. "You must know that you are not alone, Henry. You do not have to bear the world all by yourself."

Their eyes met. In a few swift strides, he closed the distance between them, his hands finding her waist and pulling her to him with an urgency that stole her breath.

"Evelyn," he began, but the plea in his voice was lost as she leant in, closing the final distance between them.

Their lips met in a tentative kiss, a soft brush at first, like a whispered caress, testing the boundaries between them, but that light touch was

110

enough to send shivers rippling through her, awakening a slow burn through her centre. The taste of him was warm and rich, like spiced wine.

In that instant, time ceased to exist, and the world around them dissolved into nothingness. It was only them, suspended in that fragile stolen moment.

His hands tightened on her waist, drawing her flush against him, their bodies pressing together as if neither could bear the space between them any longer. He threaded his fingers through her hair then, tangling in her chestnut strands, tilting her head to deepen the kiss with a hunger that left her breathless.

She sighed as his lips moved over hers, slow and insistent, drawing her further into the heady sensation of being utterly consumed by him. Her world narrowed to the heat of his mouth, the way his hands gripped her as if she were the only anchor to keep him from unravelling.

But then, he stilled. His lips hovered near hers for a heartbeat longer, the warmth of his breath mingling with hers. Just as swiftly as the moment had ignited, he pulled back, his fingers slackening as he drew away. His chest rose and fell with laboured breaths, his eyes dark as they searched hers.

"We shouldn't," he murmured, his voice rough, the heat of his breath still grazing her lips.

"Why not?" she challenged, her lips still tingling from the kiss, the taste of him. She did not step away. "What is there to fear when it feels so terribly right?"

Henry remained silent, his jaw tightening.

"It is that confounded family curse, isn't it?" Evelyn suddenly pulled away from him, shaking as she pushed his hands off her. The cool air of the room seemed to rush between them. "You have allowed a foolish story to control your life."

Henry's gaze flickered, revealing a flash of pain before he masked it with his familiar veil. "It is not that simple, Evelyn. There are consequences to all of our actions – curse or not."

"That seems like a coward's way out," she murmured, her chest heaving with the weight of her frustration, though she knew she was being petulant.

Still, she could not stop herself. She wanted to shake him, to break through whatever walls he had built around himself.

I barely know this man, she thought. *And yet* – there it was again, that inexplicable pull, sharp as hunger, deep as longing. She was drawn to him against all logic and sense, as though some unseen thread tethered her to his sadness, his silence, his maddening restraint

Henry's expression darkened. "It is not cowardice," he shot back, balling into hands into fists at his sides. "I am protecting you. If you knew the truth! If you understood the danger – "

"Then tell me! I do not need your protection. I deserve to know the truth of whatever truly plagues you."

He is being utterly insufferable, Evelyn thought, her temper flaring despite her best efforts to remain composed. *Always speaking in riddles and shadows, as though the mere act of confession might bring the house crumbling down upon us both.* It was galling – condescending, even.

Henry's hand raked through his dark hair, trembling with the effort of restraint. He paced before her like a restless animal trapped in a cage, every line of his face tight with conflict.

"Please," he said, his voice raw. "You don't understand the burden I carry. You cannot become part of this legacy."

Evelyn stood her ground, her breaths coming fast and shallow as she drew herself up. "I refuse to let fear and fiction dictate my life." Her voice was hard, but inside she was trembling. She did not want to push him away, but she could not stand the half-truths and riddles any longer.

She could see his defences falter for a moment – how her words cut through the fortress he had built around himself. His eyes softened, his body swaying towards her as though he might wrap her in his arms, pull her close, and never let go.

Might he kiss me again? she wondered.

But just as quickly, he turned away.

"I cannot," he whispered, the words barely audible, more to himself than to her.

Evelyn felt something within her snap. That soft restraint she always held, that polished composure expected of ladies – it fractured under the weight of his persistent despair. She could not bear to see him retreat again, could not watch him bury himself in his self-imposed prison of doubt.

She reached out for him.

"Help me understand," she begged, her hands hovering just inches from his back, aching to touch him. "There is no curse, Henry. Logic and reason tell us it is simply impossible. Why do you shut yourself away in this lonely manor? Why do you torture yourself with thoughts of a burden that does not exist? Travel! See the world. Love and be loved. The world is yours to explore as a man – embrace that freedom. There is no curse, Henry."

Why does he not see it? she thought, despairingly. *He is young, wealthy, intelligent. He is a man! He could go anywhere, be anyone. If I could only shake him loose!*

Henry let out a wild, bitter laugh that sent a shiver down her spine. The sound was sharp, hollow, tinged with something close to madness. It startled her.

He turned, his eyes gleaming with an intensity she had never seen before. The air between them seemed to crackle, alive with something raw and dangerous.

"Come with me, then." His eyes bore into hers. "If you want the truth."

Before she could answer, he grabbed her wrist – not harshly, but with enough force to pull her towards him. His touch sent a thrill through her, a sharp contrast to the icy dread curling in her stomach. Her pulse quickened, her breath coming in short gasps as she stared at him.

He's going to show me, she realised. *Whatever madness he harbours, whatever secret keeps him pacing these halls like a penitent, he means to reveal it.* And if she saw it, perhaps then she could reason with him, untangle fact from fear, dissuade him from this obsession with curses and shadows.

"Show me," she whispered. Her voice was barely audible, but she knew he heard her.

There was no turning back now.

∞∞∞∞

113

The echo of their hurried footsteps seemed to vibrate through the ancient stone walls as she struggled to keep pace. The lit candle sconces along the walls cast long, wavering shadows, their glow doing little to dispel the gloom that seeped into every corner of the manor.

Evelyn glanced around nervously, wondering what the servants might think if they happened to witness this scene: Henry Sinclair, heir to the manor, dragging a young lady through the manor's corridors with no explanation. The very idea was scandalous; entire drawing rooms could dine out on it for weeks.

I ought to pull away. I ought to demand he stop. I ought to care more about what this looks like. This is madness, and yet…

The thrill of it sent a shiver through her, one she could neither explain nor resist. *Where is he taking me? What truth has he concealed beneath his tortured silence? And why, heaven help me, do I want to desperately to know?*

Henry's grip had changed from her wrist to her gloved hand. They were in the East Wing, where Clara had warned of flickering lights and strange happenings. Evelyn could almost sense it: the soft rustle of fabric, a fleeting silhouette at the edge of her vision, a chill that crept along her spine.

You do not believe in ghosts, Evelyn Ward, she chided herself, but the thought ran hollow.

At last, they reached a door at the far end of a long hallway. It was old, the wood warped with time and the paint peeling in large, uneven patches. It looked untouched and forgotten, like something that had been left to rot, some secret buried and abandoned. Henry paused only for a moment, his breath heavy with a tension that mirrored her own. Then with a firm push, he forced it open.

The hinges groaned as the door swung inward, releasing a sickly, damp smell that hit her like a wave. Evelyn instinctively recoiled, her hand flying to her mouth to stifle a gasp. She hesitated, her eyes wide, but Henry was relentless. Without so much as a backwards glance, he tightened his hold on her hand and drew her inside, pulling her across the threshold.

The door clicked shut behind them, the sound echoing in the small, dark room. Shadows clung to the walls, the feeble light of a single candle casting a trembling glow. It barely penetrated the gloom, revealing only the edges of the space: a broken chair sagging in the corner, a thick layer of dust blanketing everything.

A shape in the centre of the room drew Evelyn's eye: an object covered by a tattered, moth-eaten sheet.

What is that? A statue? A trunk? A coffin? Her rational mind scrambled for explanation, but nothing seemed to fit.

The cold crept beneath her gloves and into her bones. Her senses were overwhelmed with the dimness, the stillness, the strange, oppressive weight of the room pressing down upon her like a held breath.

She could feel Henry's presence beside her, could hear the roughness of his breathing. He had let go of her hand.

Why now? she thought, disoriented by the loss of his touch. *Why bring me here and then abandon me to this silence?*

"Henry," she whispered, her voice trembling despite herself. "What is this place?"

He said nothing. His face remained shrouded in shadow, his eyes dark as he moved silently towards the shrouded object in the centre of the room. He reached out, his hand hovering above the ragged sheet, and Evelyn felt her stomach drop.

Do not do it, she wanted to say. *This room has teeth. It remembers things!* It was terribly illogical, she knew, and yet the thought persisted.

Whatever lies beneath that fabric, she realised, *it is a piece of the truth he's buried for years. The thing he fears will make me run – or make him fall apart.*

She could not look away.

Henry paused for a breath, as if he were steeling himself for the truth about to be unveiled. His voice, when it finally came, was barely more than a ragged whisper: "You wanted to know the truth. Here it is."

With a swift tug, he pulled the sheet away.

Beneath was an old bed, its wooden frame sagging with age. The mattress was thin, no more than a threadbare cushion, but it was the figure in the bed that sent a chill racing down Evelyn's spine.

The man lying there was barely human – more shadow than substance. His skeletal form was stretched tight with skin so pale it seemed almost translucent, and his chest rose and fell with laboured, shallow breaths. Indeed, the faint rise and fall of his chest was the only indication that life still clung to him. His face was gaunt, a death mask etched with years of agony. The pallor of his skin was sickly, ashen, as though every ounce of life had been drained from him long ago, leaving behind only the shell of a once-living man.

Evelyn's stomach twisted in revulsion, yet sympathy rooted her to the spot. This wasn't just decay; it was torment – a suffering that ran deeper than flesh, beyond time. This was not merely death inching its way towards him; this was a kind of torment that transcended the body, a soul trapped in suffering that had no release.

"Henry…" The sight before her felt too much to bear, dread curling like a serpent in her belly.

"This," Henry said, "is my true grandfather on the Sinclair side."

Evelyn's brow furrowed. *His grandfather?* No – the Baron Sinclair was his grandfather.

"I… I'm afraid I do not understand."

She glanced at Henry, his profile carved in candlelight, and felt the awful weight of realisation press against her ribs.

There is something wrong in the bloodline, she thought. *Something hidden. Something shameful enough to be buried, quite literally.*

"Tell me what you mean, Henry Sinclair," she said, though she was not certain she wanted to hear the answer.

He exhaled slowly, as if the weight of the truth bore down on him with every breath. Without a word, he reached into his coat pocket and withdrew a small, oval case. He handed it to her.

Evelyn hesitated, then took it, her gloved fingers grazing his in the exchange. She unlatched the case carefully.

Inside, behind a thin glass pane, was a finely painted portrait. It showed a much younger Baron Alistair Sinclair with features still softened by youth. He held a small child – *Henry,* she realised – smiling as though the world

116

was full of promise. Behind them stood a third figure: a man, regal and commanding, his posture straight and expression composed.

"Who is this man?" Evelyn whispered, her eyes tracing the brushstrokes that captured his likeness. She looked toward the figure lying silent in the room's centre, swathed in the tattered sheet. "It cannot be…"

Henry nodded, the shadows deepening in his expression. "It is. The years have not been kind."

Evelyn studied the miniature portrait again: Henry as an infant – so clearly him, with that same solemn set to his eyes. Alistair, a young man, and then a man who stood behind them both.

"Alistair is your father," she breathed. "But… how can this be?"

"The Sinclair curse," Henry said, his tone hollow. "It affects us all differently, but it always brings suffering. Baron Alistair Sinclair – my father – may appear old and frail now, but at that moment, in that portrait… he was as young as I am now."

It made no sense – no sense at all. The man behind them in the portrait looked to be in his late fifties, perhaps sixty at most. He was not young, certainly, but strong – and yet the figure lying before her – the thing beneath the sheet – was a ruin. He was not merely aged, but broken… collapsed inwards like something rotting.

And the smell… Evelyn swallowed hard. *It would take more than thirty years to reduce a man to that.*

She looked up at Henry sharply. "How long has he been like this? How old is he?"

Henry's face twisted with an emotion she could not place: grief, anger, perhaps both. "Not old enough to be a living corpse," he muttered bitterly.

Evelyn's mouth parted, forming a reply, but before she could speak, the thing in the bed gasped, convulsing with a sudden, ragged breath. She flinched, stumbling back a step. *Dear God.*

Every instinct screamed to flee, to turn and run from the impossible thing that should not move or breathe, but then, as if compelled by something beyond fear, she found herself stepping forwards instead.

What am I doing? she thought, her breath shallow. *What madness compels me to go nearer?* Her fear was not gone – it trembled in every limb – but something else had taken hold: a grim, inexplicable compassion, as if the sheer pitiful state of the creature before her demanded kindness, even now.

Her eyes fell upon a dusty glass of water on the bedside table. She reached for it without thinking, her hands moving with a strange steadiness even as her stomach roiled.

It is just a man, she told herself. *A man, wasted by time or illness, but a man all the same. How cruel to leave him under a sheet.*

Carefully, she brought the glass to his lips. The skin there was cracked and grey, the mouth slack, the throat working feebly as a few drops slid in.

His eyes fluttered open, clouded and unfocused, but alive. He mumbled something – a sound, not a word – his voice barely more than breath. He was still in there, whatever was left of the man.

"If the curse persists without being broken," Henry's voice came from behind her, cold and distant, as though he were reciting a passage memorised long ago, "the Sinclair heirs will be trapped in a state between life and death, eternally yearning for love and connection but never able to attain it."

His words hung in the air, thick with despair. Evelyn turned to face him, her mind whirling as she tried to arrange his meaning into something comprehensible.

He cannot truly believe this to be a curse.

She glanced back at the skeletal figure on the bed, and wave of pity washed over her. She knew there was grief in the house – oh yes, she could acknowledge that… sorrow and silence and rot. That much was real. *But this? This talk of curses and eternal longing?*

No – it was far too much.

An old man on his deathbed – frail and wasting away in illness and neglect – did not prove the workings of a curse. It was a pitiful sight, yes – a stark reminder of mortality's cruelty – but it was not the evidence she sought. Sickness, age, the slow decay of the body... these were the natural sufferings of life, not the workings of some sinister enchantment.

"This makes no sense, Henry," she said, her voice shaking as she struggled to speak against the rising unease within her. "Curses are but tales – nonsense conjured to frighten children. This man is merely old and ill. The notion that some... unnatural force could be responsible for his affliction – it is beyond reason. It defies all logic." She shook her head as if trying to dispel the notion entirely. "People do not wither away from curses. There must be a rational explanation. Something grounded in truth."

There must be.

Henry's expression hardened, his jaw tightening as if her words struck a nerve. "Are you slow? It defies reason because it exists beyond it," he snapped. He stalked across the room. "You think I want to believe this? I would give anything for it not to be true! But look at him, Evelyn! Look at what this curse has done."

She flinched at the raw intensity in his voice but held her ground. "But where is the evidence?" she pressed.

She was not trying to anger him – she was trying to make sense of the madness, trying to weave all the threads together into something that resembled truth. "You cannot attribute your family's suffering to magic. Your grandfather is suffering, and you hide him away in a room while pretending to be cursed!"

Henry took a step towards her, his movements sharp, his eyes dark with barely contained emotion. "Do you think I enjoy carrying this?" he said, his voice low and fervent. "I have shared my truth with you, and you still refuse to accept it. Why can you not see? It is not about logic or reason or evidence – it is about the weight of generations pressing down upon me!"

Evelyn stepped back. She could feel the anger radiating off him – but more than that, she sensed his deep, inescapable pain, and that he truly believed what he spoke.

You cannot reason with madness, she thought helplessly. *You cannot argue with someone who has wrapped their soul around a myth.*

It was not condescension she felt – no, worse than that. It was fear... though whether fear that he was mad, or fear that he was right, she did not know.

119

Evelyn sighed and turned away, walking to the door. "I just... I cannot reconcile what I see with what you are telling me. It is too... too fantastical."

Henry let out a bitter laugh, shaking his head. "Fantastical?" he repeated. "Perhaps. But if you cannot believe me in this, how can you believe in anything we might share?"

Her heart ached at the pain in his voice. There was no artifice in him, no manipulation. She wanted to believe him – she truly did – but her mind rebelled, clinging to reason like a shipwrecked sailor to driftwood.

This cannot be real, she told herself. *It cannot. If I accept this – if I follow him down into this madness – what does that make me?*

"I want to believe you, Henry," she whispered, her voice breaking. "I really do... but I need something more than mere words and sorrowful eyes to grasp this reality."

She paused, turning back to him.

"What do we even share, Henry?" she asked softly. "Each other's first names? A single kiss? We are strangers – you with your secrets, and I with my doubt."

He said nothing, and the silence stretched between them like a chasm.

Her chest tightened as she turned away again. She did not want to go, but staying felt like sinking.

Behind her, Henry remained still, his eyes fixed on her back, but he made no move to stop her.

Chapter 15

Clara

The servants had been whispering again, spinning tales of shadows that danced in the corners, and of strange noises emanating from the attic and the East Wing. Old Mr Haroldson, in his trembling age, had sworn he saw the woman in white with his own two eyes. He claimed she glided through a corridor, a lantern swaying in her grasp, with hollow eyes. The very thought sent a shiver down Clara's spine.

And then, always, there was the scratching – the dreadful scratching. It came each night, like nails against the wood, dragging through the silence as though something – or someone – was trapped within the walls, trying to claw its way out.

"A curse," the servants said. "The Sinclairs' legacy."

Those words followed her as she flitted about, tidying Miss Evelyn's room. She moved too quickly, tugging the linen tighter than necessary and rattling the washbasin as she set it down. She could not settle. She simply could not still her hands or her thoughts.

The image of Miss Evelyn coming downstairs that morning with her cheeks flushed, chin set, eyes burning with purpose haunted her more than any ghost or curse ever could. Miss Evelyn had wanted answers –

demanded them, and she had asked the servants for help as though they were not already trembling beneath the weight of what they knew, or rather, did not know.

She knew – oh, she knew – her mistress meant well, but she was too clever by half, and far too curious. Miss Evelyn thought she could fold everything into neat little facts, explain it all away, but she was wrong – so terribly, terribly wrong.

When Miss Evelyn entered her chamber, Clara's heart sank at the look on her face.

"Miss Evelyn," she greeted, forcing a bright smile that quickly faltered. "What troubles you?"

Her mistress sighed, sinking onto the edge of the bed, her gown pooling like a sea around her. "I do not know what to think anymore," she murmured.

Oh no – no, no. The sound of Miss Evelyn's voice – so quiet, so lost – unnerved her more than raised voices ever could.

She forced her voice to remain even, though it came out thinner than she meant. "What is it? Did you... did you go into the attic?"

"No, I could not find it. But Mr Sinclair showed me... something else. Clara, as my lady's maid and my trusted friend, I must confess something to you. I know not what my heart truly feels, but I cannot deny my attraction to Mr Sinclair. I am torn between my interest in him, and the dread that he... may not be right in the mind – that this supposed family curse has driven him to the brink of madness."

"Madness?" Clara stepped closer, her eyes wide. "You think him mad?"

Oh, she had feared this – feared the way Miss Evelyn looked at the man, the softness in her voice when she said his name. Madness wore many faces, and love made women blind to most of them. Clara had no illusions about the sad words men used to draw sympathy.

"Yes." Miss Evelyn's voice was barely a whisper, as if the word itself were a sin. "What if the true curse of the Sinclair family is not just an old tale, but something that could truly consume him? What if insanity is the real darkness he carries?"

Clara's heart ached for her mistress – truly, it did – but even that ache was tempered by something harder. She nodded thoughtfully, masking the unease growing at the base of her spine.

"My Granny once told me that love is a powerful force that can light up even the darkest of nights. And yet," Clara took on an Irish accent, lowering her voice to quote her grandmother, "fear possesses a might even greater. It can twist love into shadows... leadin' those we cherish into depths we dread."

It was almost a comfort to speak her Granny's words aloud, though they rang too true for comfort. Clara had watched women disappear under the twisted love of men – not literally, no – but inch by inch, year by year, until they were ghosts of themselves, haunting kitchens and drawing rooms and marriage beds.

Miss Evelyn smiled at the accent, and then nodded, leaning back against the pillow. "What if I am drawn into that darkness, Clara?" she said, looking up at the ceiling. "What if I lose myself in the chaos of his mind?" She paused, as if remembering. "We shared... a moment. But it feels fraught with confusion. I need you to keep it a secret."

Clara's eyes widened slightly, and she took a seat on the edge of the bed. She nodded, and patted her mistress's head gently, wondering what hidden sins the moment might have entailed. A kiss? A touch? A word too tender, too binding? She did not ask – no, she never did.

Miss Evelyn drew a deep breath, pulling the sheets up around her despite the daylight filtering in. Just then, the black cat emerged from the shadows and jumped onto the bed.

"I only wish I could see a clear path ahead," Miss Evelyn sighed, resting a hand on the cat's dark fur.

"Perhaps it will reveal itself in time," Clara offered gently, but inside, her mind reeled. *The path she walks now leads straight into ruin.* "But, Miss Evelyn, you must tread carefully. The deeper you delve into the mysteries of the Sinclairs, the more entangled you may become in their web of despair."

As Miss Evelyn closed her eyes, Clara felt the weight of the manor pressing in. The connection her mistress felt with Mr Sinclair was like a candle's flame in the night – flickering but vibrant. Clara could not shake the worry that this flame might not guide Evelyn to safety, but rather draw her further into the shadows of the Sinclair curse.

"Promise me you will remain vigilant. Your heart may lead you to him, but the shadows here hold secrets that could ensnare you both. Promise me you will never turn your back to the dark."

"I promise," Miss Evelyn whispered, her eyes still closed tight, though her uncertainty lingered in the air, a heavy mist that neither could dispel.

Chapter 16

Evelyn

Evelyn had promised to remain vigilant, and so she would. Her resolve intensified as she wandered the dimly lit halls of Rosehill Manor, determined to unearth the truth behind the rumoured Sinclair curse and the illness that afflicted Henry's grandfather.

With the old diary still missing and the attic lost in the labyrinth of the manor, her options were dwindling. The enchanted rose, once a source of wonder, now seemed to mock her with its silence. She could feel it calling to her, and yet, its secrets remained locked away, just as Henry's heart and mind felt closed to her.

Her thoughts drifted back to Henry Sinclair, as they so often did. Her heart ached as she thought of him, the way he looked at her with such longing, as if she were the only light in a shadowed room. He seemed to teeter on the brink of madness, burdened by the same illness that had claimed his grandfather and now loomed ominously over his father. What had befallen the men who once ruled Rosehill Manor with such strong bodies, now reduced to mere whispers of their former selves?

She imagined the young boy Henry must have once been, playing in the gardens. Did laughter ever escape his lips? Had he ever known the sweet, unrestrained joy of childhood?

She supposed he had never known a mother's tender embrace, nor the warmth of a sibling's camaraderie. There were no cousins to chase through sun-drenched meadows, perhaps not even friends to weave tales of adventure. She imagined him as a solitary figure, a boy burdened by a destiny he had not chosen, his innocence overshadowed by a legacy steeped in sorrow. Had he ever played at all, or was he left to wander the halls of Rosehill Manor alone, a ghost of his own youth, longing for the laughter that never came?

She paused in front of a portrait of Baron Alistair Sinclair, the man whose visage seemed to watch her with both pride and despair. If answers were to be found, they lay with him.

Henry had revealed to her the existence of his grandfather, wasting away in the East Wing, neglected and hidden from view.

Why had Baron Alistair Sinclair never spoken of him – his own father? With a slow, cold clarity, she realised that the man rotting in that bed was still – technically – the Baron Sinclair, and yet it was Alistair who ruled in his place and bore the title. The son had stepped into the father's shoes long before the man was cold in the ground.

How could no one know? How had society, the estate, even the household itself accepted this without question?

Had Alistair simply turned a blind eye to his father's suffering, locked him away like some shameful secret? Or was it worse: was he the cause of it?

The man was clearly sick. Yes, it was an illness. But what manner of illness afflicted him? Evelyn's thoughts swirled with possibilities. Madness? Poison? Some inherited affliction of the mind, or the blood?

She shivered, for the same thing must have begun in Alistair Sinclair. How had he aged so terribly since the miniature portrait? Her thoughts darkened further. Would it take Henry next? Would it devour him too, inch by inch, until he too was locked away in some shuttered room while his son smiled in his place?

The questions gnawed at her like rats at the edge of reason.

She must speak to Alistair Sinclair. She must look into his eyes and see what they held: remorse, horror, or something colder.

"The truth is out there," she murmured to herself, "hidden among the shadows. I *will* find it."

The grand staircase loomed before her, its dark bannisters curving upwards into the heights of the manor. She spotted a footman idling in the gloom. Approaching him, she spoke in a hushed tone, as though the very walls might overhear her inquiry: "Pray, could you direct me to Lord Sinclair's whereabouts?"

He shook his head in confusion. "I'm afraid not, Miss. I haven't seen him for some time."

"Not at all?" she pressed, hoping for a glimmer of information, a single clue to guide her through the labyrinthine halls of the manor.

"No, Miss." He glanced over his shoulder, wary of unseen ears. "Some say he's taken to the upper floors, though no one knows for certain where he goes. It seems he spends most of his days lost in solitude."

Evelyn frowned. Where could Lord Sinclair be disappearing to? What further truths was he concealing?

Before she could reply, Mr Blackwood emerged from the shadows, his tall figure framed by the dim light. "Ah, Miss Ward. I find you in search of the master, I presume?"

Evelyn's heart leapt against her ribs, startled more by how close he'd been than by his voice. *How long had he been standing there?*

She nodded, trying to steady her breath. The air around the butler seemed charged with a peculiar energy. It was not hostile – no, Mr Blackwood was far too polished for overt menace – but nevertheless, she could not shake the feeling that he understood far more than he ever let on.

"Indeed, Mr Blackwood. I was just asking after Lord Sinclair. Might you assist me?

"Certainly." A slight smile curled at the corners of his lips. "His study, if I am not mistaken, is where he retreats to deliberate upon matters of the estate. However, I must caution you, Miss Ward, that he is not one given to idle conversation, particularly of late." He gestured down the hall, and the shadows around them seemed to deepen, thickening like a suffocating fog.

"The Lord Sinclair has taken to himself more than is usual," Blackwood continued as he led Evelyn through winding corridors and through so many turns that she almost lost count. "But the mind of a Sinclair can often be a treacherous place. Perhaps it is best left unexplored."

He stopped by a door a last, and pushed it open slowly.

The chamber beyond was dimly lit, revealing a sanctuary of dust-laden tomes, and at the centre of the room sat the baron.

"Do not keep him waiting, Miss Ward," Mr Blackwood warned. With a subtle nod, he stepped back, allowing her to cross the threshold. Just as she opened her mouth to offer a word of gratitude, he slipped away, leaving her alone with the baron.

"Lord Sinclair," she began, her voice steady despite the fluttering in her chest. She had rehearsed this moment countless times as she wandered through the manor in search of him. Yet now, standing before him, she felt a rush of foolishness. "I find myself compelled to inquire about the woman in white and the rose, about your *son*, Henry – and the curse that plagues your family. It is of the utmost importance to me, and I beseech you to share whatever knowledge you possess. I fear that, without your guidance, I may be ensnared in a darkness I can scarcely comprehend. Please, I beg of you – reveal to me the truth, devoid of all fiction."

The baron's gaze bore into Evelyn, and the intensity of his scrutiny was almost palpable. "What is it that you truly seek, Miss Ward? This is no trifling matter, and I would not have you wade into murky waters unprepared."

Evelyn met his stare, her heart pounding. "I seek understanding, my lord. I must know how the thread of Seraphina's tale weaves into your own. What happened to your own father – who I have seen withering in the East Wing – and what fate awaits your own son?"

A flicker of something – regret or perhaps excitement – passed across his face. He glanced away, as if considering her request.

"Very well," he finally said, each word vibrating in his throat, slow and drawn out. "You must understand that the truth is often shrouded in shadows, much like this manor itself. But I will share with you what I know." He shifted in his chair, fingers steepled before him.

"It is a story passed down over centuries – twelve generations of Sinclairs… each retelling has been cloaked in the mist of time, yet it always echoes the same haunting refrain: When Seraphina learned of her lover's betrayal, her heart shattered, much like the fragile petals of the rose that bears her name.

"You see, Seraphina fell in love with my ancestor, Edmund Sinclair, the heir to this estate. Their love blossomed in the hidden corners of the garden, nurtured in secret, growing quietly away from prying eyes." He paused, looking towards the window, where the rain lashed against the panes. "But Edmund… Edmund was not content with love alone. He craved power, status – things that Seraphina, a humble healer, could never offer. On the night Seraphina believed he would ask for her hand, she discovered the bitter truth. Edmund had already promised himself to another: a woman of wealth, influence and beauty far beyond Seraphina's reach."

Evelyn furrowed her brow as she settled uninvited into a chair by the hearth. *The man who spurned Seraphina was a Sinclair.*

It was a seemingly insignificant detail, yet now, it was a connecting puzzle piece. She had heard the story before, of course, but it held new meaning now.

Still, it was merely one piece, a fragment in the tangled web of secrets. Evelyn's fingers tightened around the edge of her chair. She sought fresh revelations – new insights into how the past intertwined with the present, of how it would impact Henry's future. What dark burden had caused him to retreat so tightly from her, as if love itself was a threat? What path awaited him, and where did she fit into it?

"Heartbroken and betrayed," Alistair Sinclair continued, his voice quieter now, more intimate, as though he was confiding in the very stones

129

of the manor itself, "Seraphina fled into the garden. Her tears soaked the soil, watering the roots of the rose she had so carefully nurtured. In her anguish, she cried out, unable to contain the sorrow in her heart. Words of grief spilled from her lips, and with them, unknowingly, a pact was made with the very spirits of the earth. Magic twisted her pain into power, binding the souls of the Sinclairs to the rose, condemning them to a fate as lonely as her own broken heart.

"From that night on, the rose would bloom only under winter's moonlight, once a year. If the heir of the Sinclair family did not find true love by the time the last petal fell, they would wither away, just as the rose. And so it has been, year after year, generation after generation. The Sinclairs have been haunted by that curse ever since, always searching for true love, but rarely finding it."

Evelyn shook her head with a long sigh. She longed for something tangible, a reality beneath the myths. What did it matter that the rose bloomed only in winter's moonlight if the truth remained obscured in darkness?

"But what does that truly mean for the Sinclairs?" she persisted. "What ailment troubles your father? Has he ever been attended to by a physician? Do you bear the same affliction? And what of Henry?"

Lord Sinclair regarded her with a sombre intensity, as if weighing the significance of her questioning. Still, Evelyn sensed the wall of silence surrounding him, guarding secrets that still danced just beyond her reach.

"Ah, Henry – is that not the heart of it? Seraphina's curse was born of betrayal and sorrow, a legacy that would ensnare every Sinclair who dared to love."

Evelyn's frustration simmered beneath her composed exterior. Though the baron had recounted the tragic tale of Seraphina, he had withheld the very essence of the ailment that afflicted the Sinclair lineage. How could she confront the darkness that loomed over Henry without grasping its true nature?

"My lord, your words are but riddles. I seek not merely a recitation of the stories, but a glimpse into its implications for the present. What, precisely, does Seraphina's supposed curse entail? How does it bind Henry to such despair?"

"The curse is not so easily defined, Miss Ward. It lingers like a shadow in the hearts of the Sinclairs, manifesting in ways most subtle and insidious. Betrayal is its core, yes, but the ramifications twist and turn, ensnaring those who love without caution."

She could have screamed. She breathed deeply, forcing herself to speak calmly. "Are there no means by which this... curse may be lifted, no action to be taken that could alter its course?"

He leant back slightly, his gaze distant, as if looking through her to some long-forgotten sorrow. "To challenge the curse is to court danger itself, Miss Ward. One must be prepared to sacrifice, for love demands its own price. The heart is a treacherous thing, but..." He hesitated, something inscrutable crossing his features. "Perhaps true love – the kind that transcends mere affection – might hold the key to breaking this darkness. Yet, such love is rare, and few truly find it."

At his vague explanations, Evelyn's resolve deepened; perhaps it was not only Henry who teetered on the brink of madness, but all the Sinclairs! Yes – ensnared by the shadows of their own minds, trapped in a web of sorrow and insanity spun long before her arrival.

Chapter 17

Henry

Henry Sinclair sat in the dim light of dawn, brushing his fingers against the strings of the grand harp in his music room. It was an odd hour to be awake, but sleep had never been Henry's companion. The soft notes that filled the room offered a peace that nothing else in his small world could. He closed his eyes, letting the music transport him from the heavy gloom that hung over Rosehill. He sustained a single note, letting it fade into the stillness, before drawing out another, weaving together a melody that echoed the weight in his chest.

As he played, Henry found himself lost in the memory of kissing Evelyn, a fleeting moment that lingered like the echo of a haunting song. The warmth of her breath had caught him off guard, but her gasp had ignited a wildfire in his veins. He recalled the softness of her lips, the way she had leant into him, her body pliant and eager, as if they were drawn together by some unseen force. The curve of her hips had pressed against him, awakening a primal urge that roared to life with a single touch.

But the warmth of that connection had dissipated too quickly, leaving behind a chill that clung to him. The curse hung over him like a dark spectre. He could still feel the tremor of uncertainty in her voice as she challenged him, that gentle defiance that only deepened his resolve to keep her safe.

The harp's strings thrummed beneath his fingertips. Each note curled through the air, soft as a whispered lullaby, filling the empty corners of the manor with something like life. Henry played with a practised ease, his touch gentle, coaxing out melodies that spoke of longing, of places far beyond the heavy stone walls that enclosed him.

He had learnt the harp as a boy, a gift from his mother before he was born – a small, humble instrument – but it had opened a door to another world, one he longed to step fully into. He had always imagined himself as a musician, playing to grand audiences, or sitting in an opera house, letting the swell of the orchestra carry him away. Such things were beyond him now, confined to the pages of books and the tales of travellers who passed through Rosehill. His life had not allowed for such frivolities as opera or ballet; the only music apart from his own was that of fleeting guests, those who brought their talents along with their polite conversation.

As a child, when the nights grew long and the scratching sounds plagued him, he had taken to his small harp. He would play until his fingers ached, each note a shield against the noises that crawled through the walls. The scratching noises had unnerved him as a young boy, like whispers of some hidden torment; but as the years passed, it became as much a part of the house as the creaking floors and the cold drafts. He barely noticed them now, so entrenched were they in the fabric of the manor.

Here, in the early hours before Rosehill awoke, he could still find solace in his music. The notes shimmered, rising and falling like a distant breeze, and for a moment, the shadows seemed to recede, drawn back by the music, but as the final note faded, the stillness that returned felt heavier, as though the house itself sighed, waiting for him to stop.

Henry's thoughts drifted back to Evelyn – this time, in her disbelief of the curse that plagued him. He had shown her the truth: his grandfather, withering away before their very eyes! A man who should have been old but not ancient – and still, she still did not believe.

It gnawed at him, this doubt of hers. The curse was not some fanciful tale spun to frighten children. It was real, a shadow hanging over him, creeping closer with each passing day. He had thought showing her would make her understand, but her scepticism remained, like a quiet wound that bled into his thoughts, making him wonder if anyone could truly comprehend the weight of this legacy. It was a burden he carried alone, with no solace in sight.

He caught a glimpse of himself in the distant mirror. Grey had begun to bleed into the corners of his dark hair, creeping like a silent invader at his temples. It was a quiet reminder that the curse marked him too, just as it had ravaged his father and grandfather before him. He turned away from the sight, a bitter taste rising in his throat. The curse, it seemed, would not be content until it claimed them all.

He had devised a plan to make Evelyn believe. His grandfather's old journal, kept hidden away for years, filled with ramblings and ink-smudged drawings. Henry had sought it out the night before the flower bloomed, desperate for answers, something to confirm the curse's grip on the Sinclair line. He had pored over the pages, but most were indecipherable – a madman's scrawl. The frustration of it had made him throw the book out the window, convinced he could glean nothing from its crazed script.

That journal now felt like his last hope. Perhaps Evelyn would see in its broken words and frantic scribbles what he could not explain on his own. Even in its fractured state, the diary might show her that the curse was real, something that even she could no longer dismiss.

He had spent hours over the past day and night poring over the pages once more, scribing down every line related to the curse that he could find. His fingers ached from the effort, and ink stained his hands. He filled three whole pages of parchment, weaving together the disjointed fragments into an ominous tale that echoed the despair he felt coursing through his veins.

Today would be different. Today, he would confront her with the truth, with real evidence. He would lay bare the horrors of the Sinclair legacy, forcing Evelyn to understand that the curse was not just a figment of imagination.

He imagined her reaction: her wide eyes absorbing the revelation, her disbelief faltering in the face of undeniable proof. He wanted to shield her from this cursed lineage, to convince her to leave this dreadful place behind. How could he risk loving her, knowing the darkness that shadowed him? Knowing the fate that may befall her? He would show her, and then convince her to leave Rosehill – to flee to the safety of her home in London.

He resolved to be steadfast. Evelyn deserved to know the truth, even if it meant shattering the fragile connection they had begun to forge. Today, he would show her the words of a madman, and in doing so, he hoped to reveal the depths of their shared fate.

Chapter 18

Evelyn

Evelyn stirred to find herself still in her dress from the previous day, having missed dinner entirely. Though her sleep had been long, it had been restless, haunted by nightmares. In her fevered dream, her nails splintered against the wood of a coffin, her screams swallowed as soil rained through the cracks. Blood seeped down her thighs, warm and sticky against the grit beneath her.

Clara bustled into the room breathlessly. "Miss Ward, there's a carriage pulling up to the manor! I believe guests have arrived."

She stood and moved to the window, her breath fogging the glass as she squinted in the morning light. The dark silhouette of a carriage was rattling along the twisting path. An unsettling feeling washed over her. Who could be arriving at this hour, disturbing the fragile peace she had sought to reclaim?

In many ways, she felt less like a guest and more like a true inhabitant of the estate, weaving herself into its fabric with each passing day. She smoothed her gown, trying to compose herself as Clara approached her with a clean gown and a brush in hand.

"You shall need to look your best," Clara said, setting to work on her hair. "For all we know, it could be a duke arriving, or a prince! Oh yes, much better than a baron's brooding son, wouldn't you say?"

After Clara's fussing, Evelyn gathered her composure and made her way downstairs in a dress of light blue muslin and simple pearl earrings.

As she descended the grand staircase into the foyer, she spotted her father and Charles already waiting by the doors. Charles rested his weight slightly on a polished cane, his leg still healing, but bearing less of a burden with each passing day.

Henry, too, was present, leaning against the marble mantelpiece with his gaze fixed on the window, watching the approaching carriage. A faint frown creased his brow, deepening the weary shadows under his eyes, as if he were bracing himself.

Pale sunlight filtered through the grand windows, casting elongated shadows across the marble floor, and Evelyn felt an unexplainable sense of dread wash over her. As the carriage drew nearer, her heart raced in tandem with the rhythm of hooves on gravel.

After some time, Mr Blackwood stepped forwards and opened the door ceremoniously, revealing a striking young woman at the bottom of the stone staircase. She stood poised, dressed in a gown of emerald silk that flared gently at her ankles. Soft blonde curls framed her face like a golden halo in the morning sunlight. Behind her, an older woman loomed in austere black, her sharp eyes scanning the grounds.

As they walked up the stone staircase towards the manor, the blonde woman maintained an air of elegance, her gown trailing and the older woman following closely behind.

Henry stepped forwards with a stiff formality. "Lady Arabella Ravenwood," he said through a tight smile. "It has been many years since our childhood. Welcome back to Rosehill Manor."

Lady Ravenwood curtsied prettily, looking up at Henry through long eyelashes. "You remember my Aunt Agatha, do you not, Mr Sinclair?"

The woman in black stepped forwards and Henry bowed deeply. "Of course. Welcome, Dowager Countess. It is a true honour to have you grace this manor again. You are most welcome to stay for as long as you desire. Lord Sinclair is presently resting but shall be pleased to receive additional guests." He turned with practised grace. "Allow me to introduce the baron's esteemed guests, the Wards. This is Mr Edward Ward, a renowned botanist, accompanied by his daughter, Miss Evelyn Ward, and his son, Master Charles Ward."

Evelyn felt Lady Ravenwood's eyes linger on her, appraising her dress and pearl earrings. "Rosehill is such a charming little corner of the world, is it not? I can only imagine how dull it must seem for you compared to your life in... London, is it? One can easily spot an ambitious society woman among the wealthy and titled country folk."

Evelyn straightened her posture, keeping her eyes steady. "How splendid to meet you. Indeed, I am from London, Lady Ravenwood. Nevertheless, I find the tranquillity of the countryside refreshing, far removed from the noise of ambition. The country possesses its own beauty – one that does not require titles to appreciate."

"Indeed," Lady Ravenwood replied with a sly smile. "But do call me Lady Arabella – we are to be friends now, are we not?" Her eyes lingered on Evelyn, then shifted to Henry. "I trust your company remains as delightful as ever?"

Evelyn could sense the tension in the air, the unspoken history that hung between them. Lady Arabella smiled, but there was an edge to it, a sharpness.

"It must be such a *bore* here during the long winters. I've come to bring a bit of excitement to this quiet estate once more. After all, we cannot let the ghosts of the past consume us, can we?"

As Lady Arabella and her aunt stepped further into the grand foyer, the subtle scent of foxglove wafted through the air.

"Now, do tell me, Miss Evelyn," she continued, her voice honeyed. "Do you have any talents? Perhaps you play an instrument? You must entertain us while my aunt and I are here."

Evelyn's cheeks flushed slightly. "I dabble in music, though I must admit I have no true talent. I find more joy in observing the artistry of others than in performing myself. There is something lovely about listening, don't you think? It allows one to appreciate the nuances of a piece without the pressure of the spotlight."

"Such a modest response," Lady Arabella purred. "But modesty can only go so far in society, can it not? One must showcase their talents to truly shine." She dismissed Evelyn with a wave of her hand and turned to the servants. "If you'll excuse me, I would like to be shown to my chambers. I trust the accommodations are suitable?"

The servants exchanged glances before hastily moving to comply.

Evelyn noticed Henry looking between the two women. He shifted his weight, tapping his fingers against his thigh.

"Miss Ward," he said, his voice rising just a fraction too loud. "Would you do me the honour of joining me in the drawing room? I would like to show you something I have been working on."

Lady Arabella's eyes narrowed, but she swiftly masked her irritation with a gracious smile. "Oh, do take your time," she said sweetly. "I shall instruct my maid to unpack my belongings and refresh myself before we convene. After all, there is much to discuss regarding the local society, Miss Ward. And I daresay we have quite the catching up to do, Henry."

The use of his first name was like a blow to Evelyn's stomach, though she forced a polite smile. *What history was there between the two?*

Henry straightened his back further, now clenching his hands tightly behind him as he tilted his head in silent agreement.

Lady Arabella's smile remained, though her eyes were calculating as she turned to leave. "I shall be in my chambers, then."

As she swept from the room, she leant in closer to Henry, his arm in a gesture that felt far too intimate for mere acquaintances.

Evelyn watched as Henry stiffened, a faint flush creeping up his neck. He quickly cleared his throat.

"Shall we?" he asked, turning to Evelyn.

∞∞∞∞

As they entered the drawing room, Evelyn settled into a plush chair. Her father sat at the far side of the room, engrossed in a heavy scientific volume.

He adjusted his spectacles, the lenses glinting in the soft light. Charles had hobbled off to play marbles in the courtyard after the mystery of the new arrivals had passed.

Evelyn tucked a loose strand of hair behind her ear, stealing a glance at Henry as he leant against the mantel. He was a study of silent struggle, his shoulders tensing and releasing in an unsteady rhythm.

Silence hung between them, suspended like a breath held too long.

"Lady Arabella," Evelyn said quietly, at last. "She is quite the presence, is she not?"

Henry shrugged. He remained silent for a time, the embers of the hearth reflecting in his eyes. "We were acquainted in childhood. She is not as imposing as she appears. Rather unremarkable, really."

Evelyn raised a brow, but before she could press further, Henry reached inside his coat and withdrew a small leather book.

The diary!

"I have been working on something," he began, his voice low and earnest. He left the hearth and took a seat opposite her, the subtle scent of wood smoke and cedar on him. "It concerns a family diary."

"Your grandfather's diary!"

He stilled, his eyes widening in surprise. He held the book firmly, his grip tightening along its worn edges. "How do you come by this knowledge?" he whispered.

"It is of no consequence," she replied hastily. "I once happened upon it in the library, but when I returned to seek it again, it was gone. I suppose you've had it all along. Come now, tell me more."

Henry pursed his lips and then leant forwards, his eyes darting briefly to where her father sat, still absorbed in his book. He lowered his voice. "Then you would know my grandfather wrote of the curse. Pages and pages – most of it nonsensical, but at times, oddly profound. I have been transcribing all the passages that pertain to it. There are entries that speak of the rose – of its power and the legacy it carries." He paused, studying her reaction, and she saw something behind his gaze: determination, perhaps, mingled with fear.

"What does it say?" she urged, leaning in closer as he withdrew folded pages from his pocket.

As he unfolded the parchment carefully, she noticed the slight tremor in his hands. A swell of guilt washed over her. How could she have doubted him when he had held so firmly to his convictions? Even if one were deemed to be mad, their fears still warranted belief. Didn't pain still deserve compassion, even if its source could not be named? Perhaps... yes, perhaps she ought to apologise.

"Henry," she tested. "I am sorry for my scepticism. I will try... to approach this matter with an open mind and... a willingness to comprehend the truth, however unsettling it may be."

He nodded, almost ignoring her apology. He leant in even closer, shifting in his seat, the fabric of his coat brushing against her arm. His brow furrowed as he scanned the text, inscribed by his own hand.

"Here," he began. "This entry speaks of a time when the rose was said to bloom, but once a generation. My grandfather warns that his heirs may find themselves ensnared in a fate worse than death."

"And you truly believe this?" she asked, her voice shaking, caught between her own disbelief and the sincerity in his gaze.

"I do not know what to believe," he whispered. "But I cannot dismiss it, Evelyn. We watched the rose unfurl – it could only be that rose. And I have witnessed the effects of the curse firsthand. It is not simply an old wives' tale to me... and I would not share this with you if I did not feel it was significant."

Evelyn looked into his eyes, acutely aware of the way his knee brushed against hers.

"There is more," he said quietly, pressing on. His fingers tightened around the edge of the pages, his knuckles paling. "An early entry reads: *'Tonight, I had a dream – a vision of a rose, drenched in moonlight. In it, I heard my grandfather's voice warning me: "The rose will reveal your heart's desire, but it shall also unearth your darkest fears." I awoke trembling, unsure of what to make of this omen. I feel a sense of urgency; the truth lies within reach, yet it eludes me still.'*

"You can see how my grandfather unravels into madness through his diary," Henry whispered, his voice thick. "It becomes more difficult to read the further it goes."

He thrust the pages into her hands, gesturing for her to continue.

"*It is too late,*" Evelyn read, "*The curse has claimed me, entwining my fate with Seraphina's. I feel her presence everywhere in this manor, watching me, even in the shadows. I watch my wife, my son – dear Alistair – suffer, knowing that my actions have brought them to this fate. If only I could turn back time.*" She flipped the page, searching for more. "*Their scratching fills the ceiling. They mock me. They know my fate, as do I. It is an endless loop. We are each destined to repeat it.*'

"This is just madness," she breathed, glancing up at Henry. He looked older somehow, worry deeply etched into his brow and the lines around his eyes.

"Keep reading."

"*I have solved the...*" she continued, noticing Henry had scribed sections that were not fully legible, but together, painted a chilling story. "*Each generation... a fleeting moment where love presents itself... squander it. Time after time, the same mistake... as if the curse itself compels us... destroy the very thing that could save us. History will repeat itself... A cruel game... no escape. There are... in the attic. I dare not speak of them openly... those who came before... a warning to the living. Beware... desire... love.*"

She looked up at Henry, his face obscured by his hands. His broad shoulders, usually so steady, slumped with weariness. It was only then she noticed the subtle streaks of grey at his temples – a man burdened by more than his years should allow. How had she never seen it before? She longed to reach out, to rub the aches out of his shoulders, to smooth the lines around his eyes.

"You have shared a part of yourself with me," she whispered. "I see you, Henry. I see how you are striving to unravel this wretched curse – how you wish to make me understand, to make me believe... But what troubles me so," she continued, her tone gentle but insistent, "is what holds you back in your own mind. What prevents you from allowing yourself the fullness of life, of love? There is something, something buried deep in your own soul that weighs upon your heart. It keeps you from surrendering to… to happiness, from allowing yourself to feel… to love." She held her breath for a moment.

Let me see you, she thought. *Not the heir. Not the cursed. Just the man.*

He looked up, his eyes creased in pain, as though her words had touched upon a truth he had long avoided.

"Is it fear, Henry? Do you fear that you will follow the same fate: to grow old and ill before your time, like your father? Forgotten, like your grandfather?" Her question hung between them, delicate, fragile. "Is that what keeps you from giving yourself fully?" She watched him, searching his eyes for the answer she feared to hear.

For a moment, he looked as though her words had pierced him deeply. His expression tightened, a flicker of pain crossing his face. But then he turned from her, his jaw set, as though could not bear to confront the truth she had laid out before him.

"You are trying so hard to uncover the source of your torment," she murmured, running her fingers along the pages of his writing. "I cannot help but wonder: will you ever allow yourself to let it go?"

He leant forwards, his elbows resting on his knees, his hands clasped tightly. His gaze lifted to meet hers again, and she saw fear, deep and unshakeable fear.

"I fear you still do not see. What if this is more than mere madness?" he whispered, his voice strained and raw, shaking as he spoke. "What if I cannot let it go? What if it cannot be relinquished? You speak as though I am the one clinging to this curse, as if I am the mad one. But what if its fingers are wrapped so tightly around me that I cannot escape, even if I tried?"

His fear pierced her heart, and in that moment, she knew he would not be so easily convinced to let go of it. If he could not bear the weight of his fear alone, then she would have to shoulder that burden for him. She would have to engage in his silent struggle, to battle the monsters that lurked in the corners of his mind for him.

Yes. Yes, I shall pretend I see it all as he does. I shall nod and watch and speak of the curse as though it is true… And perhaps… perhaps in doing so, I shall find the truth of it myself.

"Perhaps…" she began, "perhaps we shall regard this as a puzzle to be solved… composed of many pieces which must interlock. Or like a composition on your harp, where each note must work in harmony to create the melody."

His gaze bore into hers, searching for reassurance amidst the shadows that clouded his mind. There was a fragility to his face, a vulnerability that made her heart ache. It was as if he stood on the precipice of despair, his spirit weary from fighting an unseen foe.

"The diary speaks of the rose, and the curses. And Seraphina," she continued, her heart quickening with each word. "The same woman your father spoke of in his ghost stories. He told me she was spurned by your ancestor, a Sinclair. And there are references to the strange scratching noises. Perhaps these are clues, fragments of a larger puzzle we must unravel."

She leant in closer, their faces mere inches apart, her breath mingling with the warmth of his against the cool morning air. "And then," she added, her voice dropping to a whisper, "there is the attic."

Henry sat back and shook his head, a bitter laugh escaping his lips. "I have lived in this manor my entire life." He paused, raking a hand through his hair in frustration. "I have never seen an attic. I am not even certain one exists. The attic is but a ghost, like the woman in white."

The vision of the woman in white loomed large in her mind, and a chilling question formed: had she, in some way, begun to descend into the very madness she feared in Henry? Perhaps she was not merely playing along in his world of shadows; perhaps she was caught up in it, too, and not even realised it…

But still, she needed to tell him.

"I must confide something else to you," she hesitated. "Something quite fantastical. You mustn't laugh. I have seen her… the woman in white."

Henry's eyes widened and then narrowed slightly as if he were trying to discern the truth behind her words.

"The woman in white? Surely, you jest."

His doubt stung. It struck her as a cruel twist of fate that *she* now stood as the harbinger of the extraordinary, while Henry seemed to falter in his belief.

"I scarcely wish to believe it myself," she admitted. "Yet, there she was, ethereal and haunting, drifting through the garden. What if she is connected to all of this, Henry? What if it is Seraphina herself?"

As she spoke, the memory of the encounter washed over her anew, each detail sharp and vivid. Could it be that her own mind had begun to weave threads of delusion, blurring the line between reality and the ghosts of her imagination?

"Seraphina?" He breathed. "You cannot be serious."

"I am. What if this apparition holds the answers we seek? Perhaps she knows of the... curse. And more of the rose! If we are to confront this mystery, we must seek her out – whether in the attic or wherever she may dwell. What if she could guide us?" She reached out, brushing her glove hand against his forearm.

Henry's gaze shifted to where her fingers lingered, the uncertainty in his eyes replaced by an awareness of their proximity. She felt him inhale deeply, his arm tensing beneath her hand like a taut bowstring.

"You would face whatever might be lurking in the shadows of this manor?" he murmured. "You would follow me into the darkness?"

She paused, the moment but a breath.

"I would follow you anywhere, Henry."

∞∞∞∞∞

There was no need for words now; the air between them hummed with a quiet understanding. They slipped quietly from the room, careful not to disturb her father, who still sat engrossed in his book.

Evelyn felt the warmth of Henry's presence, the brush of his coat sleeve against her fingers as she slipped her hand into the crook of his arm. Together, they moved, their steps light and sure, leaving the hearth's dying

146

glow behind. The manor was quiet, save for the ticking of the grandfather clock in the hallway.

They passed door after door, each one leading to rooms that seemed too familiar, too ordinary: drawing rooms filled with dusty relics and furniture draped in white sheets, ghosts frozen in time, and the occasional study overflowing with tomes, their spines cracked and yellowed.

After some time, they came upon a small corridor tucked away in the West Wing. At its far end, a narrow door stood slightly ajar, beckoning them forwards. Henry pushed it open.

The door creaked on its hinges, revealing a cramped storage closet filled with old linens – faded, moth-eaten fabric that hung in thick folds, damp with the musty scent of disuse.

"This cannot be it," he murmured, but Evelyn followed him regardless, tracing the walls, searching for something – anything. As she stepped into the cramped space, the door shut behind her with a thud, sealing them in the closet.

Darkness enveloped them, shadows swallowing the details of the tight room, leaving only the faintest outlines of each other's faces.

Suddenly, she was acutely aware of how confined the space was – how closely they stood to one another. Henry's figure loomed over her, filling every corner and overwhelming her senses. His eyes pierced through the shadows, and the air between them thickened, every movement slower, more deliberate, as if time itself had begun to bend around them.

"We ought not," he murmured, his voice low and thick, though he didn't step back.

"Hm?" she breathed. "Ought not do what?"

He lifted his hand to her cheek, brushing away a loose strand of hair. "This."

Before she could say another word, his lips were on hers. His kiss was heated, urgent – far more than the one they had shared before. It was as though every emotion he had been holding back finally broke free, and in that suspended moment, nothing else mattered. He gripped her waist, pulling her closer until she was pressed against him.

In the darkness, where only shadows danced, Evelyn melted into him, clutching the fabric of his coat as if it were the only thing tethering her to the floor. She felt her body respond to his every touch, the heat between them searing, almost unbearable. Her hands found their way to his shoulders, feeling for the solid strength of him.

He moved his mouth against hers, hungry and unrestrained, as if he was trying to pour all his feelings into that single, all-consuming kiss. His hands moved against her behind, pulling her closer still, their bodies entwined so tightly it seemed there was no space at all between them. She clung to him, feeling the rhythm of his heartbeat match her own, and in that intimate darkness, the world outside ceased to exist. They were simply Henry and Evelyn, entwined in a dance as old as time.

His mouth trailed from her lips to her ear, his breath hot against her skin, and then to her neck with a slow, burning intensity. A soft moan escaped her lips unbidden.

Of course, as suddenly as it had begun, he pulled away, his breath ragged. He rested his forehead against hers, his eyes tightly shut.

"We ought not. I ought not," he repeated, this time with more conviction, each word a plea to the darkness around them. "I cannot... I will not do this to you. Not with the curse hanging over me. You read the words. *History will repeat itself.*"

As she opened her eyes, Evelyn found him looking more beautiful and haunted than she had ever seen him.

Her chest ached at his words, but she refused to let him pull away entirely – refused to allow him retreat into the shadows of his fear. She reached out, catching his hand gently in hers, feeling the warmth of his skin against her palm.

"Then do not allow it to," she whispered. "We will not *allow* history to repeat itself."

Though uncertainty clouded her own belief in the curse, she knew Henry believed, and perhaps, if nothing else, she could help free him from the grip it held over his heart and mind. She saw a faint glimmer of hope in his eyes, as if her words had struck a deep chord within him. Still – *still* – it was as though he remained tethered by an invisible chain, too burdened to reach for the light she offered.

"I cannot risk it," he croaked, his voice strained. "Not with you."

Without another word, he opened the door and strode from the closet, the hinges creaking softly behind him as he disappeared down the dim hallway.

Evelyn stood alone in the darkness, her chest heaving. His absence settled around her, his words ringing in her ears.

He walks with it always, she realised, pressing a hand to her breastbone as though to calm the tremor within. *His fear. It is not a fleeting emotion, but a constant companion. It drains him. It follows him like a ghost.*

As she stood there, alone, one thing became painfully clear: the curse wasn't the only thing they were fighting. Henry was at war within himself, and until he found a way to break free from his fear, from the chains he had forged in his own mind, the curse on him was stronger than ever.

Chapter 19

Henry

The kiss had unravelled him, truly and completely. The taste of her remained on his lips, a delicate sweetness that reminded him of wine and summer blossoms. He could still feel the softness of her skin, the gentle curves of her body pressed against him, the way her breath had quickened, and how, in that fleeting moment, all his fears had lifted.

He sat by the hearth in his chambers, swirling his glass of whiskey. It was nearly impossible to push aside the vivid image of her flushed face as she surrendered to him, the rise and fall of her breasts against him. Each heartbeat thudded in his ears, a stark reminder of how dangerously close he had come to crossing the line into something irreversibly passionate.

Nevertheless, reality pressed in on him like a vise. He knew the dangers of that intimacy, the inherent risks of loving her amidst the shadows that loomed over him. And so, in a desperate bid to shield them both from the heartache that seemed destined to follow, he had turned away. He tore his lips from hers and wrenched his hands free, as if their touch might ignite a fire too dangerous to contain. He had fled the cramped darkness of that closet, like a coward, taking with him only the echo of her breath and the ghost of their kiss.

The very idea of losing her completely twisted in his gut like a knife, each turn sending fresh waves of torment through him. Her desire to uncover the fullness of the curse stirred a deep fear within him; he knew all too well that no good could come of it. He wanted her to believe him and *leave* for her own safety, not weave herself further into the curse's grasp, not to follow him into the darkness. What a fool he was for entertaining the premise, for encouraging her. He could not bear for her to suffer, for her name to join the whispers of cautionary tales amongst the servants, a name no one dared utter aloud, a name like his mother's.

And so, his heart heavy, he resolved to turn his attention to Lady Arabella that night at dinner. The very thought of it made his stomach twist.

You are a fool, he told himself bitterly. *A coward playing at martyrdom.*

The idea of pushing Evelyn away clawed at his heart like thorns tearing through flesh. He could already see the confusion in her eyes, the hurt she would try to mask behind polite conversation. She would not understand – not at first... perhaps not ever.

Still, he clung to the hope that that it was the only way to protect her. If she believed him cold, distracted, uninterested, then maybe she would return to London... forget this place... forget him. Perhaps she would be safe. That knowledge alone would be enough.

It was a heart-wrenching decision, born not out of indifference, but out of a fierce need to shield her – to shield himself – from the inevitable heartache that came with loving too deeply and losing too much. He had seen what the curse could do... what it had already done. If she stayed, it would take her too, in one form or another.

Yes. Yes – he knew that enduring this short suffering might spare them both from a far deeper agony. Sometimes, brief anguish was necessary to shield the ones you love from the darker shadows of fate. It was a sorrowful sacrifice he must make for the sake of her future.

Let her hate me, he thought. *Let her turn her back and never look back. If that means she lives untouched by this wretched legacy, then I shall bear it gladly.*

He closed his eyes for a moment.

Let me be the villain in her story, if it keeps her safe.

He threw his whiskey glass into the fire, watching as the glass shattered against the embers.

∞∞∞

Henry sat at the dining table that night, wearing his mask with practised ease, like a stage actor in a tragic comedy. Each smile was a carefully curated performance, a desperate attempt to drown out the echoes of Evelyn's name that haunted his thoughts.

"Tell us, have you finally taken an interest in political affairs, Mr Sinclair?" the Dowager Countess teased. An imposing figure even in her advanced years, she carried herself with a regal air that demanded attention and respect. Henry remembered her from his childhood, her sharp eyes often settling on him like a hawk sizing up its prey, always eager to match him with her simpering niece. "Or are you still too preoccupied with your music to notice the world around you?"

Henry forced a smile, the mask he had donned becoming heavier with each inquiry. "I assure you, my lady, the world has not escaped my notice. Although I fear I am still a humble servant to my harp. It keeps me too busy to bother with the trifles of politics." He turned slightly, allowing his gaze to wander in a purposeful manner to Arabella, who laughed lightly.

"Oh, but surely there are matters worthy of your attention, Mr Sinclair," Lady Arabella chimed, her voice lilting as she leant closer, deliberately nudging the space between them. "Perhaps a certain charming lady in our midst?" She shot a glance at Evelyn, a sly grin spreading across her face.

Henry's gaze shifted to Evelyn before he could stop it, drawn to her as if by gravity. She sat straight-backed and composed, but he saw flush creeping up her neck, blooming across her cheeks like the soft blush of early dawn. That delicate pink had no right to stir him as it did. *She is beautiful,* he thought helplessly. *God help me, she is so bloody beautiful.*

His eyes lingered too long, and he wondered if the buds at her breast were that same rosy hue. Her gown clung to her form, showing the soft curves that had haunted his thoughts since their kiss. He tore his eyes away, forcing his fingers to curl into his palm beneath the table.

No, not now. Not here, he silently chastised himself. *She is not your concern.*

153

The lie rang hollow, for she was already everything: light and warmth and the future he dared not imagine.

"Lady Ravenwood, your boldness knows no bounds," Evelyn said. Her tone was light, teasing almost, but Henry could hear the tension beneath it.

He blinked, dragging himself back to the performance, forcing himself to shake off the desire that had no place in his resolve. He needed to push her away, to keep her at a distance, yet every fleeting glance felt like a betrayal of his intentions.

He cursed himself. *Fool. You cannot have her and keep her safe. You cannot do both.*

"Just a bit of fun, dear Evelyn," Arabella replied, her tone light, though the edge of her words cut deep. "Surely you must agree that our Mr Sinclair possesses a certain… charm?"

Henry seized the moment, though bile rose in his throat. He turned to Arabella, masking himself. This was his chance, his opportunity to shift the dynamic and turn Evelyn away from him. He must let her believe he was just like every other man of his class: fickle, flirtatious, faithless. He would play the part of the charming suitor and bury the ache that thrummed in his chest.

"Indeed, charm is a most elusive quality," he said as he leant closer to Arabella, conjuring a smile he did not feel. "Though I must admit, it pales in comparison to your wit, Lady Arabella. You have a remarkable talent for lightening the mood."

He felt Evelyn's eyes on him: sharp, assessing, quietly wounded. *Good,* he thought, though it nearly undid him. *Let her turn away. Let her believe I am unworthy. Let that be what keeps her safe.*

The Baron Alistair Sinclair cleared his throat, attempting to guide the conversation back to safer waters. "Let us not forget the state of the estate, shall we? With the thaw of winter upon us and spring lurking just around the corner, there is much to discuss regarding the upcoming planting season."

Henry settled back in his seat. *Coward,* he thought, not of his father, but of himself. Across the table, he could feel Evelyn's confusion like a physical

154

weight, such a contrast to Arabella's gloating smile which danced across her lips like a victory flag.

The baron coughed gruffly, casting discerning eyes around the table. "We must consider our crops and the state of the orchards. Mr Ward has brought my attention to a new variety of apples that may thrive in our soil."

Henry only half-heard the words. Talk of apples and orchards felt absurdly distant.

Lady Arabella, ever quick to seize an opportunity, shifted forwards. "Ah, but do we truly want apples when there are so many delightful flowers to consider?" Her voice dripped with playful seduction, as if the mere suggestion was a private joke shared among conspirators. "Perhaps we ought to plant something more... enchanting. And speaking of enchantment, I expect the blooms would pale in comparison to the beauty of the company we keep tonight." She looked pointedly at Henry.

He caught her gaze, and though it twisted something sharp in his chest, he steeled himself: *Stay the course. Finish this painful charade.*

"I daresay, Lady Arabella, your choice of flowers might inspire more than just a bountiful harvest. Perhaps a garden of such enchantment would attract a rare breed of admirer – one who appreciates beauty and thrives on laughter."

She laughed lightly. "Is that so, Mr Sinclair? And what sort of admirer do you suppose would catch *your* eye?"

"Someone who possesses the charm of a wildflower – unpredictable yet captivating," he said, his eyes lingering on Arabella, even as his thoughts spiralled back to Evelyn. *Her stillness. Her silence. It is she who would catch my eye.* "A lady who knows how to weave her magic into the air."

As his words hung in the air, he could not resist glancing at Evelyn, just once. He saw the flicker of hurt before she masked it with a smile so polite it nearly shattered him. Guilt rose hot in his throat. *This is for her. You are doing this for her.*

He turned back to Arabella, desperate to drown the tension in frivolity. Arabella's eyes sparkled with delight, clearly pleased by his attentions.

"Mr Sinclair, you do know how to flatter a lady. But tell me, do you often find yourself enchanted by wildflowers, or is it merely *my* particular brand of magic that has caught your fancy?"

The table had gone quiet. All eyes were now fixed on them.

"Perhaps it is both," Henry said, a tight smile curving his lips. He refused to look again at Evelyn, who sat still as stone across the table. "After all, who could resist the allure of something so beautifully chaotic? A wildflower's charm lies not just in its beauty, but in its defiance of convention, wouldn't you agree?"

He sensed Evelyn shift, could almost hear her spine stiffen. *She's hurt. She's furious. Do not stop now.*

"Tell me, Lady Arabella," he continued, forcing a more rakish tone, "if one were to wager on a wildflower's survival in a garden, would you consider yourself the best choice?"

"Only if you promise to cultivate me, Mr Sinclair."

At that moment, Mr Ward choked violently on a mouthful food. He spluttered and gasped, earning himself a hearty thump on the back from a footman who rushed to assist, barely suppressing a smirk.

A quiet, seething rage crept across the baron's face, his lips pressed into a line so thin it might have vanished altogether. He looked as though he longed to throttle someone – possibly everyone.

"Lady Ravenwood," he interjected slowly, "I daresay we ought to steer our conversation back towards more sensible topics."

At the far end of the table, Charles sat blissfully unaware of the tension in the air, so absorbed was he in his succulent meal. "This roast is delightful, is it not?" he exclaimed with a wide grin.

"Quite so," Mr Ward managed, sipping wine to clear his throat.

Henry's gaze shifted across the table. Evelyn sat with her shoulders slightly hunched, absently tracing the embroidered edge of the tablecloth. The spark in her eyes – the sharpness, the quiet fire that he so loved – was gone, and its absence struck him like a blow.

What have I done?

When dinner at last concluded, she rose and excused herself to her bedchamber. As she turned to leave, her mask faltered for the briefest moment, and in that slip, he saw it all: the pain she refused to show, the disappointment she had buried behind her smile. Her eyes, when they met his, were storm clouds ready to burst, brimming with unspoken words she would never say aloud.

His heart sank. The diary's words surfaced unbidden: *It is an endless loop. We are each destined to repeat it.*

He stood frozen, caught in the tempest of this thoughts. He considered running after Evelyn, grasping her hand, pleading for her forgiveness. Instead, he remained rooted in place with his hands curled into fists at his sides.

You are a coward, he told himself.

The dining room felt colder now, emptied of her presence, and as her silhouette slipped beyond the doorway, he could almost hear the echo of that warning: *History will repeat itself.*

In the end, he had chosen silence over confrontation. It was a foolish, failing sort of honour – but it was easier than risking what he could not control.

The chaos of the evening pressed in against his ribs: longing, regret, guilt all swirling like a tide he no longer had the strength to swim against. His thoughts tangled, snarled with impossible threads.

He resolved to distance himself from both women. It was too much trouble, too much pain, and he was weary – so very weary – of the battle waging within his heart.

But Evelyn... He pressed his fingers to his temple, as though he might press the thought of her away. *Sweet, stubborn Evelyn. I love her.* The truth landed with quiet devastation.

And I am a fool.

Oh, a fool indeed for loving her, and a greater fool still for believing that love might be enough to shield her from the weight of what surrounded him, and the inevitability of what lived within him.

It will hurt her less in the end, he told himself. *It has to.*

And so, he slipped deeper into the shadows, convincing himself, with each hollow step, that retreat was the only option left to him.

Chapter 20

Evelyn

Evelyn tossed and turned beneath the heavy quilt, her mind and body a tempest of unrest. The memory of Henry's kiss still clung to her like a stubborn shadow, a bittersweet echo that refused to fade. She could still feel the heat of his breath against her lips – that moment, that softness, when the world had quieted and only they existed. It felt like a dream, half-remembered and already slipping through her fingers..

She knew he was pushing her away, but how could she leave? How could she, when she had already crossed the threshold of caring?

She rolled onto her side, burying her face in the pillow, hoping to suffocate the memory of it.

It was not the kiss that truly tormented her. No – it was dinner... the sight of him leaning in towards Lady Arabella, his shameless banter, that careless charm in his smile. A sick twist bloomed in her stomach.

It wasn't just the performance – for she knew it had been one -- but how convincing he had been: his flirtation, his ease, his wretched civility. Was that all she had ever been to him? A passing fancy. Something to be kissed in the dark and cast aside in the light?

Tears stung behind her eyes, but she refused to let them fall.

159

I will not cry over a man who cannot decide if I am his salvation or his ruin, she told herself. *Let him hide in his shadows. I will not chase him there.*

Still, her hands clenched in the bedsheets and her heart ached with every breath. She forced herself to focus on the storm brewing outside – the rattling windows, the hiss of wind slipping through the shutters – as though anchoring herself to the weather might silence the storm within.

She yearned for clarity amidst the confusion, but each thought only spiralled her deeper into despair. The warmth of their kiss now felt like a cruel taunt, an illusion conjured in the dark and scattered by the light of his easy laughter with Arabella

Betrayal clung to her now. *Had it all meant nothing to him?*

"*I cannot risk it. Not with you.*" His words echoed ceaselessly, refusing to fade with the night.

Not with you.

Each repetition struck her chest like a blow. She buried her face in the pillow, as though darkness might erase memory, but it only grew louder, the echo bouncing off the walls of her mind, drowning out all else.

Not with you.

She shifted in the bed, kicking her feet in frustration, her body thrashing beneath the warm sheets and quilt. *Why could she not sleep?*

It was more than grief, more than anger. It was the memory of his lips against her neck, the trail of his breath along her skin, the maddening *pause* where he might have gone further. She had wanted him to continue. *God, she had wanted him to.*

She inhaled sharply, the thought of it lighting a fire low in her belly. Her body was foreign to her now – heated, alive, aching in places she did not know could ache.

Desire.

It was word whispered in forbidden conversations, spoken of with lowered eyes and embarrassed smiles. The diary had warned her: *Beware of desire* – as though it were a storm, a thing to fear.

And yet, here it was, burning low and insistent and dangerous, making her skin feel too tight, her breath too quick. She pressed her hands to her face, willing the sensation away, but it lingered, pulsing softly like the distant beat of a drum. The rational part of her mind scoffed. *This makes no sense.*

She had no experience, no frame of reference. She was untouched, innocent in the ways of the world, and yet her body knew what her mind did not. It was yearning, aching... *but for what?*

"For him?" she whispered into the darkness, breathless at the thought.

A sharp pang of longing answered her. She shook her head fiercely, as if the motion alone could scatter her thoughts like crows from a field. She closed her eyes tightly and willed herself to sleep, though she knew no peace would come.

As the night wore on, sleep eluded her. She tossed and turned, until the echo of his words merged with something deeper, something primal, stirring within her a desire she neither understood nor could quell.

The quilt felt too heavy.

She pushed it aside, the cool night air caressing her skin through the thin barrier of her nightgown. She brushed along the curve of her collarbone with her bare fingers, then lower, tracing a path with a feather-light touch that left her breathless. Heat bloomed low within her, spreading like fire caught in dry leaves.

She closed her eyes, surrendering to the sensation, letting memory become fantasy.

She let her hands wander, learning herself in the stillness, guided by instinct and the ache he had awakened. Each breath deepened as she strained towards something she could not name but somehow *knew*. It was like a song she had never heard but remembered all the same.

In her mind, he was beside her: his hands replacing hers, his lips at her ear, the heat of his body against hers, the promise of more. he imagined him teasing her, coaxing her closer with every touch.

A soft sound escaped her, and she bit down on it, no from shame, but from how much she wanted him. The world outside began to fade away, leaving only the haze of her desire. In that moment, she embraced the yearning, the longing that threatened to consume her entirely.

A wave of heat and light rushed through her like a storm breaking over a field. Her body arched and quaked, the coil within her unravelling with pleasure she had never dared to name. She surrendered to the moment, succumbing to the tide as it swept her away.

When it passed, she lay silent and trembling.

She turned her face into the pillow and let herself imagine it: Henry's arms wrapping around her in a tender embrace. It was a dream – a beautiful, dangerous dream – and she wanted it so very much.

Chapter 21

Alistair

The baron sat in his darkened study, silence gnawing at the edges of his mind. The embers in the hearth sputtered weakly, throwing fleeting shadows across his careworn face. He sighed heavily, for he could not escape the sense that time was a noose around his neck, drawing ever tighter with each passing day.

Across from him, Blackwood stood in stillness, surveying the room with a predator's patience. He said nothing, waiting, as if sensing that his master's thoughts were not yet fully formed. The only sound was the low crackle of the dying fire, that insistent reminder of how fragile light was in the face of encroaching darkness.

"This is becoming untenable," Alistair finally murmured, watching the fire with the intensity of a man searching for meaning in the ashes. "Lady Ravenwood... that woman is an unwelcome thorn in my plans. She meddles where she ought not! Uninvited guests are the bane of my existence."

Blackwood stepped closer, his coat sweeping against the stone. "Lady Ravenwood is inevitable," he said, smoothly. "But inevitability, my lord, has its limits. She is merely a distraction."

"A distraction we cannot afford," Alistair muttered. "Henry is slipping away. She circles him like a vulture."

"Indeed, my lord. Nevertheless, distractions can be managed. Redirected." Blackwood took another step closer. "Think on this: what if, instead of retreating into the darkness, we bring light to the situation? A distraction of our own... one grand enough to turn Henry's attention elsewhere?"

Alistair's fingers stilled. "Speak plainly, Blackwood."

"A ball," the butler said softly. "Something grand. A spectacle to dazzle the eyes and stir the heart. Lady Ravenwood would attend, naturally, but so too would Miss Ward."

"You believe she may succeed where others have failed?" Alistair's voice was low, barely more than a growl in the dim light.

Blackwood's expression did not change, but something gleamed in his eyes: a quiet certainty that unsettled even Alistair. "With the proper conditions, yes. It is at such moments when the young often glimpse beyond the surface." He paused, allowing the weight of his words to sink in before adding, "And I know precisely how to ensure those conditions."

The notion hung between them, hovering on the edge of absurdity, yet Alistair found himself contemplating the idea... A ball. It was reckless, bold – far too bold for his sensibilities. He knew all too well that the Sinclair family had ever been drawn to the same trifles: power, influence, society's glittering veneer. Lady Ravenwood – and a society ball – embodied all of which tempted them, time and time again.

Still... Miss Evelyn Ward was different. She was not part of that world, not seduced by its hollow allure. Yes, she was something altogether different. Quiet, to be sure, but not frail. There was something in her that had caught Henry's eye, though he likely did not comprehend it as yet. The notion of creating a moment where that connection might deepen – where Henry might glimpse something beneath the surface – was almost too tempting.

Slowly, almost unwillingly, Alistair's fingers began to drum against the armrest. "A ball," he muttered, as though testing the word. "Yes, it may work... if the timing is right."

Blackwood's smile deepened, though it was no less unsettling than before. "Precisely. The grand hall has not seen such life in centuries. The whispers of the past will be masked by laughter and dance. Lady Ravenwood's charm will pale in comparison to something deeper, something stronger. Miss Ward's connection with Henry is nascent, but given the right spark, it could burn brighter than any fleeting infatuation."

Alistair leant back, the old chair groaning under his weight. He had spent his life trying to control the unpredictable, to bend fate to his will. This would be no different, though the risks were far higher.

"Very well," he said at last. "Send the invitations. Prepare the hall. But mark my words, Blackwood – if this fails, the consequences will be yours to bear."

Blackwood inclined his head, his eyes gleaming in the dim light. "Leave the details to me, my lord. All will fall into place."

As the fire died, plunging the room into a cold, suffocating darkness, thin tendrils of smoke curled like ghostly fingers into the air. Shadows crept along the walls, shifting as if they had a life of their own, watching, waiting. Soon, the grand hall would stir with life again.

Chapter 22

Evelyn

The morning sun streamed through the tall windows of the dining room, casting a glow on the mahogany furniture. The breakfast spread at Rosehill Manor was a feast for the senses. Delicate china plates overflowed with an opulent display: fluffy scrambled eggs, golden-brown pastries, crisp bacon, freshly cut fruit – strawberries, plump figs, and slices of ripe melon – jars of preserve and creamy butter. Servants moved quietly about the room, pouring tea and offering warm bread.

Evelyn sat quietly, nibbling on a pastry. The remnants of last night still lingered on her skin, drawing a feverish blush up her neck as she replayed those fleeting moments of unguarded pleasure.

Lady Agatha, the Dowager Countess, was seated at the other end of the table, engaged with the baron in reserved conversation. Her tone was measured and lofty as she recounted tales of her last soirée. The baron chuckled at her anecdotes, though the sound was hollow and distant. It was painfully clear that his thoughts lay elsewhere.

Across the table, Lady Arabella sat back her back straight, her laughter ringing like silver chimes as she watched Henry.

"Mr Sinclair, you simply *must* join us for a ride later," she purred. Her voice dripped with a sweetness that grated against Evelyn's frayed. "Young Charles informs me that you have some truly magnificent horses."

Henry, however, remained aloof, his dark brows knitted together as he stared out the window. He offered no response.

The sight of him disregarding Arabella was a soothing balm to Evelyn, a small, secret victory against the unwelcome ache of jealousy, yet that brief reprieve was swiftly overshadowed by a rising tide of concern – a nagging dread that twisted in her gut.

She stole furtive glances at Henry, but each time their eyes met, a chill washed over her. *He is looking straight through me, as though I am not even here.*

It unsettled her far more than his flirtation had.

She had risen early this morning with foolish hope tucked beneath her bodice. She'd thought perhaps they might exchange a glance – just one would do – that would mend what had frayed between them. Perhaps he might meet her gaze with the quiet intimacy he once had, and remind her, without words, that what passed between them was real. Yet he remained oblivious, haunted, ensnared in the labyrinth of his own thoughts.

She swallowed a bite, but the pastry turned to lead in her throat. The room was warm and the sun gentle, and yet she felt cold.

How could I have been so selfish? she thought bitterly, forcing the food down. *Indulging in thoughts of kisses and yearning when he is so dark and troubled?*

She could not name the thing she felt, not precisely. It was part fear, part grief, and perhaps the strange, creeping sensation that he was slipping further into the recesses of his own mind – and once it was gone, she would not get him back.

Evelyn shifted uneasily in her seat, acutely aware of Lady Arabella's laughter cutting through the air. The woman was insufferable – so self-satisfied, so utterly transparent in her pursuit of Henry.

"Surely, you would not decline a ride, would you, Mr Sinclair?"

"Indeed, I would. I have other matters to attend to," he replied tersely.

The chill of his dismissal hung in the air. Arabella's smile faltered for a moment as she registered his indifference.

A small flicker of satisfaction sparked in Evelyn's chest.

Good. Let her feel the sting of being ignored.

Still, the warmth soured almost instantly. Henry's detachment was more profound than mere annoyance at Arabella's advances. Something was falling apart inside him.

Was he becoming madder? It was a chilling thought, yet the more she observed him, the more it felt like a creeping truth. He oscillated between fleeting moments of passion and deep despair, caught in a perpetual cycle of hope and despair. It was as though he was being pulled apart by invisible forces. Evelyn longed to reach out, to pull him back from the brink of whatever abyss threatened to swallow him whole, but each time she tried, he slipped further away. She ached to understand him, to unravel the mystery of his soul, yet his walls seemed to rise ever higher.

He is not well, and I do not know how to help him.

Her fingers trembled around her teacup, for desire had blinded her. She had let herself be swept up in longing, in aching and wanting, when perhaps... perhaps what he needed most was not her affection, but her strength.

With a resonant creak, the old baron rose from his chair. He cleared his throat loudly. "Ladies and gentlemen," he intoned slowly, "I have a momentous announcement to make. We shall host a grand ball at Rosehill Manor."

At once, Lady Arabella clapped her hands together. "A ball! Oh, how splendid!"

Her aunt, though more reserved, could not entirely conceal her pleasure. "Indeed, this shall be quite an affair. Rosehill Manor has long awaited such a gathering."

Evelyn remained quiet. *A ball?* It surprised her, for it felt so oddly out of place. She cast a sidelong glance at Henry and caught a look of astonishment in his otherwise impassive face – a crack in his cold façade – but just as quickly, the mask of indifference returned.

"Might I offer my assistance in the planning, my lord?" Arabella crowed. "The intricacies of such an event are staggering – every detail demands perfection. The decorations, the music, the carefully curated guest list! What a night it shall be!"

"It is all arranged, my dear," the baron declared, raising a hand to silence her with an air of finality. "Invitations shall be dispatched this very morning to families of suitable standing – those of the landed gentry and their esteemed connections. Families such as the Ashfords, the Whitcombes, and the Harringtons, who dwell within a reasonable distance of our estate. It has been far too long since we have basked in the company of such distinguished guests, and I have no doubt that this occasion will rekindle the spirit of festivity our manor has sorely craved."

Lady Arabella's smile flickered, her excitement extinguished as she cast a desperate glance towards her aunt. Lady Agatha met her with a stern shake of her head, a silent warning her not to press for more. Arabella's shoulders slumped.

Evelyn could not shake the disquieting sense that something was amiss. *Why now? Why a ball?* The very idea seemed foreign to Rosehill, to the Sinclairs, like a jarring note in the sombre melody of their lives.

"Pray tell, has there ever been a ball at Rosehill Manor?" she ventured.

Baron Sinclair regarded her with a piercing gaze. "Not in living memory, I assure you. This manor has languished in silence for far too long. Oh yes, it has been an eternity since it felt the pulse of such gaiety."

At that moment, Evelyn's father lifted his eyes from his crumpled newspaper and removed his spectacles. "A ball, you say? How utterly curious."

Meanwhile, Charles, who had been sitting silently at the table, suddenly twisted his mouth into a grimace. "And I shall not be permitted to attend, shall I, Father?" he pouted, crossing his arms. "What good is a celebration if I am left out?"

Evelyn shared a knowing glance with her father. After a brief moment of silent communication through his eyebrows, he returned to his newspaper as if to say, *You ought to handle this one, my dear.*

170

"Fear not, brother," she said gently. "I shall ensure you receive a most generous portion of the refreshments. Perhaps a slice of the finest cake and a few sweetmeats, just for you."

The corners of Charles' mouth twitched upwards, though his arm remained defiantly crossed. "You will?"

"Indeed, I shall," she replied, nodding. "I will make it my mission that you are well-fed with all the delights from the evening's festivities. Just think of it – a grand ball to regale us, and while the adults dance, *you* will indulge in all the delectable treats, relishing every bite as if you were right there with us."

"Very well, but you must bring me the best!" Charles said sincerely, unfolding his arms and returning to his plate of pastries and eggs.

As the news of the ball settled in the air, a rustle of movement stirred among the servants. One maid hastily departed the room, her footsteps a whisper against the ancient floorboards, as if the manor itself held its breath in anticipation of the news she would share. Outside, a footman stationed by the door raised an eyebrow as he glanced curiously towards the gathering in the dining room.

Lady Arabella shifted closer to Henry, her voice a whisper that travelled through the room. "Oh, Mr Sinclair, do you not find the prospect of the ball *thrilling*? Just imagine all the splendid decorations and the delightful music." Her eyes sparkled as she blinked up at him from beneath her cascading blonde curls.

"Yes." Henry replied, his tone flat. "Quite."

"And what of you, Miss Evelyn?" Lady Arabella continued, her voice dripping with sweetness, a veneer so thin it could hardly disguise the venom beneath. "I hope you will be joining us for the festivities. It would be such a shame for you to miss it."

"Of course, Lady Ravenwood," Evelyn replied stiffly. "Why ever would I choose to miss it?"

"Oh, I merely thought you might be inclined to return to London soon, where your prospects in the marriage mart may be… more favourable."

"I am not at Rosehill Manor for the purpose of securing a match," Evelyn said sharply as the others – save for Henry – watched on with wide eyes, "but rather as a guest of Lord Sinclair, whose interests in botany align with my father's. It seems rather fitting to prioritise scholarly pursuits over frivolous schemes to secure a husband, would you not agree, my lady?"

There was a momentary crack in Lady Arabella's polished facade, before it was swiftly concealed beneath her practised smile. "Your family's dedication to botany is truly commendable. And I daresay – perhaps you could even assist with the decorations! Your penchant for arranging flowers might prove quite useful."

"Or perhaps I might choose to enjoy the ball as any guest should, free from the burdens of planning."

Lady Arabella's smile tightened, her eyes narrowing. "Well, I shall be sure to dance with Mr Sinclair a great deal, then," she declared loudly against the hushed silence of the room. "He deserves a partner who appreciates the finer things in life."

Evelyn, feeling the weight of Lady Arabella's challenge, chose silence as her shield. The room held its breath, waiting as the silence stretched thin.

With a barely suppressed sigh, Henry rose abruptly.

"I have pressing matters to attend to," he muttered before striding from the room.

Evelyn's eyes darted to Lady Arabella, whose victorious smile had faltered, its brittle edges betraying the fragility of her triumph.

As breakfast drew to a close and the last of the plates were cleared away, Evelyn felt a restless energy swell within her. She excused herself from the table, aching for the solitude of the gardens. In a near flight from the manor, she rushed outside, the door swinging open to reveal the vast expanse of newly blooming life.

Sunlight spilled across the grounds, casting rays across the cobblestone path. Still, the beauty around her did little to lift her spirits. Each step felt laden with the echoes of the morning's tension, and she longed for a refuge where the chaos of her heart could quiet among the petals.

Moments later, as if drawn by the gravity of her distress, Clara approached, her brow creased with worry as she smoothed the dark fabric of her skirts.

"Miss Evelyn, are you quite well?"

"I am well enough, Clara. Just lost in thought." Her words felt hollow, a poor cover for the tumult within.

Clara stepped closer, threading her arm through Evelyn's. "It is only a ball, my lady. I daresay it is not worth such distress. You are beautiful, and I shall ensure you shine brighter than any other lady. You shall impress all the gentlemen, I am certain of it."

Evelyn paused, letting the words wash over her like a gentle breeze. She had not considered that it may have been the ball that unsettled her so, but rather Henry's strange behaviour and Arabella's rivalry. Yet, the thought of the forthcoming ball, with its delicate lace and twinkling chandeliers, felt like a bittersweet reminder of her tangled emotions. Would it merely serve as a backdrop for the unspoken distance that hung between her and Henry, a reminder of all that felt just out of reach?

She did not feel like explaining all this to Clara, for the weight of her emotions was difficult to articulate, and she feared that her worries might sound insipid.

"You have a talent for lifting my spirits, dear Clara," she replied softly. "Yet, I must confess, I have never enjoyed balls. The music, the dancing – it all seems part of a grand performance in which I am but an unwilling participant. And as for the prospect of impressing any gentleman other than Mr Sinclair..." She hesitated, her thoughts tangled. "I cannot say with certainty that I desire to. I find myself lost in a tangle of emotions, uncertain not only of my own heart, but of his as well."

Clara's voice was soothing murmur as their steps fell into rhythm beside each other. "I am sure the social whirl must be overwhelming, particularly when it seems as though all eyes are upon you. Perhaps this particular ball shall prove different. *This* ball presents an opportunity, not merely a performance."

173

Evelyn sighed, plucking a petal from a nearby flower as they walked. She watched it flutter to the ground. "Perhaps. Yet, there is something unnerving about the prospect of being paraded about with my every movement subjected to scrutiny."

Clara nodded thoughtfully, a spark of mischief dancing in her eyes. "Then let us turn that uncertainty to our advantage. If you wish to be more than a mere spectator, we shall ensure you shine like the stars, even if you have no intention of impressing the gentlemen. Simply imagine Lady Ravenwood's ire at being so overshadowed!"

Evelyn chuckled softly, the tension in her shoulders easing ever so slightly. "You always seem to have a scheme brewing, Clara. Yet, I fear no amount of finery can alter what lies within."

"Ah, but beauty is as much about confidence as it is about appearance," Clara said dutifully. "Together, we shall weave our magic. You will be a vision, and perhaps, amidst the festivities, you may discover a way to enjoy the evening after all, my lady."

Evelyn sighed. "Very well, Clara. I shall permit you to work your magic, but do not expect me to dance with great fervour. I merely wish to endure the evening."

Chapter 23

Clara

As the whispers of the impending ball swept through the manor, the household servants burst into frenetic activity. The air thickened with the scent of lavender and beeswax, wrapping around them as they dusted the ornate furniture until each surface was gleaming in the sunlight that streamed through the tall windows.

"Look at the way the sun catches on the crystal chandeliers!" Sarah, one of the younger maids, exclaimed, her cheeks flushed with excitement. "They will look simply enchanting when the ballroom is alive with candlelight."

Clara nodded, looking to the chandeliers that hung like dark jewels from the ceiling. They sparkled and glimmered, each crystal prism refracting the light into a kaleidoscope of colours. Yet, as the sun's rays shifted, the shadows deepened, twisting and curling in a languorous ballet that cloaked the hall in an ominous play of light and dark. It was all so carefully arranged, so deliberately grand, yet to Clara, it felt as though someone had dressed a corpse in its Sunday best.

Like rouge upon the cheeks of the dead, Clara thought, a chill feathering down her spine. *No amount of light could bring warmth back to such a place.*

As the servants toiled, Clara observed them fluff the drapes that framed the windows. They manoeuvred with precision, ensuring the fabric would billow gracefully in the evening breeze.

"Each arrangement must be flawless," Mr Blackwood intoned, his voice echoing in the grand hall. "Position them to draw the eye yet ensure they do not eclipse the beauty of this hallowed hall."

The maids exchanged furtive glances. Sarah ascended a stepladder to wrestle with a particularly stubborn drape, while Bess polished the golden candelabras until their surfaces gleamed like captured sunlight.

"Do you think there will be music?" Sarah mused.

"Of course," Clara replied, her mind weaving a tapestry of ghostly melodies. She could almost see the evening unfolding: guests descending in their splendid finery, their laughter bubbling like champagne in the air, mingling with the whispers of the past that clung to the walls like phantoms.

"Aye, it shall be a sight to behold," Sarah said, her eyes sparkling, as though she were imagining herself twirling through the grand hall in a gown of her own, the fabric swirling around her like a dream. "Yet I must confess, I hope the guests pay even greater heed to Miss Ward than to the lavish décor or finery." Her voice lowered to a whisper, laced with earnestness. "She deserves to shine in the glow of admiration, to be the jewel of the evening."

As Sarah spoke, she leant too far over the edge of the ladder, her balance wavering for a heartbeat. Clara's breath caught in her throat as Sarah flailed, clutching desperately at the air before regaining her footing. "Oh, good heavens!" Sarah exclaimed, a flush of embarrassment colouring her cheeks.

"Perhaps," intoned Mr Blackwood, his voice low and unwavering, "you should focus on keeping yourself upright rather than daydreaming." His piercing gaze lingered on Sarah as she steadied herself on the ladder, before he stalked from the hall.

Old Mrs Hargroves bustled past, her brow furrowed as she shook her head at Sarah. With a knowing glance at Clara, she tilted her head and lowered her voice. "I have overheard Lady Ravenwood boasting of her gown and the admiration she expects to receive at the ball," she remarked dryly. "I would not wish for her to overshadow your mistress. We must show that beauty alone cannot secure a place in Master Henry's heart. Though Miss Ward is certainly a beauty."

Clara offered a polite nod, but her thoughts churned. *Master Henry's heart?* She wasn't so sure he had one left to give. There was something cold about him, something distant and bruised. And Miss Evelyn had said she had no desire to parade herself for the sake of male attention.

Still, Clara's heart swelled with pride and quiet resolve. It had not taken long for the house to see what Clara had known from the first: the goodness in Miss Evelyn's heart, the gentleness behind her composure. Already, intricate plans began to swirl in Clara's mind, each detail crafted not to win a gentleman's admiration, but to let Evelyn be truly seen as the most captivating presence in the grand hall.

The ball would be no mere evening of idle waltzes. It would be a stage upon which those with power, with beauty, with entitlement, vied for notice. Clara did not care for their games. What she wanted was for someone like Miss Evelyn, someone kind and steady, to be the one who drew every eye.

Let them see her, Clara thought, tightening the ribbon she had been smoothing. *Let them all see the grace that does not shout to be noticed. Let them see what I see.*

Though she thought neither poorly nor highly of Mr Sinclair – he was too handsome, too haunted, and altogether too dangerous – Clara cared deeply for her mistress. This was her chance to help Miss Evelyn rise above the fray, to shine not just for the sake of vanity, but to reclaim her own narrative in a world that often sought to overshadow her.

Clara would make certain the gown shimmered just so, that each curl fell like poetry, that when Miss Evelyn entered that grand hall, the hush would be audible. She would see to it that when the last candle was extinguished, it would be Miss Evelyn who stood triumphant, her heart unscathed amidst the chaos of rivalry.

A young footman, James, leant in. "Well, confidence can be a double-edged sword, can't it? A little mishap might remind Lady Ravenwood of her place," he quipped, a sly grin spreading across his face.

Mrs Hargroves chuckled softly. "Let's hope she remembers to keep her wine glass steady, then."

"Imagine Lady Ravenwood as the lady of the house," another maid exclaimed with dismay. "The thought alone is enough to make one shudder."

A low murmur of assent sounded amongst the servants.

"Miss Ward possesses a genuine kindness," James added, leaning casually against the polished banister. "She brings a breath of fresh air to this manor, wouldn't you agree?"

Another murmur of agreement rippled through the group, and Clara felt another swell of pride for her mistress. Mrs Hargroves nodded thoughtfully, her expression turning serious. "Indeed, kindness is a rare quality in these times. Perhaps Master Henry might benefit from being reminded of that."

Clara ventured, "I do wonder if we might assist Miss Evelyn – offer her the chance to truly flourish. If we can help her feel beautiful and at ease, she shall naturally outshine the rest."

Within moments, the hall transformed into a small council of conspirators. They envisioned a gown of soft blue silk and delicate lace that would flow like water. Sarah proposed a pair of silver slippers, glimmering just enough to catch the light but never overwhelm.

"And as for her hair," chimed Bess, "it must be arranged in gentle curls, perhaps entwined with fresh flowers that reflect the garden's beauty."

Even Millie, usually too shy to offer opinions, whispered, "And a touch of lavender at her wrists. For calm."

Clara smiled, her heart swelling with purpose as the vision took root – not of some gaudy display, but of Miss Evelyn as she truly was: luminous, gentle, worthy of every glance the room could offer. She could already see it: Miss Evelyn stepping into the ballroom like sunshine breaking through storm-clouds, her presence silencing every cruel whisper and dismissive look.

"Let them look," she murmured, not realising she'd spoken aloud. "Yes, let them all look."

Chapter 24

Evelyn

The arrival of spring brought a refreshing breeze, a gentle whisper that beckoned the inhabitants outside, promising an escape from the confines of the manor's dark walls.

Inside, servants hurried to prepare for the upcoming ball, their voices weaving together in a symphony of chatter that echoed through the grand hall.

With a twinkle of youth in his eyes, Evelyn's father proposed a picnic on the estate's expansive grounds.

"Let us take advantage of this glorious day!" he declared with a wide smile. "Just imagine! Spreading a chequered blanket beneath the blossoming cherry trees, where the sunlight filters through the leaves like golden lace..." He sighed wistfully. "The petals shall fall like confetti, showering us in soft hues of pink and white. Does that not sound utterly delightful?"

Evelyn sometimes thought her father would have been a wonderful poet, were he not such a dedicated scientist. As he spoke, she envisioned the warmth of the sun on her skin, the taste of fresh strawberries and cream, and the sound of birds serenading her from their hidden perches. Winter would recede, and all would be well.

The idea was met with a hum of approval by those present in the drawing room, particularly by Arabella, who clapped her hands in delight. "What a splendid notion! It shall serve as the perfect backdrop for some light-hearted games!" she exclaimed, casting a pointed glance towards Henry.

He occupied a nearby chair, his posture relaxed yet distant, intently reading the newspaper.

Lady Arabella's laughter seemed to flutter around him like a butterfly, a sharp contrast to his stillness. "Perhaps you'll join us, Mr Sinclair? I can already see you participating in a game of charades, bringing forth your usual charm."

Evelyn almost rolled her eyes. The prospect of witnessing Lady Arabella fawn over Henry all day twisted her stomach into knots. She envisioned herself tucked away in the grand hall instead, her sketchbook propped open on a polished table as she captured the likeness of flower arrangements in watercolour. Each line from her quill, each stroke of her brush would be an act of rebellion, a way to reclaim her own narrative amidst the unfolding drama. She could lose herself in the beauty of it, allowing her art to speak the words her heart could not.

And yet, as spring's vibrant embrace filled the air, the garden called to her, beckoning her towards the open air. The thought of spreading a blanket beneath the cherry trees offered a fleeting escape from her worries. And perhaps, amidst the laughter and light of the day, she could carve out a moment with Henry.

∞∞∞∞

As they settled upon the lush grass, Clara and another maid arranged the picnic blankets and baskets, untethering the soft fabric to reveal an array of treats. The gentle hues of the day seemed to dance around them as the staff paused their bustling preparations for the ball. Nearby, fragrant tea steeped in porcelain pots, while a pitcher of lemonade glistened in the sunlight, casting reflections against the imposing silhouette of the manor.

Charles quickly suggested a game of croquet. Evelyn gestured to his wooden crutch and his splintered leg with a raised eyebrow, but he swiftly leapt up, using his crutch to twirl around on his good leg.

"I only need one hand for my crutch, and the other for a mallet!" he exclaimed. "I'm very practised at hopping now, you know."

Evelyn smiled and shrugged.

As expected, Lady Arabella eagerly volunteered to partner with Henry, her voice lilting with false innocence as she cast a sly glance in Evelyn's direction.

A pang of jealousy surged within Evelyn, a fierce tide she fought against with all her might, reminding herself that such feelings were neither in her character nor a quality she wished to embrace. She had always prided herself on quiet dignity, on rising above such petty rivalries.

You are being foolish, she told herself firmly. *This is nothing. He owes you nothing. You are not a girl to pine after glances and smiles.*

But even so, she found herself glancing at Henry, hoping – quite stupidly and desperately – that he might refuse Arabella and look at her instead. He did not, and the ache beneath her breastbone deepened.

With a forced smile, Evelyn accepted Charles as her partner, tousling his hair. The four of them strolled – or hobbled, in Charles' case – onto the lush expanse of grass.

Her father, the baron, and the dowager countess settled into their seats beneath the cherry trees to watch. As the game commenced, Arabella was particularly animated. She leant into Henry with practised ease, brushing her gloved hand against his arm with a casual intimacy.

Evelyn watched as Henry began to relax in the warmth of the sunlight. He struck his croquet ball through the first hoop, sending it gliding across the lawn with a precision that drew appreciative cheers from their spectators.

The game settled into a lively match, brimming with banter as Charles cheered his sister on.

"You can do it, Evelyn! Show them what you're made of!" His childish laughter floated through the air, a melodious sound that mingled with the gentle thwack of mallets and the soft clinks of balls colliding.

As Arabella playfully nudged Henry, he responded with a genuine laugh, the kind that seemed to illuminate the space around them. The sight of their easy connection twisted in Evelyn's chest. She gripped her mallet tighter, the wood pressing into her palm.

Be glad for him, she told herself fiercely. *He is smiling. He is at ease. That should be enough. Let him have this moment of peace, even if it costs me mine.*

She watched as her father strolled away from the shade of the cherry tree, smiling as he approached the croquet lawn. The sun caught the silver strands of his hair as he made his way towards them. "Is it too late for me to join?" he called out.

Evelyn felt a rush of relief. "Not at all, Father! In fact, why don't you take my place? I could use a break."

With a smile that crinkled the corners of his eyes, he accepted her mallet and joined the game beside Charles, who did look to be tiring.

Evelyn slipped away, opting for a solitary walk along the garden path where fresh blossoms lined the hedges. The vibrant colours felt muted as she strolled. She wished she had brought her sketchbook to turn this ache into art. The sunlight fell in dappled gold through the trees, illuminating petals with a painter's grace.

As she circled the lawn, she caught sight of Henry and Arabella engaged in their partnered game of croquet, their laughter carrying on the breeze like a haunting melody.

He looks happy, she reminded herself. *Is that not what you wanted?* She should be glad. She *was* glad, or so she told herself again and again, like a prayer. The warmth of the sun felt stifling now. She clenched her fists at her sides and kept walking.

The sun dipped lower in the sky as the afternoon wore on. The lively game of croquet eventually drew to a close, with Henry and Lady Arabella emerging as the triumphant pair. Evelyn could only watch and force a gritted smile as Arabella basked in the attention of Henry's low laughter.

The servants laid out a spread of finger sandwiches filled with cucumber and cream cheese, savoury quiches, and freshly baked scones, topped with clotted cream and strawberry jam.

Evelyn watched as Henry lounged on the picnic blanket, the golden sunlight casting a glow on his features. He looked so at ease: his head tilted back in a lazy smile, the lines of worry smoothed from his brow as he chatted with Arabella, who inched ever closer to him. Her golden hair shimmered in the light as she handed him a sandwich with a flirtatious flourish.

Evelyn felt a knot tighten in her chest, and she forced herself to look away. The cheerful murmur of voices around her faded into the background as her gaze wandered to the horizon, where the sunlight met the trees.

As the picnic settled into a comfortable lull, Charles pointed with a grin to the baron, who had slumped asleep in his chair with a sandwich still dangling from his hand. Even Henry laughed at the sight.

They all sat in silence, watching as the clouds slowly covered the afternoon sun. Lady Arabella's voice broke through the stillness, turning to Henry with a smile that bordered on coquettish.

"Mr Sinclair, would you do me the honour of taking a walk around the garden? I've heard the roses are particularly lovely this time of year."

Of course they are, Evelyn thought bitterly. *The roses, the sunlight, your entire curated existence… it is all just blooming, isn't it?*

She silently cursed herself once more for not having brought her sketchbook, for she longed to disappear into the solitude of the grand hall to draw. Instead, she found herself tethered to this moment.

Henry glanced at Arabella, his relaxed expression shifting to one of polite acquiescence. "Very well, Lady Arabella," he replied, rising to his feet and brushing the crumbs of his sandwich from his waistcoat.

Arabella's eyes sparkled. "Aunt Agatha," she trilled, "would you mind accompanying us as a chaperone?"

Aunt Agatha gave a regal nod, rising with the slow grace of one who had waited years for just such a moment. Evelyn watched the trio disappear down the flower-lined path, Henry's tall figure flanked by silks and propriety. The ache in her chest deepened with each retreating step.

Charles turned to her with a teasing grin. "It seems the Sinclair heir is rather taken with Lady Ravenwood," he remarked, his tone light. "Careful, sister; you might find yourself out of the running."

She shot him a sharp glare, her cheeks flushing hot. "Charles, that is not funny."

He only shrugged, entirely unbothered. "Only stating the obvious." He popped another pastry into his mouth, the sugary glaze dusting his fingertips. He grinned at her, licking his fingers one by one.

Before she could snap back, their father, who had been observing quietly beneath the cherry trees, set down his teacup.

"Evelyn," he began gently. "I can see this weighs heavily on you."

She hesitated, the words threatening to spill over. She was unsure of how much to expose in the presence of her father and Charles. She was afraid that if she tried to say even a fraction of what she felt, it would come out all wrong. She felt cracked open, peeled back, laid bare beneath Henry's indifference and Charles's easy teasing. The notion of being 'out of the running' stung more than she cared to admit. *As if I ever entered some dreadful contest. As if I ever wanted to be chosen like a prize.*

When she finally she spoke, her voice was tight. "It is only..." she paused, forcing down the swell of bitterness. "It feels as though I hardly exist today." The admission came out sharper than intended, and the hint of vulnerability stung her pride. She hated how small and petty the words sounded, but they were the truth, and they burnt in her throat.

Charles grinned, reaching for yet another pastry. "We could always start another croquet game, and this time, you should stay. Then you should be part of the action."

Evelyn shot him a sharp glare, her patience fraying. "That's not what I meant, Charles," she snapped. "Go and play now – you have had enough pastries."

"I was bored anyway," he sneered, sticking out his tongue. He grabbed his crutch and hobbled to his feet, hopping away over the grass to the stables.

As they watched him go, her father gave a long-suffering sigh and took off his spectacles, polishing them with a handkerchief. When he looked up at last, he squinted at Evelyn, as if seeing past the composed exterior she tried to maintain

"Oh, my dear. Do not let his nonsense rattle you."

Evelyn stared down at her gloves, twisting the edge of the wrist seam between her fingers.

Her father sighed again. "Sometimes... yes, sometimes... it can feel as though we are eclipsed by the light of others. Louder voices, brighter personalities, shinier shoes." He paused, frowning at his own phrase. "Hmm. That sounded rather more profound in my head."

That also earned a smile from her.

He tapped his spectacles gently against his knee. "But that does not dim your own light, Evelyn. Not in the least. You may not shout for attention, but your presence is no less felt. You will find your moment, my girl. And when it comes, it will be wholly your own... and all the more dazzling it.

His words were wrapped in clumsy affection, but they were earnest, and Evelyn felt the tenderness behind them. Still, her heart resisted the comfort.

What if I do not want to dazzle? she thought. *What if I only want to be seen as I am, without needing to sparkle like a blasted jewel in a ballroom? And what if my moment has already come, and it slipped through my fingers, disguised as a kiss that meant more to me than it ever did to him?*

She could say none of that aloud.

"I suppose," she said carefully, "it is difficult, at times, not to feel... invisible. Especially when others are so charming and effortlessly admired."

"Ah," her family said with an owlish smile. "The curse of not being an opera singer or a conjuror."

She gave a soft laugh and bit the inside of her cheek.

Her father smiled, the lines around his eyes crinkling with a warmth only a father could offer. "My darling girl... you are not a performance to be

187

applauded or forgotten. It is natural to feel insecure, though you must remember that the bonds we form, if true, are not so easily swayed by momentary distractions. The people who truly see you will never be distracted for long."

Evelyn hesitated, the words on her lips feeling too heavy, too dangerous to speak aloud, but she could hold them back longer. After a pause, she said in a whisper, "And if this is not a momentary distraction? What if Mr Sinclair's heart already belongs to Lady Ravenwood?"

Her father's smile faded into something more thoughtful and distant. For a moment, it seemed he was somewhere else entirely.

"If that is true," he said gently at last, "then it shall reveal itself in time. But even so – it changes nothing of your worth. Others might be drawn to glitter and spectacle, yes... but love – real love – is not fooled so easily. It knows substance. It recognises home, my dear. Relationships are like plants, you see... they require patience, care and understanding to flourish."

Evelyn took a deep breath. She looked out towards the garden, where Arabella and Henry were just visible through the hedges.

Her father reached out, brushing a wayward curl from her forehead. "Remember, patience, my dear. Oh yes, patience is a virtue in matters of the heart. Observe the dynamics around you without letting them overshadow your own feelings. Sometimes, taking a step back allows us the clearest view of what truly lies ahead. And sometimes," he added, with a twinkle, "a clever girl has already captured a heart... and simply hasn't realised it yet."

∞∞∞∞

That evening, after dinner had drawn to a close, Evelyn found herself in the orangerie, where the last of the twilight slanted through the glass panes and bathed the citrus trees in gold. The air was heavy with the scent of ripening oranges and lemons, yet the beauty around her did little to lighten the weight in her heart. She stood very still amongst the greenery, with her arm folded against her chest.

At dinner, Henry had not looked at her once. His words had been clipped, his posture stiff, a stark contrast to the carefree laughter and warmth that had been so easily given to Arabella in the garden.

She had tried to be gracious – truly, and to listen to her father's advice. *Patience*... but oh, what a brittle virtue it was, so utterly useless in the face of Henry's sudden coldness.

With each passing moment that he ignored her, the shadows of doubt crept deeper into her heart. *Have I imagined it all?*

Had he ever truly cared for her, or had it all been mere illusion? Had she misread the signs from the very beginning? The madness of these thoughts began to unravel her, tugging at the seams of her sanity.

She left the orangerie, winding her way through the gardens until the crunch of gravel gave way to grass and the towering old oak tree stretched above her. The secret garden lay head, tucked behind hedges and time – her quiet sanctuary.

Kneeling beside the rosebush, she pressed her fingertips into the cool, damp earth. The soil gave way beneath her hands.

"Why do I feel so lost without him?" she whispered. "I never wanted love."

She had not meant to say it aloud, yet the words slipped out, soft and aching. The admission felt traitorous somehow, as though she were confessing a weakness – but it was true. She had never longed for romance in the way other young ladies did. She never fashioned daydreams of courtships or kisses or marriage – but her heart was a thing of its own. It had not asked her permission before attaching itself to him.

In response, the rose before her seemed to shimmer in the dusk light, as if in quiet sympathy.

A sudden rustle nearby interrupted her.

She turned, heart quickening, to see Henry standing a few yards away. His coat was unbuttoned and cravat askew, as though he'd left the house in a hurry.

Has he followed me here? Or is it merely chance?

Swallowed hard, torn between the urge to draw closer and the instinct to retreat. "Henry..."

He took a step closer.

"Evelyn," he replied, his voice low and rough with emotion. "I did not expect to find you here this evening."

She blinked at him, unsure whether to believe him. *Then why are you here?* she wanted to ask. *Did you hope to find me? Or had you hoped to be alone?*

"I come here to think," she said instead, trying to keep her tone steady. "It is my escape."

"As it is mine. You should not be out here by yourself so often."

"Why not?" she countered, suddenly bristling. "Is that not what you desire? For me to be away from you?"

Henry flinched as if struck. His face was taut, the lines beside his eyes deeper. In the fading light, he looked suddenly older... haunted, even. "I wish it were that simple."

"Then what is it?" Evelyn rose to her feet, brushing the dirt from her skirts with shaking hands. "Did you ever truly care for me, or was it all just... a moment's amusement? A fleeting diversion? Was I merely another tale in the long line of your family's cursed fates?"

She had not meant to say so much, but the words spilled out like blood from a wound bound too tight. Her heart raced as she searched his face for an answer.

"The kiss we shared in the closet..." She faltered. "It meant something to me. It felt real."

His silence was deafening.

She turned from him before the tears could rise, before he might see how deeply she bled from that stillness

Behind her, there was another rustle of leaves – far too deliberate to be the wind. Evelyn stiffened as the slender figure of Lady Arabella stepped into view from beneath the archway. Her laughter rang out, bright and mocking, as though she had been listening all along and was rather delighted to have done so.

"Miss Evelyn! " she purred. "Henry! What a delightful surprise to find you both here."

Evelyn quickly dabbed at her eyes. She forced a smile, but it was brittle on her lips. "We were merely enjoying the garden," she said, though a tightness in her throat made the words ache on the way out.

"Oh, I can see that," Arabella crooned, glancing pointedly at Henry, who remained still. "And what a charming little garden! How secretive... how quaint."

She strolled further into the garden, scanning the space with an air of superiority, as though every bloom were arranged for her pleasure.

Evelyn drew her shoulders back, willing herself not to cower before Arabella's gleaming confidence.

Arabella stopped, her smile dying as she saw the rose in the centre of the garden. "What is...?" she breathed, with sincerity this time, stepping closer to the rose. "I have never seen anything so... stunning." Arabella took another step. The glow of the rose caught in the folds of her gown. "Absolutely magnificent."

Evelyn's heart raced, not merely from the fear of what Arabella might do to the rose, but from something more primal. The rose had been her sanctuary, her secret with Henry... and now Arabella looked at it with covetous eyes, as if it were hers to admire and pluck.

No. Not that. Not that, too.

As Arabella reached out to touch the rose, her fingers poised to claim a beauty she had no right to, Evelyn opened her mouth to speak – to stop her – but nothing came out.

Henry moved first.

"No, wait – !" he said sharply, but it was too late.

Even as his warning sliced through the air, Arabella's fingers brushed the bloom.

The first petal detached, floating gently to the earth. Evelyn watched it fall, transfixed. It seemed to shimmer as it descended, like moonlight caught in a drop of water, before settling in the grass.

The atmosphere shifted.

A pulse of energy rippled through the garden. The glow of the remaining petals flickered in response, like the last heartbeat of something once alive and precious.

Chapter 25

Evelyn

The season continued to change around them, spring erupting in a riot of colours. Evelyn forced herself to ignore the rose in the garden, its first fallen petal like a silent harbinger of Henry's fears. In the wake of Arabella's careless touch that fateful night, Henry had stormed back to the manor in silence, leaving the two young ladies suspended in an unspoken confrontation. Arabella, sensing the peculiar gravity of her misstep, had fled the garden as though pursued by an unseen force.

Evelyn had remained, her fingers shaking as she reached for the single fallen petal, a fragile token of beauty now tinged with heartbreak. She pressed it into her sketchbook the next morning.

Heeding her father's advice, Evelyn counselled her heart to withdraw for a time, to cease scanning doorways for his figure, and abandon the hope that he might speak. *Patience is a virtue in matters of the heart.*

Indeed, she had resolved to distance herself from Henry, imagining – foolishly, perhaps – that absence might soften the ache that sharpened in his presence. It proved no great difficulty, for she scarcely saw him beyond mealtimes, and even then, he spoke little, answered sparsely, and rarely lifted his eyes from his plate.

Still, spring advanced in cruel splendour as though the very world conspired to remind her of the love she yearned for but could not grasp: the garden bloomed with blush-pink roses, the trees swayed with birdsong, the sky was so heartbreakingly blue it felt like a jest at her expense.

She sought solace herself in her studies, as she once had in happier times, poring over botanical volumes and meticulously sketching leaves and petals in her sketchbook. She labelled each specimen in careful handwriting, though the activity brought her little joy. She had hoped to preserve her dignity in silence – but silence, she was learning, could be as savage a thing as longing.

Meanwhile, Arabella's pursuit of Henry grew bolder by the day. She manoeuvred through the manor like a queen in borrowed robes, instructing the servants as if they were hers by right – not a guest, but a mistress returned. Her laughter, once merely grating, now echoed oddly in the high-ceilinged halls.

One evening, with the sun dipping low on the horizon, Evelyn approached her father with a heavy heart "Do you believe it is time for us to return home?" she inquired softly. "After the ball, of course."

Her father regarded her, the corners of his mouth turning down as he considered. After a long moment, he nodded slowly. "Yes, my dear. I believe it may be time." His assent settled over her like a gentle sigh.

He agreed to inform the baron of their impending departure, vowing to instruct the servants to commence the packing of their belongings.

Evelyn slept deeply that night, lulled by visions of safety and the quiet stillness of their London home – a fragile illusion that shimmered just beyond the grasp of her dreams.

∞∞∞

The manor was in a frenzy of movement the next morning, as preparation for the evening's ball consumed the household. Servants buzzed with urgency, darting about like bees stirred from the hive.

In the kitchen, the aroma of warm butter and sugared fruit wafted through the air, along with the sharper scents of citrus and clove. Cooks bustled about in a hurried whirlwind, deftly decorating tarts with slices of

194

peaches and blood oranges. Scullery maids flitted between them with arms full of fresh herbs and spices.

Evelyn could picture Charles amidst the bustle: his leg propped up on a stool and a charming smile as he pilfered pastries from the cooling trays. The cooks would scold him, of course, but would not be able to suppress their laughter at his antics.

Above stairs, footmen burnished the silver until it gleamed with an almost unsettling brilliance. Maids hurried past with florist blooms of roses and lilies and great clusters of peonies. Though the chandeliers remained unlit, their crystals caught the last of the afternoon light, glinting like ice. Garlands of crimson roses and trailing ivy draped across banisters and mantels, their fragrance weaving a heady spell that hung thick in the air.

A long oak table groaned under the opulent display of gleaming platters and sugared confections, while crystal goblets stood empty, poised in perfect rows.

In the drawing room, Evelyn's father hunched over a stack of correspondence forwarded from their London home, oblivious to the chaos surrounding him: maids darting back and forth in a flurry of taffeta and linen, footmen arranging the chaise longues in precisely the right configuration, only for Arabella to change her mind yet again. Through it Mr Ward remained perfectly still, murmuring the occasional "Hmm" or "Dreadful business" as he shuffled another envelope open.

Evelyn wandered the quieter halls of the manor, biding her time until the ball began. She paused at the end of a long passageway and released a heavy sigh. Somewhere below, the strains of a waltz floated up as musicians rehearsed, but up here – buried deep in the manor's ribs – there was only silence and the echo of her own unrest.

In the quiet moments, Evelyn found her mind spiralling back to the rose, and the curse that had once consumed her thoughts. She had invested so much time and energy into it, driven first by curiosity, then by the wild, foolish hope that she might somehow save Henry from himself. What once felt like purpose now seemed like quiet madness. Henry did not want to be saved – or perhaps he no longer believed in salvation.

The rose still haunted her thoughts, when she allowed it, and the haunting memory of the woman in white... Had she truly ever seen her? Or had grief and longing spun her into being?

Evelyn wrapped her arms around herself, though the corridor was not cold. She did not know what she longed for anymore: truth, or knowledge or simply peace. All she knew was that the threads of her world, perhaps even her mind, were loosening, and she had neither the strength nor the will to tie them back into place.

"Miss Evelyn!" Clara's voice sliced through the silence, echoing off the panelled walls. She appeared at the top of the stairs. "There you are. I have been searching high and low for you. We ought to begin dressing you for the evening, miss. The hour grows late."

Evelyn sighed heavily. The thought of attending the ball felt like slipping into another skin to conceal her true self. She had long since mastered the art of graciousness, of being what others wished her to be – and tonight, as ever, she would not disappoint. She inclined her head with quiet resignation and followed Clara down the long, winding corridor.

"We must make haste," Clara urged.

In the guest chamber, a small army of maids awaited. Evelyn took her place before the mirror and allowed herself to be surrounded by them, like attendants to a queen. She sat motionless as they worked. She felt strangely removed from it all, as if she were standing beyond the moment, watching herself from a distance.

As the maids began to arrange her hair, Evelyn let her mind slip away, her eyes unfocussed somewhere beyond the reflection in the glass. Her thoughts wandered to London, to the carriage that would soon bear her away, and to the finality of leaving Henry.

The ball felt like a distant reverie, little more than a charade. She had not confided her plans to Clara. She had told no one but her father, for it felt to fragile to speak aloud, as though naming it might splinter her resolve. Perhaps the servants already knew, and her trunks were being prepared even now. The very thought turned her stomach.

She sat still beneath the maids' hands as they twisted her chestnut hair into careful curls, and she even managed a smile. It barely touched her lips, and not at all her eyes.

What will Henry say, she wondered, *when he realises I am gone? Will he notice? Does it matter?*

"It is time for your gown, Miss Evelyn," Clara announced softly.

Evelyn nodded. With practised hands, the maids lifted Evelyn's day dress over her head and set it aside. She stood bare save for her linen shift, pale and still

The maids exchanged glances, their eyes gleaming as they presented the gown for the evening.

It was magnificent, a masterpiece – perhaps the most exquisite gown Evelyn had ever seen. It was pale blue, so light it seemed to hover between sky and water, and almost iridescent, as though it had been spun not by human hands but from moonlight and sorrow.

"It was made for you, miss," Clara said gently, holding the bodice open. "Commissioned from Madame Leroux's atelier in town. Your father gave the order, but we... well, we took the liberty of consulting on the particulars."

"It is exquisite," Evelyn said quietly, though she felt a world away. "Truly. Thank you."

The words seemed to please the maids, who slipped the gown over her shoulders in delight. The fabric encased her like a gentle cloud, cascading to the floor, where it pooled around her feet in rippling waves. Lace trimmed the puffed sleeves, while floral embroidery wove along the hem. The maids fastened the row of tiny buttons down her back with the care one might reserve for handling a precious jewel.

Then Clara knelt before Evelyn and presented a pair of silver slippers, their soft sheen catching the light just enough to echo the shimmer of her gown.

"Oh, they complement the gown perfectly," Sarah whispered. "I have outdone myself."

With the last adjustments were complete, the maids guided Evelyn back to the dressing table, as though they were preparing a masterpiece for its grand unveiling. One of the maids brushed a touch of rouge onto her cheeks, and another applied a rose tint to her lips.

Clara approached with small velvet box.

"These were your mother's," she said, opening with care. "A pearl pendant, and matching earrings. Your father thought tonight... well, he said it felt right."

Evelyn nodded, too overcome to speak. The silver settled cold against her collarbone, but the sensation grounded her.

"You are ready, my lady," Clara said softly, stepping back.

Evelyn stole a glance at her reflection in the mirror, her breath catching in her throat. The gown shimmered like starlight as though a spell had been woven into the silk itself. She turned slightly, and the vision moved too: an elegant creature of moonlight and embroidery, but a stranger. Yes, a beautiful, breaking thing.

"Like you've just stepped out of a painting," Clara whispered.

Evelyn's throat tightened. Was this who she was meant to be? The dutiful daughter, the vision in silk? A girl made pleasing for the eyes of others?

The maids beamed behind her, their smiles warm and proud, as if they had conjured a vision from the very depths of a dream. Evelyn summoned a smile for their sake. They had laboured with such care and devotion – how could she not reward them with even that?

I feel as though I am floating outside myself, Evelyn thought, watching the girl in the mirror with a curious detachment. *Is this how Henry feels, when his eyes go distant? When he looks at me and sees nothing at all?*

Perhaps this was what love truly was.

A beautiful madness, she named it silently. *Something that seeps into the blood and will not let go.*

With a final look, she turned from the mirror, uncertain if she was stepping into a dream or descending into chaos.

Chapter 26

Henry

The night was a tapestry of shadows as carriages glided up in succession beneath the watchful gaze of the moon. Their forms emerged from the mist like ghostly figures, wheels crunching on gravel with a sound that grated along Henry's spine. Lanterns flared and flickered, but they only seemed to cast longer, darker shadows.

Henry stood just inside the tall windows of the entrance hall, tugging absently at the knot of his cravat. It felt too tight and precise, as if it had been tied not by his valet, but by the hand of fate itself, intent on strangling him with civility. His reflection in the glass stared back pale and strange, the image of a man playing at being whole.

It is only a ball, he told himself. *A gathering of music and wine and inconsequential conversation.* He sighed deeply. *Like I am being buried alive in charm and obligation.*

The evening stretched ahead like a corridor without end.

As he stood in the great hall, the low hum of voices and the rustle of silk enveloped him. Guests drifted about in awe, looking up to the chandeliers that glittered like captive stars above. Garlands of roses and dark ivy lined the walls, their fragrance so potent it felt stifling. Somewhere, an orchestra had begun to play, a haunting waltz curling through the laughter like a memory clawing its way back from the grave.

Henry sunk into the corners of the hall, his tailcoat nearly indistinguishable from the shadowed panelling. A cluster of young gentlemen passed, bowing stiffly in deference. He inclined his head in return, offering nothing more. Their voices faded into the distance, replaced by the soft clinking of champagne glasses and the flutter of fans. He felt detached from it all, as though he were merely a spectator in a play, a ghost moving through a world of the living.

Another carriage rolled to a stop outside. He watched as the gentlemen offered their arms to the ladies, trailing behind them as they stepped daintily across the threshold. The whispers of anticipation grew louder, though none of it reached Henry. He was no more part of it than the statues watching from their alcoves.

His thoughts drifted, unbidden to the stairs.

Would she come down soon?

The thought struck like an arrow loosed from nowhere. *Evelyn.*

No, he ought not think of her. He had told himself as much, again and again, until the words grew dull from repetition.

She must return to London. She must forget me. I must let her go.

Still, here he was, his breath caught on a name he dared not speak aloud. It was an ache he had buried, too fearful to confront yet impossible to ignore. He lived suspended between two torments: the pull of her presence, and the relentless shadow of the curse. One promised ruin, the other redemption, though he no longer knew which was which.

Then, as if summoned by the darkness itself, or by the dreadful clarity that comes in moments just before the fall, Henry's eyes were drawn, slow and helpless, to the top of the grand staircase, where Miss Evelyn Ward stood.

Her dress caught the light like liquid moonlight, a soft blue shimmering like silver beneath the glow of the chandeliers. The fabric clung to her form, flowing with each breath she took, as though she were woven from the very shadows. The chandeliers above did not so much illuminate her as bend around her, drawn to her as he was. She descended the staircase slowly, with a grace too still for this world.

Henry's heart tightened as he watched her, for the way she held herself struck him as almost mournful... resigned yet luminous, like a star dimming just before dawn. But oh, she was a vision of ethereal light, descending into the very depths of his hellish world.

She was not merely beautiful tonight.

She was haunting.

He moved without thought, drawn forwards through the gathered throng. The crowd parted before him, the swirling colours of silks and brocade blurring into insignificance. The room could have burnt to the ground around him, and he would not have noticed.

She reached the final step, and their eyes met.

"Miss Ward," he said, extending a hand. Why he did so, he could not say. He certainly should have bowed, offered some pleasantry, and disappeared into the shadows where he belonged – but instead, he led her into the centre of the hall to dance.

The orchestra began to play.

With quiet grace, he drew her into his arm. One hand found the curve of her waist, and the other enclosed her gloved fingers as they began to move. They swayed in unison, each step effortless, as though they had danced this waltz a thousand times before.

In that single, aching moment, time itself seemed to stop. There was no ballroom, no music, no voices. There was only Evelyn, and the terrible clarity of holding what he could never allow himself to keep. He did not deserve to touch her, but God help him, he could not stop.

Out of the corner of his eye, he caught a glimpse of Lady Arabella, her face a tightly controlled mask of fury. Her jewelled gown sparkled in the light, yet her beauty felt cold and unyielding, like a diamond shrouded in ice. He did not care. All that mattered was Evelyn, cradled in his arms. This moment, this dance – it belonged solely to them, and though he knew it could never last, still he held to it.

He tightened his grip slightly, feeling the soft fabric of her gown beneath his fingers. The music swelled, rising to a crescendo, and he spun her. With each turn, her gown billowed around them like a cloud of moonlight, and for a heartbeat, it was as if they danced on air.

If this is madness, I would surrender to it gladly.

As the final notes faded and silence bloomed in their wake, Henry did not release her – but nor did she retreat.

One more moment, he thought. *One more breath with her before the dark creeps back in.*

"Evelyn," he murmured over the rising noise of the ballroom. "Would you do me the honour of stepping outside for a breath of fresh air? I find myself quite stifled by this throng."

I need you near, if only for a short while longer.

With a stiff nod, she accepted his invitation, and together they slipped away from the noise and lights of the ball.

Stepping onto the balcony, they were greeted by the night's cool breeze that rustled the leaves of the sprawling gardens below. Henry leant against the wrought-iron railing, glancing out over the gardens, while Evelyn stood beside him, her silhouette framed by the soft luminescence of the moon.

An awkward silence unfurled between them. Henry sensed a lingering sadness in Evelyn's eyes, a melancholy that clung to her like a persistent shadow. He longed to bridge the distance, to dispel the weight that hovered in the air.

"Strange, isn't it?" he began, his voice sounding odd even to himself. "All these guests, drawn from far and wide across the countryside. Most have come merely out of curiosity regarding the reclusive Sinclairs, while others… well, they seem more intent on presenting their daughters to the unmarried heir of Sinclair estate." He forced a light laugh, though it echoed falsely, jarring in the stillness. He wished he had not spoken.

Fool, he thought. *She does not care for your inheritance or your name. She never did.*

Evelyn turned to him, her gaze drifting past the gardens to the inky depths of the night sky. "Yes, it is peculiar. So many eager faces, yet none of them truly see us."

Henry studied her profile in the moonlight: the graceful line of her neck, the quiet conviction in her voice.

She sees too much, he thought. He had let her draw close, close enough to glimpse the rot beneath the gilt, and now he feared it was already too late to keep her from it.

As the shadows of the garden danced in the moonlight, they stood side by side, grappling with unvoiced thoughts.

Evelyn broke the silence first. "This cannot be your first ball. Where did you acquire such skill in dance?"

Henry turned to her, letting a wry smile touch his lips. "One of my governesses. She was a strict taskmaster, I assure you. I was caned for every misstep."

Evelyn chuckled lightly, as though she too hoped to bridge the invisible chasm between them. "Will you tell me of your childhood?"

He hesitated, memories swirling within him like shadows in the night. What could he give her? The truth? The pale, incomplete shape of it? There was so little worth sharing: no warmth, no mischief, no golden summers spent laughing in fields. Still, he answered her.

"It was a rather lonely existence. I had neither siblings nor childhood companions to share in the joys of youth. Lady Arabella visited infrequently with her aunt, and others like her. They did not want my companionship, but merely to set up a marriage of convenience for my family's wealth or title. My formal education was overseen by a succession of governesses, yet none remained long enough for me to form any true affection.

"Thus, I often sought solace in the pages of books, losing myself in worlds far removed from my own. I would wander the gardens, where the flowers offered silent companionship. Music became my refuge; I spent countless hours with my harp, or at the piano, or with the violin nestled beneath my chin. In those moments, the solitude felt less oppressive, as if the notes themselves lifted me from my isolation, if only for a brief while."

"I had no idea you were proficient in more than just the harp," she replied, with a hint of surprise.

"Indeed, I play several instruments – the piano, the violin, the viola, and even the clarinet. You may find it hard to believe, but I have dabbled a bit with the trombone as well."

As he spoke, the tension in his shoulders loosened. The burdens of duty and the ghost of the curse seemed to fade, if only for a moment, leaving behind the simple joy of sharing his passion. "Music has always been a comfort to me, a means of expression beyond words. Each instrument possesses its own voice, its own story to tell, and I find great joy in exploring them all."

Evelyn's expression grew wistful, a shadow passing over her features. "My mother was a gifted musician," she said, her voice soft and wistful. "She played both the piano and the violin as if each note were a gentle caress. Not only did she perform beautifully, but she also composed a great many original pieces. I cherish the sheets of music she left behind, though I possess no talent to render them faithfully."

Her words struck him deeper than it ought to have. Why did it feel like a confession? Why did it feel like she had given him a part of herself? He imagined her as a girl, curled in the corner of some sunlit drawing room, clutching those fading pages, listening to silence where her mother's music used to be.

"If you would allow, I would be most honoured to play them for you one day," he offered gently. "Perhaps I might breathe life into those melodies once more, if only to honour your mother's legacy."

"That would mean the world to me," she replied softly. He could hear the soft tremble in her voice. "To hear her music played would be like feeling her presence beside me once more." She paused, relishing the cool night air, her eyes fluttering closed. A gentle breeze tousled her chestnut curls, framing her face as she turned slightly towards him. "I wish I could express myself through music as you do. It seems an art that transcends the barriers of time and space." She clasped her hands together, fingers intertwining, as if holding onto a distant dream.

204

"Perhaps you could. I have seen how your hands move with such grace over a sketch, as if the flowers themselves come alive under your touch."

Evelyn's cheeks flushed, and she instinctively tucked a loose curl behind her ear, avoiding his gaze. "I am merely an amateur."

"I do not believe that at all. I have seen your drawings, and they are nothing short of remarkable." He paused, searching for the right words. He stepped slightly closer. "You possess a rare talent, one that truly deserves celebration. You should publish your work one day, a study of botany."

She smiled, yet a sadness remained in her eyes. She titled her face to the stars, and for a moment, she seemed to be counting them, or searching for something lost.

Henry watched her in silence.

God help me, I love her.

She was unlike any soul he had ever known. She was not merely kind, but gentle in a way that quieted the room around her. She was not simply intelligent, but inquisitive. Her mind was keen, but never boastful, and quick-witted, but never striving to outshine. She was beautiful – yes – but it was a beauty that seemed to glow from within, like moonlight caught in glass. The only word that dared approach the truth of her was *luminous*, and she was slipping from him, as stars are wont to do.

Stay with me, he thought. *Stay with me, beautiful star, if only for a moment more.*

"Tell me about your home in London," he said, his words offered like a hand extended in the dark. "Your garden. The room where you keep your books. I should like to picture you there."

Evelyn did not reply at once. Her eyes remained in the endless stretch of night.

"It is a lively place," she said at last. "Our street is wide and tree-lined, always filled with the rattle of wheels and the clipped calls of coachmen. One cannot step outdoors without encountering a dozen voices at once. Merchants hawking their wares, children at play, the ever-present noise of Society turning in on itself."

She paused, and he waited. "Our house sits just beyond Kensington Gardens," she continued, "tall and narrow, with ivy creeping along the southern wall. My mother always kept the parlour filled with light, arranging the chairs so the sun might fall directly upon the pianoforte."

He smiled as she spoke, for her voice was so very soft and gentle.

"I spend most of my time in the upper rooms," she added. "There is a small chamber at the back with shelves lining the walls, all crammed with books and pressed flowers, and drawings I never seem to finish. The window overlooks our little garden. Mostly herbs and lavender now, since my mother's roses refused to return last spring. I sit there for hours, with the city pressing in all around, and yet it feels… apart. As though I am quite alone in the world, and glad of it."

She turned her head to look at him at last, glancing at him from beneath lowered lashes. "I think I crave quiet, even in the midst of noise. I do not belong to the bustle, not truly. I think I was born for solitude, in some gentle place that does not exist."

You belong here with me, Henry thought, so draped was she in moonlight and sorrow that it seemed she was fashioned in the same haunted air as the rest of Rosehill Manor.

Suddenly, the moment was shattered by raucous laughter and the cheerful clinking of glasses. A group of guests spilled onto the balcony with drunken cheer.

Evelyn glanced at the approaching figures, straightening her shoulders with that quiet grace he had come to revere. Like a pane of glass shattering in a chapel, the stillness was broken.

"I must bid you farewell," she said. "I shall be leaving Rosehill Manor. Perhaps in the morning."

No. No, not yet.

The plea rose like a scream inside him, but he could not voice it. He had sent her away himself with his silence, his restraint, his damnable devotion to her safety.

Before he could make sense of the chaos inside him, Evelyn turned and slipped back into the ballroom, the flickering light and laughter consuming her.

This was what he had wanted. Was it not? To protect her and thereby to free her, and ensure she lived a life untouched by the rot that clung to the Sinclair name.

Then why, he thought bitterly, *does it feel like dying?*

He gripped the railing until his knuckles turned white. He could not let her leave – no, not without one final breath stolen from the edge of goodbye.

With a sharp inhale, Henry turned from the balcony and stepped back into the candlelit haze of the ballroom. Satin and lace blurred around him, laughter dull against the blood rushing in his ears.

I only need one last look. One last touch. One last kiss to carry into the dark.

"Henry! There you are!" Lady Arabella's voice pierced through the din. Her smile blazed across the room like the flash of a polished blade – radiant, yes, but curiously out of place, like a rose blooming in a graveyard.

"Lady Arabella," he replied coolly, forcing a bow. There was no time. Evelyn was vanishing with every heartbeat.

"I should very much like a word," she said sweetly. "If you please. It is a matter most urgent."

Before he could step aside or make his excuses, she was upon him, seizing his forearm and curling around the fabric with alarming strength.

"I said, if you please," she repeated, her voice as light as lace, though her eyes glinted. "We should not make a scene, Mr Sinclair. That would be most improper." She dug her fingers deeper into his arm. "Come now. Do be a gentleman and oblige me."

As Arabella pulled him along, Henry cast one last look toward the ballroom. Evelyn was gone – swallowed by light and noise and everything he had failed to hold.

∞∞∞

Henry tugged at his cravat, struggling for breath.

Lady Arabella had swept him inside the dark drawing room with the soundless grace of a wraith. Her grip on his arm was like iron forged in ice, and only now, as the door shut behind them, did she release him.

"Mr Sinclair... Henry," Arabella began, her voice a sultry whisper that echoed in the stillness, drawing closer to him as if weaving an enchantment. "There is a truth I must confess to you. I have, these many years, regarded you with the most tender affection. Surely, you must have sensed it. I hold you in the very highest esteem... and more besides."

Her eyes shimmered in the dim light, and Henry felt an instinctive urge to step back.

"I appreciate your candour, Arabella," he said, trying to remain calm despite the unease rising in his chest. His eyes darted to the closed door. "But I am not interested in your schemes. Whatever it is you believe you are arranging, I want no part in it."

Arabella's expression faltered for a heartbeat, but she quickly masked it with a charming smile.

"You do me an injustice, dear Henry," she purred, stepping closer still, the distance between them collapsing. "I ask only for what is already ours." She stepped nearer still, her gloved hand ghosting along the sleeve of his coat, light as cobwebs.

"A kiss," she whispered, eyes gleaming. "Nothing more. A mere token... to seal the bond that lies already between us."

Henry's breath came shallow and sharp. His heart beat a frantic rhythm, the kind one feels when darkness brushes too close and reason begins to falter. Every instinct urged retreat, but his limbs remained unnervingly still. "Arabella, this is not what either of us desires. I cannot return the feelings you claim to hold, and I will not pretend otherwise, even out of courtesy."

She only smiled and bit her lip.

Henry looked again to the door. "Please, let us not mar what little remains of our acquaintance with false hopes or cruel delusions."

Arabella rested against the window, moonlight catching her in a way that was too perfect, her silhouette too still, as though she weren't entirely human. Her silks clung to her like a shroud, whispering faintly, though the room held no breeze. With a languid smile, she caught his hand and pressed it against the bare skin at her collarbone, the pulse beneath it disturbingly irregular.

"Henry, dear," she purred, drawing closer still, her breath warm against his throat, "consider what we might accomplish together." She tightened her other hand around his, digging crescent moons into his skin with her nails. "With my wealth and your lineage, we could shape society to our liking. We would be untouchable... admired, envied, feared. Is that not what you were born for?"

Henry's stomach turned, a nausea rising that felt deeper than mere revulsion. The walls seemed to shift, the wallpaper writhing as if alive, shadows stretching and contorting in the corners of his vision.

"Enough," he growled. "I seek no alliance with you, Lady Ravenwood. Not in power, not in affection, and certainly not in anything resembling love."

Arabella stilled. Her expression faltered for a breath, then twisted into something darker. "Are you so certain?" she whispered, pressing closer until the fabric of her gown brushed against his coat. "Do not pretend you haven't imagined it... my lips on your neck, my hands unfastening the buttons of your shirt, my body – "

"I said enough," he snapped. "You mistake me entirely if you think desire can be coaxed where none resides."

Her eyes gleamed, dark and bottomless, and her smile widened, too far, stretching unnaturally as though her very face mocked him. "You would spurn me? We are not so different, you and I. You walk through this world like a man already buried, Henry. Don't think I have not seen it."

"You know nothing of me."

Henry's hand still rested against her collarbone, kept there as though by force, but now he felt something beneath her skin: a pulsing, writhing movement, as though something alive squirmed just beneath the surface. He gasped audibly, and she laughed. It was low and hollow, echoing unnaturally, as though it came not from her throat but the walls around them?

Who is this monster beneath the woman?

As he made to pull away once more, he caught a flicker of movement at the corner of his eye: a figure at the door, now slightly ajar.

No, he thought, dread clawing through him. *God help me – please, not this.*

Evelyn stood frozen, her hand still on the door as though she had only just pushed it open. Their eyes met, and in hers he saw the raw and unguard hurt of a someone betrayed. Her eyes dropped, just briefly, to the place where his hand still rested against Arabella's collarbone, to the unsettling closeness between them. He knew it could only be misread as a lover's embrace.

A low hum began to vibrate beneath the floorboards, as though the house itself had drawn a breath. Arabella smiled, but it was no longer the smile of a mortal woman. It stretched too wide, too sharp, twisting into something feral. Her teeth gleamed unnaturally white in the dim light.

"It would appear," she whispered, tilting her head with eerie poise, "that we are not quite as alone as you believed, dear Henry." Her voice echoed strangely, as though spoken not just once but again and again, layered with the whispers of something that had slumbered far too long. "How very unfortunate."

"No," Henry breathed, but it was far too late.

He looked back to Evelyn where she stood, her eyes wide with something beyond horror or betrayal. A small sound escaped her before she turned and fled, her silken skirts vanishing like smoke into the corridor's waiting dark.

Horrified, Henry tore himself free from Arabella's grasp. Her skin clung to him like frost, as though her touch had leeched even the warmth from his bones. Behind him, she laughed, low and distorted, no longer fully her own. The sound vibrated through the walls like a chime rung in hell.

"Run to her, Henry," the voice from her mouth crooned. *"She is already lost. And so, my love, are you."*

Henry bolted into the corridor, Evelyn's name on his tongue, but the house seemed alive, shifting around him. The walls groaned as if exhaling, their surfaces buckling and rippling like flesh. The once-familiar hallways stretched impossibly. Wallpaper bubbled and blistered, bleeding patterns that twisted into clawed shapes, eyes, mouths that gaped and grinned.

Candle sconces sputtered as he passed, snuffing out one by one, plunging him into darkness broken only by a ghostly glow far ahead – a glimmer of pale blue.

He ran towards it, but when he turned the corner, the floor beneath his feet gave a long, agonised groan and dropped an inch, like a mouth opening to swallow him whole.

He stumbled, catching himself on the wall, only to recoil. The surface beneath his hand was no longer smooth but cold and clammy, like damp flesh. It pulsed beneath his palm, and he yanked his hand away, bile rising in his throat.

Arabella's warped laughter echoed around him, a sound like wind moaning through a crypt.

"You belong to us, Henry," the voice hissed. *"You cannot save her. You cannot even save yourself."*

Chapter 27

Evelyn

Evelyn tore through the manor's winding corridors, her breath ragged. Panic thundered in her chest, louder than her footfalls, louder than reason. She could not stop, for the image pursed her mercilessly: Henry with his hand against Arabella's chest, caught in an embrace. Still, it was not the betrayal that undid her, but the thing beneath Arabella's skin: a monster draped in silk, looking upon Henry with hunger. Evelyn's vision blurred with unshed tears, and still she ran, deeper into the manor's bones, as though the house itself might swallow her before fear could.

Her breath hitched as she stumbled into a narrow staircase. In her frantic flight, she climbed quickly, without thought, her silver slippers slipping on the worn steps. The higher she ascended, the more the air grew thick, stifling, as though the manor itself were holding its breath, watching her.

At the top of the stairs, she stumbled into an open room – a space that seemed to expand and contract around her. The space loomed, dark and foreboding, lit only by feeble shafts of moonlight struggling through the dusty windows. A chill gripped her, for Evelyn knew without a doubt: she had finally stumbled into the attic.

Forgotten trunks and broken furniture lay strewn about, draped in tattered sheets that clung to the pieces like mourning veils. The hairs on the back of her neck stood on end. She felt eyes – cold, unseen eyes – watching her every movement. Her chest tightened, the air growing heavier with every breath, as if the room itself was exhaling foul breath. The kitchen maid's words echoed in her mind, "*Stay away, miss.*"

A low, creaking sound echoed from the far corner of the attic – a sound like old bones cracking. She turned towards it and saw nothing but the empty darkness, until something moved.

It was an indistinct shape, flickering just out of the corner of her eye. The room seemed to warp again, as though the very air were distorting, bending with the weight of something unseen.

A whisper brushed against her ear, cold and wet, like breath from a grave: *"You cannot run, Evelyn Ward. You belong here now."*

She froze, her blood turning to ice, for the words had not been heard so much as felt. No, it was not a voice in the ordinary sense, but something deeper, darker, echoing through the marrow of her bones and the recesses of her fear. She scanned the room frantically, searching for the source, but the attic was empty, save for the dark relics of forgotten time.

Her eyes were drawn to the far corner of the room, where a tarnished mirror leant. She knew, instinctively and without question, that she ought not approach it, and so – of course – she did.

The glass was fractured, warped from time and cold. It reflected the room behind her, but something felt terribly wrong. She beheld herself – or some ghastly semblance of herself – staring back. Her visage was pale, her features drawn and hollow, her eyes deep pits into which the light dared not venture. The fractures distorted her face into a grotesque semblance of womanhood, as though the mirror fought to contain her shape and could no longer manage the burden.

The voice came again, closer now, like water pressing against a sealed door. *"You are already trapped,"* it whispered, *"just as she was. Trapped in the attic. Trapped in the manor. Trapped in the skin you wear."*

It was her own voice, but distorted, as though some malevolent thing had learned her tone and twisted it to mock her. It came not from the air, but from the mirror itself.

The reflection of her face contorted into a grimace, curling its lips into smile that held not warmth, only knowledge. Its eyes were sunken and hollow staring into hers with an intimacy that chilled the blood.

Slowly the reflection began to move – not Evelyn, but the thing within the glass. Its fingers twitched once, then lifted to the edge of the mirror, as though testing the boundary between their worlds. The cracked surface groaned beneath the strain, and the splinters multiplied, webbing outward like frost across a pane

"You are already a part of this place. You always have been."

Terror surged through her. She staggered backwards, her mind reeling, desperate to escape, but every step only led her deeper into shadow. The attic walls seemed to close in, and the ceiling stooped lower. Evelyn turned again, and again, but every direction was the same: darkness without end, despair without exit.

She pressed a hand to the wall – was it stone or wood? – but it yielded like damp paper, breathing beneath her palm. She jumped back and realised with a start that she was standing in front of the mirror once more.

No, it could not be. She had fled, hadn't she? She had run from the mirror, and the voice, and the impossible grin that had been her own – and yet, she now stood in the exact place, as if she had never moved at all.

With a trembling breath, Evelyn raised her eyes, torn between the fear of seeing her warped reflection, and the greater terror that it might no longer be there.

What met her was neither. The frame remained, but where once had been fractured glass, there was now no mirror at all. It had been replaced by oil and canvas. Her likeness remained, but it was painted – *painted* – and the sight of it chilled her blood. The woman in the portrait wore Evelyn's face, yes, but not as she had moments before. It was not her expression, yet it belonged to the face in the portrait.

"I do not – " she stuttered. "How is it me? I do not understand."

Suddenly, older words echoed in her mind, unbidden, as though planted there by the house itself: *"They say that those who go into the attic come back changed, or not at all."*

Chapter 28

Clara

Clara sank into the worn chair, her limbs heavy with exhaustion, hoping for a moment of peace while Miss Evelyn was at the ball. She had scarcely slept, driven not by obligation alone, but by a deep, quiet wish: that her mistress might shine tonight, and perhaps, if the stars were kind, feel herself again.

Miss Evelyn had looked exquisite in her gown, the fabric cascading around her like a waterfall of soft colours, but Clara had noticed the what others did not: the melancholy behind her mistress' eyes. What had Mr Sinclair done to dim her so? He was too silent and brooding by half, and that Lady Arabella was a snake if Clara had ever seen one.

Yes, Clara thought, pressing her fingers to her aching temples, it would do them well to return to London. The city was loud and unkind in its own ways, but it was familiar. Miss Evelyn belonged to familiar faces and insipid drawing rooms, not to the dark and gloom. And Clara – well, she longed to see her younger brothers again, to press a portion of her wages into their hands, to hear their voices and know they were safe.

She rubbed her brow again, tracing the dull throb that had become all too familiar. *Just a moment's rest,* she told herself. *Just a moment, and then I will return to my duties.*

A soft sound jolted Clara awake. She cursed herself, for she had organised everything – every ribbon, every fastening, every blasted button – but what good was that if she could not keep her eyes open? She sat bolt upright, shame burning hot in her chest.

There was a noise outside the door, and a glow leaking beneath it. It must have been what awoke her. Someone, or something, was moving through the darkened halls of the servants' quarters.

Clara pushed herself from the chair, her feet bare and ice-cold as they touched the wooden floor. Her mind screamed at her to be sensible. What if it was Miss Evelyn? What if she had needed her? And Clara, foolish Clara, had been napping like a child with no more spine than a stray leaf.

She crept to the door and pressed her ear to it, straining to separate imagined fear from real sound.

Nothing.

Swallowing hard, she eased the door open with shaking fingers – just an inch, then another – until she could see into the corridor, and what she saw nearly stole the breath from her body.

There – gliding soundlessly through the corridor – was a woman. She was gaunt, swathed in white, her gown rippling like fog on a moor, with long hair loose around her shoulders. She held an oil lantern in one pale hand. Its flame flickered softly, casting tremulous light that danced across the walls, where shadows bloomed and twisted like spectres caught mid-sigh.

Clara's heart jolted, slamming hard against her ribs. She pressed back into the doorframe, cold wood biting through her dress.

Move, whispered something primal within her. *Flee.*

But she could not – all she could do was watch.

The ghost floated on, her gown trailing behind her like mist dragged on a tide. She made no sound now – not the creak of a floorboard, not the swish of fabric. There was only her lantern, swaying and beckoning.

Clara had heard the whispered tales of the woman in white, lost to grief, or guilt, or rage – no one agreed which – but to see her with her own eyes was a terror beyond anything she had ever imagined. It was one thing to whisper about her by candlelight with the maids, and quite another to see her.

Her Granny's voice rang in her mind, steadier than her own thoughts: *"Never turn your back on the dark, my girl."*

She did not understand those words then, but she did not. The dark did not chase – it waited. Waited for the careless, the weary, the ones who flinches. If you turned your back, it would swallow you whole.

No, Clara would not turn. She would not flee, for when the darkness called, one could not turn away; it must be faced. It was a promise, a reckoning of sorts, and she would heed it.

And Miss Evelyn might be out there – lost, afraid, or worse. Clara had slept, like a child too soft for the world she lived in. No, she would not be found wanting again.

With shaky breath, Clara pushed away from the wall. Her breath was shallow as she ventured deeper into the darkened corridor. The flickering light of the lantern swayed ahead, a beacon guiding her into the unknown.

Clara's mind raced with the old superstitions her grandmother had whispered to her as a child: how the dead, when wronged, could not rest… how their grief clung to the walls of a place, soaked through like wine in linen… how sorrow seeks sorrow.

Still, Clara followed.

The woman in white moved slowly, too slowly, as though willing Clara to keep pace, as though wanting to be followed.

But why? To what end?

The answer hovered just beyond reach, like a word on the tip of the tongue or the echo of a dream.

The ghost passed soundlessly through the great doors, and Clara, heart hammering, stepped out after her. The chill of the outdoors wrapped around her, the air thick with mist and the scent of damp earth. She hesitated, glancing over her shoulder at the manor, its dark silhouette looming against the moonlit sky. Part of her longed to turn back – to shut the door, crawl into her narrow bed and pretend this night had never happened, but the woman in white did not stop, and so neither could Clara.

The ground beneath her bare feet grew cold as she crossed the overgrown lawn, the damp grass curling around her ankles. The woman in white moved on without pause, crossing the line of ancient oaks that bordered the estate's boundaries. Behind her, the manor was all but swallowed by the mist. Somewhere within its stone walls, music still played, faint and far off, like a dream dissolving at dawn.

Clara pressed on. The grass gave way to soft, sodden earth. Brambles tugged at the hem of her dress, thorns catching like small, cruel hands. The path, if it could be called that, was no more than a suggestion, simply a winding trail veiled in wildflowers and undergrowth. The woman never slowed, her lantern a pale flame suspended in the dark, pulling Clara deeper and deeper into the trees. They had left the estate behind entirely.

After what felt like an eternity, the path opened into a clearing that revealed a hidden cemetery. Its wrought-iron gates stood open, waiting like a gaping mouth. The woman in white passed through, her figure ghostly against the line of crooked gravestones. Clara's heart pounded faster, her courage dwindling with each step.

The woman stopped before a particular grave, her white gown billowing slightly in the breeze, as if beckoning Clara closer. Clara's legs trembled, fear clawing at her throat. She dared not read the inscription. She dared not move any closer.

The gravestone stood taller than the rest, its surface adorned with faded carvings – ivy and angels, o perhaps weeping faces. Clara could not tell.

The woman in white drifted closer to it, lantern held steady in one hand, the other outstretched with a lover's reverence. She bent forwards and in a voice soft and strange and echoing through the brittle graveyard, she began to read: "Here lies Lady Margaret Sinclair, wife of Baron Alistair Sinclair, born 1766, died 1790."

The words struck Clara like ice down her spine. *Wife of Baron Alistair Sinclair.*

She staggered back a step, her hand flying to her mouth. The woman in white was not just any ghost; she was the late baroness, reading her own gravestone inscription.

The woman in white turned slightly to reveal another gravestone beside it, smaller and marked with a headstone curved like a cradle. "And here lies Eliza Sinclair, born 1 April, 1788, died 1 April, 1788."

Clara's breath snagged in her throat. The cold settled deeper in her bones, but it was something else that made her shiver now. She *knew* that voice.

Or – no, she didn't, she couldn't. It was impossible – but it was there, nestled in the space between memory and dream, like hearing a lullaby you were certain had never been sung to you, but your bones still knew the tune.

"Eliza lived but a day," the woman in white murmured sadly. "And the baroness died giving birth to her son, Henry."

Clara swayed, for none of it made sense. Her son, Henry? Was the woman in white not his grandmother, the wife of the Baron Alistair Sinclair?

"Look around you," the woman urged.

Clara's mouth opened, but no sound came. Her pulse roared in her ears. She felt like a rabbit cornered in some godless warren, frozen between flight and the terrible need to understand. She wrapped her arms around herself and trembled, every nerve screaming retreat – but still, she did not run.

Why would the ghost want her to look upon the graveyard?

Clara Byrne was many things in that moment – frightened, yes; unprepared, certainly – but she had been raised to be obedient, and if the dead had summoned her here, then surely... surely, she was meant to bear witness.

Slowly, she stepped into the cemetery. The gravestones rose up around her, their shadows long and solemn in the lantern's flickering glow. As she looked closer, a wave of cold dread surged through her, crashing over her like icy water. Every stone bore the same name: *Sinclair.*

Baroness after baroness. *Margaret. Beatrice. Catherine. Louisa.* The dates changed. The titles shifted, but they were all wives. All women. All gone.

Clara's breath turned sharp in her lungs. Her gaze fell to the smaller stones nestled beside the larger ones—half-hidden by moss, so easy to overlook. So many. Too many.

The horror sharpened to a point.

Each of the smaller headstones belonged to a baby girl, with a single date etched into each one. They all were born and died on the same day. *Eliza. Josephine. Rose. Aveline.* Many had not been named.

A bone-deep chill coursed through her, a visceral jolt of despair sinking deeper into her very marrow. The inscriptions were not just words; they were echoes of despair, the chronicles of a lineage steeped in loss.

"Why?" she gasped, barely aware she was speaking aloud. "Why were they all taken so soon? And why are there no men? No sons?"

"The burden of the Sinclair legacy is an unbearable weight, dear Clara," the woman intoned. "Each daughter born under the cursed name is doomed to a fleeting existence, their lives snuffed out before they could even draw their first breath in this cruel world." She paused, her gaze sweeping over the grave markers, each one a silent testament to a life lost too soon, a mirror of her own heartache. "But the tragedy deepens, a curse that mercilessly stalks the Sinclair heir. It is a fate far more cruel: a legacy of loneliness that condemns him to a life devoid of a woman's love – not a lover, not a mother, not a sister.

"The Sinclair baroness is destined to lose all her daughters, to bring forth only a son, and ultimately perish in the agonising act of bringing him into this world."

Clara stared at her, blank, stricken. Her mind tried to form sense from the words, but it was like trying to stitch silk with shaking fingers. *Destined. Perish.*

It was not just a tragedy. It was a pattern. A design.

"A curse," Clara whispered.

"Each generation bears this sorrow like a scar," the woman in white continued, her face still shrouded in shadow, "a cursed mark of the Sinclair name. Oh yes, a relentless cycle of loss that feeds upon itself, leaving behind only a man shackled by grief and solitude."

Clara's thoughts splintered.

No daughters. Only sons.

No wives. Only widowers.

The women – gone. Every time. Always the women.

Her eyes darted across the graves again, frantic now. The names swam. The dates bled into each other. The weight of it hit her like stones tumbling from the sky.

Had these women known?

How many had felt the stirrings of life inside them and wondered if it would kill them? How many had prayed for a daughter and buried her within hours? How many had screamed themselves hoarse in childbed, knowing they would not survive the night?

Oh, God.

"What of Evelyn?" Clara whispered, her voice trembling with fear. "What will become of her?"

The wind moved through the cemetery with a hiss, rustling through weeds and bones, like a voice that had run out of words.

"Your mistress is ensnared in the same web, dear Clara. The curse hungers for her, just as it has devoured all Sinclair women before her. If she cannot shatter this cycle, she too will be swallowed by the shadows of Rosehill, lost to the darkness as they were."

Clara wanted to scream. To shake someone! To wake up in her bed with her feet warm and dry and the world back in its proper shape.

But wait… wait.

"How do you know my name?"

The woman in white stilled.

In that moment, the light of the lantern caught her face, peeling away the shadows. The woman's expression softened, and she stepped closer. "I am no ghost, Clara. I am merely a servant of this household – someone who loved Margaret Sinclair deeply. Like a mother to her. I witnessed the heavy price she paid."

Clara stared.

No. No, it couldn't be –

"Mrs Abernathy?

The woman looked up, and in her eyes – oh God, in her eyes –Clara saw it: the recognition, the sorrow, the unbearable truth. Tears shimmered in those tired eyes, catching the lantern's glow, and for one disorienting heartbeat, Clara could not tell if she was speaking to the living or the dead.

The woman sighed, and the spectral veil seemed to lift.

There, before Clara, stood no ghost – only an old woman in a nightgown, her face drawn with grief, and hands shaking beneath the weight of memory.

"Yes," Mrs Abernathy said quietly. "I come here often. To remember all the women who have succumbed to the Sinclair curse. For if I do not remember them, Clara – who will? If I do not speak their names, who will? They deserve to be honoured. To be known. Even in death."

Clara began to shake. The chill of the night felt suddenly different. Not cold, but *hollow*. She wrapped her arms tight around herself, not to stay warm, but to keep from falling apart.

"Margaret Sinclair was like a daughter to me," Mrs Abernathy went on sadly. "I loved her. I watched her suffer, and I was helpless to stop the inevitable. It pains me to see history repeating itself, as it has done for so long."

Tears welled in Clara's eyes. The night no longer pulsed with terror, only grief... deep, staggering grief that reached into her bones and sank its claws in.

She felt a shiver run through her, as if Mrs Abernathy *was* the true haunting of this place: not a ghost, but the echo of so much sorrow left untold. Yes – she knew it now with bone-deep certainty: the most terrifying ghosts were not the dead drifting through walls, but the pain that remained living in the hearts left of those left beneath.

No, grief did not vanish. It settled into the cracks of a house, a name, a person... and Mrs Abernathy stood not just as a witness, but as a keeper of sorrows, a reminder that mourning could haunt more than any phantom.

"You have born this burden alone for so long," Clara murmured.

"Aye." Mrs Abernathy inclined her head with glistening eyes. "But I shall not to let them fade into obscurity. However brief their lives, they mattered. They are part of Master Henry's story, and now part of Miss Evelyn's fate. They must be remembered. They must."

Clara stood in the graveyard, her feet now numb with cold. Her thoughts were splintering now with the weight of what she had seen – or what she believed she had seen. The lantern's glow flickered in the mist like a dying star, and somewhere in the branches above, a bird stirred and fell silent again.

She looked to Mrs Abernathy – no longer ghostly, but solemn and earthbound – and a new thought struck her: *If the ghost was not real... then perhaps the curse is not real either. Oh God... what if the haunting is a lie? A tale passed down to hide something darker?*

What if Miss Evelyn had been right all along?

"What if..." Her voice shook as she gave the thought shape. "What if it is all a fabrication? What if the Sinclairs are not cursed, but simply mad? What if – " she drew in a sharp breath – "what if they are *murdering* their wives and daughters, playing out a tragic farce and calling it fate?"

Mrs Abernathy let out a soft, sad laugh.

"Oh, my dear girl," she said, her voice steeped in ache that went beyond sorrow. "To believe it so would be a mercy... far less terrifying than the truth. Madness and malice are horrors in their own right, but at least they are human. This – " she shook her head, dropping her voice low – "this is not."

Clara's heart sank. Somehow, the thought of murder was easier to digest than the supernatural. She wanted something she could name, confront, rage against. The idea of knives in the night, of poison slipped into wine – that, at least, made sense. But a curse?

"A curse does bind them, Clara," the old cook continued, as though hearing her thoughts. "It holds the Sinclairs tightly. It weaves through their bloodline, wrapping grief around each generation like winding sheets. And the harder they try to escape it, the deeper it burrows in." Mrs Abernathy stepped closer as the lantern quivered in her hand.

225

"The truth," she whispered, "lies in the attic."

"In the attic?" Clara repeated.

"Yes. But heed me, Clara Byrne." The cook's voice dropped lower still. "If you go seeking, do so swiftly. The curse has already begun its work, and it may already be too late to save your mistress from its grasp."

Chapter 29

Evelyn

Evelyn's heart pounded as she stood alone in the attic, the darkness coiling around her like a living entity. Shadows danced in the corners, drawing her ever closer to the painting that seemed to pulse with a life of its own.

Still, as she moved closer, she let out the breath she had been holding. It wasn't her, and yet – God above – it was.

An exquisite figure looked back at her, clothed in Medieval dress of deepest black, as though in eternal mourning. Cascading chestnut curls framed a face that bore an unsettling resemblance to her own... yes, the likeness was uncanny, as though the artist had known her long before she was ever born. The woman's expression was not one of serenity or grace, but grief... power... a terrible knowing. Evelyn recoiled slightly, a chill crawling up her spine; the woman in the painting looked like a witch.

A Cailleach.

Where had she heard that before? She searched her memory as her pulse pounded in her ears, but she could not place the word.

Her thoughts raced, grasping at fragments: a storm, a fire...

Yes – the Baron Alistair Sinclair's story! The woman who roamed these grounds: *Seraphina.* Slowly, slowly, the pieces were connecting.

The figure within the painting – so like herself it made her stomach twist – did not feel like mere coincidence. There was meaning here, some forgotten history hidden beneath the dust.

Evelyn took a slow breath, counting to ten to still the thundering in her heart.

Paintings often bear inscriptions, do they not? A title, a name, a date… There was no signature or flourish of the artists' hand. That in itself felt strange. *Could there be something on the back?*

With trembling hands, she heaved it to the side. The canvas groaned and dusted billowed into the air, but there, nailed to the back, was a scrap of parchment.

Evelyn's breath caught in her throat as she read the name: *Miss Seraphina.* The surname and date were smudged, obscured by time and neglect, but still – that single name pulsed before her like a wound. It was not merely a name now, but a key.

Seraphina.

Evelyn staggered back, her heart racing anew as a wave of nausea washed over her. She spun around, stumbling back against a pile of boxes that wobbled precariously, and then crashed to the floor. She stretched out her hands, seeking something steady to hold, something to grasp onto. Her throat constricted as she realised.

All this time – *all this time* – she had thought herself a bystander.

No – she had not been a mere observer, standing apart from the curse. She had been woven into it, thread by thread, like a figure caught in the heart of a storm. All this time – she herself was ensnared in the fate of Seraphina and the Sinclairs.

"Did I not tell you? You are already a part of this place. You always have been."

That voice, distant yet omnipresent, seemed to hum from all directions, twisting the air around her. The walls of the attic seemed to close around her. She was being watched.

She felt it now – ancient eyes observing her every move. She knew, in her bones, that she was not alone.

Another voice, softer, gentler, seemed to whisper through the oil-painted figure in the grand frame. The painted lips trembled, though no breath passed between them.

"*Run*," the voice breathed, faint but unmistakable. "*Flee before the darkness swallows you whole.*"

Oh, heavens above.

Though she could not say why, Evelyn forced her eyes from the portrait, and there, in the far corner, sat an old man, watching. She opened her mouth to scream, but no sound emerged.

Had he been there all along?

The Baron Alistair Sinclair was seated in a high-backed chair with threadbare fabric, as if it had been his refuge for decades. His face, though lined with age, appeared almost softened by the moonlight.

But no – he was not watching her. He was watching beyond her. His eyes were fixed on the portrait of Seraphina, lost in some distant reverie. Time seemed to stretch, each heartbeat echoing in the stillness.

"Lord Sinclair?" she whispered at long last. "What, in heaven's name, are you doing up here? Why are you here?"

He stirred slowly, like a man roused from a long and troubled sleep. There was a haunting sadness in his eyes – something she could not decipher, but felt in the marrow of her bones.

"I often come here," he said quietly, his voice rough with weariness, as though each word was a weight he had carried for far too long. "To think. To remember."

"Did you hear them? The... voices?"

She could not shake the terrible feeling that he had been sitting there, unseen, as everything unravelled – or perhaps as if he had always been there.

He looked back to the window, where a blade of grey moonlight pierced the grim. He nodded slowly.

"I hear them," he murmured. "At night, most often. Though they come during the day as well, when the house is still. Murmur, whispers, never quite full words... I have become accustomed to it... but they never stop. Never."

He looked at the oil portrait with clouded eyes.

Evelyn's voice shook as she gestured at the painting with trembling fingers. "Who is she?" she demanded. "Is that Seraphina... the Seraphina from your damned stories? Because she – " her breath hitched, "she looks like me. Why does she look like me?"

He hesitated, parting his lips as though to speak, only to falter.

"It is she," he said at last. "Seraphina..." He swallowed hard.

"She was... is... entwined with this place. As much a part of its walls and shadows as the stones themselves. The curse – yes, she bears its mark.. But she is also... connected to you. The likeness you see – it is not happenstance. You are not merely her reflection."

"What do you mean?" Evelyn breathed. "What is *she* to me?"

The baron did not answer at once. He turned his face away, his eyes lost to shadow again.

"Her name is Seraphina Ward," he said at last. "She is... was... your forebear. The blood that courses through your veins... it is the same blood that ran through hers. The very same."

The name hit Evelyn like a physical blow, knocking the breath from her lungs. The room seemed to tilt around her, and for a moment she thought she might be sick.

"Ward?" she gasped. *"Ward?"*

"Yes," the baron said quietly. "I invited you and your family here because I... I hoped." He paused. "I hoped you might be the key to breaking the curse. I hoped – foolishly, perhaps – that something in you, in your blood, might be enough to unpick the sorrow threaded through this house.

"I did not know how, of course. I thought perhaps you and Henry... But no, I never imagined... never dreamed you would look so much like her."

230

"Why didn't you tell me this sooner? Why wait until now? Does Henry know?" Her voice rose, echoing off the attic walls that felt suddenly too close.

"No," he said simply. "Henry does not know."

He hesitated, then added, "I thought... if you remained here long enough, if Henry loved you truly, if the house accepted you, something might change. That you might discover the way to lift the curse without needing to be told." His gaze dropped to the floor. "I never intended... for it to unfold like this."

Evelyn took a deep, unsteady breath. "So you brought me here without knowing *how* I am supposed to help?"

His silence was answer enough.

"Seraphina," she murmured, forcing herself to look back to the portrait. The woman's eyes seemed to pull at her soul. She wanted to look away, but she could not. "I still do not understand. I remember the tale you told by the fire... but this – " She gestured helplessly around the attic. "The voices, the reflection... It is real, and I... I cannot make sense of it." Her voice shook, but she pressed on. "What is happening? Please – *please* – help me to understand."

The baron coughed, a deep, chesty gurgle that echoed in the stillness. "It is difficult," he said, "to determine what is truth and what is fiction, when it comes to Seraphina Ward. The tale has been passed down in fragments... changed, or perhaps misremembered through the centuries. It has become more legend than story, more myth than reality. I cannot say if there was ever true magic, or if the rose is merely a symbol. And the Sinclairs..." He exhaled heavily. "We have always been unreliable narrators."

He settled back into his worn chair, the wood creaking beneath him as he seemed to fold inwards. His gaze turned distant, fixed somewhere beyond the dimly lit attic, as if he were searching for something lost in the recesses of his mind.

When he finally spoke, his voice was heavy. "I was not always like this, you know," he began sadly. "There was a time when I was full of life. I wanted a family... oh yes, sons to hunt with, daughters to twirl." He smiled, though the gesture held no joy. "But the curse... it was always there, lurking in the shadows. I saw what it did to my father. He just... withered away. Not from age, no... emptiness. Loneliness made flesh... it ate him alive. And I swore I would not let it take me as it took him."

Evelyn stood still, his words settling in the pit of her stomach, but she remained silent, waiting for him to continue.

"There was a time," he said, softer now, "when I believed it could still be undone. That love alone – true love – would be the key."

He looked to Evelyn.

"The year was 1785. I was but three-and-twenty, and still young enough to believe I might outpace the curse. Her name was Eliza Merrick. She was... radiant. Unlike anyone I had ever met. She was American, of course – her father a merchant of no consequence in polite society, though he'd made his fortune in shipping. New money, you see, but no title or lineage to speak of... And so, of course, he was determined to see his only daughter well-matched." He gave a brittle laugh. "And I, of course, was the prize. Landed, titled, unmarried... A barony in my name, and no mother or sister to interfere with the arrangement. I That I had not left the estate in over two decades was of no matter. Sir Thomas heard what he wished to hear." He paused, as if the words that followed required permission. "I fell in love with her. Not because she was offered to me, but in spite of it. Oh, she was full of fire. Laughter that rang like music in the stillness of the night. She made me believe I might be more than what this house had made of me. She wanted me to run away with her... to Bath, to London, across the sea, perhaps. Anywhere with sky enough to feel free. I promised her 'soon'... soon."

Evelyn could picture the scene in her mind – two lovers, hidden among the rose bushes, speaking in whispers beneath the stars. Like herself... like Henry. Yet even in her imagination, there was a cold breath on the back of her neck. The ending, she suspected, was not happy.

"I believed she was the one," he continued, his voice growing more distant, as though he were speaking to himself. "I was certain of it. The rose was near bloom. I thought if I declared my love on that night, it would

break the curse. Oh yes – I thought foolishly that love might be enough."
He paused. "But I hesitated. I was young, and although my love for her was
real, I was also a Sinclair… shackled by fear, by duty. I waited too long."

His hands gripped the arms of the chair, knuckles turning white as he
relived the pain of that moment, still raw after so many years. "On the night
of the bloom, I went to meet her, to finally profess my love, to ask her to be
mine." His voice cracked. "But she was not there."

He shook his head slowly. "Her father had secured her a far grander
match. A duke, no less. He was old and widowed, but respectable. And
when I did not run with her, when I chose the manor over freedom, she
chose her future."

Evelyn's heart ached as she listened, understanding all too well the agony
of love lost.

"I found her in chamber, folding dresses into a trunk. She did not weep.
She said, *'If I must marry for duty, I'd sooner wed a duke than a man too frightened to
cross his own threshold.'*" He paused, as if the words still ran in his ears. *"At
least a duke can take me to London,'* she said. *'You won't even take me past the garden
gate.'*

"She left that night, and I never saw her again." He looked up at Evelyn
with haunted eyes. "I returned to the garden alone. The rose bloomed,
brilliant and full of magic. I declared my love to the night, hoping – praying
– that it might still be enough. Of course, the curse remained."

Evelyn watched him sadly. "Why did you not try again?"

His smile was sad and bitter, a shadow of a man. "I tried – with Henry's
mother. Margaret, her name was. I thought… perhaps there might still be a
chance. But it does not work that way, Miss Ward. I had my chance with
Eliza, and I lost her. And the curse… it took Margaret in the end, just as it
has taken so much from our family. I watched her fade day by day – as the
light in her eyes was extinguished. And when our daughter was born still
and silent, it finished its work. It claimed them both."

In the stillness that followed, Evelyn understood the full cruelty of it:
not simply that the Sinclairs were cursed to suffer, but that they were made
to hope first. Perhaps that was why the baron had never told Henry… Yes

– hope, once kindled, was a more exquisite torment than fear. Perhaps in his own twisted way, Lord Sinclair had believed his silence to be a mercy.

"When I first laid eyes on you," the baron continue, "I knew… Oh, you were the very likeness of her. I thought my mind was playing tricks on me… But no – there you stood, as though the painting had made its way down from here.

"It began some years ago, when I happened upon your father's name, Edward Ward, in a published treatise on native English flora… something on the propagation of rose varietals, if memory serves, but the name… it caught at me. I recognised it at once. I appeared in one of the housed in the library. A common enough name, certainly, and yet… something in me would not release the thought. Could it be the same Ward line, the same blood?

"I wrote to your father. It began, as such things often do, as polite correspondence… remarks upon his published observations, shared interest in botanical scholarship. Then over time, our correspondence became more familiar. In truth, I found the letter comforting. But when he mentioned, almost in passing, that he had a daughter – a young lady of marriageable age – I…" He trailed off, ashamed.

"I invited your family here under the guise of hospitality – friendship, even. But in truth, it was an odd chance… a flicker of mad hope I had no right to chase. Madness, perhaps. But the moment you stepped into this house, Miss Ward, I knew…

"I hoped," he said quietly. "Fool that I am… I *still* hope."

Evelyn's mind raced to keep pace. She believed him – all of it: the Sinclair curse, the voices, the haunting legacy of Seraphina Ward, the enchanted rose that held their fate. She struggled to grasp the enormity of it all, the realisation that she was now entwined in a tale that transcended time, one that demanded more from her than she ever anticipated. She was no longer a guest in Rosehill's story, but its continuation.

Then, a faint scratching sound interrupted the silence.

It was a sound Evelyn had grown all too familiar with during her nights at Rosehill Manor, a sound that had burrowed itself deep into her mind. It was the same relentless, gnawing noise – soft, yet persistent, echoing through the walls.

It was closer now, so much closer than she had ever heard it before. The noise scraped against the very bones of the house, reverberating through the warped wooden beams, as though something – or *someone* – was clawing at the heart of the attic, desperate to break free.

"Ignore it," the baron said sharply, his voice low and unnerving.

The baron remained seated, his eyes fixed forwards as if the sound was all too familiar to him, but Evelyn could not dismiss it. She could not turn away.

The scratching grew louder still, relentless and maddening. A cold, creeping dread unfurled within her, winding around her spine, sinking deep into her bones. Her pulse quickened, and her breath came in shallow gasps. Her eyes flicked towards the far end of the attic, where the sound seemed to originate. Beyond the forgotten furniture and dust-choked relics, there was only darkness, but the scratching persisted, growing louder, almost as if it was impatient.

"What is that?" she breathed.

The old lord rose shakily from his chair, yet he made no move towards the sound. "There are matters, Miss Ward, best left undisturbed. Pray, do not seek what, once found, cannot be forgotten."

Still, the scratching persisted.

It clawed at Evelyn's mind, a jagged, insistent sound that rattled her bones and made her heart race. Every fibre of her being screamed for her to turn away, to leave the attic and never return. Yet there was something else – a dark, insidious force, stronger than fear itself, that wormed its way into her thoughts, binding her will. It tugged at her, pulling her forwards, towards the source of that dreadful noise.

She approached a stack of long, coffin-shaped boxes, thick with dust and cloaked in cobwebs. Each box was tightly sealed.

"Do not open them, Miss Ward. I beg of you. You have no idea what lies inside." The baron's words were desperate and pleading, but he did not approach, as though he were afraid.

The sound of the scratching drowned him out, urging Evelyn closer. She knelt by one of the boxes, brushing her fingers against the old, rusted nails that held the lid in place. With a force she barely recognised as her own, she began to pry it open. The wood protested with a sickening screech, nails splintering against the wood.

"Leave it be! Some truths are best left undisturbed!" The baron's voice cracked as he shouted, but his plea was drowned by the creaking of the lid, louder than it should have been.

With one final pull, the lid popped free, sending a groan through the attic. Evelyn peered into the dark, hollow interior of the box. The stench hit her first: a fetid odour that seemed to come from the depths of the earth itself.

Then, in the flickering light, she saw it.

What lay before her *should* have been a skeleton, but the sight defied every natural law. The bones were brittle, yet somehow still animated by a grotesque force. Slowly, they shifted. The hollowed ribcage rose and fell, as though the wretched thing still clung to life, still drew breath.

Eyeballs – still intact – stared back at her from gaping sockets, wide and unblinking, filled with a terror that transcended death. Thin tendrils of decayed muscle clung desperately to the skull, an unnatural grip that held the remnants of what was once human. A silent, hideous groan bubbled from its lipless mouth, but it was not so much a noise as a feeling – a scream so deep and awful it filled her mind, a soundless agony that seemed to gnaw at her very soul.

Its skeletal digits twitched weakly, as if trying to reach for her, to claw its way to her. Its eyes begged, pleaded for mercy, but there was nothing left in them but despair.

Evelyn staggered backwards, a scream frozen in her throat. Pure, unrelenting fear surged through her veins, colder than death itself. Her vision blurred, her skin crawling as the very room seemed to close in around her, suffocating her with the weight of that *thing* in the box.

With an unholy crack, she crashed into the beam behind her. Her head rang with a dull thud, but the horror before her continued.

The baron's voice, cold and hollow, pierced the air behind her, sending fresh shivers crawling up her spine. "I told you not to open it! This is what the curse has done, what it will do – unless it is broken."

The words echoed in the space, distant, as if they came from a time long past. The baron lifted a finger, pointing towards the living nightmare before her. "These were once men, like me. Like Henry."

Evelyn's blood ran cold, her stomach twisting into a sickening knot. His words crashed into her, dawning with horrifying clarity: The curse was not a shadow. It was not even a haunting. It was alive – a living, breathing nightmare that would never let them go.

Chapter 30

Evelyn

Panic surged within Evelyn as she bolted from the attic. The horrific image of the moving skeleton – a thing that defied reason – was burnt into her mind, its ragged breathing and pleading eyes echoing in the darkest corners of her mind. The manor was alive, its very walls groaning, bending in on her like a living creature, conspiring to trap her within its decaying bones.

She stumbled through the winding corridors, the floorboards creaking beneath her as if they, too, were alive – shifting, groaning, reaching for her. Every fleeting shadow seemed to stretch and twitch in the corners of her vision, as though the skeletal creatures were closing in, their hollow eyes following her every move. The walls seemed to hum with a low, guttural whisper, the sound of dry bones scraping against stone, just out of reach, but so close.

Too close.

Her breath came in gasps as she tore down staircase after staircase, each step a race against the nightmare clinging to her heels.

The air itself seemed thick with the scent of decay, and every breath tasted of something foul – like the stench of death, but closer now, wrapping itself around her, tighter and tighter and tighter. The whispers grew louder – darker, more insistent, like slithering tendrils winding into her thoughts. They were chasing her, or perhaps calling her, beckoning her to return to whatever dark fate awaited.

She thought she heard a voice calling out to her, but her terror drowned the sound, rendering it a mere figment of her fraying sanity. She refused to slow down, even as her legs began to buckle with exhaustion.

The grand foyer came into view, its oak doors standing wide like a gateway to freedom, but as she neared, a sudden, sharp crash echoed from behind: a low, sickening scrape – the sound of something dragging across the floor – like skeletal fingers dragging themselves closer, inch by agonising inch. The air seemed to hold its breath, and Evelyn froze, her chest tight with dread. She whipped her head back, expecting to see the creatures crawling towards her – but there was only darkness. Only the smell of rot.

The ball spilled from the grand hall into the night across the lawns, where clusters of guests mingled and carriages lined the backdrop of a night sky heavy with clouds.

Evelyn dashed through the garden, her heart pounding in time with the distant music, her gown billowing behind her like a ghost in the moonlight. Her mind raced – had they followed her? Were they right behind her?

She heard a soft rustle in the bushes, something *scraping* against the stone path, like bones dragging. And then, somewhere – *somewhere* just beyond her reach – came a sound that froze her in place: a soft, mournful whisper, just a breath in the air.

"Come back."

Her pulse roared in her ears, but she kept moving, her mind focused only on escape. She could see the stables ahead, the darkened shape of the doors waiting.

With shaking hands, she wrenched open the door and stepped inside. Even as she stood there, gasping for breath, the darkness seemed to creep in, silence wrapping itself around her like a waiting predator. The scratching... the whispers... the *things* – she could feel them just beyond the door, dragging themselves ever closer.

In a frenzy, she scrambled up onto a tall, dark horse. Its muscles twitched beneath her, as if it, too, sensed the danger closing in. There was no saddle, no comfort – just the raw, quivering beast beneath her, and the fear that gripped her chest. The fabric of her gown caught as she swung herself onto the beast's back, but the surge of adrenaline burnt through her, giving her strength she didn't know she possessed.

With one sharp kick, she urged the creature forwards. As it bolted into the night, rain began to fall.

The wind and rain lashed at her, forcing her to lean into the animal's neck, gripping its dark mane for dear life. She was flying – *fleeing* – but the wind felt like a thousand grasping hands, pulling at her gown, tugging at her very soul.

The hooves beat faster, louder, like a frantic drum, as though the horse knew they were racing not just the storm, but something far worse. The rain came in torrents, soaking through her gown, drenching her to the bone. Each gust of wind sliced through her, cold as death, but she could not stop. She would not stop.

God above, they're behind me.

She could feel them, and the awful clawing reach of the estate, dragging at her spine like crooked fingers. In her mind's eye, she saw the skeletal things, all bone and hollow eyes, crawling, dragging themselves through mud, mouths open in silent screams.

They're coming for me. They want me back.

She thought she heard her name – soft, almost a whisper – carried on the wind like a distant lament, drowned out by the deluge. The manor loomed behind her even from a distance, dark and towering, and despite herself, she glanced back just once.

There, at the gate, stood Henry, drenched by the downpour, breathless and dishevelled, his chest heaving as if he had traversed a thousand storms to reach her. He was a spectral figure against the moonlight, his hair wild and wet against his face, his cravat fluttering loosely at his throat. It was as though he were caught between this world and another, yearning to reach her, yet tethered to the shadows that surrounded him.

"Evelyn!" he called, his voice rising through the storm like a haunting melody, but he remained rooted to the spot, as though bound by invisible chains.

She turned away, unable to bear the sight of him standing there – the embodiment of her longing and heartbreak, a figure suspended in time, forever haunted by the past. And yet, she longed for him to follow, to surge forwards and pull her from the horse, to envelop her in the safety of his arms where the darkness could not reach them.

Evelyn pressed her heels into the horse's flanks, urging it onwards. She rode into the night with no thought of direction, no sense of where the path might lead – only the desperate need to flee. The rain and chill seeped through her gown, and only then did she realise she had not even taken a cloak. She had fled the house bare-armed, breathless, hunted.

Still, as she rode deeper into the night, each raindrop felt like a release, washing away the remnants of her fear. Her thoughts, once a storm of their own, fell silent. In their place came the rhythm of the gallop, the hiss of rain through trees, the wind singing mournfully through the branches – a symphony of flight.

Even as the hooves drummed against the sodden ground, the faces of her father and Charles crept into her mind.

Oh, what would they think?

She had fled without a word, vanished into the storm on horseback like a madwoman. Would they search for her? Wait at the manor's gate until the lanterns burnt low.

For a moment, she faltered. With her father's face came the sweet ache of belonging. His voice, so kind, so calm, seemed to whisper though the wind: *Let us return to London. Let all this be forgotten.*

It tugged at her, that voice, with the promise of safety, of sense, of things that could be named and measured. The notion of returning – of finding Clara, of falling into her father's names, of bringing Charles a sweet treat from the ball – suddenly felt like a distant, fragile thread, and oh, how she longed to seize it.

Her grip slackened on the horse's mane. The beast, sensing her hesitation, began to slow – but before her resolve could settle, the storm surged.

A flash of lightning illuminated the night sky, striking a nearby tree with a deafening crack that echoed through the stillness. The heavens seemed to tear apart, and the thunder that followed was not a sound – it was a violent shock that reverberated through her bones.

Time seemed to fracture.

Her horse reared, its hooves striking the rain-slicked ground, and for the briefest instant, Evelyn thought she saw something in the flicker of lightning: a shadow, stretching unnaturally long, crossing the path ahead of her.

She felt herself lifted from reality, suspended in that moment, limbs flailing in a cold dance with gravity. In an agonising breath, she tumbled through the air, an ephemeral figure caught between earth and sky, before the ground rushed up to meet her.

The world spun wildly as she landed with a muted thud in the mud. Dazed and disoriented, she struggled to sit up, but the chill seeped deep into her bones, numbing her limbs and clouding her thoughts.

She lay there unmoving as the rain poured down upon her, time slipping away like a dream. The world felt distant and surreal, as though she were suspended between two realms – one of reality and one of nightmares.

She could not say how long she lay like that, adrift in the cold and dark, but through the haze, she felt arms – strong, steady, and achingly familiar. They enveloped her, lifting her gently from the sodden earth. There was a terribly familiar scent: a mixture of damp wool, warm skin and heartbreaking comfort.

Her heart knew it before her mind could speak: *Father.*

Chapter 31

Henry

Henry had watched as Evelyn disappeared into the storm, swallowed by wind and rain before he could reach her. He had called out – once, twice – but the howl of the tempest drowned his voice.

He barely registered the flurry of guests and carriages spilling from the grand hall. The laughter, the music – it all blurred into a meaningless din beneath the roaring in his ears.

Evelyn.

When he reached the stables, his chest was burning and his lungs raw. She was mounting one of the horses, God help him – the animal skittish beneath her, stamping its hooves on the hay-strewn floor. She moved with a fear that sent a stab of dread through Henry's chest.

"Evelyn!" he shouted, her name a desperate prayer against the gale. It was no use. His voice was pulled apart by the restless hooves and rising wind, and she did not turn.

She did not even falter.

The moonlight glinted off her rain-dampened gown, the fabric billowing like a ghostly veil as she urged the horse forwards.

Henry ran, his boots sinking into the sodden ground as he pursued her, his clothes sticking to his skin, his hair wild from the downpour. He was relentless, his legs carrying him as fast as they could over the uneven earth, but Evelyn was faster, her silhouette shrinking in the distance as the horse galloped away.

Just as Henry reached the estate gate, an invisible force slammed into him, crushing the breath from his lungs. He staggered, clawing at his chest as the curse unfurled itself, a living, writhing thing. Tendrils of darkness slithered up his arms and legs, pulling him back, coiling tighter with each frantic movement. He thrashed against the spectral bonds, trembling as he fought against the creeping paralysis. The shadows tightened, their grip icy and searing all at once.

"You cannot save her."

"Evelyn!" he cried out again, as she disappeared into the inky blackness. The storm clouds blotted out the moonlight, as if the heavens themselves conspired to swallow her whole.

The force tightened around him, dragging him back another step. His knees buckled, the ground beneath him slick and yielding.

"Do you feel it, Henry? The weight of your sins? Your family's sins? This is your inheritance. This is your fate. This estate is your tomb."

Rain lashed against his skin, and his clothes clung to him like chains. He stood motionless with shallow breath.

"Turn back, Henry. You cannot save her."

For a single, shattering heartbeat, he wavered. His shoulders slumped, his fists slackened. Evelyn was gone, devoured by the storm. The curse had won.

Then he turned sharply on his heel, the manor rising before him like a beast silhouetted against the storm. Its windows flickered with a trembling glow, like the last breath of a dying soul. The curse loosened its grip, its tendrils unwinding from his chest as he began to run back towards Rosehill Manor.

"Damn you!" Henry's voice tore through the night, raw and broken. "Damn this!"

His wet clothes clung to his skin, rain blurring his vision, but he sprinted forwards, the curse's taunts echoing in his mind.

He had to find Evelyn's father. He had to find a way to bring her back before it was too late.

He could not lose the woman he loved.

∞∞∞

Henry's stood at the estate's entrance, drenched to the bone, rain slicing down in unrelenting torrents. The storm seemed to mourn with him, the heavens wailing their grief into the night.

His eyes strained against the darkness beyond. Where were they? Had Mr Ward reached her? Had he even known where to look?

The minutes dragged on, stretched to agony. Henry could hardly breathe around the fear.

What if she had fallen? What if the horse threw her – what if her skull had cracked open on the rocks, and she was lying broken in the mud with twisted limbs and eyes wide and glassy? What if she was out there still, soaked and lifeless, waiting to be found only by the crows?

And then, through the thick curtain of rain, a figure appeared. At first, it was little more than a shadow against the storm, staggering towards him.

Please, he thought. *Please, let it be her. Let her be alive.*

Henry's breath hitched as lightning forked across the sky, illuminating Mr Ward, soaked and staggering, cradling his daughter's limp body in his arms.

Evelyn.

Another bolt of lightning tore across the heavens, casting the scene in a stark, ghostly light. For a heartbeat, Henry thought she looked more like a phantom than flesh and blood. Her skin was deathly pale, her hair slicked to her face, her gown clinging to her like a burial shroud. For a terrible moment, he could not tell if she was breathing.

"She is dead, Henry."

The words came from nowhere and everywhere: whispered from the walls, murmured by the ground, beaten into his skull with every drop of rain.

"She is dead because of you. Broken because of you. You brought this upon her."

Henry staggered beneath the weight of it, as though the sky itself sought to drive him to his knees. The voice reverberated through the storm, seeping into his bones, lodging behind his ribs.

"You cannot deny it," the curse crooned. *"She lies cold because of you. This is your burden, Henry – your punishment."*

"No," he breathed, but the word cracked.

"Yes," the manor hissed, the syllable dragging like a claw through his chest. *"Your family doomed her the moment you let her step foot on these grounds. You let her go. You let her die."*

He wanted to run – to tear her from the storm, to feel the warmth of her skin and prove the lie wrong – but his legs refused him. He stood paralysed, soaked, trembling, his mouth forming her name again and again. *Evelyn. Evelyn.*

His breath came in ragged gasps as Mr Ward reached him, the storm battering them from every side.

Please, he thought. *Let her open her eyes. Let her breathe. Let her speak.*

"Give her to me," Henry rasped. His hands trembled, his heart screaming in denial even as the curse's words gnawed at the softest part of his soul.

"You will never escape me, Henry. Even now, you clutch at hope, but it will slip through your fingers like sand."

Mr Ward hesitated, tightening his arms around his daughter as though afraid to let her go. The wind howled between them, and for one harrowing moment, Henry thought he would be refused. But then – slowly, with a look of hollowed-out grief – Mr Ward stepped forwards and placed her into Henry's arms.

She felt so cold, so fragile in his arms – God, so light, as if her very soul had slipped away. Henry gathered her close, cradling her against his chest, the cold rain mixing with the warmth of his tears.

"This is your doing, Henry. Your family's sins demand their price, and tonight, they claimed her."

248

He stumbled towards the manor. The guests from the ball stood frozen in the courtyard, huddled beneath umbrellas and coats. There was no laughter, but their whispers carried through the storm as they witnessed the future baron carrying a woman like a fallen angel through the night.

"Is that the Ward girl?"

"He's carrying her – my God, is she dead?"

"She rode into the storm! Alone – madness."

Henry heard none of it. Their voices and eyes meant nothing. He felt only the chill of her skin and the brush of her soaked hair against his wrist.

Doctor!" Henry's voice cut through the downpour, raw and thunderous. "Someone fetch the physician, now!"

It rang across the courtyard, reverberating off the cold stone walls of the manor, silencing what little breath remained among the guests. It was no longer a plea, but a command a storm within the storm.

"She is gone, Henry. She will not wake. And you will live with this forever."

"Servants!" he roared. "Bring the physician!"

Henry carried Evelyn up the grand staircase, his muscles taut with the effort of controlling his fear. Her head lolled against his chest, her skin ghostly pale, her breath barely there. He could feel the weight of the curse crawling along his skin, urging him to stop, to give in. That he would never reach the top of the stairs. That she would die before he could even place her in a bed.

No – he would not yield, not while she lay in his arms, not while breath still lived in him If he must drag her back from death with the last thread of his soul, he would.

At her chambers, he laid her gently upon the bed, her rain-soaked gown leeching chill into his fingers. He lingered there, shaking, unwilling to let her go even now.

"Maid!" he called out, his voice breaking. He pressed his palm to her cheek, brushing back the sodden strands of hair that clung to her brow. Her skin was like marble – too pale, too still. "Miss Clara!"

Clara burst through the door, soaked to the bone as though she, too, had battled the storm alongside her mistress. Her eyes widened in terror, her hands flying to her mouth in a stifled sob.

"Miss Evelyn – oh, sweet saints," she breathed, stumbling to the bedside. "What's happened? What's happened?"

Mr Ward followed closely behind, his face hollowed by grief, though he clung to what little composure he had left. He knelt at his daughter's side and bowed his head, pressing his lips to her temple.

"Evelyn, darling," he whispered. "My clever girl. My brave girl. You must wake now."

"She will not wake. You did this, Henry. You could not protect her. She is beyond saving now, and you will carry this burden for as long as you live."

From the shadowed corner, a black cat emerged, moving with liquid grace as if conjured by the storm itself. It leapt onto the bed without a sound, curling beside Evelyn as though it had always belonged to her, and perhaps it had. Its green eyes, sharp as shattered glass, locked onto Henry's, and the air turned heavy. The cat hissed, a low ghostly sound that cut through the stillness like a knife.

A commotion stirred at the door as the physician burst into the room, summoned from among the guests.

"Clear space, if you please," he said briskly. "Miss – maid, fetch blankets. We must warm her."

Henry moved to stand at the doorway as the physician attended to Evelyn, with her father and Clara nearby. His eyes never left her, and though the storm raged outside, the world had narrowed to this room, to the fragile figure lying so still upon the bed.

As Henry stood there, watching the fragile rise and fall of Evelyn's chest, a truth settled into him like breath returning to a drowned man: she was alive. Not whole, not well, but still alive.

The curse still pressed against him, but there was something in the room held the darkness at bay: perhaps her father's touch, her maid's devotion, or the cat's unblinking vigil.

Henry's heart ached with the force of it all.

She was alive – and as long as she drew breath, there was hope. Even if it was only a flicker, it was enough.

He would not leave – could not – leave her side until he knew she was safe.

Chapter 32

Evelyn

Evelyn's eyes fluttered open to the dim, wavering glow of candlelight casting soft shadows across the chamber. Her body felt leaden, aching with chills that seemed to sink deep into her bones. The air carried the faint scent of herbs, and Shadow slept peacefully beside her.

She turned her head, slow and stiff, and found her father seated to her other side, his face etched with lines of concern. He brushed damp strands of hair from her brow, his touch gentle, but she felt no comfort in it – not here, not in this cursed place.

"My sweet child," he murmured, "It has been three days. The fever has broken, I believe, but you must rest."

He held a small cup of steaming liquid to her lips. The warmth of it spread through her, though the chill within her would not relent. It soothed her parched throat, but not the growing dread that twisted her insides. The storm, the lightning, the howling wind – all of it rushed back in a cruel flood, each memory more suffocating than the last. She shivered, not from the cold, but from the shadows that still clung to her.

Her father's gaze softened as he noticed her trembling. He took her hand, and she flinched at the touch.

"Evelyn, my darling girl," he said softly. "What could have driven you to such a thing? Out into the storm, alone... What frightened you so badly that you would risk your life to escape it?"

How could she explain the fear that had no name, no shape? She could scarcely bring herself to speak of the dread that had settled deep inside her, but the gentle insistence in her father's eyes bade her to continue.

"There is an evil within this manor, Father," she croaked. "Something I dare not speak of. I feared I should leave at once, with no thought for you, nor for Charles, nor for Clara," her voice broke.

He felt her forehead, as if wondering if she was still feverish.

"You're still old as ice." He said nothing for a long while, and Evelyn wondered if he understood at all – or if, like her, he feared the truth might shatter them both.

When he spoke, his voice was low, almost a whisper. "Evelyn dear, listen to me. You've been through a terrible shock – I see it in your eyes. But I need to understand: what evil do you mean?"

When she opened her mouth but no words came, he continued gently, "Is it the kind that wears a human face? Has someone harmed you? Tell me truly, and I shall take you from here this very instant."

She shook her head quickly.

"You should know," he began, his words carefully chosen, "Mr Sinclair sat at your door each night, waiting for you to awaken. He was afraid, my dear. Though he said nothing, I sensed it in him. A fear as deep as your own."

"Afraid?" she whispered. "Afraid of what?"

"I cannot tell," he said softly. "Was that young man terrified to lose you... or terrified you might wake?"

Evelyn struggled upright, clutching at her father's hand. "No, Father – it is not as you fear. He has wounded my heart, yes... but not my body. Never that. I am not afraid of Henry Sinclair."

Her father regarded her for a long moment and then nodded solemnly, though she was not sure he was convinced.

"I know his heart, father. It is not he that frightened me, but what lies within this house. There is a darkness here. Something far older than Henry. It is a shadow he did not summon but must bear all the same."

There was a soft knock at the door, and Evelyn's heart fluttered painfully in her chest. She turned her head towards the doorway, where Henry stood, framed in the dim light of the hall. He appeared much more weary, so much older, than when she had last seen him. The curse had left its cruel mark upon him, etching deep lines around his eyes, adding strands of silver at his temples – an aging that had nothing to do with time. Despite the change, however, he remained undeniably striking, a presence that filled the room in ways she could not explain. She felt her pulse quicken as he stepped into the room, but she knew – foolishly, perhaps – that she must appear a sorry sight after three days of illness.

With a warning look at Henry, her father quietly retreated to the far side of the room, busying himself with preparing more herbal remedies, granting Henry permission to approach.

He crossed the threshold swiftly and settled at her bedside.

"Do I look a fright?" she whispered through cracked lips. The question escaped before she could catch it – absurd and vain, perhaps, and yet, it mattered to her... or rather, he mattered. She needed to see what lived in his eyes when he looked at her now.

Henry shook his head and his eyes – those eyes that seemed to see more than anyone else could – held her in their depths. He did not flinch at her appearance, but saw her as she was – afraid, bruised and half-lost, but still did not look away.

"You are pale, I suppose," he murmured with a flicker of humour, though his eyes were pained. "But even so... you possess a beauty that cannot be dimmed."

His words reached her like a lifeline, and she clung to them, despite the gnawing fear that still churned within her. He tried to smile, but then it faltered. His voice dropped to a whisper.

"The baron – I confronted him and pressed for the truth. He told me everything. About our... ancestors... in the attic. Their affliction. Of

255

Seraphina Ward. That she is your blood. Why he invited you and your family here."

Evelyn nodded slowly, a dull throb echoing in her temple. "Would you... might I trouble you for some water?" she asked feebly. The words, weak as they were, felt like a fragile bridge between them – a moment of normalcy in a world that had fallen apart.

Henry's expression softened as he quickly retrieved a glass from the bedside table. His fingers brushed against hers as he held the glass to her lips, tilting it just enough for her to drink. The cool liquid soothed her dry throat, and she sighed with relief. He pulled the glass away and looked at her with an intensity that made her feel as if he could see straight through her, past the fear and the illness, to the heart of her.

"I am glad you spoke with your father," she murmured. "I did not want to explain why I fled in fear that night, nor see the look upon your face when I did."

"You owe me no explanation, Evelyn. Fear has a way of stealing reason – I do not fault you for it. What matters now is that you are returned to us... safe."

"Am I?" she whispered. "Safe? I have seen what lives within these cursed walls – if such a thing could be called living at all. The curse remains unbroken, and I fear I am now as entrapped as you are.

"I believe it now," she confessed. She wanted to look away, but she could not. "All of it. I see it clear as day, and I am sorry – so very sorry – for having doubted you before. For thinking you mad, or tormented by fancies." She gave a hollow laugh. "Or perhaps I am now as mad as you are."

Henry's hand found hers, warm and strong against her trembling fingers. He brushed him thumb across her knuckles. "I do not hold it against you, truly," he said. "There have been countless nights when I wished it were all mere madness, some fever of the mind or tale dreamt up in the dark." His expression grew sombre. "But no delusions could conjure the horrors that truly dwell within these walls. Nor the true fate which awaits me. I suspected, but I did not know."

His expression darkened, grief drawing new lines beneath his eyes. "I am sorry – more than words can express – that my father ever summoned you here. I would never wish for you – for anyone – to carry the weight of this curse, nor the expectation that you might be our saviour. This is my curse to bear. I fear I have entangled you regardless.

"Evelyn – you must know – there is nothing between Lady Ravenwood and I. Nothing. What you witnessed that night – "

"It matters not," she interrupted.

"It does," he insisted. "I know that what you uncovered in the attic eclipses all else, and rightly so… but it matters to me that you know the truth of what passed between us – or rather, what did not. Lady Ravenwood sought to tempt me, to ensnare me into a marriage of convenience, but my affections were never hers to claim." He looked at her with a long, searching look. "My heart has always, irrevocably, belonged to you."

He exhaled shakily. "When I pushed you away, it was not out of indifference, but in a foolish attempt to protect you from the curse. It was fear… fear that I might bring ruin upon the only light that has ever dared shine into this darkness."

The rawness of his admission struck Evelyn like a blow, and for a moment, she was unable to speak. She squeezed his hand, as if to anchor herself to the present, to the man whose truth now lay bare before her.

She supposed she had always known, in fleeting moments – those times when his eyes lingered just a second too long, or his voice softened to a hush when he spoke her name. She had loved him before – perhaps even from the first, though she had never dared admit it to herself – but now, as the fear and darkness of the manor closed in on her, she understood the depth of it. She loved him with a desperation that was both her salvation and her damnation. She could not leave now, not even if she wanted to.

The fear that had devoured her now felt small, dwarfed by another, fiercer urgency: the need to remain beside him, to face the gathering dark by his side. She did not know what lay ahead, only that she would not abandon him to meet it alone. Perhaps, too, she needed to prove to herself that she was no longer the frightened girl who fled into the storm, but a woman capable of choosing her fate, even when that fate was bound to his.

Still, even as his confession wrapped around her, a memory stirred... The rose, the petals... They had once seemed like symbols, but if the curse was real – truly real – then so too was the flower's terrible promise: a reckoning measured in falling petals.

"How many petals remain on the rose?" she whispered, as if afraid the question itself might summon the end.

Henry exhaled slowly. "I cannot say with any great certainty. I have kept watch by your side, day and night, unwilling to leave you, even for a moment. I thought it of little consequence. But now..." He paused, dropping his eyes to their entwined hands. "Now I see it for what it is. The last petal will fall no matter how we fight against it. The curse... it cannot be undone."

Evelyn's chest tightened at his words. She pushed herself further upright, wincing as she did so. "No. We must go to the rose at once, Henry. Whether it saves us or damns us, we must face it."

He made to protest, but she shook her head. "We must try."

"Evelyn, you are still weak," he said, looking stricken. "You are trembling with the mere effort of sitting upright. No. You are in no condition to – "

"Henry." She fixed her eyes on his, a silent plea in them that spoke of everything she could not put into words. "I shall stand in the secret garden in a quarter of an hour. You may choose to meet me there, or not – but I will go. If I must stand there alone, then so be it. The choice is yours." The tone in her voice brooked no argument, and for a moment, she saw a flicker of admiration in his eyes, even as worry pulled at the corners of his mouth. He opened his mouth, but she had already turned her head towards her father.

"Father," she called, forcing her voice to steady, "pray send for Miss Clara. I shall require her assistance to dress."

Her father frowned, but with a look at Henry, he relented, nodding once before departing the room to find her lady's maid.

As Henry stood to follow, he hesitated at the threshold, turning back to her with an intensity that stole her breath.

"You are everything to me," he said, his voice a husky whisper that sent a shiver down her spine. "You are the pulse within my veins, Evelyn. The breath in my lungs, the beat of my heart." He was leaning against the doorframe, gripping the wood until his knuckles turned white. "Even the stars could not tempt me from your side, for they hold no light compared to you. But I am afraid," he admitted. "Not of death, nor of the curse, but of what this love may bring upon you. I would endure every torment tenfold to spare you a single moment's pain. Yet I fear I may be the very thing that brings it."

260

Chapter 33

Alistair

The clock in Alistair's study ticked on like a mockery of his dwindling time. On and on it went, an eternal metronome that did not chime, but condemn. How long until he, too, became a living skeleton, more part of the manor than man, a hollow shell bound to the walls of this accursed place? His thoughts spiralled – too fast, too tight – and his mind wandered once more to the attic, that damned place from whence Miss Evelyn Ward had fled in horror. The image tormented him: her wide, pleading eyes, filled with terror, her hands clutching her gown as though fabric alone might shield her from the curse. The memory pierced him deeper than any blade and left an an ache in his soul that would not cease.

He had brought the girl here – lured her into the jaws of an ancient evil, believing, naïvely, that she could break the family's chain of despair. Fool that he was! He had freed no one. He had only drawn her down with them into the mire.

"Forgive me, my dear Evelyn," he murmured, his voice breaking under the weight of his own guilt. "I had hoped to protect you."

His words rang hollow, a bitter echo swallowed by the silence, lost in the endless ticking of the clock. How could she forgive him, when he had condemned her?

He had failed her. The curse, deep as the earth, would drag her into its maw. She would perish, giving birth to the next doomed heir, as had all those before her.

And Henry... Henry would inherit this curse, this eternal cycle of death and despair. The thought churned in his stomach, thick as poison.

"What have I done?" The words slipped from his lips, raw and desperate. He was trapped, as surely as they were. Neither Evelyn nor Henry could escape it now. He had only brought them closer to the precipice, to the doom that awaited them. And the walls – *the walls* – they seemed to close in around him, whispering in voices that were not his own.

It started softly, barely a murmur, but it grew.

"You have failed them. You have failed her." The voices clawed at his thoughts, hissing from the shadows, from the walls themselves, their words curling like smoke into his ears. *"She is doomed. They are all doomed."*

Alistair's breath came fast and shallow. He could not escape them, not even in this room, not even in his solitude. The chill of despair wrapped around him, cold as the grave, tightening like a noose around his throat.

"The curse is within you. You are the curse."

His fingers twitched around the knife in his hand.

What if... What if he plunged it into his heart? Would the endless ache of his guilt stop? Would the voices cease, would the walls fall silent? What if he slid the blade across his throat and let the warm blood spill out, staining the cursed wood beneath him?

He lifted the knife, feeling the weight of it in his hand.

Would he perish? Or would the blood, thick as poison, merely mark the beginning of a slower end? Would his body crumple in silence, or would his heart stutter on, stubborn and grotesque, forcing breath through a throat already torn open?

Perhaps death was the only escape. Perhaps it was the only way to break the chain.

"*Yes, yes. Do it. Free yourself. Free them.*"

Alistair's breath quickened as he rose to his feet.

"*Yes, spare them this suffering. Do what your father could not. Do what every cursed heir before you were too weak to do.*"

He raised the knife, pressing its edge against his chest. The cold steel bit into his skin as he braced himself.

"Forgive me, Evelyn," he whispered, his voice shaking. "Forgive me, Henry."

And then he drove the blade in.

The pain was immediate, white-hot, radiating through his body as his knees buckled. He collapsed to the floor, his cane clattering away. Blood seeped through his shirt, warm and sticky, pooling around him as his vision blurred. His breath came in ragged gasps, and for a fleeting moment, he thought he might finally be free.

But then, the whispers laughed. A cruel, rasping sound that echoed through the room, rising and falling like a grotesque hymn. "*You cannot escape us. Did you think death would free you?*"

Alistair's body convulsed, his vision clearing as the pain began to recede. He looked down in horror, expecting to see his lifeblood spilling onto the floor – but the wound was gone. The knife lay beside him, its blade slick with blood, yet his chest bore no mark, no scar, no sign of the mortal act he had just committed.

"*You are ours,*" the voices hissed. "*You cannot die, foolish man. You will live, and you will watch them suffer. That is your curse.*"

"No," he rasped. "No, this cannot be. This is not – "

"*It is,*" the voices whispered, deep and resonant now, layered like the tolling of ancient bells. "*You cannot end what binds you. You are the blood of this house, and this house is eternal. You will live, Alistair – long after your bones have crumbled into dust.*"

He clawed at his chest, desperate to find the wound, to feel the mark of his attempt. There was nothing but wrinkled skin. The blood pooling beneath him seemed to seep into the floorboards, vanishing like water into parched earth. The manor devoured it, as it devoured all things.

"You will not escape us. When your time comes — and it will come — you will not leave this earth. Your body will be entombed here, within these walls, where you belong. The manor is your grave, and you will never leave it."

His limbs felt leaden as he pushed himself upright, clawing his way back into the chair behind his desk. His hands shook violently as he reached for the bloodied knife. He stared at it, the edge glinting in the dim light, before sliding it into the drawer.

The knife thudded softly as it hit the wood, and Alistair slammed the drawer shut. His chest heaved as he leant back in the chair, letting his head fall against the worn leather. The ticking of the clock filled the room once more, steady and unrelenting, like a heartbeat that was not his own.

A knock at the door shattered the silence. He stared at the heavy oak. His heart raced, and for a moment, he wondered if the knock itself was a manifestation of the curse, an unwelcome visitor from beyond the veil.

"Who dares disturb me at this hour?"

The door creaked open, revealing Mr Ward and Evelyn's young lady's maid, both pale.

"Edmund?" Alistair croaked. "What brings you to my door so late?" But the question died in his throat, for even as he spoke, the walls whispered again, louder this time. *"It is too late for them... Too late for all of you..."*

"I am most gravely concerned for my daughter," Mr Ward said. "She has awoken, thank Providence, yet she is deeply unsettled after the events of the night she fell ill. I had hoped you might – "

Alistair barely heard him. The voices murmured faintly, mocking him from the edges of his consciousness. *"It will never end."*

"Unsettled?" he rasped. "No, no. It is far graver than that. I have placed her in untenable danger. This cursed bloodline – " He stopped himself, swallowing hard. "She has borne witness to horrors no soul ought ever endure."

Evelyn's maid shifted and stepped closer, wringing her hands. "My lady... she has gone into the gardens." She glanced at Mr Ward. "We believe Mr Sinclair followed her. We have already searched the grounds, sir, but they are nowhere to be found."

"If what my daughter told me is true… there is something unnatural afoot," Mr Ward said grimly. "We must find them at once, before it is too late."

Alistair sighed, for he already knew. A cold resignation washed over him, pressing down until he could hardly breathe.

"I know where they've gone," he said. With a slow movement, he rose from his chair and leant heavily on his cane.

"It is already too late," he murmured, more to himself than to anyone else. "Come."

Chapter 34

Evelyn

The secret garden unfurled under the pallid gaze of the moon. Once a haven, the garden now felt taut with dread, as though the very air strained against some unseen force. The wind whispered through the leaves, a sound too close to sighs for comfort.

Evelyn's breath came shallow. Each step was a struggle, her legs unsteady beneath her, yet she pressed on with one hand braced against the stone wall for balance. Her body ached and her vision swam, but the pull of the rose was stronger than pain, stronger than fear. It called to her, and she would follow, even if she had to crawl.

Ahead, beneath the gnarled boughs of an ancient tree, Henry stood – a spectre of grief etched into the night. Moonlight carved hollows into his face, deepening the years he had no right to bear. The beauty of his anguish was almost unbearable, a portrait of ruin that stirred something profound within her.

"Evelyn," he murmured, his voice thin, like a thread unravelling in the stillness. He stepped forwards. "It is too late."

Her chest tightened, and her vision blurred as fatigue clawed at her. Yet she squared her shoulders, forcing her faltering body to stand firm.

"No," she said, the defiance in her voice sharper than her fragile frame betrayed. "Do not say so. It cannot be too late... not when we are so close."

As Evelyn reached the rosebush, a sharp chill sliced through her, stealing the breath from her lungs. Where once the rose had bloomed in crimson splendour, deep as blood, there now remained only a gnarled, lifeless stem. Its leaves, once lush and green, curled inwards like clenched fists, browned and brittle with decay. At its base, the last petal lay in the soil, ghostly pale, so thin it might dissolve in the wind.

No. No, this cannot be the end. Her heart thundered, drowning all else. *Please — whatever force governs this place, whatever power still listens — I am not ready to lose him.*

With shaking limbs and a desperate cry blooming in her heart, she turned to Henry and bridged the distance between them.

She pressed her lips to his, pouring every ounce of emotion into that kiss. It was a kiss of forgiveness, of confession, of yearning, and of a promise that transcended the curse itself – a promise that, despite the darkness closing in around them, she would not let go.

He returned it fiercely, and then he drew away with a guttural groan, a sound that seemed to reverberate from the depths of his soul.

When Evelyn opened her eyes, his face etched with anguish.

"It is too late," he repeated. "The curse cannot be broken. If it could, it would have lifted for my father – for us now. You must leave this place, Evelyn. The curse will not release me, but I cannot – will not – let it take you, too."

Evelyn's chest constricted, her breath coming in shallow gasps as Henry's words settled over her. The weight of his despair threatened to pull her under, yet, unexpectedly, a soft, almost bitter laugh escaped her lips. It sounded foreign, even to her ears – a fractured thing born of grief and defiance.

"It matters no longer, Henry," she began quietly, and then, as if the dam within her had broken, the words spilled forth with growing fervour. "The curse... the rose... this accursed place... none of it matters anymore. It is all shadows and smoke when weighed against what I feel for you. They are hollow things, meaningless things, when set beside the truth that lives in my heart."

She hesitated, twisting her fingers together before she clasped them tightly. Her eyes flicked towards the garden's edge where a movement caught her attention.

From the depths of the gloom, Shadow emerged. The cat moved with the grace of something not entirely of this world, gliding through the underbrush.

Turning back to Henry, Evelyn's voice dropped. "I never sought this," she confessed. "I did not dream of love, nor for the bonds of marriage. I fancied myself beyond such things... I believed I could outrun it, bury it beneath ambitions, dreams, anything that was wholly my own. But the truth, it seems, is no respecter of such notions, Henry. It burns within me like a fever... And it has brought me here, to you." She locked her eyes on his. "No, I never wanted to fall in love. I fought it – I scorned it – I tried with all my strength to resist it, but it claimed me nonetheless. And now, here I stand, loving you all the same, Henry Sinclair. Even if it damns me."

Above them, the night seemed to hold its breath, and in the shadows, Shadow paused, tail flicking once as if to acknowledge her words.

"I love you in ways that defy sense, in ways that terrify me to my very core. It is a darkness I cannot escape, a fear greater than the shadows in this house or the curse that binds us. But it is mine, Henry – it is ours. And I will not deny it." She searched his eyes, pleading for understanding, for him to see the truth of her heart. "Whatever fate awaits us, whatever darkness lies ahead, I choose *you*."

Henry's eyes brimmed with unshed tears that caught the moonlight like fractured glass. A shudder coursed through him, and his voice broke as he spoke. "Do not love me, Evelyn Ward. Do not speak those words." There was a rawness in his tone, a desperation that bordered on agony. "I cannot bear it. What future could we possess, when mine is already forfeit? The thought of you sacrificing everything for me... it is unthinkable. I would age before your eyes – I am aging before you now!"

Evelyn reached out to him, but he recoiled as if her touch might sear his flesh. An anguished groan escaped him, and he pressed his hands to his forehead, curling his fingers into his hair as if to claw away the torment.

"I cannot leave this place, Evelyn," he groaned. "You must understand – I do not speak in riddles or poetic tragedies. This is the plain and bitter reality. That night you fled, I *tried*... I tried to follow, but I was powerless. Something unseen, unyielding, holds me here. I am bound, Evelyn. Bound to these cursed grounds as surely as if chains dragged at my very soul.

"If you remained, you would be bound as well. Not as a guest, but as my wife – still young and lovely – condemned to this endless decay. You would bear witness to my ruin, Evelyn – to the day when I am no longer a man, but something grotesque, twisted by time and torment. Worse still, you would hear me, one day, long after sense had fled. The scratching... it would haunt your nights, invade your sleep. The sound of *my* nails upon the walls, as I clawed not for freedom, but for you... clawing at the walls of your sanity, a nightmare that would never release you."

Evelyn reached out to him once more and cupped his face, intertwining her fingers with his. Her breath hitched as she searched his storm-filled eyes.

"Do you not see, Henry?" she whispered, her voice catching on a sob. "Are you not listening? I understand now – I see it clearly. I would relinquish all else. Not for marriage, not for duty or expectation, but for *love*. For *you*. Even if this place were to become my prison, if the world beyond were to forget my name, it would not matter. If I could hold your face in my hands each night, if I could whisper your name before sleep takes me, that alone would be enough. That would be enough for me, Henry Sinclair."

For a moment, he seemed to lean into her words, into her touch, as though she might pull him from the abyss, before he clenched his jaw once more.

"You do not understand, Evelyn. There is more I have not yet confessed."

Her hands stilled, but she held his gaze as he continued.

"I believe – though I cannot prove it – that it was not merely my birth, but the curse itself that claimed my mother's life. As it claimed every baroness before her. And if... if you were ever to carry my child..." He faltered, anguish rising in his throat. "I fear it would take you too."

Evelyn did not recoil. Her grip on him only tightened, and she dropped her voice to a fierce whisper. "Then I shall never bear a child, if that is what you fear. It matters not to me, Henry. My life, my soul – my love – are yours. Wholly and without condition."

As her words settled into the air, Henry crumbled before her. He fell to his knees, like a wounded soldier, as a man broken – an offering of surrender in the face of a love too consuming to resist. His body shook with ragged breaths.

Without hesitation, Evelyn cradled his head against her stomach, weaving her hands through the dark strands of his hair.

"I love you, Evelyn," he murmured against the fabric of her dress, his voice raw and torn. "I love you. More than life. More than death. More than any salvation I might once have hoped for."

He rested there in the sanctuary of her arms. His words clung to the stillness, as if the night itself had quieted to hear them, listening, waiting for them to fade into the shadows. Still, the words did not fade. They remained, echoing in the space between heartbeats, until Henry lifted himself from her embrace, like a man risen from the dead.

As he stood, his hands found her face. He cupped her cheek tenderly with one hand, the other threading roughly into her hair, drawing her closer until their foreheads nearly touched, their breaths mingling – warm, frantic, as though they were both starved for air.

"From the very first moment I laid eyes upon you," he said, his voice low and urgent, "I knew. I knew there could be no other. I have fought this, Evelyn. Fought against it with everything I had – seeking only to shield you from a fate worse than death – being bound to me in this cursed place. This *wretched* manor. But now, I must confront the truth I have denied every day in your presence: I cannot be, if you are not mine. I cannot endure the thought of living a single moment without you. Even if I were to become a mere shadow, a wretched thing confined to the attic, it would be worth every second… knowing that I loved you, even if only for a fleeting time."

Evelyn felt herself trembling as he held her tightly. His words tore through her like a storm.

"Evelyn," he rasped, his voice thick with anguish. "You are the very marrow of my existence, the shadow that haunts my every waking thought. The world beyond you is cold, lifeless – a barren wasteland where I cannot dwell. I would tear apart the heavens themselves to keep you as mine." His grip tightened on her as desperation threaded through his every word. "You are the ink that stains my soul, the blood that courses through me, and I cannot – *will not* – let you go. Not while there is breath left in my body. You are bound to me, as I am to you, through this cursed life." He brushed his lips against hers in a whisper of a kiss.

"Be my wife. Be my salvation. If only for the time I have left as a whole man."

The words hung between them, so thick and rich with yearning. Before Evelyn could respond – before the weight of his plea could even settle – a sudden rustle stirred the stillness of the garden. It came from beyond the garden's entrance, near the shadowed archway. Both turned at once, straining their ears and eyes in the dark.

"Evelyn!" a deep voice called.

Her heart raced as her father stepped into the moonlit glade, parting the tendrils of ivy. Clara trailed behind him, her face pale in the half-light.

At the sight of them, Evelyn and Henry broke apart instinctively. Still, as if tethered by some unseen force, their fingers sought each other again, reaching out to hold hands. Evelyn's throat tightened, and she blinked hard against the tears threatening to fall.

"My girl," Mr Ward said, looking between them. "What in God's name are you doing out here in the cold? You should be abed, child!" His voice softened as he approached her. "I believed you were merely dressing for dinner. When I returned to find you gone…" He exhaled, pressing a hand to his chest. "You gave me a terrible fright."

"Well, you were right to be frightened," murmured the baron, hobbling through the archway behind Clara, leaning heavily on his walking stick. He paused to catch his breath, looking from Henry to Evelyn with a look of deep contrition.

He made his way slowly through the hidden garden. When he finally sank onto the cold stone bench with a sigh, the weight of despair seemed to settle upon him as well.

Clara looked as if she might rush to Evelyn and embrace her, but instead, she stood still with her hands clasped tightly before her.

The baron coughed throatily, and then began to speak.

"I must beg your forgiveness to you, my dear Miss Ward," he began hoarsely. "That night in the attic – when fear gripped your very soul... I have rued every hour since. Would that I could turn back the clock and undo the chain of events that brought you to such a place. The terror you must have endured... it grieves me more than I can rightly express." His gaze fell, as though the weight of his own guilt was too much to bear. "I am burdened by what I have done... by what I have asked of you. And for that, I am most profoundly sorry.

"To have brought you to Rosehill Manor was a grievous error... a choice made in haste and borne of desperation. I have longed to lift the burden of this curse and the sorrow it has wrought upon us all, but alas, I fear the cycle is beyond our power to break."

He closed his eyes as a tremor ran through him. He parted his lips as if to speak again, but the words slipped away, lost in his sorrow.

Evelyn let go of Henry's hand and crossed the garden slowly, until she crouched before the old man. Gently, she took his withered hands in her own, offering what little comfort she could for the deep wounds of time.

"Dear Alistair," she said softly, deliberately using his given name. An instinctive tenderness enveloped her, as if she were the mother he never knew, reaching across the chasm of time and grief to hold him. "You are forgiven. I forgive you."

He opened his eyes to meet hers – blue as a winter sky, fragile and clouded. A single tear escaped, carving a solemn path down his cheek.

Evelyn reached up and cupped his face, her heart breaking for the man who had borne such sorrow for so long.

"You are but a man in search of answers, Alistair," she whispered. "Wrestling with the shadows of your past. And oh, how long you have carried this weight. I can scarcely fathom how it must press upon you." She wiped his tear away with the softest motion.

"I cannot help but wonder," she continued softly, "whether each Sinclair has borne this curse in solitude, locked within the silence of your own minds. One after another, all grappling with confusion, with heartache, with grief, with ghosts – yet never daring to speak of it. Never daring to seldom share the burden with one another."

Alistair let out a soft breath, blinking away the tears from his weary eyes. "That is true," he murmured. "Too true, I fear. You possess a rare grace, my dear."

Evelyn smiled sadly. Her heart ached not just for him, but for each Sinclair who had come before, each soul marked by the same silent sorrow. She still knelt before him, holding his withered hand in one and cradling his cheek with the other.

It was Clara who stepped forwards then, her expression wavering as if she hesitated to voice her thoughts in the presence of the baron. Evelyn looked at her and nodded in encouragement.

"My lord," Clara began. "On the night of the ball, I glimpsed a figure I took for a ghost... But she was no spirit... no trick of the light or spectre. She was flesh and blood. Only a woman, haunted by her own sorrows, lost in grief so great it seemed to unmoor her from the world."

She paused to draw breathe, dropping her eyes to her hands before lifting again with quiet resolve. "It made me see clearly, my lord. It struck me so... The curse you speak of... it is indeed real, yes, but it is not only bound to old blood or ancient misdeeds. There are bonds – tangible, human bonds that also ensnare the Sinclairs. You have all become trapped in a relentless cycle, condemned to repeat the same grave errors, like moths drawn again and again to the same flame."

She glanced between Evelyn and the old baron, her words gaining strength. "You speak of curses as if they are external forces, but perhaps the greater affliction lies in your silence... in your isolation. That is what binds each of you, more truly than any curse. The unspoken grief, the unresolved sorrows... they fester inside, drawing you back to the very darkness you each try so hard to escape. You've passed this suffering from father to son, looking for salvation outside yourselves. But a curse cannot break while hearts remain closed. What festers in darkness cannot heal without light."

Clara stepped back as tears began to fall, unbidden, from the baron's weary eyes.

Evelyn grasped his hand tightly, feeling the tremor in his grip as he began to truly sob, a raw sound that reverberated through the garden.

Instinctively, she soothed him, her fingers brushing over his hand in slow, gentle circles, offering comfort in the only way she knew how – a mother's warmth, an anchor in the storm.

"Thank you, Miss Clara," Evelyn said softly. "For speaking what others feared to name."

She sighed as she continued stroking the baron's withered hand.

"I have always prided myself upon reason," she said quietly to the baron, to Henry, into the night. "Upon comprehension, upon the comfort of things made clear. I have spent my life seeking to make sense of the world through sense and order. And yet... this curse has never heeded logic nor reason. Nor, I find, does love."

She glanced at Henry then. "What I feel for you – it defies reason. It cannot be measured or explained. And still, it is the most certain truth I know."

As Evelyn turned her attention back to Alistair's tear-streaked face, something within her gaze way. The enormity of it all – the curse, the loss, the shared pain, the love that blossomed amidst ruin – it all pressed down on her chest. Without warning, her own tears began to fall.

A single droplet traced the curve of her cheek, gleaming in the moonlight as it slipped past her chin and into the soil below. It landed upon the withered remnants of the rose bed as a fragile offering to all that had been lost to time and misfortune. Beauty and grief intertwined – as they ever were in this place – now sealed in earth and silence. For what was the curse, if not sorrow preserved? And what were the Sinclairs, if not its most faithful custodians?

Chapter 35

Seraphina

In the stillness of the moonlit night, where shadows danced like whispers across the walls of Rosehill Manor, the woman in white floated – an ethereal wisp suspended between the realms of the living and the departed. Time had worn away the sharp edges of her grief, yet it clung to her still, a gossamer veil swirling with the chill of memories long past.

As Seraphina glided through the cold halls, the hollow space within her ached – not the sharp pang of fresh sorrow, but one that neither time nor torment could quell. The house knew her, as it had known her grief, her rage, her lingering wrath. The walls had memorised her footsteps, her cries, her curses. Yes, it was a silent witness to the twisted path her soul had taken, a path she could not turn from, even now.

In the dark recesses of her mind, the curse stirred, like an ancient serpent coiling in the shadows.

"Foolish girl," it whispered. *"Do you still believe you can escape the consequences of your own heart's poison?"*

She lingered unseen, observing the figures huddled in the drawing room with faces alight in the hearth's glow. That warmth – so human, so ordinary – shimmered like a distance memory. For the first time in centuries, she felt a stirring within, a yearning buried so deep it might once have borne the name 'hope.'

"*Behold thyself,*" the whispers sneered. "*So full of longing, so full of envy. You watch her – the girl who treads where you dare not. Evelyn. The living. So full of everything you once had... or thought you had.*" The voice flickered like a flame, its cold caress like ice against her soul. "*She has the love you hungered for, and she does not even know it. How oft have you watched her, hiding in shadows, your soul twisting at the sound of her laughter?*"

Evelyn, her sweet ancestor. Her own likeness. She sat gracefully, her chestnut curls cascading like a waterfall over her shoulders. She was warmth, and she was surrounded by warmth. Her laughter weaved through the air like silk. And Henry Sinclair – strong and steadfast. He gazed at her with such tenderness. How Seraphina still longed for such a love.

"*What do you suppose will become of her, Seraphina?*" the curse whispered, its voice now a twisted lullaby. "*Do you truly believe Evelyn shall be spared from the same fate that has claimed all those before her? You watched her, did you not? You wished to see it unfold – the same ruin, the same fall... the same dark end you once embraced.*"

Yes, it was true. Day by day in the manor, she had watched Evelyn from the shadows of the manor. At first, it was not pity she felt, nor kinship, but something darker: a cruel and bitter hope that history might repeat itself... Let the Sinclair men falter. Let the sorrow repeat. For if they erred again, then her own anguish might be justified. Her grief, her fury... they were vindicated each time the wheel turned anew.

But time had betrayed her bitterness, for Evelyn – with her boldness, her bright defiance, began to unmake that hunger for revenge. She had not merely resembled Seraphina in form, but in fire, in that fierce spirit unbowed by a world that sought to tame her. And in that fire, Seraphina glimpsed herself as she had once been, when hope grew wild and unguarded in her chest, like untamed blooms in spring.

Laughter rang out in the drawing room, a melody of joy among the living. In their laughter, she heard the whispers of her own lost youth, a time before anger had seeped into her bones, before bitterness had twisted her soul like poison.

"Do you hear it, Seraphina?" The curse's voice laced itself through her thoughts like smoke. *"That laughter? Oh yes. It is your penance. A reminder of what you could have had, what you squandered. She has it all — the love you could not hold, the life you could not live. And all the while, you remain, neither living nor dead, a ghost trapped by your own making."*

She gritted her teeth.

"You thought you could hide your grief, did you? You imagined you could bury your anger deep enough that the curse might forget you," the voice continued. *"Foolish girl. It was born of you. It is you. The rot of your bitterness festers in the very walls of this manor, feeding the darkness that now binds you."*

"Oh, sweet Evelyn," she breathed, ignoring the voice, as she had long learned to do. "I shall not let your fate mirror mine. I will not stand idle while the darkness stretches forth to take you, too."

Yet even as the vow left her lips, Seraphina felt it: the weight of her own heart's curse pulling at her, hungry for more, demanding its due. It had shaped her into this terrible form, and now it reached for Evelyn with the same greedy hand.

"You cannot save her, Seraphina. Not now. Not ever." The voice was a quiet hiss, yet it reverberated through her bones. *"She will end as you did. You will see to it, just as you wanted. This is the legacy you bequeathed, the ruin you nurtured. The darkness you birthed shall feast upon her as well."*

With a shudder, Seraphina turned away from the drawing room. Though she despised it, she knew what she must do. The path she had long evaded now called to her, a grim inevitability she could no longer ignore.

She made her way down the shadowed hall, the cold grasp of the manor pressing in from every side. As she moved, her body shifted, shrinking and slinking, muscles folding and bones twisting, until she became once again the creature she had so often wore: the cat.

Her paws pressed lightly to the creaking boards. Before her loomed the attic, a yawning maw of darkness, a place she had long avoided, too wretched to confront. The curse was alive here, as much a part of the place as the dust and decay that filled the air.

Her shape began to shift again, the sleek feline form melting back into the pale, translucent ghost she had become.

Seraphina took one last breath, then stepped into the darkness.

"Edmund," she whispered.

She could see him, the hollowed visage of the man she had once loved, a memory now reduced to nothing but bone and twisted remnants. Time had stripped him of all that had been human, leaving only the bleached remnants of his former self. The very sight of him was enough to make her heart twist, but she did not flinch. She had long learned to bury her grief beneath the weight of her vengeance.

As if stirred from a nightmarish slumber, his skull twisted slightly, the darkened muscles that still clung to the bone trembling with a feeble recognition. His eyeballs twitched, and for the briefest moment, Seraphina thought she saw something like sorrow there.

"Seraphina…" His voice was a rasp, the sound of dry bones scraping against eternity. "You have come."

She did not move, nor did she respond. Hours – perhaps even longer – passed as she stood there, caught between time and the endless void of memory. The world outside had ceased to matter, as had her own sense of existence. "I have remained. Not by choice but haunted by the echoes of what once was."

Edmund's skeletal form shifted with a creaking ground, a sound like cursed laughter.

"And now, you are but a whisper, as am I," he murmured, a rueful smile hollowing the bones of his face. "Trapped in the liminal space between life and death, between hope and despair."

She remained silent. Oh, she saw him now, pitiful creature that he was… No, not the man he had once been, but something less, something more. He was not quite alive, and yet not fully a ghost – a fading soul, neither bound to the earth nor freed by death, caught in a state of eternal limbo.

280

"I have had ample time for reflection, Seraphina. The curse you wrought but naught but a mirror of your despair... And now, it is you too who bears its chains."

A cold shiver ran through her, the words striking a deeper than she had expected. He was right, for the curse – *her curse* – was no foreign infliction, no cruel spell cast upon her from without. It had sprung from within, born from her own torment, from the poison she had kept in her heart for so long. It had become her, and she had become it.

"Do you not see? Bitterness binds the soul tighter than any chain. You have condemned yourself to a fate worse than death. It is *you* who shall never know peace."

The words were a dagger, driven deep into the very core of her being. *Never know peace.*

"Peace," she repeated in a whisper. "I believed... oh, I believed I could outrun the pain. That through silence, I might deny its power... But I was mistaken. I have *become* the very torment I sought to escape."

Edmund tilted his skull, an almost tender gesture. "I was a flawed man... prideful, blind. I loved you, and I wounded you more than any other. Yet it was never silence you needed, Seraphina. It was the healing you refused to seek."

Her spectral form trembled, but she did not answer. There were no words left to speak, no absolution to be had.

"And yet, you stand before me," Edmund's voice rasped. "Your wrath, once just, has morphed into a poisoned draught, infecting all who dwell within these walls. I alone ought to have borne the burden of your ire. Those who followed should not. They are innocent of my sins. What of your descendants? What of mine? Will you permit your darkness to taint their hearts as well? Set me free, Seraphina. Release me from this cage of bones."

She sighed, long and deep, though there was no breath in her lungs. ""I have borne your betrayal as a stone upon my heart these many centuries, Edmund, and permitted it to shape the very marrow of my being. I became the vessel of my grief... and in so doing, I ceased to be anything else. And still, even now, you speak of freedom not as atonement, but as reprieve. Your own. There is remorse in you, yes, but it dances too close to self-pity to be pure."

She sighed once more. "And yet… in our descendants, I have witnessed love untainted by fear, by ambition, by pride. I did not know it could exist. In their hearts, I glimpse the light I once extinguished… and perhaps, if I am brave enough, I might yet tend to its flame."

"Then allow that light to guide you. Forgive me, not for my sake, but for yours. In forgiveness, reclaim your soul. Release me, Seraphina, and in doing so, release yourself."

Her heart – a ghost of a thing, long abandoned – ached with the truth of his words. They echoed through the chambers of her soul like a haunting melody. She had been adrift for so long, imprisoned in the quiet fury that had hardened her.

Edmund was perhaps unchanged – still casting his sins in softer light. Even now, he sought absolution not entirely for her sake, but his own. Still, what mattered was not the purity of his regret, but the clarity of her own. The curse had never been some distant affliction, but something she had wrought from her own festering grief. The voices in the shadows, the darkness that had clung to her like a second skin – it came from her own heart, feeding on the bitter marrow of her pain.

The whispers surfaced, familiar, accusing. "*You will never be free. You are naught but the sum of your bitterness. You will fade as you have lived… haunted, empty, unloved and unforgiven.*"

With a low, almost imperceptible growl, Seraphina silenced the voices. She summoned the single, unspoken thought forth with the strength of a woman who had suffered too long: *Enough.*

The silence that followed was heavy, like the settling of dust after a storm. The voices faded, no longer able to claw at her, no longer able to speak their poison. She stood still and unbound, her presence as fragile as a shadow at the edge of dawn.

I am not this.

The realisation came like a whisper of wind, quiet and unspoken, but profound. She was not this endless sorrow. She was not this curse. She had been many things – daughter, lover, mother, wronged, wrongdoer – but this... this shadow, this prison of her own making... she would inhabit it no longer.

Into the stillness of the night, she cast a silent prayer. It was not to any god who might deign to hear her, but to the aching remnants of a life once lived.

First, she offered forgiveness to Edmund: for the wounds he had inflicted, for transgressions that had once defined her misery, for the love that had withered in his keeping. And then – more tentatively, and more tenderly – she turned that grace upon herself: for the sorrow she had mistaken for strength, for the years spent nursing her anger, for clutching so tightly to the bitterness that had become her only companion.

Turning her gaze once more to the skeletal figure before her, or what little remained of the man who had once held her heart.

"May you find peace at last in the embrace of death, Edmund Sinclair," she said softly, a benediction for the man she had loved and lost. "Breathe your last tortured breath."

And for the first time, she felt the darkness lift, just enough to allow a sliver of light to creep through.

∞∞∞∞

Seraphina drifted across the gardens at the far edge of the estate to the hidden realm cloaked in vines and ancient oaks. There, amidst the tangled undergrowth, rested the remnants of her cottage, rotted into the soil.

Once, nestled amidst the blossoms and greenery, her cottage had been a haven, a sanctuary where laughter danced through the air like sunlight. At its heart had bloomed her roses, which she had nurtured so many centuries ago, her fingers so often stained with earth as she pruned and cared for them.

Now, the solitary dead rose seemed to echo her grief, its skeletal stem stripped bare. Still – *still* – despite its loss, the rose still clung to the earth, its roots buried deep within the soil.

Tears, glistening like dew, slipped down her spectral cheeks.

"If you can endure this death, then perhaps I can too," she whispered, brushing her ghostly fingers against the barren stem. "You have lost all your petals, yet here you remain."

As the rising sun bathed her ethereal form, she felt the chains of her sorrow begin to shatter, each link dissolving into the cool dawn air.

"I have held on for too long," she murmured into the mist.

She heard them: Henry and Evelyn, with their laughter spilling from within the manor. In her minds eye, she saw them too: Henry's arm encircling Evelyn's waist, drawing her close; Evelyn leaning into him with a tired smile. How beautiful they were together, how pure – like the first rays of sunshine breaking through the morning fog.

"You deserve this," she said softly. "Your love deserves to flourish, free from the shadows of the past. Let the thorns of old yield to the beauty of new growth. From the ashes of sorrow, you will rise, and you shall bloom anew."

In her final moments, she drew one last breath – not from necessity, but from the essence of their joy. It was a breath woven from the threads of laughter that echoed in the stillness of dawn, a hymn of hope that coursed through her spectral form. She knew, at last, that she was ready to be more than a whisper in the dark.

She was Seraphina, a woman forged in the crucible of love and betrayal, and now – at long last – one who could forgive.

Chapter 36

Henry

Morning sunlight poured through the arched windows of the grand hall, bathing the dark wood panels in a golden embrace. As Henry Sinclair stepped into the room, he almost gasped, for the hall – once a canvas of shadows – now radiated with vitality, as if each beam of sunlight were a painter's brush lifting the gloom and revealing a thousand hues.

For the first time in all Henry's years, the manor breathed.

The long breakfast table, draped in white linen, stretched across the centre of the room. Silver trays glinted in the sunlight, laden with an array of pastries, fruits, and meats. Footmen moved about the room, tending to the guests who had remained since the ball. Some had already taken their seats, quietly conversing over tea, while others filtered in, their expressions softened by the night's rest.

Henry paused for a moment, his eyes sweeping over the scene. The tension that had knotted his shoulders for as long as he could remember began to unravel. Something in the air felt different, lighter. Though he could not articulate it, he sensed the shift. The curse had lifted, if only slightly, its weight easing enough to be felt in the gentle murmur of the room, in the buoyancy of his step, and in the warmth of the sun, which had long been hesitant to grace Rosehill Manor.

Henry made his way to his seat at the head of the table, catching a glimpse of Evelyn as she entered the room, her figure illuminated by the soft morning light. A question danced in his mind: *did she, too, sense the change?* His gaze lingered on her for a moment longer before he turned to one of the waiting servants.

"The manor feels different this morning," he said quietly as a cup of tea was placed before him. "Do you feel it too?"

The servant nodded with a polite smile, yet Henry knew they could not understand the depth of what he meant. The change he sensed ran deeper than mere atmosphere; it was a stirring in the very heart of the manor itself.

As Evelyn took her seat across from him, their eyes met. Henry rose from his chair, and the quiet conversations around the hall faded into silence as all eyes turned to him.

"Good morning to you all," he began, his voice resonating through the grand hall. He took a breath, allowing his gaze to linger on Evelyn, who offered him a reassuring smile. "I have an important announcement to share with you all this morning. It is with the deepest joy that I declare Miss Evelyn Ward and I are formally betrothed."

For a heartbeat, the room held its breath, stunned into silence as his words settled over them. Then, like the release of a bowstring, a wave of applause erupted, rippling through the hall. The loudest cheer came from the far end of the table, where Lord Alistair Sinclair stood, his hands coming together with a force that reverberated in the air.

Henry's gaze drifted to the baron, and for a moment, he could scarcely believe his eyes. It was as if the burden of years had been stripped away overnight. The deep lines etched into his face had softened, and the heaviness that had bowed his shoulders for so long seemed lifted. His eyes, once dulled, now sparkled with a long-lost youthfulness. It was a flicker of the man he had been before the darkness took hold.

When the baron met his son's gaze, his smile widened. For the first time in years, Henry allowed himself to smile back.

As the applause subsided, he spoke again. "Let us gather, then, in celebration of this joyful new chapter in our lives, surrounded by the affection and goodwill of those we hold dear. It is our intention to be wed in the coming weeks, and it is my earnest hope that you will remain with us to share in the occasion. Your presence is a source of great comfort and happiness to both the Sinclair and Ward families. To those who would choose to stay, know that you shall be received not merely as guests, but as cherished companions in the days leading to our union."

As he returned to his seat, a low murmur filled the room, conversations resuming as guests discussed the engagement. Evelyn glanced across the table at him, and in that instant, a peace settled over him – the kind he could scarcely remember feeling.

∞∞∞∞

As the dishes began to clear and guests stumbled wearily back to their chambers, Henry remained seated for a moment longer. He looked to the baron, who now stood near the great hearth, absently tracing the rim of his goblet.

"Do you perceive it?" Henry asked, though he already knew the answer. "The change... in the very air around us?"

The baron took a long breath, setting his glass down on the mantel.

"For the first time in decades," he said softly, his voice almost reverent, "I do not hear the voices. I heard nothing last night. No scratching at the walls. No whispers in the dark. No cold breath upon the nape of my neck." His eyes seemed to drift beyond Henry, as though searching the manor's walls for the unseen presence that had haunted them both for so long. "It is... vanished."

Henry swallowed hard. "Father," he said, feeling the truth of the title for the first time in his life. Something in him settled at it, as though a wound, perhaps, had begun to heal. "We must pay a call upon my grandfather. Come. Let us go to him."

As they walked, Evelyn came into step beside them, slipping her hand into Henry". They paused in the drawing room, where Henry picked up an old, worn diary, and continued to the far East Wing of the manor, where his grandfather's room lay. At the threshold, Henry hesitated and then steeled himself as he pushed the door open.

They found him lying in a neatly made bed, his frail form swathed in soft blankets. The atmosphere felt different now – less ominous, devoid of the terror that once filled the room. The shadows of fear had retreated, revealing merely an old, lonely man. Though age still marked him deeply, he appeared less skeletal than before, as if the shadows that had lingered for so long were lifted at last.

Henry approached cautiously, clutching the diary tightly. "Grandfather," he began, though the word came out in an odd croak. "We come bearing news of great importance." He glanced at Evelyn, for her presence offered him strength. "We believe the affliction that has long plagued our bloodline – the curse, as it has come to be known – has at last been broken." His voice steadied as he spoke, gaining conviction. "The shadows that once haunted these halls have lifted. There were no whispers in the night. I believe, with all my heart, that the darkness has been dispelled."

At first, he was unsure if the old man had heard him.

Slowly, his grandfather's eyes flickered open, revealing a glimmer of life beneath the years of weariness. He inhaled deeply, filling his lungs with the air, as if savouring a taste he had long forgotten. The old man's gaze wandered between Henry and Alistair – his grandson, his son – his eyes brimming with unshed tears.

Henry stepped closer, gently placing the diary on his grandfather's chest. The old man drew in a long, steady breath, his eyes falling shut as he exhaled softly. The gentle rise and fall of his chest grew shallow, the moments stretching into a serene stillness.

With one final, quiet breath, he slipped away, embraced by death's peaceful grasp at last.

Henry, Alistair, and Evelyn stood vigil at his side, their hearts entwined in a bittersweet weight – heavy with sorrow yet lifted by the end of suffering.

"The rest of them," Evelyn finally whispered, her voice a fragile thread breaking the stillness, "they will be at peace now too."

"We must bury them," Alistair replied. "Lay them to rest."

Henry nodded, his heart heavy with the gravity of the task before them.

Chapter 37

Alistair

Alistair stood in the cemetery, encircled by freshly turned earth. The graves of his ancestors awaited beneath the brightening sky. He had never entered the cemetery on the outskirts of the estate, bound to Rosehill as he had been. He had never been able to mourn his mother, his wife, his daughter – all lost to the shadows. Perhaps once they were done here, he might ride a horse along the bridle paths skirting the estate. Perhaps he might journey further still – beyond the edge of the woods, down to where the land met the sea, and let the wind carry away what sorrow remained.

He cast a glance at the coffins resting nearby, their dark wood catching the morning light. Each one contained the remains of a man who had suffered under the curse, their stories now woven into the fabric of his own. Soon, they would be laid to rest beside their wives and daughters, mothers and fathers, their sons, their sisters – those they had never been able to love fully.

He recalled the gruelling effort of carrying each coffin down from the attic, Henry at one end and he at the other. They had pried open the lids one by one, exposing the bones that had languished in their wooden prisons for far too long. With each coffin they carried down, their breaths came ragged, muscles aching beneath the weight. It was a struggle, yet Alistair felt it was a burden meant to be borne together, one that belonged to no one else. The scratching that had once haunted the manor was now silenced, replaced by a profound stillness that felt almost reverent.

As they had set the last coffin down in the cemetery, a wave of peace washed over him. The years of despair – the curse that had loomed over his family like a dark cloud – seemed to lift as he gazed at the mounds of earth. He could sense strength returning to his bones, the heaviness beginning to lift. The aches in his back and shoulders, though still present, felt different – less like the weariness of age and more like the exhaustion of purpose.

Henry knelt beside him, wiping the sweat from his brow. "We did it," he said.

"Yes, we did," Alistair replied. They had carried the weight of their ancestors together, and now they would finally lay them to rest, granting them the peace they so richly deserved. A cool breeze rustled the leaves of nearby trees, lifting the hair at his temples and brushing against his cheeks. Even the earth seemed to sigh.

With care, they began to cover the coffins with soil. Each shovel of dirt felt like a promise: a vow to honour those who had come before them. It was not absolution, not entirely, but it was something near to peace.

Evelyn and Mr Ward entered the cemetery clothed in black, with sombre faces. As Alistair straightened, brushing the soil from his hands, he nodded to them in silent gratitude. His son stood steadfast at his side, the sun casting a pale gold light upon them all.

"On this day," Alistair intoned slowly, "we consign our forebears to the earth – not as relics of the past, but as cherished spirits whom we hold within our hearts and minds. They have suffered long enough, trapped in the shadows of a curse that has ensnared our family for generations. No longer."

He paused to survey the freshly turned soil, the breeze stirring the edges of his black coat. "These coffins do not merely mark their final resting place. They are monuments to the anguish they endured. Forgotten men, living skeletons. Entombed not by time alone, but by grief and fear and silence. Today, we do not bury their memory. We release it. We honour it. In laying them to rest, we break the yoke that has bound us for generations."

His voice grew softer, filled with reverence and sorrow alike. "Let their spirits be at peace within the bosom of the earth. And let us, the living, carry their memory forward – not as a burden, but as a blessing. For the Sinclairs yet to come, may this be the dawn of something new."

They stood in silence for a time, before Evelyn stepped forwards, her gaze flitting between the fresh mounds of earth and the solemn faces of those around her.

"I confess," she said softly, with quiet strength, "I did not fully comprehend the breadth and burden of your family's history – our history – until but a few days past. And yet, through fear and revelation alike, I have come to understand. They are free at last, those poor souls who were forgotten. And in their release, we too are free."

With that, they moved to gather around the final grave, the last resting place for Alistair's father – the sole coffin yet untouched by the earth.

With solemn care, Alistair and Henry lowered the coffin into the waiting ground. The soil cradled it, enfolding it as a mother might a wayward son returned at last.

"Rest now, Lord Aelfric Sinclair," Alistair said. He placed the worn diary atop the coffin, and it felt like a final offering, a bridge between the past and the present. "May your spirit find peace beyond the grounds and the grief that held you."

With the coffin now nestled in its earthen bed, Alistair and his son began to cover it with soil, sweat beading on their brows in the warmth of the morning sun.

Evelyn stepped forwards, cradling a bundle of young bulbs in her hands. She knelt beside the grave, sinking her fingers into the dark soil as she planted the bulbs with care.

"May these flowers bloom brightly," she whispered upon the still air. Henry smiled at her sentiment, grasping her soil-covered hand in his as she continued: "Let them rise as a testament that from the ashes of sorrow, beauty may emerge once more."

Chapter 38

Evelyn

In the fortnight leading up to their wedding, Evelyn was surprised and slightly disappointed by Henry's restraint. His eyes often lingered on her with an intensity that ignited a slow burn within her, yet he approached their courtship with caution, apparently determined to offer her a wedding – and wedding night – worthy of her status as the future Baroness Sinclair. His kisses were sweet and brief, each a tender promise rather than a full embrace. He would bid her goodnight just before passion could sweep them away.

Lady Agatha loomed over them like a hawk, determined to remain at the manor with her pouting niece until the wedding. Ever vigilant, she flitted about with the sharpness of a knife, ensuring that propriety reigned during their short engagement. Arabella trailed in her shadow, now a pale, fluttering thing with the presence of a wisp. Her eyes were glassy, her hands always folded, as if afraid to touch the world lest it splinter. Evelyn had once tried to approach her gently, but even that had been too much. At the sound of her voice, Arabella had recoiled, shrinking into herself like a creature who had wandered too close to the edge of something unspeakable, and returned not wholly intact.

Evelyn and Henry often found themselves wandering through the garden to seek refuge from the assortment of guests left roaming the manor. It was a pleasant sort of company but often overwhelming after so long cloaked in solitude. In the dappled sunlight, they stole precious moments together, fingers brushing, glances lingering, where silence spoke more sweetly than words.

As the wedding day approached, the gardens were a hive of activity. At Henry's request, the once-secluded walls of the secret garden had been pulled down, revealing its hidden beauty to all, and indeed, the perfect setting for a wedding.

The centrepiece of it all was the rosebush, which had burst into full bloom with petals cascading in rich shades of crimson and pink. Every rose seemed to nod in approval, as if nature itself had prepared for the occasion.

The ceremony passed in a blur of soft vows and whispered promises. Their kiss was met with a hushed awe before the crowd erupted into applause.

That evening, the garden transformed into an enchanted realm, with strings of lanterns suspended between branches, flickering like stars above the gathered guests. Laughter mingled with the music of a string quartet, and the scent of roses and honeysuckle filled the air.

Evelyn, radiant in her ivory gown, moved through the crowd with her new husband, accepting kind words from well-wishers. She glimpsed her father and the baron in animated discussion with faces alight.

"Would you do me the honour of a dance, my lady?" Henry asked, his voice low and warm as he took her hand. With a playful glint in his eye, he drew her gently towards the patch of grass that was their makeshift dancefloor.

As the music swelled, Henry twirled her around, their laughter ringing out like music of its own. She felt weightless, caught in a moment that seemed to stretch into eternity.

Nearby, Charles clapped his hands in delight, his face aglow with pride as he cradled a small bouquet of flowers.

"Pray, look at them!" he exclaimed. "They appear to have stepped from the pages of a storybook."

"Indeed, they do," Clara replied, her eyes shimmering as she stood slightly apart.

Other couples took to the dance floor, and Henry's eyes widened for a moment at his father, twirling the Dowager Countess, their eyes alight in concealed joy.

Henry smiled and leant in close to his new wife. "Do you believe this is real?" he murmured, his breath warm against her ear as he spun her slowly in circles. "That you are truly mine?"

She looked up at him, the word spilling from her lips like a sacred prayer: "Forever."

They moved through the dimly lit corridors like children sneaking away from prying eyes, their footsteps light and quick. Henry's hand closed around hers, and she let out a breathless laugh as he pulled her along. She stumbled once, her feet still clumsy from the endless twirls and waltzes, but Henry caught her, steadying her with a soft chuckle. The sound of their laughter echoed off the stone walls, mingling with the distant murmur of their guests still celebrating in the gardens below. Her fingers, damp from the excitement of dancing, slipped in his, but he tightened his hold, glancing back at her with a grin that sent her spiralling into another bout of laughter.

The door to his chambers creaked open, and the heady scent of roses embraced them. A cool breeze teased through the open window, stirring the curtains in a deliberate dance. Henry paused, his eyes on hers, a softness there that made her stomach dip. Then, in one smooth motion, he swept her up effortlessly.

A laugh escaped her, bright and surprised, as he carried her over the threshold. The world felt lighter in his arms, though her heart was anything but.

The bed met her back with a gentle thud, and the cool coverlet kissed her bare arms, sending a shiver through her that had nothing to do with the temperature. She looked up at him, parting her lips to say something, but instead his lips brushed hers, and she found herself smiling against his mouth, her heart still dancing with the same lightness that had carried them through the halls moments before.

His kiss slowed to become passionate, drawing her deeper, until her thoughts blurred and the world outside ceased to exist. She pressed herself against him, curling her fingers into the linen beneath her. He tasted of wine and something sweet she could not place, and with each gentle press of his lips, she felt the space between them shrinking, vanishing, until nothing else mattered but this moment, this touch.

His hands moved over her dress to wrap around her waist. When his fingers found the delicate buttons of her gown, she stilled, her chest rising and falling with shallow breaths, suddenly aware of how little separated her from him.

One by one, the buttons gave way, the cool air of the room meeting her bare skin as he revealed more of her. Evelyn's pulse quickened as the last of her gown slipped free, leaving her exposed and vulnerable before him in a way she had not expected. The soft candlelight danced over her bare skin, and for a moment, she instinctively drew her arms inwards as a flush crept up her neck.

The look in Henry's eyes stopped her – so full of reverence – as he paused to take her in. His eyes traced every line, every gentle curve. He knelt over her, smoothing a palm over the length of her arm.

She arched into him, her nerves settling, surrendering to the way he looked at her – like she was something precious, something beyond comprehension. The uncertainty that had fluttered in her chest softened, replaced by a quiet thrill, knowing she held his complete attention. His lips hovered just above her collarbone, his breath hot as it skated over her skin, and she sighed softly, her body coming alive under his adoring gaze.

Evelyn pushed herself up to sit, but before she could gather her thoughts, Henry's hands found her breasts. His breath hitched, and she could feel the quiet marvel in his touch, the way his palms lingered, his eyes darkening with desire. He traced in gentle circles, sending a sharp pulse of heat through her that made her gasp.

He leant in, capturing her lips in a kiss that was no longer tender, but deep and consuming, his passion unravelling her as his hands roamed over her body, claiming every part of her skin as though it were sacred.

But even as her breath caught, something shifted in her mind. She wanted more than his touch. She wanted to explore him, to feel *his* skin under her hands, to undo the finely tailored clothing that clung to his broad frame. She pulled away just enough to see him, her lips parted as she gazed upon him. She wanted to undress him herself, to take control of the moment, to feel every inch of him as she peeled away the layers between them.

Evelyn's fingers trembled slightly as they traced the edge of Henry's tailored coat. She untied his cravat, letting it fall in a soft heap on the bed, her eyes never leaving his.

She moved her hands moved lower, skimming over the crisp linen of his shirt, feeling the heat of his skin through the thin material. She lingered at his chest, spreading her fingers wide to feel the strength beneath, savouring the way his muscles tensed under her touch. She could feel the rise and fall of his chest, the steady thrum of his heart beneath her palms. Her hands deftly worked their way down, unfastening the buttons with steady intent.

She waited at the hem of his breeches, the fabric tight against his body, the last barrier between them. Just as she finally brushed the buckle, he pushed her hand away, a teasing smile dancing across his lips.

In a heartbeat, he was over her again, his warm chest pressing against her bare breasts. With a swift movement, he pushed her onto her back. He captured her lips in a passionate kiss, a searing intimacy that consumed her. The kiss deepened, urgent and demanding, a fervent language that spoke of hunger and desire.

He slipped his hand between her legs, exploring with a gentle caress that sought the sensitive heat nestled between her thighs. He moved with an artist's touch, each stroke deliberate and tender, as if playing a harp, seeking out her point of pleasure.

She moaned, and she felt the deep rumble of his pleasure resonate from his chest in response. Encouraged, his fingers danced with increasing confidence, coaxing her hips to rise and meet his hand. She surrendered fully to his touch, parting her legs wider, allowing him to explore the depths of her yearning.

The bulge of his breeches pressed against her thigh, a reminder of his own desire, yet he remained entirely devoted to her pleasure. His mouth trailed a sultry path from her neck, exploring the delicate curve of her collarbone before descending to her breast. He enveloped the soft bud of her nipple with his lips, drawing a breathy moan from her as pleasure surged through her body like a wave.

With each kiss, he journeyed further, his lips descending to her navel, then trailing down her thigh.

So this is pleasure, she thought, her senses swirling. *This is desire.*

He kissed her inner thigh gently, and then replaced his finger with his mouth between her legs, kissing her deeply, his tongue moving in slow, languid strokes. She pressed her hips against him, desperate for more.

As his tongue explored her, he grasped the flesh of her thighs, his pulling her ever closer. He moved a hand to her centre, slipping in a single finger. A soft moan escaped her as he curled his finger, beckoning her closer.

Lost in the intoxicating rhythm, she felt herself unravelling, her body responding to his every move, aching for release as the world around them faded away. A tight coil began to twist in her stomach, pleasure rising with each movement. She tangled her fingers in his hair, pulling him closer against her, lost in the sensation.

He moved his fingers, plunging deep within her, and she moaned, panting into the cool night air. He shifted to kneel between her legs, and she opened her eyes to meet his smouldering gaze. Desire burnt in his eyes, a fierce hunger that mirrored her own.

Her breath hitched as she caught sight of the unmistakable bulge straining against his breeches, a vivid reminder of the need that coursed through them both.

"I want you," she murmured, her voice thick with longing, a delicate thread of delirium woven through her words. "Please."

A low groan rumbled in his chest. He withdrew his fingers for a moment, the heat of his absence lingering like a ghost of pleasure. As he freed himself from the confines of his breeches, she drew in a sharp breath, her heart racing at the sight of him. His cock sprang forth, thick and straining, the velvety skin glistening in the dim light.

"Are you sure?" he breathed, leaning over her, his voice husky with need.

"Mm-hmm," she nodded, her heart racing. Yet even as doubt hovered at the edges of her mind, her desire eclipsed it, compelling her to want it all the same.

His breath caught in his throat as he guided himself to her core, the thick head of him brushing against her slick heat. With a gentle pressure, he pushed inside her, and she gasped. For a moment, he remained still, their bodies locked together, as if savouring the intimacy and gathering his own breath. She could feel the heat radiating from him, pulsing in time with her own heartbeat.

Then, with a deliberate slowness, he began to move, each thrust deep and measured. She wrapped her arms around his back, feeling the heat of his body beneath her fingertips, every inch of him pressing against her, enveloping her. She sensed his restraint, the way he held himself back.

"It is alright," she whispered.

At her soft encouragement, he leant down and kissed her, their mouths moving together in a slow, languid dance. A low moan escaped him, echoing through his lips and into hers.

In a moment of daring, she slipped her hand between their bodies, seeking her own pleasure. She began to rub slowly, revelling in the sensations that blossomed within her. He seemed to notice, and a deep, urgent groan escaped him.

With renewed fervour, he quickened his movements, thrusting his hips against her with a desperate urgency. She felt the pleasure rising within her once more, a tide of sensation that threatened to break free. Then, he groaned – a deep, guttural sound that reverberated through his body.

"Evelyn," he moaned, his voice thick with desire. "I need to – I cannot – "

In that moment of urgency, she kissed him fiercely, tangling her free hand in his hair, pulling his head roughly to hers.

As his pleasure erupted, his body moving wildly against hers, she followed suit, a wave of ecstasy crashing over her, blackening her vision as twilight stars exploded behind her eyes. A deep, primal instinct took over, igniting every nerve as she surrendered completely to the moment, her body arching and writhing against his.

As their bodies began to slow, their breathing calmed into a shared rhythm, a gentle symphony of heartbeats echoing in the stillness.

He let out a soft laugh, a gentle sound that danced in the air around them. She could not help but join him, her laughter bubbling up as his weight settled heavily on her. It was a comforting heaviness, like a soft, warm blanket.

With care, he shifted to his side, wrapping his arms around her in a protective embrace that felt like home. In that tranquil moment, he kissed her – slow and sweet, no longer driven by need, but infused with tenderness. He trailed soft kisses across her nose, her eyelashes, her forehead.

He pulled away for a moment, leaving her to bring the sheets up to cover her nakedness, a shiver of vulnerability dancing along her skin. She watched in awe as his form moved away from her, the light cascading over his broad shoulders and sculpted back, tracing the defined muscles that rippled beneath his skin. Her gaze travelled lower, admiring the curve of his firm behind.

He disappeared for a moment before returning with a warm cloth.

"Be still, my dearest," he murmured, low and gentle. He cleaned her tenderly, the soft cloth gliding over her skin as he removed the evidence of their passion with care.

Once he was finished, he crawled back into bed, drawing her back into his arms.

"I hope you are not overly sore?" he asked, his voice both teasing and sincere.

She shook her head, smiling as she traced the contours of his chest, feeling the way his muscles shifted beneath her touch. "Perhaps a little. I might be on the morrow."

He frowned. "I was determined to only bring *you* pleasure," he admitted. "But when you said *please...*" His frown melted away, replaced by a wide grin.

She grinned back, revelling in her power over him. "Is it always thus, between a man and a woman?"

He chuckled, a light sound that danced between them. "I cannot say. I have not had much experience."

"But you have courted other ladies, have you not?" she pressed, more intrigued than anything else.

He paused, a thoughtful look crossing his face.

"No," he replied at last. "I could not leave the manor, and there were few guests whom I deemed worthy of my affections, and fewer opportunities."

"So, it seems we were both quite innocent?" She laughed softly, and the teasing lilt of her words caused a blush to rise upon his cheeks.

He glanced at her from the corner of his eye, a smile playing at the edges of his lips, yet he did not answer her question.

"Well," she teased, rolling onto her stomach and propping herself upon her elbows to admire him more fully. "I daresay we acquitted ourselves rathe admirable for a first attempt, did we not?"

She took in the broad expanse of his chest, the soft curls of hair that graced it, but she knew her eyes sparkled with mischief. "Tell me, husband – how often do you suppose a newly married couple engages in such... intimacies?"

He grinned at her, reaching out to brush a stray curl of hair behind her ear, lingering there. "As often as they desire, I should think," he replied, his gaze holding hers with newfound intensity.

A thrill shivered down her spine, though she matched his look with one of teasing boldness. "I believe we shall be quite busy, indeed."

Epilogue

1817

Henry and **Evelyn**

The sun dipped low on the horizon, casting a golden hue that danced across the lush gardens of their seaside retreat, transforming the landscape into a scene from a dream. The young Sinclairs had settled for a short spell into a charming villa along the coast of Devonshire, where the gentle sound of waves lapped against the shore. The air was filled with the briny scent of salt and the sweet perfume of blooming wildflowers.

Evelyn sat at a wrought-iron table nestled beneath a sprawling oak tree with a collection of leaves and petals spread before her. In her hands, she held a freshly published volume she had hastily unwrapped – *The Enchanted Rose: A Study of Botanical Wonders.*

"Henry, come! You must see it!"

Her husband approached and settled beside her, leaning in to examine the book. "Ah, the famed author herself. Let us see what marvels you have conjured within these pages."

As she opened the book to reveal the delicate illustrations and poetic passages, her heart swelled with joy.

Henry looked through the book intently for a long time before looking up. "You have outdone yourself, my dear. Your passion and intellect shines through every line... every illustration." He turned another page, his brow furrowing in mock seriousness. "And here, I see you have dedicated a section to the *Rosa Sinclaire*."

Evelyn laughed, a sound as melodic as the ocean breeze. "I could not resist, could I? After all, it was that fated rose that brought us together." She moved closer, resting her head on his shoulder.

"Indeed," he murmured, his voice rich with warmth. "And what a fortunate twist of fate it has been. To love and be loved so freely... to travel the world hand in hand with you by my side. It is a wonder I never dared to imagine."

Just then, Clara emerged from the cottage with a small bundle in her arms. "Your ladyship," she said warmly. "Little Margaret is ready to be nursed."

Evelyn's heart swelled as she reached out, taking the babe into her arms. The tiny girl, named in honour of Henry's mother, cooed softly as she settled against Evelyn's shoulder.

Henry leant in closer, kissing the top of Margaret's head. "I cannot remember a moment so perfect."

Clara observed the tender scene for a moment, then nodded. "I shall leave you three to enjoy the evening. Should you have need of anything, you need only ring."

As the gentle sounds of the ocean filled the air, Margaret nestled against Evelyn's breast, her tiny body growing heavy with sleep. The sun dipped lower, painting the sky with shades of pink and lavender. Evelyn smiled softly, brushing her fingers over the babe's sweet face.

"Shall I carry her within?" Henry offered softly. He lifted his daughter gently from Evelyn's arms, cradling her close, and with a tender kiss on her forehead, he promised, "I shall see her settled with Clara. You shall be safe and sound, my little one."

Evelyn watched as her husband disappeared into the cottage, her heart swelling with love for the two precious souls. She marvelled at the profound changes in Henry. He was no longer the brooding figure burdened by the shadows of the past; instead, he radiated warmth and joy.

He returned with a lightness in his step, taking her hand with a familiar ease. As twilight deepened, the first stars began to twinkle overhead.

Hand in hand, they wandered towards the gentle waves, their voices mingling with the soft murmur of the tide, a symphony of joy that danced upon the cool evening air. Their spirits soared like the gulls overhead, unrestrained and luminous in the twilight.

As a full sky of stars winked into existence, casting their ethereal glow upon the shoreline, Henry and Evelyn knew in their hearts that all was well. Their future stretched out before them like an endless sea.

Afterword

I cannot thank you enough for taking the time to read my work. *The Haunting of Rosehill* is my debut novel, and it has truly been a labour of love. I sincerely hope it has met all your expectations.

When I embarked on writing this novel, it was titled *The Enchanted Rose* – a sweet Regency romance infused with a touch of magic. However, as all good stories tend to do, it took on a life of its own. What emerged was a dark gothic tale, intertwined with steamy romance and just a hint of Regency charm, mainly for Henry Sinclair's unfurled cravat and open shirt in the rain.

I owe my heartfelt gratitude to my husband, who loves me dearly, but who often exclaimed, "Do I have to actually read this?" and who once, when I read the first paragraph aloud, played the meme sound "Boring!"

As punishment, I dedicated this book to him.

And to my toddler, who graciously allowed me to type away on my laptop each night while she snacked and watched cartoons – thank you for your understanding.

A special thank you to my sister-in-law, Gwynn, my Regency and writing buddy, for her enthusiasm and encouragement. To my sister Bonnie, who listened to Seraphina's curse and said, "that's a bar and a half, Sam!" I still don't know what that means, but thank you. And to my older brother Josh, who said Seraphina needed to speak to Edmund one last time – I hate to say it, but you were right. Thank you to my family; your unwavering support has meant the world to me.

I also urge my parents and in-laws to never read Chapters 20 or the latter part of 38 – and if you've already ventured there, to kindly erase it from your memory.

I hope you will follow my author account on Goodreads and my social media accounts at @samanthablok.author for more updates and novels!

Thank you again for reading my book, and if you found joy in it, please consider leaving a review – as an independent author, I rely on your good opinions and reviews to help my work find new readers.

With love,

Samantha Blok

About the Author

Samantha Blok is a hopeless creative, hailing from sunny Sydney, Australia. By day, she's tethered to her laptop, weaving through the labyrinth of policy writing from the quiet corners of her home office. But in the spaces between the keystrokes, she dreams of escaping into worlds of romance, pulse-pounding adventure, and just the right hint of spine-tingling horror.

As a devoted wife to a sports enthusiast, mother to a wild toddler, and companion to a spirited border collie, she seizes every spare moment to escape the bustle of domestic life through her writing. Whether penning a sweet Regency romance or a gothic adventure, her stories reflect her passion for weaving intricate narratives that keep readers enchanted.

If you crave more, the haunting is far from over.

Clara survived Rosehill Manor… Dunmore Grange might not be so kind.

The Heir of Ravens: A Gothic Horror Romance

1820 Ireland. A crumbling abbey. A man bound to the darkness.

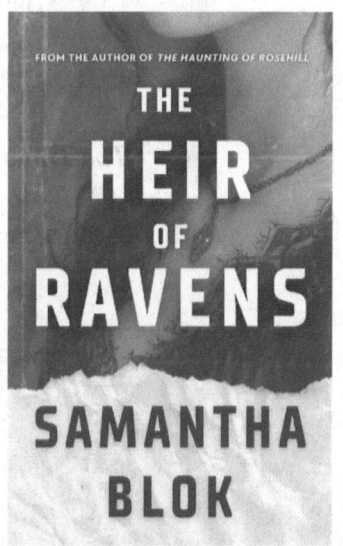

When Clara Byrne arrives at Dunmore Grange, she expects only duty: to care for a dying woman and secure a future for herself. But deep in the woods, in the ruins of Ravens Abbey, something is hungry.

Ciarán Fane is a man of shadow and blood. There's something unnatural about him, something that calls to the darkest parts of Clara, parts she has long since buried.

She came in search of a future. She did not expect to find a love so all-consuming, so ruinous, so utterly inescapable that leaving would no longer be an option. Not when she has finally tasted the hunger that has haunted her all her life.

Not when he is the one who burns for her in the dark.

The Abbey does not forget, and it does not forgive. It takes. It keeps. It devours.

Novels by Samantha Blok

GOTHIC ROMANCES:

The Haunting of Rosehill
The Heir of Ravens

REGENCY ROMANCE SERIES:

The Trouble with the Tollivers:
(1) A Most Dreadful Guide to Ruin
(2) The Matchmaker's Most Disastrous Scheme

A sweet, laugh-out-loud, friend-to-lovers Regency romance for lovers of *Bridgerton*...

A Most Dreadful Guide to Ruin

(Book 1, The Trouble with the Tollivers)

London Society demands perfection.

Hetty Tolliver is about to deliver absolute chaos.

As the eldest of five sisters, Miss Henrietta Tolliver is everything a proper young lady ought to be: elegant, accomplished, and endlessly agreeable... and she is utterly, mind-numbingly bored of it. If she must smile sweetly through one more pianoforte recital or suffer another dull dinner party spent discussing drainage, she might very well scream. Her solution is simple, and entirely improper: she shall engineer a scandal so ruinous

that no respectable gentleman would dare offer for her hand.

Theodore Winslow, the Earl of Langley, is her childhood friend, London's most notorious flirt and precisely the sort of man foolish enough to help.

Theo considers Hetty's plan absurd... which makes it all the more irresistible. After all, what harm could come from a few stolen dances, a scandalously low neckline, and perhaps a duel or two?

Unfortunately, what begins as a mock courtship soon unravels in a most inconvenient fashion: Hetty is declared the Diamond of the Season, suitors flock by the dozen, and the gossip columns swoon over their tender romance. Somewhere between moonlit kisses, an accidental shooting and a faux engagement that refuses to remain pretend, Hetty discovers that the true danger is not in scandal... but in falling hopelessly, disastrously in love.

A riotous Regency romantic comedy bursting with banter, bedlam, and one increasingly besotted earl.

Read now on Amazon

www.ingramcontent.com/pod-product-compliance
Lightning Source LLC
Chambersburg PA
CBHW011452170626
46814CB00009B/3014